William Kirkus

Frederick Rivers

SALZWASSER
VERLAG

William Kirkus

Frederick Rivers

Reprint of the original, first published in 1864.

1st Edition 2022 | ISBN: 978-3-75259-203-0

Verlag (Publisher): Salzwasser Verlag GmbH, Zeilweg 44, 60439 Frankfurt, Deutschland
Vertretungsberechtigt (Authorized to represent): E. Roepke, Zeilweg 44, 60439 Frankfurt, Deutschland
Druck (Print): Books on Demand GmbH, In de Tarpen 42, 22848 Norderstedt, Deutschland

FREDERICK RIVERS;

INDEPENDENT PARSON.

BY

MRS. FLORENCE WILLIAMSON.

1864.

CONTENTS.

FREDERICK RIVERS.

CHAPTER I.

STONECROFT.

"There is a river in the ocean;" bluer, salter, warmer, swifter than the waters through which it flows. It will not mix with those waters a moment sooner than it must; and a ship may sail in mid-ocean, half within and half without this mystic gulf-stream. Yet, for all its wondrous separateness, it gives and takes, until at last the whole ocean is aware of its presence, and even the shores are gladdened by its genial warmth.

And there is a stream no less mysterious beneath the surface of human character and life; a current of deeper passion, warmer affection, swifter and more irresistible thought and purpose than any careless observer would dream. It were well indeed if this under-current of human nature were always genial and benign; only thawing the ice of conventionalism, and nourishing those timid and beautiful affections which, like the delicate creatures of the sea which are cherished by the warmth of the Gulf Stream, cannot live in the bleak and nipping air of the common world. Alas! it flows too often like a torrent of molten lava, scorching, withering, killing, bursting up through the smooth surface of the proprieties, bringing desolation and death. Perhaps everybody's life is sometimes tragic, or, at the least, what we call romantic; but when I first saw Effie Holmes and Frederick Rivers, they seemed so quiet and *un*romantic—so like the people about them, or differing from them, if at all, by a greater unobtrusiveness and shyer modesty—that I scarcely thought they could have a history worth writing. They seemed far too gentle to fight, even in the quiet battle-field of common life; and I should have thought them the most yielding and conquerable of human beings.

At the same time, I remember, I often noticed that there was in their quiet affection an almost unearthly solemnity; in their tenderness—as indeed there is in all genuine tenderness—a *strength* capable of any achievement. Sometimes, when they merely called each other by name—*Fritz* and *Effie*—their eyes seemed to beam with the recollection of innumerable experiences which raised them far above the most passionate of the lovers who sentimentalize about us every day. They lived in a world of love; but it was an awe-stricken and most reverent love, a love conscious of fierce conflict, and of a gigantic power that contains all possibilities even of destruction. I used to notice this at first, before I knew them as I do now; and others noticed it too. "How fond they are of each other" people used to say; "and yet *fond* is hardly the word. They seem to worship one another; and though they are so undemonstrative, it is plain that they have quite lost themselves in each other; every word and look seems to come from unfathomable depths of life." Is it not the fact that the meaning of words, in the actual use of them, depends on him who uses them? Do we go to the dictionary to find out the meaning of the words "I love;" and does it make no difference from what lips they come?

I may as well begin at the beginning, and tell you where Fritz was born. He was born in England, in a little village in Derbyshire. If this little village had been two or three days' express-train and fastest steamboat distance from London, it would have been visited every year by hundreds of tourists, and would have been described in Murray's Handbook; it would have cost many a Paterfamilias hundreds of pounds. But, being within easy reach, a very inexpensive place, where a family might hire a whole house for a month for less money than a week of dirt and impudence and neglect at even Margate or Ramsgate would cost, nobody knows anything about it. It is a mystery to everybody but the natives how the ordinary wants of human beings in this little village are supplied. Nobody is in a hurry. A shopkeeper will ask you "what are you short of?" and tell you he's going down the street to "The Crown," and you must just look round again "in the afternoon." The law of supply and demand, competition, buying in the cheapest market and selling in the dearest, are laws applied in this little village with much reservation. Very primitive it is, and very beautiful; for I have been there with Fritz, and with a passionate affection he showed me every nook and corner of the dear old home. It reminds me always of Gray's "Elegy;" and, moreover, there are two or three "country churchyards" not far away, where the "Elegy" itself might well have been written.

"Perhaps in this neglected spot is laid
Some heart once pregnant with celestial fire;
Hands that the rod of Empire might have sway'd,
Or waked to ecstacy the living lyre.

"Some village Hampden, that with dauntless breast
The little tyrant of his fields withstood;
Some mute, inglorious Milton here may rest,
Some Cromwell, guiltless of his country's blood."

And why are these sweet, romantic villages of England as unknown as their Hampdens, as inglorious as their Miltons? It would do no harm if admiration, like charity, oftener began at home.

In this little village of Stonecroft Fritz was born. His parents had not long been living there; and had settled in the place because it was very pretty, and old Mr. Rivers (not so old then) had a place to fill there of a somewhat "private and confidential" kind, for a neighbouring magistrate; which suited his disposition, and enabled him to live comfortably and even, for Stonecroft, luxuriously, without diminishing the store he was anxious to keep "for a rainy day," or a quiet old age. They took the best house they could get—Mr. and Mrs. Rivers, Tom, Harry, and Margaret or Peggy. They were English enough, and yet there was a tradition that they were somehow connected with some German family—of course of great nobility and wealth; though for all the good the German family ever did to them it might have been the most plebeian of beggars. Perhaps that was the reason why Frederick was not called Freddy but Fritz. The house they lived in when Fritz was born was by no means elegant. It was the house which had just been vacated by the death of a very old dissenting minister, about ninety-two; whose affectionate flock thought him (and themselves) very hardly used that he had not been taken to Abraham's bosom at least thirty years before. It was a white house, a little above the village, in a most delicious valley, sheltered from the north winds by a high hill, beautifully wooded, running on for some five miles east and west. Between the house and the hill were a lawn, or, at any rate, a broad piece of grass—across which the high road passed—and a shallow, rapid, brawling river, turning scores of water-wheels as it hurried along to join, at last, the Mersey. The house was surrounded by tall trees—ash, copper-beech, elm, sycamore. At the back were three good meadows (with a brook running through them, joining the river lower down at the beginning of the village) which did not indeed belong to the white house, but were as free to the juveniles as if they did. The front-door was studded with huge iron nails, like the door of a prison. There was a damp, cold parlour, which no fire seemed able to warm; and a "house-place"—a large room, half-kitchen, half-parlour, which was, in fact, the ordinary "living room," always warm, cheerful, and homelike. But there was another room in the white house shrouded with a fearful mystery; for therein, years ago, the son of the aged divine, at last elevated to Paradise, had, after much forbearance, been "squelched." The report had never been cross-questioned by any competent physician, and it never occurred to the unsophisticated villagers that "squelching" might have been treated with unnatural suspicion and severity by the law of the land—but the report was, that the parson's son had been bitten by a mad cat, that he exhibited all the ordinary symptoms of hydrophobia, that at last he wandered about the house mewing horribly like a cat, till the parson and his household could bear it no longer. Was he happy, this poor mewing wretch? Was anybody else happy that had to listen to him? Would it not be better for everybody if "the Lord took him?" Of course it would. They drugged him with pitying opiates, they laid him sleeping on the mattress, and they laid the feather-bed on both, and——he never mewed again. They call that "squelching" in primitive rural districts; and at any rate it was in the room where the poor parson's son was smothered that our little Fritz was born. Even his very beginnings were unconventional.

"The child is father to the man;" but you don't care to hear all about Fritz's babyhood. He was "brought up by hand;" he had the usual share of ailments; of course he had to struggle through his teething—and, in truth, he was so like other children, that I have nothing to say of his babyhood that you may not see for yourself in any nursery you like to visit. He was only seven years old when his parents left Stonecroft. But he often revisited it, and it had an unquestionable effect on his character. While Mr. Rivers lived at Stonecroft he could afford to be genuine. *Real* happiness, and not the mere appearance of happiness, was what the whole family sought and found. There was not even the *temptation* to make a great display; it would simply have alienated Mr. Rivers from all his neighbours, and imprisoned him in a lonely grandeur which not a single inhabitant of Stonecroft would have either envied or admired. And we sacrifice our real happiness for admiration, and the ignorant envy of those who do not know us, and whom we do not care for. If we could not get that we should most likely throw away our affectations, and take what we really like, and not only what we wish other people to think we like. When Mr. Rivers moved to Manchester he never forgot the "rainy day;" he never wasted his money beyond what he could afford to waste; he did not know that he was wasting it at all. But he bought "appearances" instead of realities. And little Fritz could not play about in the Manchester streets as he could in the lanes round Stonecroft. The people were much more polite, but not nearly so kind as those he had grown up among. They seemed to have a much less rough way of speaking; but they never pressed him to their hearts and kissed him, and made him understand without saying a word about it that they loved him, and he might feel at home among them. For a long time he felt quite miserable in Manchester. People stared at him, and called him a "very odd little boy;" and he began to think that polite people must always be fools. At the same time his Stonecroft life had shown him another side of unconventionalism. We were walking together, he and I, not very long ago, along the road that winds round the meadows at the back of the white house, and were coming almost close to the village when he stopped me. "I shall never forget this spot," he said; "I know it by that tree bursting into the old wall. But if that were gone I should remember it still. Just here, when I was a little mite about six years old, I found a woman lying drunk, cut, bleeding. I ran away, screaming; and people asked me what was the matter, and went back to fetch the poor, miserable creature home." We walked on to a point where the brook behind the white house takes a sharp curve, and flows under a bridge to join the river; and where we could see the road which passes the front of the white house, enter the village. "She lived there," he said, pointing to a miserable house; "she was married to an Irishman. The last time I saw her she was shouting, cursing, banging at the door, trying to force her way in. For an instant the door opened. Her husband raised his hand and struck her on the head with a large hammer. She fell down, like an ox in a butcher's slaughter-house, stunned and bleeding. She was not killed, and the constable at Stonecroft never interfered with his neighbours if he could help it. But I was an odd little boy; and I thought—mother is never drunk in the road, and father never hits her on the head with a hammer—don't fathers and mothers *always* love one another?"

What an odd, disjointed world it is, when even little Derbyshire Stonecroft could suggest such questioning! And, perhaps, after all, Fritz *was* an odd little boy.

CHAPTER II.

GOING TO SCHOOL.

At any rate he was very sorry when the time came to go to boarding-school. He didn't care much for Manchester, and he had scarcely a single boy companion; which may account for his meditativeness and love of books, and a sensitiveness and warmth of the affections almost feminine. Men will grant to women that advantage even over themselves; they will allow that they are at any rate very loving little fools, and that their instincts may be trusted, sometimes, even further than the wise generalizations and cogent reasons of the stronger sex. Tom and Harry Rivers were older than Fritz; their school-days were over, and some part also of their apprenticeship. They were at home only for about a fortnight in a year, and their way of life was getting more and more removed from the tender girlishness of their younger brother. It was not for their sakes, therefore, that the Manchester home seemed a garden of Eden, and school a little patch of the outside wilderness full of the toughest, prickliest thistles. Peggy was the Eve of Fritz's paradise. A year younger than himself—she was nine now, and he was ten—they played together, sang together, read together, took their walks together, in the Stonecroft time, and even in the grimy streets of Manchester. He seemed incapable of doing anything well or happily unless she were with him. So one evening in January, they were sitting together by the piano; Peggy played, and both were singing one of their favourite songs. No stranger would have cared to listen to them, perhaps; though Peggy played well for a little child, and both their voices were sweet, and blended well together. But they were not singing for applause; they sang as larks do, for the love of song and for the love of each other. His arm was round her waist as he bent over the music to see the words.

"I remember, I remember, how my childhood fleeted by,
The mirth of its December, and the warmth of its July;
On my brow, love, on my brow, love, there are no signs of care,
But my pleasures are not now, love, what childhood's pleasures were.

"I was merry, I was merry, when my little lovers came
With a lily, or a cherry, or some new-invented game;
Now I've you, love, now I've you, love, to kneel before me there,
But you know you're not so true, love, as childhood's lovers were."

"Oh, Peggy, Peggy," said Fritz, weeping passionately, "I don't want to go to school."

She could speak no answer; they sat by the piano till it grew quite dark, with their arms about each other. They could sing no more; it was some time even before they could talk.

"No, no; I don't want to go to school. Tom and Harry say they liked it; but they are bigger and different, and they never can have been quite like you and me, Peggy. They never sing as we do. And boys are so rough: and if they hurt you so much that you can't help crying, they only hurt you more because you cry, and laugh and call you a coward. And I don't care half so much to play at some rough game as to sit still and read a book. And, Peggy, what shall I do without *you?*"

"Well, you'll be very dull, darling, for awhile; not half so dull as I shall be. I can't bear to think how lonely I shall be when you're gone. But you know, Fritz, you want to be clever; and even now we often find pieces in our books that we don't understand. And Tom and Harry said the boys were very nice fellows; and they have such jolly games, and such a large playground, and you're sure to like it very much after a week or two."

"Peggy, I shall never like anything so much as sitting with you at the piano, and singing our prettiest songs. And every afternoon, when it gets near tea-time, I shall think of you. I wish we could *hear* one another think, don't you?"

"I don't know. Don't you remember telling me you thought Mrs. Atkin a very disagreeable woman, and that she didn't mean what she said? Perhaps if she'd heard your thoughts she wouldn't have liked it; and besides——"

"Well, I don't mean that, Peggy, do I? But I should like to hear *your* thoughts, and I should like to be able to make you hear mine. How often will you be sure to think of me, darling?"

"I'll think of you, Fritz, in the morning, the time I always kiss you and say 'good morning;' and at breakfast; and when I'm reading; and when I'm practising; and when I'm saying my prayers;—and oh, dear, dear Fritz, how dreadfully dull I shall be!"

With many tears, they "promised and vowed" to be true to each other, and to live in love with each other always, however widely they might be separated; and so a gleam of pure light from heaven and Him who is Love, brightened the darkness of that evening, when these two felt for the first time the full bitterness of their parting. For it *was* bitter; and such partings will and ought to be bitter to the end of time. They were entering on a new life, both of them. She would have no other, for long years to come, to whom she could speak her very thoughts with perfect unreserve, as she could to Fritz; and she would feel the need of fellowship all the more as her thoughts grew wider and deeper. Perhaps this is why girls often grow so shallow and frivolous. They cannot tell their thoughts to men, who alone, as education and social arrangements now are, could guide and strengthen them, correct their blunders, check their too hasty generalizations, and give them that very foundation of facts which they need to change their air-built castles into the solid structure of truth. A man will very seldom believe that their mere sincerity is the disinterested love of truth, and the simple claim not to be excluded from God's beautiful and good because they are women. He thinks they are only baiting traps to catch a husband, and that what they really want to know is the way to a comfortable settlement in life. Poor little Peggy had soon to find that out; or, at any rate, what meant that. There was a little Willie Smith, who was just sufficiently like Fritz, even in face and figure, to make Peggy often look at him and try to know him. And he, too, was delicate and meditative, not averse to books and music. So somehow they were often together, and he would talk of her in a simple, brotherly way at home, and praise her cleverness, and ask his father for answers to the questions she had asked. Was it not getting dangerous—a girl of nine and a half, a boy of nine? More mischief lurks in books than either printer or bookbinder puts there; and Mr. and Mrs. Smith regarded them with peculiar suspicion.

"I don't think it's quite the thing, William, that our Willie should be so much with Peggy Rivers; she's getting a big girl now, and it's not exactly the thing."

"Well, my love, perhaps it isn't; though Peggy's a nice enough little chick in her way."

"Oh! you think so, do you? I'm not quite so sure about it. I'm rather inclined to think she's just a little forward. What business has a girl to fasten herself on our Willie, under pretence of reading books with him? That girl, in my opinion, will need a very tight rein, or she'll grow up decidedly odd and disagreeable. Why can't Mrs. Rivers set her to darn stockings, or teach her to make a shirt, or help a little in the kitchen, or in making the beds, instead of cramming her head with a lot of stuff out of books? I'm sure Willie had better give up going there."

"Well, Jane, of course if you think so; but there's Willie crying over his book instead of reading it."

Thereupon Mrs. Smith petted Willie, and said Peggy was a very nice little girl, and he might go sometimes and see her, but it wasn't quite the thing to read books with a little girl, and papa and mamma knew best, and he would understand it all when he grew up, and much more to the same purpose—as the devil gave her utterance. So once more that cruel divider of men from God and from one another, gained a victory. Of course Willie told Peggy Rivers what he could remember of the conversation. What could she do? She just said, "Well, Willie, I didn't know it was wrong; I always read books with Fritz; but father would be very angry if I asked you to do what would grieve your mamma. I wish the holidays would come and bring Fritz back to me." Perhaps if Fritz, at his desk a hundred miles away, could have *heard her thinking* then, it would have filled his exercise with blunders.

But that was nearly half a year after Fritz had gone from home. He went away the morning after he and Peggy had with tears, in the deepening darkness, promised to love one another, as sister and brother should, for ever and ever. It was a bleak, clear morning, with a nipping frost; and Fritz was to travel to a quiet town in the north on the top of the coach. The railway was opened part of the way, but Mrs. Rivers was rather afraid of those great, puffing monsters which have now become so thoroughly domesticated among us; and besides, there would have been much changing of carriages, and Fritz was to travel alone. He was very unhappy and lonely; but he was, after all, a boy; and the ride, the changing horses, the novelty of his position, the good-natured chat of the coachman, the bugle of the guard, all helped to cheer him. At last as it grew dusk and very cold, they drove into Huddersfield; and Fritz found that the coach was going no farther, and he was still some thirty miles from his destination. It was market day, however, and another coach would take him on late at night. The landlady of the inn where the Manchester coach "put up" took him into her cosy little parlour, and petted him as if he were her own child. He never forgot her beaming face; and it reminded him of Stonecroft, and the people there who were so genuine and hearty, though they had a much rougher dialect than the respectable people in Manchester. There was yet one more accident before the day was over. The Huddersfield coach reached the town to which Fritz was going after midnight. The boys who had been sent from the school to meet him had waited till they dared wait no longer. It was impossible at that time of night, even if he had known how to set about it, for Fritz to hire a conveyance to take him and his boxes to his new home. He was quite bewildered, cold, worn out by fatigue; and he turned with imploring countenance to a gentleman who had been a fellow-traveller from Huddersfield. He asked the gentleman what he was to do.

"Do, my little man? Why, there's not much to be done, for what I see. You'd better let me take you home with me, and I'll see you safe to your school to-morrow."

So a basin of hot bread-and-milk, and a soft, warm bed in a good man's house, was the end of Fritz's first day away from his own home. It was a good beginning to find such love among mere strangers; and years afterwards, when Fritz was a thinker and a writer, when his heart was chilled and disappointed, when he was inclined to say in his haste, "all men are liars," and build society on the rotten foundation of selfishness and distrust, the ready hospitality of the stranger-gentleman, and the motherly fondness of the Huddersfield landlady, rebuked him. He dared not frame a theory of life or morals which should have no place for them.

Was there any connexion between the care which Fritz was receiving and the common life of the home from which he came? Perhaps none;—is not our age far too scientific to retain the obsolete superstition that any good can come from prayer? At any rate, that night, as usual, Mr. and Mrs. Rivers, Peggy and the servant, were what Mr. Rivers used to call "gathered round the family altar." We can scarcely help being sincere when we pray; and so it comes to pass that the grief we have smothered all day long, and covered over with the show of happiness, will burst forth in genuine manifestation when we kneel down in the presence of Him "unto whom all hearts be open, all desires known, and from whom no secret is hid." So all were weeping bitterly, while the father on earth sobbed out to the Father in Heaven a prayer like this:—

"Oh God! we are not ashamed that Thou shouldst see us weeping, for Jesus wept; and it is love that makes us weep, and Thou art Love. Our little Fritz has left us, and we are all very dull and sad. It's a great and dreadful thing, oh God! to have the power to choose our own way; and we don't know what our darling boy will choose. Wilt Thou show him, Thy little lamb, where the meadows are green and safe, and keep him from harm? Provide friends to love him, and make him always deserve their love. If he is crying now because he is far away from us, do Thou dry his tears and comfort him, and send him back to us in due time wise and strong, to do Thy work in the world; even as He did it in whom we see Thy glory and know Thy love. Take care of him and all of us, this cold, dark night, Thou who givest Thy beloved sleep; and to-morrow may we try more than ever to be kind, and true, and good, for Jesus Christ's sake. Amen."

CHAPTER III.

SCHOOL AND HOLIDAYS.

Going to boarding-school is often the first event that makes a boy clearly understand his power of *choice;* the earlier days at home are passed among relationships which were appointed for him, and which he could not alter. He could not choose who should be his father and mother, his brothers and sisters, but at school he can choose his friends; and they also can choose or refuse *him.* The gentle discipline and watchful affection of home conceal our freedom and ease us of the burden of responsibility; the stern work of life brings both into the utmost prominence. School is that first halting-place where we try our powers under a discipline severe enough, though not unfatherly, to make us understand that the world will not be very tolerant of our errors, or pet us back again, as our mothers would, into good behaviour; but will punish or reward us according to our deserts, not from the impulses of self-denying love.

The school to which Fritz was sent was an old established grammar school, in Yorkshire. It bore no kind of resemblance, however, to Dotheboys

Hall. It was so far a proprietary school that it was under the control of a committee, and the head-master was not exposed even to the temptation of diminishing the comforts of the boarders to increase his own profits; for he received a fixed salary, guaranteed by the committee of management. The boys were well fed; their bed-rooms were large, and light, and airy; their playground was a large field of about nine acres, and there were many quiet walks, and a "plantation," which were also considered within "bounds." All the boys belonged to families of respectability; that truest respectability, which comes not from the possession of money, but from education and true human culture. Their fathers were, with scarcely an exception, clergymen, lawyers, physicians, literary men; often poor enough, but with correct taste, lofty ideals, and a habit of considering "a man more precious than gold, even than the golden wedge of Ophir." So the school was not, in either of the ordinary senses, a "commercial" school; it did not exist for the sake of pecuniary profit to the masters, and it did not exist for the sake of fitting the young men who were trained there to get on in the world, whatever they might be themselves. For the first half-year Fritz was merely finding out where to begin. He knew nothing of Latin. Indeed, his father, though a man of considerable culture, was no classic. The only Latin book he had was a Virgil; which

Fritz always took for a history of George the Third; probably from seeing "Georgic. III." on the first page he happened to look at. But after the midsummer holidays he was put into a class, and began forthwith to make sure and rapid progress. Many boys worked harder, and so far deserved higher praise; but none were so completely successful. For Fritz heartily enjoyed his work; it was far better to him than play. He stayed at his desk in play hours, because he really liked his books, and read them with a keen relish. Even grim old Euclid was a favourite; at any rate Fritz would be second to nobody in the two great departments of the grammar-school studies, classics and mathematics. But unquestionably it was the classics which then, and always, suited best his temperament and course of thought. The Q. E. D.'s and Q. E. F.'s of real life are not, like Euclid's, to be obtained by the application of undisputed definitions and postulates and axioms; and real human life was what Fritz cared most for, even from his earliest boyhood. Moreover, he loved beauty everywhere. To learn Horace's odes by heart was no task to him; for he admired their wondrous neatness and polish, their faultless rhythm, their perfect form. The grand yet gentle flow of Virgil's hexameters thrilled him with an inexplicable delight; and the lines fastened themselves upon his memory, almost without an effort of his own. But, above all, his Homer! That majestic roll of song mastered his whole spirit. He himself fought every battle; and when he read of Hector, and Andromache, and Astyanax, he thought how his mother would weep if his father had to go into the very jaws of death; and how she would tell him to think of her and Peggy, and save himself if with honour it might be. No wonder that he was top of his class. It was no great merit. Was it any merit in Helen to be beautiful? And he made no boast. There was not a schoolfellow who might not reckon on his help, and his nearest rivals loved him.

But, merit or no merit, he was making rapid progress; and very proud his father, and mother, and Peggy were when he brought home his prizes, and the assurance of his master that no boy in the school gave so rich a promise of future eminence. Peggy's delight and pride knew no bounds—their own Fritz! The whole world would know him one day, and love him and honour him almost as she did. Dear, trusting Peggy, it is not with such eyes of sisterly love and truth as yours that "the world" looks even upon real worth. But on the other hand, it is not for "the world" that any human being lives. Years afterwards Fritz had his fair share of honouring, and even of flattery; as he had also his fair share of trouble. But it was not the world's flattery he cared for, and he could rise above its calumny and cruelty. Still he cared more for Peggy than for all the praise or blame of an unknown multitude who did not, either for good or evil, truly know him. But Peggy was then married, living far away, with cares and claims of her own. And he had found another who was near him, and loved him utterly, and whose spirit his spirit claimed by eternal irresistible affinities—one who had known his troubles and losses, and wept with him over the grave where the cruelty of his enemies had buried his best beloved. "Effie," he used to say, "do you hear what these people say and write of me? They say I am a cold, hard, scornful man, conceited and vain-glorious, meanly eager to be notorious, no matter for what. What do you think of it all, darling? You ought to know me well."

There was not much logic, perhaps, in kisses and tears; so Fritz was none the better for them, was he, in his hour of grief? But at any rate he had them, and Effie said—

"Fritz, my own darling, if *I* did not know and love you there would be a better love than mine to shelter and honour you. But I think I do; I think if not another heart in the whole world were true to you, I should cling to you still. I don't know, but I *think* I should cling to you all the closer."

"Yes, dearest, I *know* you would. But I hear far other words sometimes, and God knows I need such love and help as yours. Yes, I can fight it all out now."

If we are unable to rise above the world, if we dare not brave its anger and sacrifice its applause, we can do it no true service. Fritz owed much of his courage and high principle in literary life, to the judicious and really noble discipline of the Yorkshire Grammar School. At the end of every school-year, before the midsummer holidays, the prizes were distributed, and the master used to make a speech. The speech he made the year that Fritz was leaving was surely worth remembering, and his favourite pupil never forgot it.

"You know, my boys, I always try to say something to you before you go home that may be worth your while to remember. I like to explain to you my plans, as far as you may be able to understand them; and above all to show you what it is that you come here for. The world is full of dangers for all of us; and one of the greatest dangers we can meet with will be the temptation to try to succeed without deserving to succeed—to think more of what we can get, than of what we are. But if people thought you clever when you were not, their good opinion would really be very painful to you; you would almost feel that you were sneaks, that there was something mean and deceitful in your characters, you would be in constant fear of being detected and put to shame. That is the reason why we have so many examinations, that you may know whereabouts you *really* stand. We are often very much surprised.

Those whom we thought the cleverest are often far down in the list; and those whom we thought dull, because, perhaps, they were timid and slow of speech, by their accuracy and care get a very high place. In the real world you will have, some time or other, to choose some trade or profession; and that will require much, by far the greatest part, of your time and thought. Many very interesting subjects you will be then unable to study; and you will be in danger of forgetting what belongs not simply to doctors, lawyers, merchants, tradesmen, but to *men* of all kinds. At school we have to do with what concerns everybody. When we read Virgil, or Horace, or Homer, we don't ask what use it will be in trade. "A thing of beauty is a joy for ever," and a joy for everybody. When we read Livy and Thucydides we are reading about our fellow-creatures; and we cannot help feeling that we and they are brothers, though they lived before Christ came into the world, and knew nothing about geology and chemistry, steam-packets and railroads. Try, each one of you, to be a good, a brave, a wise, a righteous, a kind-hearted man; and then you are sure to be a good lawyer, doctor, clergyman, tradesman, merchant—good, whatever you are. Good-bye, my boys, and God bless you. I wish you a merry holiday—a happy year of work to those who come back—a good and happy life to all of you."

Fritz was to spend a few weeks, after leaving

school, with the magistrate for whom his father had acted as confidential agent at Stonecroft. His name was Moses Holmes—Moses Holmes, Esq., of Shiloh. His family had a strange fancy for scripture names, and bestowed them with great liberality both on persons and places; Moses, for instance, had a brother Abraham, who called his house Salem. Abraham was, perhaps, the richer of the two, and more a man of the world than Moses. Salem was oftener prepared for company than Shiloh, and boasted grander visitors than Shiloh ever knew. The grandest visitors at Shiloh were two far-off cousins, old maids, long past the possibility of affecting to be young. They used to come in a large old-fashioned chariot, and they always brought with them a black servant. Then the shutters of the drawing-room were opened, and a huge fire lighted there, such as only country-people know how to make; for in truth a fire was needed. Shiloh was a bleak place; and a room shut up and darkened for about ten months in the the year has a mouldy, unwholesome feeling, do what you will, which only the warmest of fires and the brightest of lights can remove. But Moses was an old bachelor of sixty, and cared very little for the mere grandeur of a house, though he felt it a kind of duty to keep it up. The cousins used to come about twice a year, because they were cousins; and, moreover, they had money which they could not take away with them on their last journey, and which might as well be kept in the family as not. But for the most part Moses was a very quiet man; caring much more for the cheese-room than for the drawing-room. For the cheese-room he unquestionably did care—and such cheeses they were, stored up there—Cheshire cheeses albeit made in Derbyshire, that he might well be proud of them. Then there were the pigs, and cows, and a very fine bull, the terror of the neighbourhood, and old Dash the Newfoundland dog, and no end of cats, and pigeons, and fowls of all kinds—what did Moses want with humankind, especially womankind? For a pig is not perhaps a very beautiful animal, nor susceptible of very delicate sympathies and affections. He wants no more from his dearest friend than swill and a scratch on the back—he responds only with a contented grunt. But he never tells your secrets, betrays your confidence, cuts your acquaintance. Even if he can't grow fat enough for you to kill him with complete satisfaction, he looks quite miserable about it. And can anything be more comfortable and matronly than a handsome cow? How gratefully she responds to your caresses; what a warm, nursery-like, healthy odour there is in her clean "shippon;" how sleek and well-to-do she looks. And in all these things there is a solid satisfaction, a pecuniary, or, at least culinary, *quid pro quo*, which ordinary human friendships do not always produce. But old Moses Holmes, Esq., of

Shiloh, was not a niggardly, old scrape-up-all. Without much pretension or display he was very generous; and it was at least a good sign that boys liked to visit him, and that he liked them to come. The old gentleman's heart was yet young; or perhaps he had never gone beyond that early stage of human experience, the keen enjoyment of things seen and temporal, with a good-natured hope that the things not seen and eternal will get themselves right at last. He rode down every Sunday, on a brown horse, along five miles of rough hilly road, to the little chapel at Stonecroft; and had been one of the flock of the old minister whose son was "squelched." His square pew was snugly cushioned and curtained, as a magistrate's pew should be, even in a conventicle; and if, after his morning's ride, he sometimes nodded, it was at any rate on a good day and in a good place. He was at least perfectly free from cant; and his religion seemed neither more nor less than the honest endeavour, in which the best must often fail, to be a good man. And so he jogged on through life at Shiloh, fatting pigs, making butter and cheese, meeting his brother magistrates as occasion required, administering justice with the clear consciousness that the unhappy evil-doers brought before him were mostly his own neighbours, sometimes his tenants, for whom grim law must not forget to be paternal and humane. So he was a man well liked by the people who lived about him; no hero, awaking no passionate love, but well liked—and when he died decently lamented.

But he hadn't died when Fritz, fresh from school, just turned seventeen, came to spend a few weeks at Shiloh. He had often been there before with his father, when they lived at Stonecroft; and he knew the old rumbling mansion well, and the piggeries, and "shippons," and stables, and gardens, and the field where the bull was, and the long plantation of firs with a path through the middle of it, running along one whole side of the Shiloh estate. Above all, he knew the library, a room not very large, but covered with books, and with curiosities in every nook and corner. Many a duel Fritz fought, and many a foe had he slain, with a two-edged sword, blunt and rusted, which used to stand in the corner by the fire. With an eloquence worthy of Demosthenes, and a courage that would have added lustre to the fame of Achilles, he poured forth torrents of reproach and scorn upon his proud adversary, and dared him to the fight. He cared nothing for the blows which made him totter and reel; his wounds only served to increase his fury; till at last the moment of advantage came, and he clove the skull or pierced the heart of his foe. Then he could sit down in the old-fashioned arm-chair with gleaming eyes and dilated nostrils, and remember that his tremendous battle had been with a shadowy foe, a creature of his own imagination. Long after we have passed our hot youth do we fight battles quite as unreal, quite as real. The foe is a bodiless creation of our fancy; but it is an actual sword in our hands with which we deal real blows, and we suffer pain, and we are exhausted with fatigue and emotion, just as Fritz's flushed face, and beating heart, and wet brow, bore witness that on his side of the combat there had been grim earnest.

The books in the library were not, perhaps, very modern, nor of very exciting interest; but Fritz had a peculiar taste for a boy, and found a deep mine of treasure, a perpetual fountain of delight, in the Shiloh bookcases. There were long rows of law-books, some volumes of state trials, criminal reports, and such like, in all of which he found more than enough to interest him. He never could forget that the criminals and witnesses, judges and juries, were real people; and he used to lose himself in reveries, wondering how the unhappy culprits came to their misfortunes and crimes. But the state trials roused his bitterest indignation. He grew hot, cold, giddy, as he read those torturing examinations which were not intended to elicit truth, and those venal judgments which were often no better than the sophistical apologies for murder. Could this be British justice? And were not the actors in these solemn tragedies often the very greatest men in English history? Was that history truly written? How he wished he could have stood forward to speak the plain, unvarnished truth for men and women—gentle, tender women, wives, sisters, mothers—hunted to death, with none to help them. Then there were some medical books, books on farming, books about cattle, a few old-fashioned novels, a few of Sir Walter Scott's. There was Pope and Dryden, Shakspeare and Ben Jonson. And sometimes Mr. Holmes would ask Fritz to write something or other for him, making him a kind of secretary or amanuensis. So they grew quite fond of each other, the young and the old, with strange likenesses, strange points of contrast; and the two or three weeks of Fritz's holidays began to change themselves into months.

There was some little visiting, too, at Shiloh. The far-away cousins came with the chariot and the black servant. They were certainly rather frosty company. They were very much alike, as old maids often are. Perhaps they are made in pairs, like gloves or scissors; or perhaps by living together they acquire a resemblance that doesn't naturally belong to them. Mr. Holmes's cousins always wore gloves. They were very short and lean, with extremely bony necks and sharp elbows; and they both parted their hair at the side, like men. It was impossible to discover any real character in them, though they bristled with oddities as a porcupine with quills. Their names were Maria and Jane; and, as is quite common with a couple of old maids who have lived together from childhood, Jane always echoed what Maria said, and Maria always echoed whatever was said by Jane. They had a habit of speaking in a half-whispering, mysterious way, making the most trite and obvious remarks with a tone of reserve and suppression, as if there were much more to be said on the subject, if it were only proper to say it. And sometimes, long before Fritz discovered that any subject had been started, Maria would say, "I think, Jane, we will pursue this subject no further." And Jane would reply, "I quite agree with you, Maria; it will be better not to pursue this subject any further." But nobody wants to hear about a couple of old maids, who were very little different from other thoroughly old-maidish old maids. They had nothing to do with Fritz's destiny; and as they always rose after dinner and retired alone, in solemn pomp, to the drawing-room, and as Fritz never saw them except at meals, and as they only staid at Shiloh a week, we may bid them good-bye for ever.

Their ebony footman, whom, with the family fancy for Scripture names, they had called Shadrach, was a well-made, healthy-looking man, and, for a "darkie," even handsome; there was a vein of waggery, too, in his character. He had never been in the least trouble or difficulty, much less slavery. He had been, on the contrary, petted and spoiled from his very childhood, and found himself decidedly at a premium, because his skin was black and his lips were thick. But he knew how many pictures there were on the title-pages of tracts representing a poor black man in chains; he had accompanied his mistress to an anti-slavery society's meeting, and heard the tales of horror that the runaway slaves told to weeping audiences. Moreover, the fellow had a tropical fondness for lying, pure and simple—lying, as it would seem, for its own sake. So he thought he might at any rate try how far it was possible for Fritz to be "trotted out;" and he therefore presented himself one morning outside the library door, with the intention of communicating to Fritz the pathetic details of his autobiography, from the hour when he was torn by ruffian whites from the bosom of his mother, to the very moment when he should be producing a work of the imagination in Moses Holmes's library.

Fritz was reading, of all books in the world, "Blackstone's Commentaries." Not without a sense of fatigue, he was approaching the end of the chapter on "Title by Descent," and was reading, with increasing dreaminess, "if no issue of Geoffrey Styles be of the whole blood to John, then comes in his brother William Styles of the half-blood," when he heard a gentle tapping at the library door.

"Come in." Enter Shadrach, with a twinkling

eye, and a gleam of suppressed mirth in his white teeth.

"Well, Shadrach; what is it?"

"Yes, sir."

"What do you want?"

"The housemaid was out in the yard, sir, talking with the young man who came about buying some fat pigs; and I thought it might save trouble, sir, if I answered your bell for her."

"You're very obliging, Shadrach; but I didn't ring the bell."

"I humbly beg your pardon, sir, something must have touched the bell inadvertent—it certainly was rung."

Shadrach turns round towards the door as if departing, and privately grins from ear to ear to relieve his feelings—then turns round again.

"As I am here, sir, is there anything I can do for you?"

"No, thank you, unless you'll just put a little more coal on the fire."

Shadrach complies, drops a tract on the hearth-rug, and hastily retreats to the exterior side of the keyhole.

Fritz picks up the tract, and rings the bell. As it takes some few minutes for Shadrach to return from the other side of the keyhole, Fritz has time to examine the tract. On the cover a negro in chains, mercilessly flogged by a slave-driver; underneath the striking likeness of an ill-used fellow-creature, the well-known words, "Am I not a man and a brother?" with a choice selection of texts of Scripture, headings of the pages much in the style of a Victoria play-bill—"I am torn from my mother's bosom!" "I am whipped to the bone!" "I escape over the roaring cataract!" "Blood-hounds!" &c. &c. Meanwhile Shadrach re-enters.

"See, you dropped this."

"I'm deeply grateful, Mr. Frederick; I wouldn't on any account have lost that little volume."

"What's it about, Shadrach?"

"It's the story of a poor black" (here Shadrach begins to dissolve) "who was a slave, sir. He escaped at last, thank God." Shadrach wipes his eyes, and at the same time conceals a grin with a pocket-handkerchief—killing two birds with one stone.

"Did you know him?"

"No, sir, not to say know him. That little volume was placed in my hands by a kind lady as comes a visiting Miss Maria. 'Shadrach,' she says, 'you're black in skin, but you've a beating heart and a tender feeling, and a soul, just as much as white people. Cheer up, poor Shadrach, blacks have often escaped before now, and there may be a future of joy and liberty for you.' Those, sir, is the words she addressed to me, when placing this little volume in my hand."

"And a very nice lady she must have been—but really you don't seem to need much cheering up."

"Do you know my history, sir?"

"Is it anything particular? I thought you'd lived with the family you're with now almost ever since you were born."

"No, Mr. Frederick—I was torn, when a 'elpless baby, from my mother's breast, and sold into slavery. When I grew up I had to work in chains, and was sometimes so severely beaten, that I fell to the ground, fainting from loss of blood. At last I could bear it no longer; I determined to make my escape. I ran away in the dead of the night, and as the morning began to get light, I heard the bloodhounds barking all about the place where I was hiding."

"I say, Shadrach," said Fritz, interrupting this touching narrative, "how old do you think I am?"

"I am sure I don't know, sir; I couldn't take upon me to guess."

"Well then, I'm old enough to know the difference between a well-whipped nigger, which you ought to be; and a fat, lazy, black humbug, which you are. If you don't mind, old boy, Miss Maria will be giving you 'joy and liberty' rather sooner than you want it."

Of course Shadrach knew quite well that Fritz

would never tell Miss Maria. In fact, he felt so sure of it, that he couldn't help grinning slyly at Fritz at dinner next day—in which gross impropriety he was detected by Miss Jane, and very nearly effected his escape into freedom. The day after, Shadrach, old maids, and chariot, took their departure from Shiloh.

CHAPTER IV.

EFFIE.

THERE was another visitor at Shiloh, while Fritz was staying there, another cousin or fraction of a cousin of the old bachelor magistrate, for whom I reserve a whole chapter—though it may be a very short one. Her name was Effie—Effie Holmes. She was nearly seventeen when, this October, she came to stay over Christmas with her Derbyshire kinsman—seventeen on the next New Year's day. I suppose I ought to describe her; but I'm not at all like Lord Byron, and "description is" *not* "my forte." Suppose I say she was of average height—one of those girls who acquire at about sixteen a womanly three or four-and-twenty look, which they keep till they are three or four-and-thirty—that her hair was light brown, and her complexion absolutely faultless, with a skin almost transparent—her eyes, her nose, her mouth, her chin—suppose I could tell you all about them, or put a photograph of them into the margin, what would you know about them after all? Would any photograph be better than a poor caricature; or would any words express that wondrous expressiveness that made her face so fascinating? Fritz never could describe her. I once asked him to try to write for me a description of his heart's idol. When I saw him again he said to me—"I've been writing something about Effie, but it will not answer your purpose. He who would see an object must have light; but, above all, he must have *an eye*. Nobody can see Effie as I see her, unless he has my eyes. When I look on her dear face I do not see the features which a photograph might copy: I read a history. I do not judge her by her face—though that seems always to me most beautiful: I judge her face by *her*, for she masters every feature, and compels it to show forth some portion, some mood, of her own very self; and inhabited by any other spirit even her fair form would seem to me little better than a corpse, or a lying, deceitful image. I cannot help you to describe Effie. You want to describe her to strangers: strangers have neither the light nor the eye with which to see her."

So I wont try to describe her. Take it for granted she was rather more fair than dark, much more pretty than plain, with very good features, and an ever-varying expression. There were, indeed, some women who could see no peculiar attractiveness in her; but, perhaps, women can't explain one another's attractions. We seek for a manlier type of beauty—a beauty that cannot be separated from strength. Let it be enough, then, that no *man* in her circle of friends and acquaintances ever approached Effie without a strange feeling of reverence and admiration, and utter confidence. No *true* man; there were flirts innumerable, and commonplaces of masculine humanity, and lovers and "offers" enough to turn the brain of any girl less noble. But, somehow, she smiled them all away. They felt, one after another, her mystic power. *She* knew *them*, *they* did *not* know *her*. She was above them. And in her modest way she must have known it. She never consciously put it to herself, when some new admirer came—"I am far superior to him;" but she felt while he flattered, and offered such admiration as he was capable of—she felt while she reckoned up his attractions, money, connexions, and the like, that her inmost soul was hungering and thirsting for something which was not in him, that her spirit was beholding a glorious ideal that he was far unlike.

But I am forgetting she is not seventeen yet, not till the next New Year's day. And here she is, at Shiloh; and though it did no harm, could anything have been sillier than for that unworldly old bachelor to let Fritz stay till Effie came? For they were, of course, constantly together; and it seemed to Fritz as if Peggy were with him, while in truth it was not Peggy; and that variation doubled at least his enjoyment and his heart's wealth. As Peggy sought out little Willie Smith, ignorant of forbidding conventionalisms, so did Fritz, though now so much older, pour out his heart to Effie, and read, and talk, and walk with her; as if it were nothing strange for man and woman to be thus at home with each other.

If the farm, the plantation, the library, had been a treasure to Fritz before, what were they now? Effie came from London, and knew nothing about farming and common country life, nor had she any knowledge of scientific botany; but she had as quick an eye as sparkled anywhere in the world for the beauties of colour and form in flowers and plants. And she took a hearty, genuine interest in all life; and she had a way of winning the heart of every servant, workman, farmer about the place, which made her a universal favourite. Much more than a favourite—they were all eager to find out what she wanted, and were positively happy in doing anything they thought would please her.

But in bleak Derbyshire Shiloh the nights were now getting long, and the days raw and cold. The library was the "holy of holies" for these two devotees. Of course Fritz could fight no duels with thin air while Effie was with him, though the two-edged sword still rested temptingly in its old corner. But he could *talk* battles, and that was better still. He showed Effie what he had been reading—those State Trials, for instance, which had made his blood boil. They read together "Ivanhoe," and "The

Lady of the Lake," and several of Shakspeare's plays —"Macbeth," "Hamlet," and "Romeo and Juliet." Fritz read to Effie Pope's translation of "The Iliad," trying to throw into it something of the glory of the original, sometimes even reading a few lines of the Greek itself, that Effie might catch the roar of "the far resounding sea," and "the dreadful twanging of the silver bow." The genial criticism of two young hearts and intellects is fresh and wise, often beyond the insight and wisdom of maturer critics, who approach their authors with less reverence and gratitude. Indeed, these two criticized not so much the drama as the *dramatis personæ;* not the novel, but its heroes. They did not ask whether Sir Walter Scott wrote well; but they asked whether Ivanhoe and Rowena, Rebecca, Locksley, and the Black Knight, were brave, or beautiful, or true. And they acquired the habit of connecting each other in thought with the heroes and heroines of the books they read. "That is just what you would have done, is it not?" said Fritz, when they were reading with a panting eagerness how Rebecca stood on the turret, threatening to fling herself down if her tormentor approached a step nearer to her. Effie, indeed, was little enough like a Jewess, and Fritz was no way like the Black Knight. But Effie seemed to think he would have been brave and true, and could see only him leading on the assailants against the Castle of Front-de-Bœuf. They read each other into everything; and that, let me tell you, is one of the ways to make books living.

But Christmas was now drawing near, and Fritz must spend Christmas with the dear folks at Manchester—father and mother, his two brothers, and Peggy. He really wanted to see them; but Shiloh had become very dear to him. There was no such library at home, and there was no Effie! They bade each other good-bye, with a strange shadow of the future on their spirits, though they knew not what it was. Why was Shiloh so dull now to Effie? Why was the plantation of firs so dreary? It was autumn, winter—surely nothing more.

> "Tears, idle tears, I know not what they mean,
> Tears from the depths of some divine despair,
> Rise in the heart and gather to the eyes
> In looking on the happy autumn fields,
> And thinking of the days that are no more."

But did autumn and winter, with fire and lamp, make the warm and cosy library cheerless and lonely? Where was the Black Knight's prowess now? Had Shakspeare lost his genius and inspiration? Had the Muse grown careless of the direful wrath of Achilles, son of Peleus? No, surely; and yet——

They were not in love; but perhaps some other day they would find love easier for the old-fashioned cosy library, and the path among the firs at Shiloh.

CHAPTER V.

CHOOSING A PROFESSION.

HOME once more! Tom and Harry were to come the week after next; Peggy was there, of course, already; and they were all to have a merry Christmas and a happy new year. It was to be for Fritz one of those quiet resting-places in life which prepare us for future and more fruitful work. Till Christmas was over he was to think of nothing but pleasure and home; then, when the old year was gone and the new one come, he was to "take stock" of his possessions, to find out whether he was round or square, and to be careful to get into his own proper hole in life, and not into somebody else's hole which he would not fit. Peggy and he sang over all their old songs, and many new ones, went all their old walks together—such walks as could be had in grimy Manchester. They visited their favourite shop-windows; coveting their neighbour's goods, in spite of the Tenth Commandment, with the most undisguised sincerity. Of course they talked over the Shiloh visit; and Peggy loved Effie already with all her heart, and wished she could see the pretty girl from Loudon who had seemed so like Fritz in taste and disposition. He told her, as well as he could remember, the tales which he and Effie had read together in the Shiloh library, not without many recollections and comments. "You should have seen her face, Peggy, when we came to that part!" And again: "It's nothing to *tell* you; you should read it. How Effie cried! Of course we knew it was only a tale; but tales are true in a way, and at any rate she cried, and I had to stop reading. Indeed there was a lump in my own throat, and I couldn't go on very well."

Then there was much to tell about school. Fritz was top of all his classes—top of the school. It was, indeed, fair enough that he should be; for he was now one of the oldest boys there. But his master had written to Mr. Rivers a most encouraging letter, telling him that Fritz's position in the school was higher even than it seemed. He sincerely hoped, if it were compatible with Mr. Rivers's circumstances and arrangements, that some profession might be found for Fritz, in which his love of literature and his abilities in that direction would not be thrown away. In fact he wrote quite affectionately. "Was there anything *he* could do for Fritz? He really loved him as if he were his own son, and had set his heart upon the success of his favourite pupil. Mr. Rivers might command his services to the utmost." Nothing was to be determined about Fritz's future, nor even gravely discussed, until after

Christmas; but they had many a talk round the home fireside—many of those blessed conferences, so unlike the hard, cold bargaining and hiring of the outside world—in which each sought only the other's good. There is nothing mean in trade, but there are very terrible temptations; not least, the temptation to measure everything by a pounds-shillings-and-pence standard. Mr. Rivers was not in trade; and, in truth, he did not ask; where would Fritz be likely to make most money?—but rather; where, being what he is, will he be most happy and do the best work? Money alone would never have made him happy; though he needed money, for he had a free hand and a not ungenerous heart. Peggy, too, and "mother," with their womanly, personal, concrete way of looking at the matter, thought chiefly what would Fritz like, what would "bring him out" and make the world understand his worth? For they had built already gigantic castles of air for him, and measured him and the world by their affection and desires. But there was time enough. Christmas was not come yet, and the bells were to "ring out the old" before they "rang in the new."

Meantime Tom and Harry came home; Tom growing a tall, stout lad, diligent in business, but diligent in so many other things at the same time, that business didn't quite prosper as might have been wished. His master liked him—who could help it?—and so did his master's sister, twice Tom's age; and altogether it was getting a little muddled. Mr. Rivers unmistakeably objected to the master's sister, be she what she might; considering that when Tom was in his prime she would be growing old and querulous, and every way unsuitable. So there was just a shade of coldness in the intercourse of Tom with the home-circle; there was a subject that could not be approached, which everybody was thinking about, though it could not be mentioned; and it was precisely the subject which, if all had been exactly as it should, would have been uppermost that merry Christmas-tide. But when Peggy remembered that Susan was only three years younger than "mother," she didn't quite feel to care to be bridesmaid. Wouldn't everybody have to dress rather oldly, lest the bride should forget she was young? And besides . . . There is always a host of "besides" to questions we can't talk our minds upon. They were all of them the sorrier because Tom was such a capital fellow—so merry and generous. It sometimes seemed plain that *he* thought Susan a mistake; but still he felt pledged to her, and it would be mean and unkind and selfish, he thought, to alter their engagement, such as it was, now it had gone so far. It had not gone very far; but Tom argued, "She thinks we understand each other, and am I to say it's all stuff and nonsense, just because we've never put it into plain words, or put it down in black and white?" So it was to go on; even now regretted by everybody but Susan—who had an eye to what men choose to make a woman's great business in life, getting a husband at any price. They do their best to make women dependent and tricky, and then, if they are a little less hypocritical than they should be, and let their tricks be found out, they hate them. Not that Susan cared for that; she could "give as good as she got:" but she meant to have Tom, and she meant it all the more, because she was considered too old and *not* too pretty.

Harry was wholly different, steady, persevering, unromantic; didn't care a straw for dogs and horses, couldn't do a tithe of the things that Tom could do; but he could do, and did, the one thing that Tom couldn't do—stick to his own business. So he was to his master a perfect treasure, and got on as fast in business as Fritz did with books. His affection, too, was not dashing and outspoken like Tom's; it was of the kind that often cannot speak a word. But he was true as steel, to be trusted anywhere, to any length. He *was*; for the grave has closed over him. First of that happy family he was called "up higher." He passed away, some ten years later, when they were all in trouble and danger; as if to tell them that their own people and their true home were in a world, to which in due time they would come, "where the wicked cease from troubling, and where the weary are at rest."

But Christmas-day came with the mirth that is not unwise. There was church in the morning; for, Dissenter though he was, Mr. Rivers couldn't see the harm of thanking God, on the twenty-fifth of December, that His Son had been born into the world to make life holy. Then came dinner, plum-pudding and such like—and a very quiet family-party in the evening, kith and kin, who might kiss even without mistletoe. The old songs were sung; Tom's bass, "by ear," making some addition of strength if not of beauty. There was perfect homeliness and freedom that night; just what mistletoe and such devices are meant to produce in larger circles. Once a year men recognise that conventionalisms are a dreary necessity; that there is in true love and genuine sincerity a better safeguard for human happiness. Once a year, within certain narrow limits, they cast the outside crust away, and try to seem what they are. Christmas-day at Mr. Rivers's would doubtless have seemed to many flat and tame; but it was the meeting together of those who truly loved each other, who were united in common experiences of the past, in common hopes for the future. A few more days of holiday followed; and then on the second of January Tom and Harry went back to business, and Fritz must begin to ask what *he* had been sent into the world to do, and how he could best set about the doing of it.

Many and grave were the consultations on this

all-important question. It seemed plain, to begin with, that it was no use putting Fritz into a trade; he was made for a different, if not a higher, work. The choice seemed to lie between law, medicine, and the Church. Either of them would have suited Fritz. But both law and medicine would have required a far greater outlay than Mr. Rivers thought his circumstances, having due regard for the rainy day, would justify. So, what about "the Church?"

First of all it *wasn't* the Church, it was only a sect. Mr. Rivers was a Dissenter; no way bitter, but unquestionably fully persuaded in his own mind. His temperament rendered him wholly indifferent to the ceremonialism of the older communions, and his slightly radical political creed had no place for bishops or ecclesiastical state patronage. He thought that an establishment of religion involved of necessity a good deal of that coercion which is fruitful of hypocrisy, and empty of genuine goodness and truth. Fritz had been brought up in the same opinions, scarcely knew what was to be said on the other side, and above all had a very slender experience of the actual working of English sectarianism. So he never once thought whether it was possible for him to become a "clergyman." He knew, indeed, that he should very greatly have preferred the status of a clergyman to any which the Dissenting ministry was at all likely to offer. He knew the difference between Oxford and Cambridge, and the little theological seminaries in which candidates for holy orders among the Dissenters are trained. At the same time he couldn't begin life hopefully with a lie in his right hand. He could not affirm that he heartily believed what he had not even fairly examined, nor did he ever askhi mself whether there might not be discovered some device by which he might *seem* to say what he really did not say. He accepted the position in which God's Providence had placed him. Everybody must begin life on some hypothesis or other, never completely true, always needing the verification of actual experience. One man's hypothesis is called Mohammedanism, another's Romanism, another's Anglicanism, another's Congregationalism; as in politics one man sets out a Tory, another a Radical. We are not responsible for the hypothesis with which we begin life, we are responsible only for the diligence and honesty with which we learn and apply the lessons of experience.

But there were other questions about "the Ministry," which to Fritz's friends were of prime importance; for the religion of dissenting sects is far more self-conscious than that of the Catholic Church—it has a stronger sense perhaps of liberty and responsibility, with a very weak belief in a divine order and Providence to which men belong whether they know it or not. Had Fritz "a call?" Were his motives quite pure? Was he thinking about the ministry only as a quiet, respectable way of getting a living, instead of being bent upon saving souls?

"I'm sure, joy, I don't know," mother would say; "do you really think you've a call?"

"Yes, mother, I think so; but you know it isn't a call you can hear with your ears, as when father calls to you out of the dining-room when you're upstairs."

"No, Fritz; and you ought to know your own heart best. I hope, love, you've the root of the matter in you. You used to write me beautiful letters when you were at school; I've quite a bundle of them tied up in the cupboard there. But you're growing almost out of my reach. I must leave you, Fritz."

"Well, mother, if I were as sure of getting on as I am that you wont 'leave' me, I should be very hopeful indeed."

"Yes, yes, joy. I shall very likely just tell you what I think sometimes; and then you'll laugh and say to yourself, What does poor old mother know about it?"

They none of them thought that Fritz was mercenary; and though it was one of the stock questions in dissenting circles whether a young man was looking to the "priest's office for a morsel of bread," the Riverses thought quite rightly that, pecuniarily, Fritz was much more likely to lose than gain by the step he had all but determined to take.

"And, perhaps, you wont get on, Fritz," said mother; "and a poor, stuttering bit of a parson with nothing to say, and nobody to listen to him, is badly off indeed. You'd better weigh tea and sugar over a counter."

But Fritz was not used to breaking down. He had always succeeded; he felt sure that in anything that needed diligence and mental application he always would succeed. He had a vast stock of hope, energy, elasticity, not yet drawn upon by the cares of life. He fancied that if only *he* were right and true as a Christian minister, his course would be one of uninterrupted happiness and success. It never occurred to him that though he might become thoroughly competent to *teach*, Christian people were by no means always willing to *learn*. He had no means of measuring the strength of ignorant prejudice, the spitefulness of bigotry, the obstructiveness of a lazy dogmatism, the cruelty and dishonesty of assumed infallibility, the mercenary dodges and auctioneering craft by which some of the greatest "religious causes" are disgraced. He knew almost nothing of "the religious world." It was well that he could begin life with hope, even if it were but a blind hope. He never doubted his "call;" but the time came when he felt that if he had known what the dissenting ministry was, he dared not have ventured upon its dangers and griefs.

Meanwhile, he was all joy and confidence. The die was cast. He applied to the Secretary and President of a neighbouring theological college, his testimonials were satisfactory, and he was to pass the preliminary examination immediately. This would involve an additional half year at college—five years and a half, instead of five; but he couldn't learn too much, he thought, nor be trained too well. One week more at home, and then with beating heart he bade good-bye once again to father, and mother, and Peggy, and set out to begin life.

CHAPTER VI.

A DISSENTING COLLEGE.

Fritz used to look back with great delight to his five years and a half at college; but none of my readers will find this chapter in the least degree romantic. Fritz's new home was a quiet retreat for pious mediocrity, anxious, by dint of much preaching, to make other people pious. There were not half-a-dozen men in the house who would have been marked out, at once, as men of originality and power, born to be leaders and shepherds of the people; very few had even received a careful and sufficient drilling at a good school. Some had come from the warehouse or factory, after some few months' cramming with a private tutor, and nothing more. The preliminary examination, itself far too slight, was rendered absolutely ridiculous by the leniency of the examiners. No "articles of religion" had to be signed; but Fritz had to make a statement in writing of his opinions at that time, on certain specified doctrines; and he was required to read before the committee a short discourse. There was no palpable heresy in his meagre sermon; and Virgil and Euclid, and the Greek of St. Luke were old and familiar friends. So he was duly admitted, a little under eighteen, to get himself ready in five years, to be the spiritual guide of a congregation of human beings, young and old, having to fight, each in his own way, the real battle of life, often in sore need of a wise general.

I must confess that the students of a dissenting college are generally seen by the outside world to great disadvantage. Their college discipline is too narrow and monastic to admit of the free development of individuality; and they are expected to appear in society weighed down by an intolerable burden of responsibility. They acquire the habit of putting on priggishness with their black clothes; they have a peculiar and unnatural face and manner for Sundays, and "going out to preach." They act as if they were, as indeed they very often are, in the midst of spies; who are watching every word and deed, that they may find out "whether that young man is likely to turn out sound in these treacherous and dangerous times." What can a poor young student do? Speech may be silver, but silence is gold, if you are not quite sure of your company. The deadest level of priggish behaviour, and the tamest assertion of undisputed platitudes, will be the best protection from failure.

And of course some of them *are* prigs, came to college *because* they were prigs; because they didn't know what to do with God's good world, but, as far as might be, get out of it, and give to it and all its belongings their lugubrious warnings and ignorant reproof. They cannot smile on Sunday, because it's the Lord's day; they cannot smile on Saturday, because it would disturb their preparation for the sabbath; they cannot smile on Monday, because they are still over-shadowed by the gloom of the day of rest. They cannot conscientiously pay their share to a college supper, because they're not quite certain that it's right; it's a little worldly; nor is it exactly consistent for a young man preparing for the ministry to drink a whole half-pint of wine in addition to a modest allowance of Bass's bitter ale. They can't smoke, and they beg you'll not let them *see you* smoke; because it's against the rules which they have undertaken to keep, not to mention that tobacco almost always makes a prig sick. They wonder you should be fond of concerts and oratorios, for where are you to draw the line? They are very great at prayer-meetings, though they are exceedingly small in classics and mathematics. Charming characters, no doubt, redolent of sanctity — but at the same time unquestionable humbugs.

I'm told everything is changed since Fritz was there; that the prigs now predominate at his old college, and the hearty workers and jolly frolickers are in a very weak minority, looked down upon by the young Pharisees, who piously wish they "could see them rather more devoted to the work." In Fritz's days, the prigs were in due subordination. So there could really be something like conviviality and good fellowship, "within the limits of becoming mirth," when the black clothes were taken off and the Sunday mask removed. In spite of conscientious Pharisees, who felt that to discharge a duty was doubly pleasant if it saved a guinea, the session was always closed with a dinner in honour of those who were leaving. The dining-hall was decorated with flowers and evergreens, there were toasts, and speeches, and songs; and when dessert was over, one end of the room was partitioned off, the butler's pantry turned into a dressing-room, and Mr. Tomkins, "presenting" an abdominous Irish schoolmaster (with a pillow under his waistcoat), made love to "Matilda Hann," *alias* Mr. Williamson, B.A., resplendent in the Sunday finery of the tallest housemaid. One game or farce followed another, till night wore to morning; and then they all joined hands in a semicircle round those who were coming back no more, and sang "Auld lang syne," not without emotion. And if any dissenter be among my readers, and groans in his righteous soul at these very mild outbursts of the "natural man," take my word for it, good sir, that there was not less of love, and prayer, and faith in that "Auld lang syne," notwithstanding the theatricals and feasting which had gone before it, than in your own more conventional behaviour when your last new minister was ordained.

When young men are brought together they will make themselves merry, even in a dissenting college, if there be any manly stuff about them. Many a joke was cracked in Fritz's "study;" a tidy room, bookcased and furnished from the paternal pocket, somewhat beyond the regulation amount, always at a temperature of at least seventy degrees. When work was over, and the regulation-supper done, and the governor safe in the bosom of his family or the blankets of his bed, then Tomkins and Williamson would come in, each with his "mild Havannah," and the frolic and jest began. At first, subdued bursts of gentle mirth; at last, shouts of furious laughter, and clappings, and cheers; till Mr. Sharpe threatened to ring the governor's bell, for he couldn't get on with his sermon (poor prig), and he was going somewhere on Sunday "with a view;" and the spherical Mr. Johns, as broad as he was long, and as red as a boiled lobster, could make nothing whatever of his conic sections, and rolled into Fritz's room to join the sport. It was all Tomkins; with his inexhaustible store of anecdotes, his twinkling black eyes, his matchless power of imitation, his comic songs, his dying brigand, dying very hard indeed, his perfect good-nature and open-handed generosity, though he was about the poorest man in the house. Where is he now? He "wags his paw" no longer in the pulpit. In a country post-office his "merry heart maketh a cheerful countenance," though it is not unwrinkled with care; which ploughs deeper furrows than time, and sooner turns black hair grey. Tomkins, unfortunately, had only one face, and was always obliged to carry his wicked, week-day eyes even into "the sacred desk." "My friends, I've much pleasure in informing you that Mr. Grubb, from London, will next Tuesday, in the Corn Exchange, address his fellow-worms on the subject of temperance. The lecture will commence at seven o'clock." Poor Tomkins! he hardly knew he was joking; but very few of his affectionate flock could remember at what hour Mr. Grubb's exhortation was to begin. On the other hand, it was with extreme swiftness resolved by the agitated deacons that there must be a special "church-meeting." With entire unanimity it was resolved that, in a most Christian spirit, the playful leopard be earnestly requested to change his spots. Alas! alas! the spots could no way be made to come out; so poor Tomkins had to go out himself instead, the victim of a pun.

But college was not all jollifying and play. Fritz did some really good work there; and though in the college course itself preaching was far more carefully provided for than scholarship, the London University examinations furnished a healthy stimulus and a valuable reward. Of these Fritz availed himself, and succeeded beyond his hopes. It is of not much use asking from what college a dissenting minister comes, nor even what are his degrees. Everything depends upon the University by which his degrees are conferred. But it was not only in regular college work that Fritz found pleasure and benefit; indeed, I scarcely can write all he has told me about the regular "curriculum." The Professor of theology was also the Principal; a not ungenial man, and well read in history, especially the history of England. He had taken a considerable part in those religious controversies that had disturbed the Dissenting world, and was by no means unknown beyond that narrow circle. He had defied the public opinion of nonconformity on the question of State education, and so far had given hostages to virtue. He had even ventured upon a feud with "the London Missionary Society," the most powerful corporation outside the Church; and, when it chooses, not much less powerful for mischief at home than for good abroad. He was "at daggers drawn" with the Professor of biblical literature in his own college; who was perhaps the best Hebrew scholar in England, either in or out of the Established Church. He seemed to have an ambition to be mediator between a certain party of free-thinkers that he considered extreme, and another extreme party which he considered, in the main, orthodox. But in college his lectures were tedious and unlearned; confined mainly to a criticism, from the modern Evangelical point of view, of the Puritan divines. His Greek was ludicrous even to his own classes. His Latin was sometimes faltering. He had little, if any, direct knowledge of the Fathers; and far too slender an acquaintance with the history of doctrines. He was a gentleman, a historian, a careful reviewer, a judicious governor of a college, impartial even to the extent of being almost chargeable with universal coldness, tolerant of everything but downright, outspoken, unconventional conviction; but he was no theologian. The men who seemed most attentive to his lectures were, alas! too often drawing caricatures of himself and parodies of his teaching.

So far as the necessity of teaching the students to preach whatever else might be neglected would allow, the classics, mathematics, and biblical criticism were in Fritz's time all that could be desired; though the Professor of classics was considered too worldly (his wife had been known to dance), and the Professor of biblical criticism too German. In this way, almost unconsciously, those students who were not prigs found themselves in a kind of antagonism to the religious world, which was by no means unwholesome. A kind of independence was quietly and unostentatiously commended to them; not perhaps less effectually because it was connected with living persons and not mere theories. Even the rebellion of the Principal against public opinion was a very healthy stimulus.

But, in many things, the *students* of a college are its best teachers. They work together, read together, talk together. Williamson was Fritz's favourite companion; in many things, also, his superior. He was a better classic, though possibly Fritz had the advantage in that intellectual power of assimilation which rendered all he read or heard his very own. They read together in their rooms, not without most friendly help from the classical Professor, more than they read in class; and they often talked in soberest earnest about that work of God which they had undertaken—talked about it in a way that might have suggested topics for the Principal's lectures, more edifying than the commonplaces he generally chose. Every Saturday, about an hour after the delivery of letters, the bell summoned all the students into the library—a summons which almost every man in the house rushed eagerly to obey. It was to hear "the list"—the list of places needing preachers the next day, and of the students who were to be the preachers.

"So you're to go to Belmont again, Williamson, and Jones to Manchester? What can it mean?"

"I suppose it means that Jones is 'more acceptable' than I am. We've made our minds up about that long ago, haven't we, Rivers?"

"Yes, in a way; but are the governor and old

Targum obliged to yield to the stupidity of those people who are always sending for Jones? *They* know, and everybody in the house knows, the difference between him and you."

"All right, old boy; but what of it? You're positively jealous of Jones; you wish you *were* Jones, that *I* was Jones, don't you? Should we read together in one another's studies then? Do you think we should really be happier than we are, if we had Jones's 'popularity'? Rivers, old fellow, I shall *never* be popular; no more will you. What do you think of that prophecy for a friend to make?"

"I think it's a true one. I very much doubt whether we shall either of us get a place at all, when our college time is over. We couldn't either of us go to Belmont, you know, even if we were invited; though I really like Belmont, in a way. It's really *something* to preach in a chapel, ugly as it is, which the people positively built themselves, that they might hear God's gospel. They were telling me all about it the last time I was there; how they were too poor to get a chapel in the usual way, so as there was plenty of stone round about the village to be had almost for asking, those of them who were masons and bricklayers set to work, and with their own hands reared the walls, in God's name, joiners and volunteers of all sorts helping till the work was finished. Besides, old Higginbotham, that we stay with, is such a genuine old cove, so much better *every way*, even in intellect, than those blessed old prigs we meet at grander places. 'Eh, Master Rivers, is it you comed again? Well, our folk 'll be glad o' that, at any rate. But, bless us all! how wet you are.' That was my greeting last Saturday night. Wet enough I was, and half perished with cold, after that five miles' walk from Bolton in sleet and wind and darkness; and, to tell the truth, I was in a horrible fright. Just by the reservoir, where the water lying at the bottom of the cliff on the right, looked as black and deep as hell, and the hard rock rises so high and steep on the left, a grim-looking wretch came up to me and asked me where I was going. I told him to Belmont, and volunteered the profound remark that it was a wild night. 'Ay, lad, damned wild! But thou'rt not him I was wanting. Mak' th' best o' thee way to Belmont.' And then he turned away, muttering something I couldn't hear, while I sweat at every pore, in spite of sleet and wind, and *did* make the best of my way to Belmont. So I daresay I'd a scared look when I presented myself to the unromantic Higginbothams; and the good, motherly missis looked up from the tub where she was washing that jolly baby, and wiped her hands on her apron, and said, 'You mustn't be well, Master Rivers; you look pale like, and sick. Sit ye down while I get you a drop o' summat warm.' So that blessed baby, with its beautiful, round, plump limbs, sat cooing and splashing in a washing-tub, a sight to see, till I got, by degrees, a bit more colour and life."

"Well, that's a cheerful tale to tell a fellow just before setting out on that dark, infernal walk from Bolton. I am not very nervous; but I've often enough had all manner of horrors passing that black sheet of deep water, with not a house or cottage for a mile in either direction. But, at any rate, I always enjoy a Sunday at Belmont. The people really want to be taught, and they want to be made better. I'm sure they make me feel the 'burden of the Lord' more than all the Manchester chapels put together, big as they are."

"I don't know about that, Williamson. Is it a heavier burden to teach people who want to learn, or to teach people *who don't want to learn?*"

At this point in the conversation there was a sharp knock at the door—they were of course in Fritz's study—and in walked Jones.

"That's capital—you're the very two fellows I wanted to see."

"Yes, it's a very fortunate circumstance that you should find us together, isn't it?" said Rivers; "and so particularly unusual."

"I hope I'm not intruding; but there's not much work done for the first hour or two after the list comes out, and I've got a word or two to say; in fact, four or five of the men—Sharpe, and Thomas, and Slow, and another or two—asked me to do it."

"Well, pitch into it, Jones, my boy—don't be bashful. What's the row? Do you smell cigars? or have you to come tell us not to read the last number of 'David Copperfield,' because it's Saturday?"

"Don't, Rivers," said Williamson; "let him say his say. You like to say *your* say, don't you, old chap?"

"And I'm sure it's with the kindest feeling I come," said Jones, while even Williamson couldn't help winking slyly at Rivers; "because, of course, what do *I* gain by it? But I know very well that both of you are standing very much in your own light. People are very particular, and it's no use offending them."

"Offending whom?" asked Williamson.

"Well, when I go out to good places——"

"Yes, *you're* a lucky beggar at any rate," said Rivers, mentally comparing Jones with Williamson, and consequently speaking less politely than might have been wished.

"Lucky or not, people ask me about the students, and sometimes about you two. Last week I was at Liverpool, and one of Sowerby's deacons asked me if it was true you were sometimes seen at the Monday evening concerts in the Free Trade Hall."

"Well, what did you say?" said Williamson.

"I evaded the question, of course. I didn't want to make more mischief than there is already."

"Then you're a very great ass," said Rivers;

"for we've been seen there very often, and, D. V., we shall be seen there very often again, unless the Church is so lost to a sense of propriety as to leave us without a shilling in our pockets."

"I wish you wouldn't go," responded the man of unimpeachable properness: "it makes a deal of scandal—in fact, it gets the whole house into ill repute."

"Not *you* into ill repute, surely, my dear old boy; why, you're going to Manchester to-morrow, aren't you?"

"Well, it doesn't alter matters to be jealous of me, Rivers; and it isn't thought consistent in students preparing for the ministry to be so fond of worldly amusements."

"Worldly amusements! Now, as you are here unburdening your conscience, Jones, let's really talk the matter over with some approach to common sense. Do you really believe that it's *wrong* to go to a concert?"

"Well, no; not the mere music—it's the example."

"The example of doing what is *not* wrong?"

"Of course not—but people wont stop where you stop."

"That's very likely; but for all that we're bound to set an example of stopping at the right place, and not a mile or two on what you call the safe side of it. Give Rivers and me credit for being as conscientious as you are, and Sharpe and Slow, and that set. We think amusements are very beneficial, and that we can work better for them, and that it is a proud disregard of God's mercies not to enjoy them when we can: so we're going to the Free Trade Hall concerts whenever we can spare the time and money; and we're going on Tuesday night to the Free Trade Hall to hear Jenny Lind in 'Elijah.' I suppose even you, and Sharpe, and Slow, have *heard* of Jenny Lind?"

"Well, Williamson, I can't help it—you'll find it out when you are leaving College, and want to get a good place. I suppose you'll be at the prayer-meeting at twelve?"

"Perhaps we may," said Williamson.

"I'm quite certain we shall *not*," said Rivers, "for we've that piece of 'The Republic' to finish; and we must take the old monkish motto for to-day —'Laborare est orare.' Ta-ta, Jones."

But, as I said at the beginning of this chapter, there is nothing romantic in a Dissenting College. The outside world knows nothing, and I am afraid will care nothing, about such still life. But, for all that, a good many hundreds of thousands of the people of England are Dissenters; and their theology and social habits, and even morality, are influenced far more than appears on the surface by the College training of their ministers.

Williamson and Rivers went on the next Tuesday

to Manchester, to hear Jenny Lind in "Elijah," at the Free Trade Hall. It was, indeed, a glorious sight; even the dingy old Hall, big, ugly, low-roofed barn though it was, looked positively gorgeous. It was crammed in every corner. The cream of Manchester society was there, and also the cream of society even from all the neighbouring towns. The ladies of Manchester are very dressy and, moreover, many of them very pretty; and on that high festival of song they had done their very best to be beautiful. Every face, too, was beaming with that anticipation of complete and unmixed pleasure which is itself one of our keenest enjoyments. People in London scarcely understand the genuine excitement of delight which the visit of a great singer gives to a country town, even so large as Manchester. At any rate, for that Tuesday, hundreds, nay thousands, had for weeks been longing and preparing, and now it had come; and they were there waiting for the sweetest voice in Europe, and the masterpiece of a composer who had come to be loved almost as much as he was admired, and who had died too soon for the hopes and wishes of his contemporaries. Nearly everybody was in good time, even the holders of numbered tickets for the best reserved seats. For some minutes there had been the not unpleasing discord of the tuning of stringed instruments; and now a few grand, solemn chords from the large organ, with more vigorous tuning and adjustment till all were ready, and the clock struck the hour at which the performance was to begin. Then there was breathless silence, and the hush of expectation; then clapping of hands, as one and another of the principal singers came up; then a perfect tempest of applause, everybody instinctively rising, half in curiosity, half in admiration—and Jenny Lind was truly there, bowing with a sort of modest self-possession to the audience, dressed in quiet black, mourning for Mendelssohn. A few sharp taps from the bâton of the conductor, and then he raised his hand, and the performance was begun. It was for Fritz one long enchantment —the prophet's solemn threat of famine in the name of the Lord; the overture, while want and misery are gathering over the people; the wailing and bootless prayers of the Israelites; the reproof of Elijah, and his assurance that they who seek the Lord with all their hearts shall surely find Him; the departure of the prophet to Cherith's brook, and the sweet song of the angels, "He shall give His angels charge over them:" the command to go to Zarephath, where a widow woman should sustain him. It was all delicious self-oblivion and irresistible fascination. But it was nothing to what was to follow; for now stood up the widow woman, wrestling in piteous, passionate entreaty with Elijah for the life of her sick, her dead son; and then the prophet's prayer, the mother's trembling strengthening hope; the returning life of the child; and the burst of boundless gratitude in which prophet and widow unite, "I will love the Lord my God with all my heart, and with all my soul, and with all my might." Fritz trembled from head to foot; his whole soul was stirred; the tears streamed down his face, the voices still rang in his ears, clear and true, through all the clamour of wonder and admiration which burst from every part of the crowded hall. "There is no breath left in him. I go mourning all the day long; I lie down and weep at night. See mine affliction. Be Thou the orphan's helper."

But everybody knows "Elijah" now, and description is not my forte. Still this was the first oratorio Fritz had ever heard, and the old emotion returned whenever he attempted to describe it. For weeks and weeks the strains were ringing through his memory, and as he opened his Bible to read in plain prose that stirring history, the page was bright with a new light and full of a new meaning.

And all the while Jones, and Sharpe, and Slow, and the prigs in general, were groaning in their dark, dull souls, that Rivers and Williamson were growing so worldly, and bringing so evil a reputation on the house. When will pious people learn that bad tempers and uncharitable judgments are far more worldly and wicked than to rejoice with thankful hearts in the rest and gladness that our heavenly Father sends us to cheer the weary cares of human life.

CHAPTER VII.

EFFIE AT HOME.

But what of the cosy autumn evenings at Shiloh, and the old-fashioned library, and the path among the firs? Did Fritz ever remember them? Had they faded quite away from Effie's heart? It is not likely; at least, no woman can think it likely. Men seem so busy, and their avocations are so absorbing, that they think of the woman they love only for a little minute at a time; but when a man has won a woman's heart, *really* won her *heart*, her life seems to become a long sweet reverie, an unbroken spiritual fellowship with him. How her soul listens for the inaudible words which still she fondly dreams he *must* be speaking to her! What passionate fondness she lavishes upon him, though he be too far away for her arms to twine about him, and for her kisses to touch his lips. She never *remembers* him, for she *never forgets*. Goethe should have loved women more truly, gently, pityingly, than he did, for he had read their hearts. He must have had a rare insight into what they are, when he put into Gretchen's mouth those few deep words which are almost untranslatable* from their very simplicity.

> "Sometimes one little moment think of me;
> And I—I've all my time to think of thee."

But what am I saying? Fritz and Effie were not in love, so why should *they* think of each other? And, on the other hand, why should they not? Can there be no intercourse between the two sexes which is not meant to end in marriage or crime? Effie and Fritz didn't intend that their intercourse should end in either; they had no communication with each other; neither knew where the other was, and not even they themselves were aware that irresistible affinities were drawing them together.

Effie was at home in London with her father and mother, and no inconsiderable tribe of brothers and sisters. Mr. Holmes was a chemist and druggist with a first-rate business—the shop being in Tichborne-street, a short street which leads across from the bottom of the Quadrant to the Haymarket end of Piccadilly. The private house was a little out of the bustle of town, in one of the suburbs now almost as busy as Piccadilly itself. It was in what Londoners call a square—that is to say, an enclosure with five unequal sides, and not one of its angles a right angle. There was a little bit of ground at

* "Denkt ihr an mich ein Augenblickchen nur;
Ich werde Zeit genug an euch zu denken haben."
—*Faust* (Garden scene).

the back of the houses, producing very little but cats; and the occupiers of the houses in "the square" had the use in common of the square garden. Effie's little garden was really the balcony which ran along in front of the drawing-room windows, and on the top of the portico of the front door. There she defied and conquered even the grime and smoke of London; and the flowers came out, sweet and bright, in their seasons, as if it were their joy and reward to be admired by her. I never saw either her father or her mother, so I can only give such part as I may need of what Fritz used to tell me about them. He used to say that Mr. Holmes was the very model of an unselfish tradesman, a man who knew quite well that if we "take care of the pennies the pounds will take care of themselves;" but who believed that there was something better in life than either pounds or pennies. He was often upbraided by his friends for being over-generous, and they used to tell him he was in a manner robbing his wife and children. Once he had really gone further than even he cared to think in utter unselfishness. A young relation had come to him in great distress. The youth had not been over-steady, and had already come to grief through his boyish recklessness; his father could do nothing for him, and nobody else would—nobody, at least, unless he could touch the too susceptible heart of Mr. Holmes. He told his generous kinsman what a random life he had been leading, how keenly he had suffered, how bitterly he had repented.

"And now, sir," he said, "there is a broad, straight way for me to honour and prosperity, if only some kind friend will open for me the 'wicket-gate at the head of the way.'"

"Which means, I suppose, Frank Walker, 'if only some kind friend will advance me a few thousands of pounds.' Of course, a good many people would be glad to set out on pilgrimage if they could be sure of getting through *that* wicket-gate."

"Indeed, sir, I shouldn't dream of asking you for anything of the kind. In truth, I've no right to ask you for anything; and I only do ask you for such confidence as I hope you will not find it difficult to give me. I have never been even suspected of dishonesty, and I only want you to believe that I will not steal."

"That's all, is it, Frank? You scarcely needed to look so grave about that."

"Thank you heartily, Mr. Holmes. I'll tell you all my plans and prospects, and then leave the whole matter to your generosity. Goulburn and Sons have offered me a good clerkship in their bank, with a much better salary than I could fairly have expected—200*l.* a year. At first they wanted a deposit of 2000*l.*, just as a protection in case of any mistake or negligence. That, you know, would really have been equivalent to offering with one hand and taking away with the other. However, they were so kind as to waive that, on condition I would find somebody to be surety for me. There is nothing to advance—there never will be anything to advance if I am steady and honest, and that I'm determined to be. Goulburns know you, and I thought——"

"Well, Frank, you thought——?"

"I thought perhaps you wouldn't mind saying——"

"Saying——?"

"Saying, that if anything did go wrong, which it never shall, you would be my surety."

"Frank, do you know *why* Goulburns want so large a deposit, or a responsible surety?"

"Because the place they offer me is one of great responsibility; a great deal of money will be passing through my hands every day," said Frank, rather proudly.

"Yes, of course. In fact, you might lose, or somehow get wrong, to the extent of many thousands of pounds; and even Goulburns can't afford to run any needless risk of that. Suppose anything of that kind were to happen, who do you think would be the sufferer?"

Mr. Holmes looked hard at Frank; and while

Frank hesitated, went on—"*I* should be the sufferer, and mother, and Effie, and the brothers and sisters—*we* should be the sufferers."

He paused; for his mouth was working with more emotion than he cared to show, and there was a fierce struggle in his soul. At last Frank broke the silence.

"You're quite right, sir," he said; "I ought not to have asked you such a favour, but—but—it was my only hope."

"I haven't refused you, my lad, and *I wont refuse you.* I know how I should bless and almost worship the man who would be kind to a child of mine. But, Frank Walker, look me in the face—if ever you bring want and sorrow into my happy home, be sure that Almighty God will require it of you."

They were both silent for a while; but Mr. Holmes was not the man to do a favour grudgingly. He shook hands with his young kinsman right heartily.

"I wish you success, my boy," he said, quite cheerfully. "Work hard; don't be selfish; try to make other people happy, and never mind yourself. God will look after *you,* if you do your duty and put your trust in Him. Tell Goulburns I shall be glad to make any arrangements they think necessary; and they may call either here or at home whenever they like. Good-bye, Frank, good-bye."

With a light heart and the best of resolutions,

Frank hurried away to the city. One of the Goulburns called on Mr. Holmes that evening, with the necessary legal instruments, and all was done. Perhaps it was silly—so Mr. Holmes's brother thought at any rate; and though it was too late to prevent the mischief, he called a few evenings afterwards to say a little bit of his mind. The evening was chilly, and Mr. and Mrs. Holmes with Effie were sitting round the parlour fire. The two brothers went into another room to talk; and Effie and 'mother' could hear voices louder than usual, speaking with a troubled kind of earnestness that rather frightened them—at last the door of the room where the brothers were was opened, and they plainly heard the words—

"Well, Robert, all I can say is, you're robbing your wife and children."

Mr. Holmes looked uneasy when he came back into the parlour. There was evidently a mystery somewhere—serious, dangerous. Effie was quite pale, and looked up inquiringly into her father's face.

"Well, mother," said Mr. Holmes, "Alfred here's been rather hard on me. I can't quite explain it; it's a matter of business, and concerns others besides myself, so I must make a bit of a secret of it. But brother Alfred thinks——well, I half believe he thinks I scarcely love you—*you*, mother, and *you*, my pretty queen."

The two looked more frightened than ever.

"Mother," said Mr. Holmes, and it was plain that he was deeply moved, "if I were dead, and you were to come, as I know you would come, to see my grave, would you like to be able to say, 'he was thought a hard man—grasping, grinding, uncharitable, and all that sort of thing; but it was all for the best; he's left us well off and comfortable?'"

"Robert, Robert, what do you mean?" said Mrs. Holmes.

"What, indeed, Emma darling! No, no; you would scorn such thoughts. You would rather be poor, and remember that your husband tried, in his poor way, to be loving and pitiful like the good God —whatever came of it."

Effie got up from her chair, and sat on her father's knee. She passed her fingers through his thin hair. She could not speak; but she kissed his cheeks and brow again and again and again, while the tears were streaming down her face.

"My Effie, my queen!" he said; "if we are ever poor, and you and your mother cannot have the little comforts you prize so much, what shall I do?"

"Hush, hush, father; you will love us just the same, and we shall love you more than ever."

But they could not talk. They drew their chairs closely together, Effie still on her father's knee, and father's arm round his wife's neck. There has been much joy that might have been glad to change places with that night's sadness. Come what might, those three could never doubt each other's love.

And Alfred? They had forgotten all about him; and when they looked round he was gone. He was walking homewards at that rapid pace which indicates so truly the hurry and impatience of the thoughts that are working within. "What a fool Robert is," he was muttering to himself; "and I know if any mischief comes out of that swaggering puppy, Frank Walker, and Robert and his family are brought to poverty, he'll expect me to help him out. And I shall have a swarm of poor relations sticking to me like leeches; and that sentimental little donkey, Effie—what's she good for? Bah! I'll let Robert know that I'm not going to rob *my* wife and family even for him."

Alfred was a very wise man, was he not, good reader?

CHAPTER VIII.

FRANK WALKER.

Frank Walker was very grateful for his kinsman's help. He felt that it was very generous in Mr. Holmes to do what nobody else would do. In fact, that was the very thing; in itself what Mr. Holmes had done wasn't much; it cost nothing, beyond a bit of stamped paper and a few dips of ink; but nobody else would do it. It didn't occur to Frank to consider deeply the reasons why people are so shy about becoming sureties even for their young relations. He simply thought the world disgustingly selfish and suspicious; and that on the whole, as people go, "old Holmes had been very plucky and goodnatured—in fact, a regular old brick." About once a fortnight for awhile he used to call at the house in the five-sided square, to say how he was getting on; and also to have a look at Effie, and quite to make up his mind whether in spite of her prettiness she was not rather a milksoppy kind of little humbug. Frank had a decided preference for much more dashing young ladies, inclining to be "fast."

She was often dashing, indeed, and quite ready on fit occasions to brave the worst that Mrs. Grundy could say or do; but then her brilliance and fiery-gentle independence had no spice of *wickedness* in it. She would be unconventional without a regret or a fear; but it was only for the sake of what was better, truer, kinder than conventionalism. So Frank made up his mind at last, and to this effect—Effie was rather a muff, but might have been made something of with a better bringing up.

For a person who knew so well as he did what to do with ready cash, loose and uncounted in his trousers' pockets, Frank's pocket-money during the first three months of his clerkship was undoubtedly shabby. It was far too little to admit of much amusement; so he had the mortification of hearing young Sparks describe the opera, and the play, and the supper, and all that came after, every now and then, just as the greenest young gooseberry from the country might have heard it. To him these delights were for awhile forbidden by the hard and dreary law in operation at Goulburn's and most other houses of business in the City—never to pay a clerk's salary till it is really due. Sparks, on the other hand, had much more pocket-money than salary. Nevertheless he seemed quite as meanly suspicious as the general world; and never could be made to understand the hints which Frank sometimes ventured to throw out, that a temporary loan, just sufficient to cover an evening's entertainment and enable a fellow to stand treat for an obliging friend, would be very satisfactory. Sparks said he thought it would be first-rate, and what a pity it was Frank didn't know somebody who'd do it for him. Wouldn't old Holmes?

"And I'll be bound," said Sparks, "I'm the lucky beggar you'd stand treat for if you got a little loan."

"Yes, you are," said Frank; meaning, in the depths of his miserable soul, that that was the interest he would pay for any temporary accommodation.

"Then," said Sparks, "I'm all the more sorry, old fellow, that I can't for the life of me think of any human being at all likely to lend it to you."

Now this didn't make Frank understand that he was setting out in a course of absurdity and danger; it didn't cast the faintest glimmer of light on the reasons why people don't like to be sureties for their young relations. It simply made him bad-tempered, and kindled within him a fierce desire to show Sparks that he could make a dash as well as anybody. He really *knew* that he *couldn't* make a dash as well even as Sparks. He was wild enough, and, for that matter, wicked enough; but he was certainly not rich enough. When quarter-day came, he would be worth 50*l.* sterling. He might have it in notes, or gold, or silver, or even copper; but he could make no more of it—50*l.*, and by no chance 50*l.* 0*s.* 0¼*d.* Then he had to pay for his apartments; there was a tailor's bill, a shoemaker's bill, a general outfitter's bill. They were not much, and they might stand a quarter; but still, what's 50*l.* Sparks wouldn't mind spending half as much, if anything were to be gained by it, on a single lark. Frank knew, and he bitterly cursed him while he thought of it, that his fellow-clerk had taken the exact measure of him; had seen to the very bottom of his mean soul and meaner pocket. But *he'd* show him. Show him what? How soon 50*l.* could be spent? What a beggar he would be when it *was* spent? Frank didn't clearly see *what* he would show him. "But the proud young devil shan't have it all his own way—that's all."

No, that wasn't all. Quarter-day came—and 50*l.*, "three ten-pound notes, and the rest in gold." He thought having to change notes would be a kind of protection against spending too fast—just a very easy drag on the wheels of extravagance. Indeed, he thought the safeguard so strong that he hesitated whether he should not ask for two notes and 30*l.* in gold, but he gave to prudence the benefit of the doubt; and he felt just as rich as if he'd saved 10*l.*, or somehow turned fifty into sixty. So on the strength of this unexpected good fortune he invited Sparks to go out with him that evening, to the theatre, to Evans's, and to whatever else turned up. Sparks would be delighted; and by way of stirring the fire of Frank's jealousy and throwing on an extra shovelful of coals, he warned him not to go wasting his money too fast, because even the best of salaries don't last for ever.

They went together to the Princess's, and then to Evans's; and after sitting till very late, listening to the music, and eating and drinking what they wanted, they had a Hansom, and Frank set down Sparks at his rooms and went home to his own. It wasn't much of an evening. It cost a good deal, dress-circle at the theatre for two, refreshments after every act, cab, supper, odds and ends, something like three pounds; for, like all green spendthrifts, Frank had simply wasted twice as much money as he needed to spend; while Sparks was inwardly grinning, and thinking how he'd tell the story to a select party of young friends the next evening, a party of which Frank was not one. But next morning came before next evening; sc Sparks met Frank as usual at the bank, in the most candid and free-and-easy temper imaginable.

"It was rather slow last night, wasn't it, Walker, considering what it cost?"

Frank was the more annoyed at this speech, because it expressed with perfect exactness, his own sentiments.

"You know, I'm rather a miser," continued Sparks, "and at any rate I like to get money's worth for my money, or else I feel in a deuced bad temper. And I'm the more anxious about that when it's somebody else's money, and I'm getting treated. But it *was* slow, wasn't it? I like to be candid."

"Well, I think it was, rather. Evans's is rather a humbugging kind of a place; and as to the theatre, when you've been to one you've been to 'em all."

The fact is, Frank expected Evans's to be very fast indeed. He'd heard a great deal of it; and in truth some of his quizzical friends had trotted him out on the subject, and made him believe that under the disguise of scrupulous chastity it was neither more nor less than a sort of ante-room to the temple of Aphrodite herself, and that going to Evans's was a cheap way of "going to Corinth." Of course he was quite mistaken; he found admirable kidneys, baked potatoes, chops, steaks, ale, porter, grog, and music, and nothing else. The proprietor himself was icily modest, so Frank was disappointed. He didn't quite mean to be bad, but he did mean to have a reputation like the two-faced Janus, looking both towards heaven and hell; and for a while he meant to give the hell side a turn. But when a fellow wants to go to hell and *can't*—there's a disappointment,. That's one of the devil's best jokes.

Not that anybody is forbidden admission to the abode of misery and shame, but he can't always go *viâ* Evans's, or any other way that he specially affects. Frank was going fast enough, however, it didn't much matter which way.

"However," said Sparks, "remember I owe you an evening, some of these days; the season's nearly over, so I daresay we shan't get out again for some months. Besides, I've such a damned lot of expenses—rooms, tailors, shoemakers, and all manner of odds and ends. But I'll owe it you, and I wont forget."

"And I wont forget," thought Frank. "I'll remember I owe you a grudge, you contemptible devil; and I'll pay you, if I perish."

Yes, "*if I perish!*"

The next "season" came; Frank was in debt, in debt everywhere—nothing was paid that could by hook or crook be left unpaid. Sparks had paid him the evening he said—at the Adelphi, the pit; Sparks said it was much the best for seeing, and (nudging Frank in the ribs) "for fun." They could scarcely go out during the play for refreshments lest they should lose their places, which were not reserved, and the house was very full. It was hardly worth while trying Evans's again for supper; why not quietly have oysters somewhere? say at Scott's, at the top of the Haymarket? Proprietor not icily modest; company miscellaneous; liberty of the British subject to resist the devil unlimited. So they tried Scott's. Frank didn't mind the mixture of vice and virtue; unlimited power to do right, combined with unlimited facilities for doing evil. Moreover, it was Sparks's object to put the best face on everything; so he laughed and talked and made fun of everybody he saw, and did succeed in making the evening less slow than it would have been under Frank's management. But waking up next morning, and thinking the evening's entertainment over, Frank could scarcely help seeing that Sparks had been doing the affair cheaply, and economy was with Frank a mortal sin. He thought Sparks a mean snob, and he was the more annoyed because he knew that his fellow-clerk had been presuming on his greenness. However, *he* would show him.

In other words, he would spend his money on Sparks *because*—he hated and despised him. He would waste his salary, quarter after quarter, for the sake of proving to Sparks that he could quite well afford *to ruin himself.* He spent, and spent; debts produced new debts; he borrowed at enormous interest; he was sinking day by day (alas! how well known are the steps on the downward journey!) to shame and ruin.

"I only ask you to believe that I will not steal." Was not that what he said to Mr. Holmes? "Is thy servant a dog that he should do this thing?" But was it stealing to advance his own salary? He must get the money somehow. Here was a writ—debt and costs—Rigby and Sons *v.* Walker—

36*l.* 2*s.* 8*d.* Only two days left, or——. Other gentlemen had grown weary of politeness; and were beginning to correspond through their solicitors, with whom brevity and six-and-eightpence are the soul of wit. It was getting very serious—a quarter's salary, half-a-year's? No—a mere nothing. And for a mere temporary arrangement he must, *just a very little,* cook the accounts. He could make all right when he paid the money back. And in the meantime, for two years he would live, lodge, eat, drink, clothe himself, and *amuse* himself—on—— thin air and good resolutions?

He meant to pay the money back; but really nobody would know whether he did or not, the accounts were adjusted so carefully. So to make assurance doubly sure, he put crape on his hat, and told Sparks an uncle had died and left him a jolly lot of money. Sparks asked his uncle's name. Thompson—that was the name—lived in Yorkshire —died at Beverley ten days ago. Sparks was rather inquisitive—Frank was rather incoherent. Sparks knew, and Frank did not know, that for a very humble payment, anybody who tells a lie about a legacy can be found out. So Sparks invested that modest amount of capital, and found out that Frank was telling lies.

But knowing where money does not come from, is a very different thing from knowing where it does come from; and Sparks was not so good a detective officer as he thought himself. He began to bully Frank in a quiet way, and drop mysterious hints, and seem to know even more than he did know, instead of pretending to know nothing. So Frank got frightened; nothing had as yet occurred to bring him under the suspicion of the firm; and Sparks dared, as yet, make no charge. One Tuesday morning a letter came to Messrs. Goulburn to say that Mr. Walker was ill; his attack was very sharp, bronchitis, but the medical man, who wrote on his patient's behalf, hoped he might return to business in some ten days or a fortnight. On Thursday it occurred to Mr. Sparks to ask Mr. Goulburn, junior, if he might see the doctor's letter. The handwriting was familiar; altered as much as might be, but still familiar. Mr. Walker was evidently his own physician. In fact, it was soon discovered that Mr. Walker was out of town, was not expected to return again to his old quarters; and that he had robbed Messrs. Goulburn and Son of ten thousand pounds.

No! not Messrs. Goulburn and Son—Mr. and Mrs. Holmes, and Effie, and the brothers and sisters of that happy home.

CHAPTER IX.

FRITZ BEGINS "THE MINISTRY."

And Fritz knew nothing of the change that had come over the prospects of his pretty and intelligent companion of those autumn evenings at Shiloh. Often, indeed, as in a dream of memory, she passed before him. Often he would happen to meet with some passage in a book, and wonder what gave it its mystic charm, till he recollected that he had read it in the old-fashioned cosy library when she was with him, and when there was in her presence a quiet fascination which spell-bound him. Not *love,* that wild turbulent power, that cruel tyrant, that most painful of pleasures, that convulsive force which flings into wildest confusion the hearts and lives of men. He did not love her—at any rate he was not "in love" with her—even now. In fact he had passed out of one stage of the poetry of human life, and had not entered the other—which second stage some never enter. He hated sentimentalism; and he was a little in danger of taking it for granted that all deep feeling was "mere sentimentalism."

So if he *had* felt very tenderly about Effie, he would have tried to subdue the feeling; he would have felt himself "a spoon."

Moreover, there was much else to occupy his thoughts. He had come to his last half-year at college; he must now expect to be sent out "with a view;" to exhibit what few attractions he might have before "vacant churches;" to preach his best sermons, and put on his best manners, and generally speaking show his points and his paces, and get as good a price for himself as he could. It wasn't much in Fritz's way. He would have scorned to preach during four "probation Sundays" his eight best sermons unless he had believed that they were fair specimens of what he might hope to do every Sunday of his life. And as to manners and Sunday behaviour and the religion of every-day life, he might have been considered very lax by the majority of the churches which looked to his college for such shepherds as they needed. For of course the sheep chose the shepherds—don't sheep always choose their shepherds? Who can know so well what pasture the sheep prefer as they know themselves? And if the sheep are mistaken and really don't know what's best for them, what's the use of being a Briton and a Protestant if you mayn't make a fool of yourself when you like? Why not have "the American Spurgeon?" Why not import or breed ecclesiastical and religious "phenomena," and have "the infant Chalmers," or "the infant Chrysostom," as well as "the infant Sappho?" Or, on the other hand, what a bore it is to be kept awake a whole Sunday; as if easy square pews were "free sittings," or to have one's mind disturbed and perplexed by being required to think! At any rate what can be better in all ecclesiastical arrangements, than the ballot-box and universal suffrage?

Fritz had looked forward for some months, with horror, to this dreadful ordeal. He was far more conscious of his defects than "the neighbouring churches" could be: but at the same time he could see that it was ridiculous for some of the deacons at whose houses he had stayed to sit in judgment even on him. They knew what they liked and disliked, but the difference between a good sermon and a bad sermon they assuredly did not know. The test they applied was very simple, and very easily applied even by the least skilful. "That was a beautiful discourse we've had this morning, Brother Swan—that's what I call the very marrow and fatness of the blessed Gospel—wine on the lees. None of your new-fashioned notions that one never heard of before. He's a very promising young man." "You're right, Brother Redford. It's just what we've heard, pretty near every Sunday, from our good old doctor for the last twenty years. Ah! he's done a good work in his day, though it's pretty near over now. Let's hope his mantle will fall on this young man."

Fritz would probably have succeeded very badly in accommodating himself to the tastes of "vacant churches," besides having an incurable aversion to being "pumped" and "trotted out." He felt also that though it might be easy to say what he believed then, it was scarcely wise to pledge himself never to believe anything else to the end of time. Even within the very narrow limits of "the Puritan divines," he found so much difference of opinion that dogmatism became every day more ridiculous to him; in fact, he was in no small danger of giving up the hope of *certainty* altogether, and did actually try for a time to build a "theology" upon a balance of probabilities. Yet even that, though far too shifting a foundation for a stable and genuine creed, was quite enough to disqualify Fritz for pushing his way to vacant pulpits. The vacant pulpits were virtually in the gift of Brothers Swan and Redford. The Thirty-nine Articles of Salem or Zion were neither more nor less than Brothers Swan and Redford's private opinions, expressed with a very complete avoidance of any such scrupulous exactness as might savour of hair-splitting. Of all probabilities or improbabilities, it seemed to Fritz *least* probable that Brothers Swan and Redford had been sent into the world and the Church to calm the strife and remove the perplexities of disagreeing scholars and divines, and settle for ever the substance and the form of Christian doctrine.

"It seems very plain and simple to me, Mr. Rivers," said Brother Swan, one Saturday evening, when Fritz had come down to "supply" at Zion Chapel, Stockport; "it's really in a nutshell, when you come to think of it. There's the Blessed Trinity," he continued, counting off that item on his thumb, "that's a great matter, though beyond us. And then there's the Atoning Blood," giving a good hard push at his forefinger, to indicate that that was number two of the essentials of religion; "what should we be without the Atoning Blood? And then there's the Holy Ghost, and the blessed influences of the Spirit poured out on the blind eyes of the carnal mind. And then," another finger, "there's Election, up to glorified, 'them He also glorified.' And then," threatening his little finger with dislocation, "ay, there's the 'Holy Bible, book divine, precious treasure, thou art mine,' on which it all rests. Yes, yes, Mr. Rivers, it's all in a nutshell *when one comes to think about it*, and them that runs can read."

"Ay, ay, Brother Swan," responded Brother Redford, who had popped in to take what he called "a knife and fork" with his fellow-deacon, on the occasion of Mr. Rivers staying at his house, "you may well say 'them that runs can read'—and the Lord chooses the foolish, and puts down the pride of intellect; that's a sweet and comforting text. Not that you're the man to say a word again learning; for never a man in all Stopput knows his Bible better nor you do."

"Maybe not, maybe not; thanks be to the Blessed Spirit. But it's all in a nutshell, when one comes to think about it; in a nutshell, Mr. Rivers."

"Yes, very possibly; but many people have found it hard work to crack the shell and get at the kernel."

"True, and it's the natural man; and that's where it is the Bible's so wonderful true. If it wasn't for the natural man and the carnal mind our Bibles wouldn't be true. And that's where it is; when they touch the conscience the pride of intellect flies in its face, and it's enmity against God."

To this coherent and lucid summary of Christian evidences, Brother Redford could respond only with a satisfied and accordant groan.

"No doubt," said Fritz, "there's a dislike of what is good in a bad man's heart; that's partly what we mean when we say a man is bad. But I was thinking of the difficulty very good and learned men find in getting the kernel out of the shell. There are so many different sects, and clever and learned books on all sides of the question, that a person might easily become bewildered and perplexed, even if he confined his readings to the Puritan divines."

"You're very right, Mr. Rivers," said Brother Swan, "and I a'most more than begin to doubt whether our colleges are doing much good to us. Stick to the Bible, sir; books may be very well, and Latin and Greek I can't have much objection to in moderation; but *God's Book*—ay, ay, that's the thing for us."

And so the conversation went on, mildly suggestive, with such pauses as might give Mr. Rivers the opportunity "of showing his real colours, you know," whatever they might be. It was far from profound; and plain answers were rendered somewhat difficult by the absence of all plainness in the questions. In the little world of Zion Chapel, Stockport, everything was on a small scale; but such as it was, in that little "cause," or, as some preferred to call it, "our little 'ill," Brother Redford had the money, and Brother Swan had the brains. The next morning, therefore, a little knot of the more influential "members," including, of course, the superintendent of the Sunday-school, and one or two of the teachers, gathered round the two deacons, to ask Mr. Swan what he thought of the "supply;" and to ask Mr. Redford what he thought Zion could afford to offer in the shape of annual stipend, in case the "supply" should suit.

"I'm not without my hopes of the young man," said the man of brains; "that was a sweet prayer he gave us at the family altar last night, eh, Brother Redford?"

"Beautiful, like any old man," said the man of cash.

"I shouldn't like to throw out a prejudice," said Swan, "nor yet a want of charity; but when I opened my Bible this morning, just shooting my bow at a venture to see what morsel of morning manna the Lord had sent me—I'm free to confess it gave me quite a turn."

"Oh, deary me!" said old Mrs. Redford, "what could it 'a been, Mr. Swan?—you've fair frightened me."

"You remember, Brother Redford, our few words about books, and how I took the liberty to remark that our best plan was to stick to the Bible, and not let our minds be troubled with human learning. Well, the portion of manna my eye just fell on, as I turned the sacred page, was in the second of Chronicles, sixteenth chapter, verse twelve. Perhaps Mr. Granger will kindly turn to it."

Thereupon, the superintendent, in a great hush of solemn expectation, read the words—"And Asa in the thirty-ninth year of his reign was diseased in his feet, until his disease was exceeding great; yet in his disease he sought not to the Lord, but to the physicians."

"Now, that rather seemed to me," said Swan, "an awful—I think I *may* say, Mr. Granger, an *awful* text, for the morning manna, dropped as it were on my way in the sacred page."

"Ah!" said the superintendent.

"Deary me," said Mrs. Redford.

It really was one of those difficulties which cannot easily be solved. The unknown chronicler might have had Mr. Rivers in his prophetic eye, when he seemed to be looking only at Asa's feet; and if nobody could prove it, it was quite equally certain that nobody could disprove it. Of course, the physicians were, in that case, neither more nor less than the books in the college library, if not even the professors themselves. But amid the "Oh's" and "Ah's" of the little prophets of Zion, in walked Fritz himself; unmistakeably not, as yet, subject to the literal affliction under which Asa was tempted to seek the aid of such medical science as was in his days available.

The sermon was over, the Sunday was over, Fritz had gone back to college, the Monday night prayer-meeting at Zion had come. Mr. Granger, superintendent of the Sunday school, aged twenty-four, had prayed that God would "guide the steps and enlighten the heart of our young friend, Thy servant, who ministered to us in holy things on the past Sabbath." Mr. Redford, being greater in finance than in public devotion, had confined his prayers to a deep-toned "Amen." Swan had taken advantage of the means of grace to convey to the

Church at Zion Chapel his private opinion about "the supply" they had heard the day before. It was all over, and the little knot of Zion notables were assembled once more in the vestry.

"Mr. Swan," said the superintendent, "I think we've not yet had the privilege of hearing your opinion about Mr. Rivers."

"No," said Redford.

"Yes," said a teacher, not meaning to contradict the man of cash, but to affirm that the opinion of the man of brains was what everybody was hungering and thirsting to hear.

"It may be the morning manna," said the oracle of Zion, "but I couldn't help thinking there was more of the physicians in his sermons, than of the Lord."

"Well, Brother Swan," said Redford, "as you've mentioned it, I don't quite feel sure whether I didn't think the very same thing."

"Couldn't we manage to get that Mr. Jones, that was here a Sunday or two back?" said Granger. "What's your opinion, Mr. Redford?"

"I rather think, Friend Granger," said Redford, "that he's just a little above our figure. *Perhaps* he might be persuaded to come down a little, but I hardly think he would. He's a young man as is a good deal sought after. He told me when he was here, when I said to him, 'I reckon, Mr. Jones, you'll soon be beginning to think of settling somewhere,' he said, 'Well, Mr. Redford, I'm not in any great hurry, indeed I've three invitations in my pocket at this very time.' "

But neither Mr. Jones nor Fritz was to be at once the guided and the guide of Swan, Redford, and Co. For Fritz, at any rate, a far other future was opening. The minister, now nearly seventy years old, of a very large chapel in London, had, in some way that Fritz never could find out, heard of him, and had written to the college to ask that he might be sent up to preach for the next four Sundays. The congregation had very wisely entrusted to their minister the choice of an assistant. He heard Mr. Rivers four or five times, he had serious and confidential intercourse with him during the month of his probation, he was satisfied and pleased; and to make a short story of it, Fritz received a letter a fortnight after his return to college, informing him that he had been appointed to be the assistant of the good old minister who had served God faithfully so many years, with the wisdom that winneth souls.

CHAPTER X.

"STOLEN WATERS ARE SWEET."

It is not wise to build life upon a single proverb; and I shall devote this chapter to showing *how* sweet the waters were which Frank Walker had stolen. Yet let me do him the justice to acknowledge that he by no means reflected how great a crime, how cruel and cowardly a sin he was committing. He never once thought of the Holmeses. He scarcely intended even to rob the Goulburns; and he really did not know, or at any rate had forgotten, how much he was taking, when he opened the cash-box, and put the roll of notes it contained into the breast-pocket of his coat. It was a mere accident that so large a sum was there; and he could scarcely have expected that his desk would have been allowed to remain locked for four or five days, even though he was supposed to be absent on account of dangerous illness. But in truth he had been very diligent and respectful to his employers; and there were certain reasons, some kind of family connexion, which had secured him, with the help of Mr.

Holmes, a position of unusual trust. He knew that Sparks hated him; he could see that he suspected him; his mysterious hints nearly paralysed poor Frank with terror. What could he do? He had only *borrowed*, he thought; but he dared not confess; he dared not run away without a penny, and face beggary and danger. He would just take whatever happened to be in easy reach, and make the best of it.

He took a ticket from London Bridge to Paris, ostentatiously labelling his luggage with his real name. He went down by the evening mail to Dover, put his luggage on board the steamer, saw it start, and then walked quietly along the shore to Folkestone. For all expenses hitherto he had found the few uppermost notes amply sufficient. But he did not intend to leave England; he thought that the safest place for him in all the world would be London—partly because of its vast size, and partly because he fancied the ticket to Paris, and the luggage on board the packet would direct the search, when search became inevitable, to some part of the Continent. He took the early parliamentary train from Folkestone, and took a ticket for Reigate. He was almost crazed with fear and shame and loneliness; but he fancied if he could get to Hastings, of all places in England, just for a few days till he got nerve to enter London, he would be safe, and even—happy. He went to a very quiet inn at Reigate, ordered what he wanted to eat and drink, read the paper (oh, how eagerly !) to see whether even already he was missed and hunted, and with Bradshaw's Guide determined, as best he could, his plans for the immediate future.

He walked to Tunbridge, and there booked for Hastings. Nobody would seek a—a thief—at a fashionable watering-place. A thief! Had it really come to that? Policemen perhaps already after him—*him*, Frank Walker—and a prison and everlasting shame before him! He arrived at Hastings about eight o'clock, and took a first-floor in one of the Marine Cottages for a month certain—"it might be longer."

"Had the gentleman any luggage?"

"Yes, three boxes."

"They are not here, sir."

"Yes, surely; has the fly driven away? I thought the man was coming after me with them, along the path at the side there. He can't be gone."

"No, sir, he isn't gone; but he says there's no boxes, sir, and you've forgotten his fare, sir."

"What is his fare?"

"Eighteenpence, sir."

"Here it is then."

"Shall he inquire after the luggage, sir?"

"Yes, of course; you don't think I want to lose three boxes, do you?"

"Hollo!" he called out, before the girl was at

the bottom of the stairs; "come back; never mind the luggage. I know now, damn it! I came here by Brighton, and dined at the 'Old Ship;' and I left my boxes there. I'll telegraph in the morning."

"Thank you, sir; we very seldom like to take lodgers, sir—asking your pardon, sir—when they've no luggage."

"Of course not; so if your mistress will just send me a receipt, I'll pay a fortnight in advance. Bring the receipt. My name is Mr. Cutting. And let me have candles and a good hot fire as soon as you can. I'll have a cup of tea, and then I'll stroll out to order what I may need for to-morrow."

He made a hearty tea. He was really hungry, and he dared not run the risk of growing weak and ill, and losing his self-command. What if he were to be delirious? What if in raving fever he were to talk of Goulburns and Sparks, of his robbery and flight, of the Calais steamer, and all the secrets he ought most sacredly to keep?

And then he went out through the streets (they were less lonely than the beach), towards St. Leonards. Just as he came to White Rock, the clouds which had been hiding the moon were blown away, and she shone forth in her most perfect splendour. The sea gleamed out before him, a mass of molten silver, restless, tossing, moaning, dashing, till again the clouds hid the light of heaven, and the sea was dark and wild as hell, and its moaning and dashing seemed the wail and useless fury of lost souls. Will the moon never shine again, to remove, were it but for a moment, that black gulf? He hurried along White Rock, lashed by the Furies, as if he were walking for a wager, not even perceiving how one and another turned round to stare at the man who had such pressing need of haste, till he had passed the houses, and suddenly felt that he was alone, that the night was dark and cold, that the rain was falling in a torrent, and that he must not present himself at Marine Cottages like a distracted maniac. Oh that the sea would be quiet, and stop that moaning, that angry dash, rising higher and louder every moment! He got back to his apartments, and the servant asked him if he had ordered anything, because nothing had yet been sent in.

"No; I forgot how late it was, and walked too far; so the shops were all shut up. Just get me a bottle of brandy and some hot water, and light my bedroom fire."

He went to his bedroom, where the fire was burnt up. Now he must determine what to do, and think over what he had done. He took out the roll of notes from his breast-pocket. He shuddered as he touched them. He counted them. He knew *now* what he had done; that *such* a robbery left him utterly without hope. And now, for the first time, he remembered what Mr. Holmes had said to him: "If anything goes wrong, do you know who would be the sufferers? *I* should be the sufferer, and mother, and Effie, and the brothers and sisters at home." He heard, as plainly as if the words were being loudly whispered into his very ear, his kinsman's solemn warning—"If you do bring any trouble upon us, be sure Almighty God will require it of you." He sat in the easy chair before the fire, with all the largest notes in his hand. He could not think; the storm was wilder than ever, the sea louder; he seemed to hear in the raging elements the angry voice of a righteous God cursing him from heaven. The room, the fire, the bed—all swam round and round; and he fell back in his chair insensible.

He soon, however, recovered; and tried to collect his thoughts. One thing, at any rate, was yet possible; he might send back the largest notes to Goulburn's—he need not say where he was—he would send them without a word of explanation—it would at least ease that generous kinsman, and the happy household in "the square." And yet there would be the postmark: they would be sure to come down to Hastings, sure to find and take him. He would leave Hastings as soon as he had posted the letter, and go off to the North of England, or according to his first purpose venture back to London, and hide himself there. And if he were caught he couldn't be more wretched than he was now.

He rose and went to the table to choose out the

largest notes. He looked again and again, one after another he examined them; not one of the largest notes was there. He could scarcely believe his eyes. He looked at the bed-room door, it was still locked; at the window, it was still fastened. A cold sweat burst out upon him. He poured out brandy and drank, for he *dared* not faint again. He stood with his back to the fire, his lips quivering, his hands restlessly clasped and unclasped, the fingers not a moment still; he trembled and shivered with that cold of utter misery and panic fear which no fire could warm. What *could* it mean? He sat down again in the easy chair, and stirred the fire.

What was that on the hearth? What bit of paper could that be that the hot cinders lighted; and those other pieces; and that little heap of paper ash so light and white? He picked them up, he looked at them with a stony stare—those little bits of paper, so thin and wavy. It was plain enough now. He remembered that he had the notes in his hand when he fainted; they had fallen to the hearth and been burned. There was no hope of saving Mr. Holmes now.

Was there any hope of saving himself? At any rate, one condition of his safety, *sine qua non*, was rest. He undressed and lay down; leaving the candles burning, and heaping up coals on the fire, not knowing what he might need at any moment.

One more glass of brandy-and-water, for he was weak and low; and then——he slept. He *dreamed* that he was at Hastings; he was with some of his old companions. They were all lodging together in Marine Cottages, walking, riding, boating together. It was a wild day, sun and cloud, with a fine, rough sea, now bright, now dark, noise and wind and dash, breeze and health.

"Roar away, old sea," he said, "what a frisky old boy you are. The winds blow and think to vex you, and you only jump, and frisk, and laugh, and call out 'hollo!' and, rude old sea, spit at the clouds and winds, and throw up your pebbles at the shore, and run back and——"

"Make a silly, sentimental old humbug of *you*," said one of his dream companions; "stop all that stupid jaw, and let's have a boat."

So they had a boat—after much demur on the part of the owner—and set out; four rowing, and the boatman steering. The boat pitched and rolled, and people on the beach stood watching, and wondering what devil of madness could possess four young fellows to risk their lives so recklessly. Before they had rowed a dozen yards they were wet to the skin; but they laughed and shouted all the louder, and pulled with all their might, defying tide, and wind, and danger. They were soon, however, convinced that rowing in such a sea was grim earnest; and that they must stop their shouts and laughter, and make the utmost use of their strength, and obey with the utmost care and promptness the directions of the boatman, if they were ever to pull the boat round without her being upset, and get safe again to shore. They were doing their best, sobered by the presence of danger; it was a moment, so Frank dreamed, when almost everything depended on his own steady nerve and vigorous stroke—when he heard hissed into his ears the words, "I've caught you at last"—and the face of Sparks appeared out of the very water, as he laughed a laugh of scorn and triumph. Frank's oar flew out of his hands into the sea, as he started to his feet. In a moment all was over, youths and boatman were struggling in the waves, and, in an agony of terror, Frank awoke.

"Only a dream!" he gasped; "I thought Sparks had me."

It was no use trying to sleep; he stirred the fire, drank some more brandy, heaped his clothes and railway rug on the bed, and lay down again to think and plan. At any rate he would leave Hastings; he would go to London. Something might turn up. Poor Frank; he had no self-reliance, no real strength of character, no strength even of badness, was in such need of the props and supports of fellowship that he had been the mere plaything of such a man as Sparks. To be alone, to have no prospect of finding any human being again with whom he would dare to be intimate, to be shut out for ever from the amusements and companions for which he had run into such awful danger—that was hell indeed. "I am alone in the world," he said to himself; "there's not a creature I dare consult. I must hide in unfrequented places. I shall soon have to beg my bread or work for my living; and I have no friends and no character." He hid his face with his hands, piteously weeping—and lay tossing and wretched with unutterable wretchedness, till the morning had grown bright, and he could venture downstairs.

"Are you ill, sir?" said the servant, staring with undisguised wonder and fear at his pale face, on every line of which terror and misery had been writing their awful records.

"Well, I don't feel quite up to the mark, thank you; I've had a very bad night, and I'm very anxious about my boxes; I must go to Brighton about them at once."

"Can't I take a message for you, sir, to the telegraph office?"

"No, thank you, Mary, it's very important; I must go myself. Let me have breakfast as soon as you can."

It was soon brought; and Mary had a pretty, loving face, quite softened to refinement by her genuine womanly pity. Poor Frank was thinking that it was perhaps the last face that would ever look kindly on him as long as he lived.

"I'll have some toast, please, Mary. No, make it here; this is a capital clear fire. It's rather dull to be alone when one's ill, isn't it?"

"I should be very dull myself, sir."

"What's your name besides Mary?"

"Why, it's a very ugly name; and I take it very hard they ever gave it me; it's Jemima."

"There are many worse names, my girl; what's your surname?"

"Holmes, sir."

He started up with a kind of shriek; while she also rose from the fire, toast in hand, looking at him with the greatest alarm and surprise.

"Oh, Mary, Mary, what a fool I am! It's all nothing now, but I knew a girl called Holmes; with a sweet face, a bright, happy girl—Effie Holmes," he said, more to himself than to Mary. "But go on making the toast."

"Has she been very unkind to you, sir? I'm sure, if she's anything of a girl, she'll be as sorry as you are by this time, though she may be too proud to say so."

"No, she never was unkind to anybody."

"Well, Mr. Cutting, you'll excuse me taking the liberty to say so, but I don't think people would start so, if she'd been *very* kind to you."

The toast was made, and Mary went away; having stirred up memories that turned Frank sick with grief and shame. In fact he was feeling seriously ill; almost too ill to venture on a journey to London, a journey into mere darkness and distraction and utter loneliness. Even pretty, good-natured, pitying Mary, seemed a very angel to him. Would this honest, kind-hearted, gentle-spoken servant girl make toast for him, and talk quietly to him by the fire if she knew what he really was? For London, at any rate, he would wait till to-morrow; a stroll by the sea or over the hills would perhaps do him good. So he rang the bell, and told Mary he was really very ill, and would telegraph to Brighton instead of going there himself. He would be glad if she would see to his dinner, and he would try if a walk would improve him.

A walk did not improve him. Before he reached White Rock he felt so utterly feeble he could go no further; he called a chair, that he might be taken quietly home, and he was led upstairs, tottering like a man already stricken with death. His landlady came to know if she could do anything for him. He thanked her, and asked that Mary might be allowed, if she would, to attend him, and he would pay for any extra help that might be necessary in the house. Would she also send for a physician?

The physician came, and ordered him to bed; indeed he was already so utterly prostrate that it was with the utmost difficulty he could sit even in an easy-chair. The physician asked where he had been living. Frank said he had been travelling.

Had he noticed any of his fellow-passengers, anybody at the hotels, ill; did anybody in the railway-carriage look as if recovering from severe illness? Frank didn't remember. The doctor recommended that the strips of carpet in the bedroom should be removed, and the woollen curtains taken from the bed; it would make Frank more comfortable. He would send the necessary medicine and give the servant all needful directions. "Yes," Frank said, "he should be very pleased if the servant would kindly attend to him; he would pay her whatever was right. But he had no friends near, and she seemed so quiet and kind."

The doctor went into the drawing-room, and closed the folding-doors which separated it from the bedroom. He rang the bell and asked for the landlady, and told Mary to stay also, that he might speak to them both together.

"I'm sorry to tell you," he said to the landlady, "that this is a serious case. I must be very explicit, both for your sake and mine, to say nothing of the patient. I know nothing of Mr. Cutting, but I will do my best; and I am sure you are quite as humane and considerate as I can pretend to be. Understand clearly, if you try to remove him you'll *kill* him; and if you take in any other lodgers for at least a month or two, you'll most likely kill *them*. I can scarcely have a doubt about the poor young man's disease; at any rate, it's highly dangerous, and I sincerely hope you'll follow my instructions carefully. To begin with, will you nurse him, Mary?"

Mary put her apron to her eyes, and began to cry and sob.

He looked at her carefully.

"You're a strong healthy girl," he said;" I don't think you'll take any harm. We shall all want somebody to do a kind action for us some day, shan't we, Mary?"

"Oh—yes—sir," sobbed Mary; "don't say a word about it. I'll nurse him, poor gentleman. But it's such a sudden thing, isn't it, sir?"

"God bless you, Mary; you're a good girl. Now do what I tell you. Take up these carpets, take the cushions and covers from those cane-bottomed chairs, take down the window-curtains, sprinkle the floor with something I'll send you—keep a little fire in the bedroom and a good fire here. Open these windows every now and then, when the bedroom door is shut; and then shut the windows and open the bedroom door, and keep the air fresh and pure. Sit in this room, where you may hear him if he calls or moves—and—well, I'll call again in the afternoon."

So the doctor went away. The poor landlady was but a landlady, a mere lodging-house keeper, a widow, a Roman Catholic—and, thank God, a woman. She cried, of course. It was very hard that this should have fallen upon her. "Why did he come here to be ill?"

"Surely, ma'am, he didn't know," said Mary.

"No, no, Mary, God forgive me; we must do our best."

So the doctor's orders were obeyed; and Mary sat in the drawing-room with the folding-doors open, listening. Soon Frank called her.

"Mary."

She was by him in a moment.

"Take a roll of bank-notes out of my breast-pocket—there, in my coat."

"This, sir?"

"Yes, Mary; it will pay for what I need. I shall never recover. I know I am on my death-bed. You'll be gentle with me, Mary, and forgive me if I'm troublesome?"

"Oh, don't talk so; don't. You'll get better, sir; and I'll take all the care of you I can."

"And if I'm delirious, you won't be frightened? People always say very wild strange things at such times."

"No, sir; I remember when father was ill I helped to nurse him, three years and a half ago come Christmas. He died of typhus fever. But you look nothing to what he did, Mr. Cutting."

"Perhaps not, Mary; but *I shall die,* and I think I'd rather die."

Poor Mary could only weep and sob, till she felt

it was only making him worse. So like a brave woman she dried her eyes, adjusted his pillow and bed-clothes, almost noiselessly stirred the fire, and went back to her solitary corner by the drawing-room fire.

The doctor came again; he could not doubt it was indeed typhus. Frank lay utterly prostrate. Then, in their awful order, came almost all the agonies and dangers that even that dreadful foe to human life can bring. In wild delirium he raved of Goulburns and Sparks; he fancied the whole room swarming with policemen; he said he must and would get out of bed, for Sparks was under the sheets trying to murder him. Then his dream seemed to come back upon him; he panted, gasped, spat what he thought the salt sea-water out of his mouth, struggled with arms and legs as if he were swimming, with all the agonizing shrieks of a drowning man. Then he sank into that calm which is scarcely less terrible than delirium itself; that awful lethargy, so like to death, and yet so unlike—almost worse than death. At last he slept, quietly and soundly, and awoke almost another man. Poor Mary looked at him with loving delight; he could understand what she said; he asked many questions—what he had said, who had been, and such like. She told him she would answer them all when he was better. He took her hand and kissed it, and poured out thanks till she was compelled to stop him, and go back with a thankful, happy heart to her corner in the next room, lest he should be over-wearied.

In a little while she heard a moaning noise, and sobs, and then in a weak, broken voice, Frank called out "Mary!"

She was at his side in a moment.

"Oh, Mary! I quite forgot where I was; surely I'm not getting better. I want to die."

"Lord bless you, sir, what do you want to die for?"

"Ah, what indeed! No, Mary, I don't want to die, but I don't want to live."

She thought he was still wandering.

"Can you write, Mary?"

"Yes, sir."

"Write to Mr. Holmes" (he gave her his address) "*when I am dead*, and ask him to come here and see me buried."

"Do you mean, say 'Mr. Cutting's dead,' and nothing else?"

Mr. Cutting! Oh, it was too true; here he was alone and friendless, but for the loving care of the poor servant girl. Mr. Cutting, indeed!

"No, Mary, never mind the surname; say Frank died here."

"Of course, sir, if you do, I'll say so."

But Mary wrote that very night, and next morning Mr. and Mrs. Holmes and Effie were wondering, guessing, and at last deciding who "Frank," *alias* "Mr. Cutting," must be.

But Frank grew rapidly worse. The typhus was gone, and he was sensible and comparatively collected. He could talk with Mary, and asked to see a clergyman. The good man came, kind and hopeful, expecting the usual clerical experience of those who try to do good for sick souls. It was with a strange countenance he went away. Not often had such confessions been entrusted to his ear. He came again twice next day, Saturday. Nothing indeed could be done to alter the dreadful past; but the message of God's priest was to the sinner, "the ignorant, and them that are out of the way." He could only point to the unchangeable Father and the infinite love. The doctor came and went with bitter disappointment. Why didn't the patient mend? What unlooked-for complication thwarted the healing fondness of nature? Sunday morning came; a bright, sunny sky, the sweet church bells, the mysterious calm of the day of rest, which even the lifeless elements seem to recognise. On his way to church, the clergyman called again. There was no time to be lost.

"Sir, I'm dying," said Frank; "and I'm going to hell."

The clergyman could say nothing to *him,* could only murmur half-articulate prayers to Almighty God.

"Father! into thy hands we commend his spirit."

They were still kneeling round his bed—doctor, landlady, Mary, and the clergyman—the bed where his dark, unhappy course had ended at last, when Mr. Holmes and Effie quietly entered the room. The clergyman told them all, and I need not try to say what followed. But Mr. Holmes sent all the remaining notes to Goulburn, and paid the landlady and doctor all they could be persuaded to take. They took Mary home with them, and went out to face that world which poor, dead Frank had made so stern for them, with the calm and hopeful courage of godly hearts.

CHAPTER XI.

EFFIE GETS HER OWN LIVING.

It *was* a stern world; Frank's sorrow had been as deep and true as his best friends could have wished; his bitter suffering and premature death might have satisfied his worst enemies. But how much misery would be prevented if we were to remember that there are troubles which neither penitence nor punishment can lessen! Poor Frank's funeral did not pay the money for which Mr. Holmes was responsible. They must reduce expenditure. They could no longer have a house in the five-cornered square. The business near the Quadrant must be sold, and such a shop and house taken as might suit their altered circumstances. And Effie? She told herself what she must do. Her father could not bear to think of his pretty queen earning her own living; but she could not bear to think of being a burden to him. What could she do? What can any well brought-up girl do in this country, when she is thrown upon her own resources?

"Be a governess." Respectable, literary, dignified,

&c., &c., &c. At any rate, she might try. She said nothing to her father about it; but she thought, surely there was something she could teach worth learning. How sadly come back upon us in our trouble the happy days that have gone! Sitting in the plainly furnished parlour, over the new shop in Islington, trying to think what she knew and could teach, she found herself, alas, too often! back again in the dear old Shiloh library, with the books that occupied, years ago now, the long autumn evenings, and the friend with whom she used to read them. Her kinsman was dead, and Shiloh had passed into other hands. But where was Fritz? Was he dead too? Would he be sorry to know what trouble had come upon them? Could he, would he, help her, if he were near and knew all? It was useless to ask; and yet, is it not a kind of comfort for us to have even in bare imagination some helper to lean on, when we feel weak and alone? To think that somebody cares for us, or would care for us if he knew our need, gives us heart, and courage and hope are themselves a victory. And as to Fritz, he was clever, or at any rate Effie thought so; and whatever men may think of women, they do not care more for coats, black or red, than for hearts and brains. The poor girl knew well enough how one "friend" after another would drop off, now her father was poor and embarrassed; but she could bear it, so long as these fickle "friends" were people who measured life and prosperity by standards she did not care for. Would Fritz dislike her if she were a mere governess, or perhaps engaged in some business less "ladylike" still? What is a "lady?" A month ago she would have been called one. In a month to come she might be governess in a family, teacher in a school, serving behind a counter. What great change would have been made in *her?* Would she have lost her own personal refinement, her education, her uprightness, her pure taste, her warmth of affection? She thought not, but——. Yes, dear Effie—gentle, loving Effie—there is a *but;* and you must henceforth think more of what *is* than of what *seems.* You must be above the poor conventionalisms of life, or they will crush and ruin you.

At any rate she would try what could be done towards becoming a governess. She read innumerable advertisements; and applied to four or five Educational Agency Offices, which furnished her with long lists of questions, more or less relevant and hopeful. She answered advertisements and wrote letters, till she began to think all the advertisements were a cruel hoax, and the very post-office in the conspiracy to despise or forget her. At one or two houses she had to "apply personally;" which was a discipline not altogether useless, though painful and irritating. Every attempt, however, was fruitless. Effie was very clever, and would have taught children both rapidly and well; but she was not "accomplished," or what was more fatal still, she measured all her attainments by so high a standard, that she could never blow her own trumpet loud enough to be heard in this world of clamorous self-assertion. Then, again, she was not a "Churchwoman;" and she had never "been out" before.

"She'd always be home-sick and low-spirited," Effie heard a mother say to her daughter, as soon as one of her many useless "personal applications" was over; "and you know we never could do with that in a governess, Fanny—moping about the house or crying."

Once, however, never having been out before might have secured her "employment," if her spirit had been sufficiently broken to take an insult with gratitude.

"So you was never out before, Miss 'Olmes?" said the wife of a "City snob."

"No, ma'am; never before."

"Oh! well, per'aps that don't matter much, especially as it's accounted for in your terms, Miss 'Olmes. Indeed, per'aps its quite as well or better. I've had a deal of experience with *all* sorts, and even governesses, when they've been out long, get tricks I can't do with. It's the way with all the people one employs," said the snobbess; with not the faintest notion that she was guilty of a very coarse and cowardly insult.

"I don't quite understand you," said Effie, in an interrogative tone; "did you say *tricks?*"

"Yes, tricks; tricks, you know; ways of rather imposing, and a haughty kind of way, not at all becoming their station in life—you know what I mean."

"Yes, madam, I rather begin to think I do now, and so I'll bid you good morning."

Poor Effie! she seemed as cool and collected as if she had received a compliment; but she hurried home, and shut herself up in her room, and wept such bitter tears as she had never shed before. She was not *surprised* by what had happened; and we are not surprised when those who have been long ill die at last. But she was none the less miserable. That gentle hearts are wounded every day she knew full well; but that bitter knowledge could not heal the anguish of her own. "Tricks!" Did she not know how patiently, to the very utmost of her power, she would have done her duty? Did she not know how in her inmost soul she scorned every kind of meanness? Had she not already, because she would not in the least degree exaggerate her own attainments, come back rejected again and again, to begin afresh the weary work of finding something to do? So it seemed that only riches can protect a woman from the reputation of trickiness; and her poverty had brought disgrace as well as sorrow.

"Be it so," she said at last, drying her eyes; "the God whom I serve is able to deliver me from the burning, fiery furnace; but *if not,* I will not worship the *golden* image which society has set up.

"Poor father, too, how little he knows what I suffer! God forbid he ever should know! His little Effie tricky—his little queen insulted and wounded! He doesn't think people will treat us differently now we are poor. He fancies the people we visited in better days were really fond of us ourselves; really, in a way, loved us. Well, well, we shall find out our *true* friends now, that's one comfort; and how I shall *love* them. How hungry my poor heart is!"

"B—by Jove!" said the City snob to his wife, too indignant almost to get his feelings into words, being in his coolest moments a man far from eloquent, "Wh—what did you say? Didn't you turn her out of doors? *I am* damned if that ain't coming it strong. You'd 'ave 'ad a nice time of it with that impident puppy in a house; a nice time of it, by Jove!"

Charming City snob! Noble and virtuous indignation! A little chit of a governess presuming to give herself airs, indeed! It was plain enough to the keen perceptions of a snob that Effie *was* up to tricks, and that "pretending to be insulted" was one of them.

"Yes, yes, by Jove, a nice time you'd 'ave 'ad of it!"

But why should Effie be a governess at all?

"Society" preferred it? It was more respectable and ladylike? More, what she'd been accustomed to? *What* was? Had she been "accustomed" to cold looks and hard words? Was she used to teaching children who considered her an upper servant, kept for their own special use and amusement? Was she accustomed to be shut out of the family circle, made a stranger to everything but the thinnest surface of the life of her home? Experienced governesses might have told her of other things that had never yet so much as presented themselves to her in thought. They would have looked at her pretty face and watched her winning manners, not with envy, but with a living pity. In fact, a friend, little knowing what she was meditating, wrote to her a little bit of her own experience; which did more even than the snobbess to determine what Effie's future was not to be.

"*Beulah Lodge.*

"My darling Effie,—I was very, *very* sorry to hear how wickedly your dear papa had been treated by that unhappy young Walker. I never liked him, I must confess; though death does much to change our thoughts—and as for you, you sweet little pet, you'd forgive anybody anything. And that charming servant, Mary *Holmes*—how funny! Perhaps she'll turn out a relation, as people do in story-books. Or perhaps it's all a mistake about the notes being burnt; and some Christmas-time, when you're playing with your grand-daughter's dolly, they'll all emerge from the sawdust in a perfect state of preservation! Even that would scarcely be so odd as what I'm going to tell you.

"Well, then, my sweet little pet, I'm going to leave Beulah! Yes, Beulah; and Mr. Thompson, and Mrs. Thompson, and the children, and the farm, and all of it! Now guess why; and while you're guessing you must think that I've got my arms round you, and am kissing your dear, dear face—how I wish it was here! Well, you can't guess? You'll give it up? I'll tell you.

"Now you *know* I'm plain, darling, don't you?—*decidedly* plain. There's my nose, for instance, just a little bit (you must admit that) inclined to curve the *wrong* way. And my eyes—you've noticed the cast yourself. And my figure, short, a little dumpy, indeed dreadful, dreadful! And yet, really, poor Mrs. Thompson is—JEALOUS! She's jealous of *me*, and I'm going to leave.

"I'm not very demonstrative, am I, my pet? But even one *frosty* day may be less cold than another; and Mrs. Thompson is very much colder than our thermometer will register. You can't think what she is. She receives her husband, who is really inclined to be 'gushing' if she'd let him, with a stiff, frozen manner, quite horrible. He comes home tired from town, and she hasn't a kind word. Presents are nothing. If he kisses her, she says, 'Dear me, Thompson, you *are* affectionate all at once; we can wait till we're alone.'

"But the crisis was last Monday. The roads were slippery, and Mr. Thompson's horse fell. He wasn't much hurt, but he was later home than usual; and that's a mortal sin. As I was passing into the dining-room, where we generally sit, the servant saw me, and told me of the accident. I hadn't seen Mr. Thompson in the morning, for he left very early; so when I entered the room he rose, shook hands, and bade me 'good morning.' I told him I was very sorry to hear of his accident, and hoped he wasn't seriously hurt, and that the horse wasn't spoiled—a fine young creature he was very proud of. 'Oh no, thank you, Miss Shaw,' he said; 'we've got over it very well this time, thank God.' Positively, my sweet pet Effie, that's *all* he said. But Mrs. Thompson 'burst into tears' (I know what that means now), rocked herself backwards and forwards on the sofa, said, 'Oh, that it should come to this, and before my very face'—with a great deal more. Her poor husband looked completely dumbfoundered, and meekly asked if she were ill. 'What is it, Annie?' 'Don't ask me what it is, Thompson—oh, oh, that it should come to this!' At last Mr. T. got rather savage; and a dark look came into his face, that has once or twice before made Mrs. T. understand that there *is* a boundary beyond which she had better not venture. He rang the bell, and ordered the coachman and gardener to bring in the invalid couch. 'Your mistress is very ill,' he said, 'carry her instantly upstairs, and tell Matilda to have everything ready. Then get the dog-cart ready and drive fast for the doctor, the young one—he's cleverest.' The doctor soon came. He just lifted his eyebrows the least bit imaginable, and Mr. T. just gave the quietest answer with his eyes (it took about two seconds), and the doctor said he'd go up and see the patient. The patient has been in bed ever since. 'Rush of blood to the head,' I heard the young doctor say; 'needs considerable depletion.' 'That's *exactly* what *I* think,' said Mr. T. And so my amiable mistress is being 'depleted' accordingly.

"However, I said to Mr. T. at supper how sorry I was (which I really am, you dear little pet); and that he must know as well as I did how very absurd the whole affair was. He said he considered it very generous of me to take the thing in that way. He would see it was no loss to me, but he thought it really would be better if I found a better place. He seemed really moved—not about me, of course; but it must be a dreadful thing for a man of spirit when his own wife makes a kind of fool of him.

"So here I am, at sea again, my darling Effie. I thought to myself, 'if it had been that sweet, pretty, winning Effie, it would have been natural enough!' Well, *you'll* never be a governess, thank heaven; and if you were to wish it, you're much too pretty to get a place—unless the 'mistress' is ill in bed when the 'master' engages you.

"Good-bye, my pet; I shall soon see you.—Meanwhile I am always your loving friend,

"FANNY SHAW."

This letter quite settled Effie, at least on one side; she would *not* be a *governess*. She didn't think herself pretty; but she didn't think Fanny pretty—and yet it was plain there were silly women in the world who could not believe in such a thing as civility or friendship—mean, impure creatures, whose very consciences were defiled. She was not the girl to contend with that kind of difficulty. So she called on a gentleman who had been a friend of her father's—and she asked if he knew any place of business where she might find employment. He spoke to her very wisely, and promised to do his best for her; meanwhile he gave her his card, and allowed her to refer to him as a friend who knew her and her family. The next day she called at the shop of one of the most "pious" men in London. She showed her friend's card, and said she wanted employment in any good business house, suitable to one brought up like herself.

"Have you been on your knees this morning, my dear young friend?" said the pious tradesman.

Effie looked up at him with blank astonishment.

"On my knees, sir?"

"*On your knees*, Miss Holmes," he repeated, with sanctimonious emphasis.

"Pray, excuse me," said poor Effie; "I don't quite understand you, sir."

"Ah, then you've *not* been on your knees;" he responded; "can we hope for a blessing, Miss Holmes, without prayer—the appointed way, the little hand of man's faith that moves the Almighty Himself—eh, Miss Holmes?"

Effie's face was crimson when she looked up at him.

"Do you mean, have I *prayed* to-day, sir?" she said; "I didn't know I should be asked such questions. But I remember father read this morning at prayers, 'thou, when thou prayest, enter into thy closet, and *shut to the door*, and *pray to thy Father in secret*.' I think, sir, I'll pray in *that* way, if you please."

"Very true, Miss Holmes, very beautiful words; but we must move our fellow-creatures, and I want it to be *known* that *my* young people are young people of prayer. Don't you think so?"

"Think how, sir?"

"Think that's right," responded the Pharisee, somewhat warmly.

"No sir, I don't," said Effie.

"Not think it right to pray! dear, dear—let me assure you——"

"No sir, thank you—I mean it's not right to make a parade of our prayers, and try to get situations by them. Anybody wicked enough to make such a use of prayer would be wicked enough to tell you a lie, sir."

The pious draper looked horrified.

"Ah, poor young woman," he said, "I fear you're in the gall of bitterness and in the bonds of iniquity. I'm quite determined to take nobody into my establishment who didn't begin the day on her knees."

So poor Effie bade him good day, wondering whether he were after all much better than the wife of the City snob. Not much better, for he *was* a City snob; but his golden calf was cant, and he devoutly worshipped it.

However at last Effie succeeded; she found a situation in a warehouse, where the work was light and feminine, and the remuneration liberal. She told her father; she said she *must* go and *would*. There were many tears, many vain regrets, many eager hopes; but it was clearly the best thing that could be done—and the next Monday Effie began the world, doing work, earning her own living, burdening nobody. God bless her!

CHAPTER XII.

THE MINISTRY.

If I had to warn my readers that there was no romance in a dissenting college, there is yet greater need to warn them that there is no romance in the dissenting ministry. And yet, on the other hand, there is romance everywhere; and even still life has its charm, if only I could tell its story truly. Some of the good, if also some of the evil, of the old mediæval priesthood lingers still even in the most iconoclastic and revolutionary sects. For is not the priest the man who can "have compassion on the ignorant and on those who are out of the way;" the man who is bound by his very office to rise above the mere fashions of the world; the man who is to testify in his own gentleness to the tender love of God? Still, as ever, there is and must be a confessional under one name or other, no matter how Protestant or how "nonconforming" we may be. There must be a confessional, until there are no longer any breaking hearts, any burdened spirits. And if I were trying to find materials for a "sensation" story, the confessional of the dissenting minister or Anglican clergyman would, I fancy, suit my purpose better than that of the Romanist priest. The secrets that are told *them* must have had force enough to burst up through the habit of reticence that no *custom* of confessing has made weak. God forbid that I should reveal those secrets, even if I knew them. In a treacherous, tale-bearing world, human beings can scarcely yet afford to dispense with the one order of men bound by holiest vows to hear their story, and to reveal it to God alone.

I am not writing, therefore, the "Diary of a late Divine;" and I shall have no thrilling stories of those patients, sick in heart and soul, who sought his counsel and help. But Fritz found the ministry far enough from mere commonplace. He stayed a year or two with the good old doctor who brought him to London, and then accepted an invitation to become the sole pastor of a congregation in one of the suburbs. In some respects the change was for the better. It was better, at least for him, at least for a time, to be alone. The congregation to which he removed was much smaller than the one over which he was first appointed; and so far might be considered more under control and guidance. At any rate, for better or worse, he moved, and at the time of this chapter had been two years in his new "sphere."

His predecessor was one of those good men who

take a congregation, or "a cause," from its cradle to its grave; and leave to their successors the corpse, the funeral, the mourning, and, if possible, the resurrection, with occasionally the suspicion also of murder. Fritz's predecessor was the Rev. James Richardson, D.D. What he was doctored for and whence his degree came were great mysteries—but a degree he certainly had. He was a little shrivelled-looking man, painfully prim and priggish, of the highest respectability, and a "perfect gentleman" in the sense of being always very stiff and cold. For the first twenty years of his ministry he was getting together a congregation, resuscitating the lifeless body that *his* predecessor had left him to restore or bury as the case might be. Under Dr. Richardson's judicious treatment the patient recovered, and in fact became very vigorous and plethoric. The chapel was twice enlarged, and was attended by more than the customary proportion of carriages and horses. For ten years there was steady, quiet prosperity; while also the doctor's energies were attaining and just overpassing their ripest maturity. The old folks still remained as long as death would let them, but after thirty years the power of the good little doctor belonged not to hope but to memory.

A most tidy little man; and if his godliness surpassed his cleanliness he must have been very godly indeed. In fact, he shaved so cleanly, and without cutting himself too, that he seemed to have a way of shaving out the very roots of his beard, and producing a perfect virginity of chin and lip. He was, moreover, an author; had produced some of the sweetest evangelical tracts, and several volumes of sermons, which I have the authority of a monthly magazine for affirming "no British Christian ought to be without." But the pulpit and the parlour were the doctor's real sphere of usefulness. Which of his hearers can forget his unimpeachable properness, the gentlemanly calmness with which he handled the most exciting and thrilling truths? Nothing had power to warm him to enthusiasm or freeze him into an icier rigidity. Who can forget his visits, when with watch in hand, and with a perfectly becoming smile playing on his smooth, clean face, like December sunshine on snow, he asked the customary questions and received the customary replies? It was the right thing to do, and a wonderful amount of work he accomplished with due method. A certain number of families can be visited every year only by giving a certain moderate maximum of time to each family. And though so short a visit as that moderate maximum allowed might seem to do very little good, yet "the people saw their pastor's face," and of course there's a great deal in that. Familiarity, also, often produces contempt; and a minister had much better occupy a region somewhat remote from ordinary intimacies and genuine hearty friendships.

Of course, I don't mean to deny that the little doctor had his intimacies; his deacons, who received as much of his confidence as was compatible with the habitual recollection that confidence may be betrayed, and that the friend of to-day may be the enemy of to-morrow, seemed in a genteel sort of a way to be unimpassionedly fond of him. At a few houses he visited on terms of comparative equality. To the outside world even those visits might have seemed slow; for the subjects of conversation were limited, and the manner of treating them more limited still. But the little doctor enjoyed them, and in a chilly sort of way slightly thawed. He was, moreover, much too well-off and much too well-bred to cant. Think of calling your footman a "dear brother!" A most excellent little man; greatly respected, sometimes feared, and a little loved. For twenty years he built up a "church," for ten more he kept it in good repair, without waste or dilapidation, for ten more he pulled it down.

Or, which amounts to the same thing, he thought he should be obliged to have some little help—he, Dr. Richardson, would have a co-pastor, who should work with him in the genial frostiness of mutual reserve and prudent suspicion. What sort of man should he look for? What did he want to have done?

"I think it wont be necessary," said the little man to himself, "that my assistant should undertake much of the visiting. Of course, our people would naturally prefer to see the senior pastor, and avail themselves of his greater experience. Besides, there might be little rivalries and slight misunderstandings, which cannot be too carefully avoided. No—I'll attend to the visiting myself."

Then as to preaching, the assistant would, of course, take the evening service; for the best of "our people" were often unable to get out twice on Sunday, and made a point of coming in the morning. He might also encourage the teachers by an occasional address in the Sunday schools, and he might undertake the week-day services.

In truth, just a very little more energy and warmth was needed; about enough heat to raise the mercury from zero to freezing point. That was the problem;—or to put it differently, it was required to place two riders on one horse so that both should drive, and both sit foremost, and one be behind. Two attempts were made to solve this problem, and neither of them was perfectly successful. There was in the problem itself an inherent difficulty, and in the particular case subjected to experiment the horse was restive, and the riders couldn't make up their minds which was back and which was front—only each was quite certain that the other was meanly trying to push him off altogether. This, of course, was extremely uncomfortable to the riders; and unhappily they were quite right in their suspicions, they *were* trying to push each other off; at any rate, each wanted the other's place, and on a horse's back how *can* that be amicably and comfortably settled? So I regret to have to record there were many "special church meetings;" that is to say, the *horse* was requested to decide which of the two riders should drive, and it decided for the old one—and, moreover, gave a parting kick to the young one as he took his leave.

So good little Dr. Richardson was to ride alone as long as he could keep the saddle. How long would that be? He determined he would sit, or lie, or be tied on, or anyhow keep everybody else off, till he was seventy years of age. The *horse*, that is to say the "special Church-meeting," agreed; and, to return to Fritz, it was when that time arrived that he, Fritz, became pastor of the "Church and Congregation," so painfully, and unexpectedly, and prematurely bereaved of the Rev. Dr. Richardson.

It was a very great honour to succeed Dr. Richardson: because the people who knew his name took it for the name of the Dr. Richardson of ten or fifteen years ago. They quite forgot that in the interval there had been two unsuccessful attempts at a co-pastorate, two "splits," and so much quarrelling and fighting that the "Church and Congregation" remaining were a mere remnant, and as it were "fag-end" of what had been. Besides that grand testimonial presented to the retiring pastor, on the principle that "to him that hath shall be given," though as much as six or seven years of Fritz's stipend, and amply sufficient to effect every necessary improvement in the old-fashioned chapel, had so dried up every river and rill of benevolence, that for a long time the seasons must needs be barren.

For a young minister to follow an old one is like a marriage of January and May. And Dr. Richardson had never been young. Moreover, he was an extreme Puritan; so bare and bald were all the services at the chapel in St. George's Road, that it was a mystery half the congregation had not turned Papists for a change from the dull monotony. The young successor, on the other hand, loved and admired the Puritan protest against tyranny in Church or State; but hated, with all his soul, the worse and uglier tyranny which the Puritans themselves had introduced. It was not well perhaps that a man should be compelled either to wear a surplice or else cease proclaiming the Gospel and administering the Sacraments; but it was at least equally bad that a man should be compelled *not* to wear one. In fact, the Puritanism of St. George's Road emptied life of all symbol and all beauty, and cut religion completely off from the ordinary duties and enjoyments of mankind.

When Fritz thought anything wanted mending, he had an absurd habit of saying so. He thought *that* was a part of the duties of his office; and, in fact, if the mending depended on himself, he used to set about the work of improvement with the utmost despatch. He was, for instance, quite decided about the services in St. George's Road; they were very much too bald and Puritanical, and he was determined they should become less so. To begin with, was he or was he not to wear his gown? It was not a matter of much importance; but if it were objected to, the objection could only be of a kind which would be far more valid against other changes which he saw would be inevitable. It would be neither more nor less than the ridiculous principle that Dissent is to reject and repudiate everything that is to be found in the Established Church, simply because it is found there. So the new minister entered the pulpit duly robed. There was much wonderment, and even a little whispering. The "fag-end" of Dr. Richardson's congregation were taken by surprise, and, in truth, could hardly realize what had happened. Two or three walked out of the chapel, with a loud, protesting stamp; and it seemed not improbable that another "split" might give a new interest to the annals of St. George's Road.

The deacons especially were extremely bewildered. Dr. Richardson had never committed himself to anything about which there could be two opinions with quiet, well-ordered people. His friends were, of course, aware that he never erred in any direction;

and even his worst enemies were obliged to acknowledge that, whatever errors their sharp eyes could detect, had all been on the safe side. The little doctor was a great admirer of principles. Was he not continually reading them in his library, and writing them in tracts and sermons? But, after all, are they not just a little impalpable? Compared, for instance, with the pew-rent of a substantial grocer, or a carriage and pair, what can you make of principles? If Mr. Tucker, with his wife and children, who took two whole pews, didn't like a gown, it might be an extremely good thing to put one on, but then two pews would be empty, and there would be a corresponding deduction from the income of the Rev. Dr. Richardson. At any rate, it was quite decisive that Thomas Thompson, Esq., objected; for he could quite easily have bought up the whole chapel.

The deacons then had never been involved in any difficulty (until the unhappy co-pastorate experiments) with their highly-respectable pastor. People stamping out of the chapel in that loudly protesting way seemed to them terribly ominous; for if things really went wrong, it would take a frightful time to make their young minister seventy years old.

"Did you see Mr. Jenkins go out of chapel this morning, sir?" said one of the deacons with a tremulous voice. The deacon's name was Bung; he was a very tall man, with a very large body, and extremely weak legs.

"No, I don't know that I did," said Mr. Rivers, "Who is Mr. Jenkins? whereabouts does he sit?"

"Dear me," said Mr. Dickson, another deacon, about as long as Bung, and about a tenth part as thick, "didn't you see him go out? I'm afraid all the congregation *heard* him; indeed I'm sure I felt extremely alarmed, Mr. Rivers."

"Jenkins himself is nobody," said Mr. Robertson, who considered himself somebody; "only one of the tradesmen here; but he's a bad-tempered fellow, and can talk, and might make some mischief. I suppose he stamped out because he didn't like the gown."

"Yes, I'm very much afraid it must have been for that reason," said Dickson, with a solemn look at Bung.

"Dear me," said Mr. Rivers, "I shouldn't have thought anybody could have been so silly; but I dare say he'll come round, and I dare say if he doesn't we shall survive it."

Spirit of Richardson! Can such random words have been uttered in the vestry from which for some forty years you were wont to emerge, clean and cold, avoiding as one of the greatest of sins the appearance of evil? Come round indeed! Mr. Jenkins was not at all the man to come round, but only to be dragged round, if at all, with extreme difficulty.

I don't think, if he had not been a vulgar boor, that Fritz would have liked him any the worse for that. Being a man of independent spirit himself, he could appreciate independence in other people. But he could see at a glance the difference between independence and the obstinacy of a jackass; and he could also see at a glance, when he called upon Mr. Jenkins, that that gentleman was by no means independent, but unquestionably was a jackass.

"Good morning, Mr. Jenkins," he said; "I'm making a few calls this morning, trying by degrees to get acquainted with my people, and you of course among them."

"Oh!" said Jenkins, "I suppose you saw me leave the sanctuary on Sabbath morning?"

"No, Mr. Jenkins, I didn't see you go out at all; I hope you're better."

"And who told you, sir, that I was ever ill?" he said; the sensitiveness of Mr. Jenkins' conscience reddening his face to the colour of a boiled lobster.

"Oh nobody told me you were ill; but I'm quite sure you wouldn't have left the chapel, which is rather disturbing to the congregation, unless you were."

"Well then, Mr. Rivers, you were very much mistaken; I went out of chapel because I was very deeply offended."

"Oh, were you, Mr. Jenkins? I'm very sorry to hear it; who can have offended you?"

"Well, sir, you're a young man I've offered a many prayers for at the family altar, and I did hope that the mantle of Elijah had fallen on Elisha; but I said long ago—if ever a gown goes up into that pulpit, I go out."

"Yes," said Mr. Rivers, "and you went out; and now really, looking back upon it, what good do you think it did?"

"Well now, come," he said, "isn't it vanity?"

"What? Mr. Jenkins."

"Vanity! A fine dress, looks 'ansome, and all that sort of thing."

The young minister almost shouted with laughing at the extremely original explanation of academical costume furnished by this highly intelligent member of his congregation; and he said, "Well, well, Mr. Jenkins, I think at any rate I can assure you it isn't what you mean by vanity; and as you've kept your promise about walking out of the chapel when the gown went up into the pulpit, perhaps the next best thing will be to walk in again."

He came back again, but only for a little while; he was very far from caring for such teaching as Fritz tried more and more to give. He was a narrow-minded, bad-tempered man; a man who never read a book above the level of a religious periodical. Argument with him, on any side of any question, beyond the routine of his own trade, would have been useless and ridiculous. But his petty and vulgar opposition to the gown set Fritz thinking; for it was typical of very much opposition which he must expect before his work was done.

Fritz had many advantages, as the minister of St. George's Road, which very few young ministers possess. It was his first "charge" indeed, but he was not wholly without experience; moreover he had not asked to go to St. George's Road, nor been subjected to the annoyance of having to show his paces to Dr. Richardson's congregation; on the contrary, they had heard of him, and had asked him to be their minister, knowing quite well that the obligation would lie, at the very least, quite as much on their side as his, if he accepted their invitation. The deacons wanted a young minister of some spirit, for only such an one could restore the suspended animation of the body which had been slowly dying out during the last years of Dr. Richardson's pastorate. At the same time they hoped, and, old as they were, were young enough to believe, that the man who had nerve and spirit enough to drive, with a very clear notion of the place he wanted to go to, and very decided opinions about the speed at which he thought it safe and pleasant to travel, would let them amuse themselves by pulling first one rein and then another, or stopping, or dawdling, or going roundabout ways to escape a thoroughfare, or miss a turnpike, or any other of the innumerable devices of timid or parsimonious drivers. In spite also of the trifling dissatisfaction and mutterings of discontent that followed the introduction of a gown into a place of worship which boasted an absolute freedom from every rag and vestige of Popery, Fritz was not altogether without success and a kind of popularity. The chapel began to fill; the seats which Dr. Richardson's co-pastoring experiments had emptied were gradually let; and Sunday after Sunday, even the frigid respectability of the Richardsonian deacons was warmed almost into enthusiasm as they congratulated themselves upon their wisdom in choosing, as the doctor's successor, a minister of youth and energy.

So by the time of this chapter, when Fritz had been about two years in his new place, St. George's Road Chapel was really well attended; and moreover the ice of the old dispensation was almost thawed away, and there was something like genial warmth, and an attempt to build a Christian society upon the foundation of mutual love instead of mutual suspicion. Fritz was a very bad visitor, and the very last thing he would have dreamt of would have been to take out his watch and stop an interesting conversation with any one of the families in his congregation because it was two minutes and a quarter past one. He visited very little; partly because he was shy, and partly because he liked sitting in his study to read; having a notion that one of the essential conditions of pulpit eloquence is having something to say. But when he did make a call, it was with the utmost frankness and unreserve; he did not care a single straw for the cold respect with which people were disposed to treat him, simply because he was a minister. He knew quite well that that was not real respect even for his office, but only another form of the superstition which in the old days of Popish darkness had divided human beings into secular and religious, and cursed the Church with hosts of idle men and women, who imagined that they were peculiarly pious only because they were peculiarly useless. He was determined that for his part he would never consent to be dressed on all occasions in black clothes; cut off from the ordinary enjoyments and interests of life; imprisoned in a frightful stifling dungeon of priggish conventionalisms, and just called in to doctor sick souls as the physician might be called in to doctor sick bodies. In his ministry and in his own person he meant to do his best to bring religion into contact with the whole of life; and he wanted his flock to receive such visits as he paid them, not as the official calls of a minister, but as the friendly and brotherly intercourse of a man.

Of course this kind of intercourse was full of danger; for though St. George's Road Chapel had been kept by the extreme carefulness of its late minister almost from knowing the existence of such a thing as difference of opinion upon matters of doctrine or ceremony, the new minister looked upon such ignorance with profound contempt and utter aversion; and at any rate no index of forbidden books was allowed to act as sentinel at the door of his own library. He received many warnings from judicious friends that this course was highly dangerous. There was in his neighbourhood, for instance, a divine about ten years older than himself, both in the ministry and in life; and far better acquainted than Fritz was with all those dodges by which skilful ministers may preserve or even restore the peace of a church. He was a charming little dandy, always as well dressed as tailor and glover and hatter could make him, with a very commonplace, not to say vulgar, expression of countenance. His sermons were always pretty, and often so pathetic as to move himself, at least, to tears. He very anxiously avoided whatever might tend to disturb the minds of his congregation, excepting, of course, those rebukes for sin which, to do them justice, the most irritable congregations are in the habit of receiving with extreme good-nature. His congregation was very wealthy; rich enough probably to buy up the parish church, and the goods and chattels of everybody that went there; and Fritz's neighbour had unhappily quite enough of the snob in him to bow down to any image that was made of gold. He looked down upon Fritz with a half-wondering kind of patronage, as a very eccentric young man, with just enough ability to make him rather dangerous; and yet perhaps at the same time, one who, under judicious guidance, might be "brought out" in the denomination, and take a fair position among his ministerial brethren. It was surely worth trying; and so the minister of twenty carriages made a point one morning of calling upon the Rev. Frederick Rivers.

He had to wait a little while in the drawing-room; for Fritz already had company, which he was receiving, according to his custom, in the very last room of his house into which any prudent minister would have allowed any one of his flock to enter—to wit, his library. The visitors were a gentleman and his daughter, very intelligent, agreeable people; and in a library their conversation had naturally enough turned upon books, and already some of those rash promises to lend and borrow had been exchanged which any minister ought to know better, in these ticklish times, than to be a party to. At last the visitors went away, and the servant ushered into the same room that smiling dandy, the Rev. John Veneer.

"Good morning, Mr. Rivers," he said; "you do me great honour by allowing me to come into your study. There are very few people that I should be disposed to trust into mine."

"Well, really, as to an honour, Mr. Veneer, I almost always have visitors in this room, unless I have some reason to suspect they would steal books."

"Ah, my dear Rivers," said his prudent neighbour, "when you've had my experience, you'll find such confiding generosity scarcely wise."

"I am afraid, Mr. Veneer," said Fritz, with just sufficient emphasis on the word *Mr.* to indicate that he was not yet prepared to be on that footing of familiarity with Mr. Veneer which is implied by calling one another by one's surname—"I am afraid I may find the world full of cheats and sneaks; but I don't want to be forced to see that a moment sooner than is necessary."

"Oh, don't you, Mr. Rivers? That's what I'm rather inclined to call an amiable weakness," said Mr. Veneer; "rather like locking the stable-door when the horse is stolen."

"Well," said Fritz, "one reason why I don't mind leaving my stable-door unlocked is, that I haven't got a horse to steal. For instance, the people who were just now in my study, by looking at the books on my shelves, and those lying on my table here, might of course run away with a limited number of my opinions."

"Yes," said Veneer; "so they might. They might, for instance, go away and say to Mr. Bung, that deacon of yours with the weak nether extremities, that they saw this book lying open in your study." And he pushed towards Fritz Maurice's "Doctrine of Sacrifice."

"Well, it *is* lying open here, isn't it?" said Fritz, with charming greenness.

"Yes it is, so far as that goes; but I dare say Mr. Bung would think it necessary to make a few remarks on the subject."

"Really," said Fritz, "I should be charmed to hear them; they would be the first remarks on any literary subject with which Mr. Bung has ever favoured me."

"Yes, I dare say; Mr. Bung doesn't look a very literary character. But you know he would not look at the thing as a literary matter; he'd simply say he was afraid you were not quite sound, and were an admirer of Mr. Maurice."

"Well then, he'd be wrong in the first suspicion, and right in the last," said Fritz.

"Well, but people wont draw those distinctions; and then they get dissatisfied, and leave, and perhaps take dozens of people along with them."

"Well," said Fritz, "if they can't draw these distinctions I'm very sorry for it, and, of course, I mean to teach them to do it. Don't you think that's part of the work of the ministry, Mr. Veneer?"

"Oh yes, of course I do," he said; "but then my way of doing it would very likely be rather different from yours; I like doing that sort of thing very gradually and cautiously."

"Oh, do you?" said Fritz, on the very brink of making some extremely uncomplimentary remark on this discretion; which, to say the truth, was, by a great deal, the best part of Mr. Veneer's valour. Fortunately, Mr. Veneer interrupted him.

"And, after all," he said, "I prefer treating these difficult and disputed subjects as mysteries, which our people ought to leave; indeed, we've bother enough with the ordinary management of our churches, without bringing upon ourselves the charge of heresy or unsoundness. I was very sorry, for instance, to hear of the trouble you have got into," he continued, "about your organ and choir."

"I'm sure it's very kind of you to be so interested about my affairs, but, in fact, I haven't had much trouble on that subject; of course there are very many people who don't like an organ, and who prefer a precentor yelling away at the bottom of the pulpit, to the best choir in the world; but you know I can't help that, Mr. Veneer; and you don't expect that I'm going to conduct the services at St. George's Road, to suit the whims of people who prefer ugliness to beauty?"

"Well, now, look here," said Mr. Veneer; "I don't mind telling you, in perfect confidence, a little bit of my own experience—my way of managing such matters. I'm as fond of music as you are;

but, with a very highly respectable congregation such as mine, we are bound just to show our best folks a little deference; so I just said to my organist, —I think we can't venture on a voluntary at present, but as we begin the service with a short anthem, you may play a rather long introduction, and introduce into it any little air you may think appropriate, and so we may gently get the thin end of the wedge in without anybody knowing it. And so that's just how we're managing the matter; and I get what almost amounts to a voluntary without offending anybody."

"I'm sure nothing can be kinder, Mr. Veneer, than your talking to me in this nice, confidential way; and, really, to return your confidence, I think your congregation must be a parcel of extraordinary fools. I really think if I believed I could impose on my congregation by so very transparent a dodge, I should scarcely think them worth preaching to."

The conversation turned to other subjects, and Fritz managed to "steal" so many of the Rev. John Veneer's opinions about books and men that he fancied, conceited little monkey that he was, that he had taken a pretty fair measure of the Rev. John Veneer, and need not be at much trouble to keep up his acquaintance. I have no doubt Mr. Veneer thought exactly the same of Fritz, and, in truth, he took occasion to say so, at a select luncheon-party in

Paternoster Row. It was a delightful little party; for it was all at the expense of a respected publisher, and there was very good wine, and a very great deal of it, and Veneer told a few kindred spirits that it wouldn't be long before there was a vacancy at St. George's Road, and that Rivers would drive every respectable person away from his chapel before another year had gone. "In fact," said Veneer, "he's a mere fool."

Perhaps he was. At any rate, with a position in life still to make, and in an age of religious panic, the wisdom of the serpent was scarcely less necessary for him than the harmlessness of the dove. Moreover, with a wife and two children (for so many hostages had he already given to Fortune), a little of Veneer's discretion would have been a good financial investment.

CHAPTER XIII.

PEOPLE WHO HAVE SEEN BETTER DAYS.

Mr. Holmes and his family were now among the people "who have seen better days." Why do we shrink away from such people? They are very much to be pitied, and we ought to draw nearer to them and comfort them. But, somehow, we don't. At any rate we meet them with suspicion; we feel sure, to begin with, that they will be peevish, disagreeable people, who probably have not yet seen the worst they deserve. In fact, uprightness, perseverance, and common sense, do generally lead to average prosperity; and "people who have seen better days" are generally either fools or knaves. *We* know that Mr. Holmes was neither, but we needn't wonder that other people were of a different opinion.

There was his brother, for instance, who unquestionably thought him a fool. Didn't he tell him so, with most fraternal candour, only a day or two after that very unfortunate transaction with Frank Walker? Didn't he say, "Well, Robert, I can only warn you that you're robbing your wife and children?" And since then had he not behaved to Robert with the frankness of an utter devil? Not that Mr. Holmes would have asked a favour from Alfred—much less would Effie. But how could Alfred know that he was safe from the importunity of a beggared relation? Was it not due to himself, his wife, his family, his remote posterity, and the whole universe, to take the utmost precautions? So he called on Robert at the new shop in Islington; not a bad place in itself, but when people have known better the positive degree even of good becomes comparatively insignificant. Alfred walked into the new shop then, one morning, the very Monday that Effie began her work at the warehouse, to relieve his mind, and to protect his beloved brother from those expectations which he had every reason to believe would be bitterly disappointed.

"Well, Robert," he said, "I knew how it would be."

"Yes, brother," said poor Mr. Holmes, "so you did; I wish that could mend matters."

"But I *can't* mend matters, Robert; I've a wife and family, and business responsibilities which quite prevent——"

"Well, well, Alfred; there's poor Effie——" He was going to say, "is already provided for," but Alfred interrupted him.

"Yes, of course there is—and I don't mind doing

what I can for her consistently with my duty to my family. So I meant to offer——"

"Thank you, Alfred," said Robert—he was half choked with anger and indignation, but he thought he might as well hear what the devilish righteousness of his brother had to offer. Even what seems the justice of such men is infinitely damnable.

"I meant to offer her a situation as our nursery-governess—*nursery*-governess; indeed, it would involve a good deal of managing the children—washing them, making their little dresses, and things of that sort; but it would be with relations, Robert, kith and kin, and it would rather keep this disgrace of yours private."

"Thank you, brother," said Robert; "I'll tell Effie."

"You'll tell her," he answered, with an uncertain look at his brother; "that's right. And she may come to-morrow."

"To-morrow—and what salary did you say, Alfred?"

"Robert," said ruffled virtue, "I'm amazed. I'm offering to put myself to expenses which are far beyond what I need, for my own sake, to incur; I offer to keep Effie, board and lodge her, and commit my children to her care, in spite of her inexperience —and you ask what 'salary!' I was scarcely prepared for ingratitude, Robert."

"I only wanted to understand, brother. Effie will,

I'm sure, be deeply grateful for your generosity—and I quite understand that there will be *no* salary."

"No, no salary, but a happy home with us, her blood relations, her benefactors in the hour of need. And what do you mean to do with the others? I can't make room for them."

"I'm trying to find something, Alfred; they must be willing to rough it."

"Of course they must; that's the most sensible thing I've heard you say for months."

"And do let me hope," continued the philanthropist who wouldn't rob his wife and children, "that this misfortune will be a warning to you. Good morning, brother—we shall expect Effie to-morrow."

I daresay they expected her, but she didn't go. Alfred thought them mad, and, moreover, was not a little vexed that it seemed harder to do a selfish and mean trick than he had expected. He knew Effie was a thoroughly good girl, and would be worth fifty of such governesses as he would be likely to hire—and she seemed far from eager to come. He meant to make a very good educational bargain under pretence of affection, and it wasn't turning out quite well. On Thursday, however, he had a letter from his niece.

"Wood Street, City.
"*Wednesday Night.*

"My dear Uncle,—I've just heard from father your proposal to take me into your family as upper nurse, without wages. As I am very comfortably settled here, with a very excellent salary, and very kind employers, I much regret that I cannot, in our present reduced circumstances, afford to do you the favour you called on Monday to ask. Hoping you may soon find a nurse-maid who will be able and willing to serve you without remuneration,—I remain, my dear Uncle, your dutiful niece,

"EFFIE HOLMES.

"*To Alfred Holmes, Esq.*"

Alfred Holmes, Esq. read this letter over many times; he examined the envelope, the postmarks, the handwriting, the signature. Yes, sure enough, was hers, "Effie Holmes," as plain as plain could be. The great annoyance of the letter was, that it clearly indicated that Effie had looked down to the very bottom of his mean soul, and felt herself immeasurably superior to her rich and shabby uncle. He hated her thenceforward with intense aversion. He would have ruined her if he had been able. He half resolved that he would ruin her if ever he became able. He might make fine speeches, put his guinea down on every subscription-list which he thought might be a good religious investment, blow his own trumpet at every corner, doing his little alms to be seen of men. But there was one human being who could anywhere put him to shame, and make him and everybody else understand that he was a mean, hypocritical humbug; and that one enemy, who had such invincible power over him, was Effie, his niece. He wanted to make a large profit out of her misery, under pretence of relieving it; and she had found him out, and scorned him.

Besides, he felt highly indignant not only at her independence of spirit, but especially at the occupation she had chosen—a shopwoman! It was just the same thing, though she might call the place where she was a warehouse. A governess would have been bad enough; but a shopwoman! Uncle Alfred was the aristocrat of the Holmes' family. His wife was distantly related to a baronet, who was known to the world chiefly as a young scapegrace, who would be treated better than his deserts if he were flogged at a cart's tail. But at any rate he had a title, and would have nothing to do with trades-people, or any such low, vulgar set. At least, he would have nothing to do with them except get as far into their debt as they would let him. He never so much as noticed Robert's family, for Robert kept a shop. Mr. Alfred Holmes, on the other hand, was "a merchant;" not on a very large scale, perhaps, but it wasn't retail, and he could talk of our "merchant princes" with a proud consciousness that he was one of them. So he felt himself unspeakably degraded by what he considered Effie's vulgarity.

"A salary! Stuff and nonsense! A girl has no business to disgrace her family for the sake of a salary." If she had been a beggar dying of starvation, or taken to the parish workhouse, her affectionate uncle might have borne it; but for Effie to turn shopwoman—to earn an honest living, instead of being the snubbed and brokenhearted dependent of a proud and selfish relation—that, Alfred Holmes, Esq. could *not* bear.

"Mark my words, Matilda," he said to his wife, shaking Effie's letter at her as if she, Matilda, had been guilty of an independent and honourable action; "I've no more to do with Robert or his family—a nasty, low lot. As to that snivelling, impudent little slut, the shopwoman, she'll go to the dogs as sure as she's born; and she'll not get me to drive 'em off if they pick her very bones. A *shopwoman* in *our* family! Good Lord!"

It was a terrible thing, no doubt; but unquestionably that dreadful calamity had fallen upon the family of the Holmeses. One female member of it was actually a brave, honest, loving woman, conquering her circumstances by stooping to them, utterly superior to those poor conventionalisms which measure the guinea by the stamp, not by the metal. It was a heart-breaking thing. They had not been without trouble before; but nothing to this. There had been idleness, cruelty, hypocrisy, even crime, in the family; but, thank God! never, until now, a shopwoman. What had they done to deserve it?

At any rate, Robert might have a shopwoman for

a daughter if he chose, but not a merchant prince for a brother. And yet when Alfred Holmes, Esq. came to think about it, wasn't he at least so far in the power of the poor deluded beggar who had run so terrible a risk for the sake of doing a kind action to Frank Walker, that somehow or other he was obliged to be his brother, whether he liked it or not. He couldn't enter the second time into his mother's womb, and be born with different kindred, though Effie was a shopwoman. Of course it was a great oversight, but it was a fact, that Alfred Holmes, Esq. had *not* been constituted the centre of the universe. He formed a part of a vast and complicated order about which he had never been so much as consulted; while, on the other hand, he was required, in the most unceremonious way, forthwith to accommodate himself to it. We should not perhaps, any of us, be the worse for thinking somewhat more carefully of these divine relationships, which are so different from the caprices of our own wayward choice.

At the same time, the coarse and false judgments of the world have so tremendous a power over us that even the best of men, in spite of innocence, are almost invariably crushed by them. There are many ways in which society gives a dog a bad name, but there are not many dogs with bad names which do not somehow come to deserve hanging. Mr. Holmes, in the days of his prosperity, had been a most generous man, both in deed and speech; and those who seemed to be his friends, at whose houses he visited, who visited him in return, seemed to be as generous and kind as himself. Mr. Holmes wasn't the least aware that it was only his own kindness that was reflected from them, and that in other company they were quite capable of making the most ill-natured remarks, and not absolutely incapable of doing shabby actions. A cynic might almost be pardoned for regarding mankind as a set of miserable monkeys, having no higher faculty than the faculty of imitation. It is humiliating to think how utterly without character most of us are. When we are in the company of men of culture and refinement, our cowardly little souls dare scarcely so much as laugh, lest we should be doing something that was not exactly proper; while spending the very next evening in the company of some good-natured, rollicking, boisterous buffoon, we, the very same poor shivering mortals that were afraid to smile, laugh till our sides are sore, and the tears stream down our faces, at jokes unquestionably coarse, and in all probability stupid. We spend an evening with Mr. Robert Holmes, and we think anybody who would hesitate to sign his name as Frank Walker's surety would be a cold-hearted, suspicious wretch; we spend the next evening with Mr. Alfred Holmes, and our contemptible monkey-nature becomes converted to the sudden belief that Mr.

Robert Holmes is neither more nor less than a fool, and that benevolence is only another name for sentimental humbug. It hadn't occurred to Effie's father that the people about him were good-natured and generous, simply because there was something in his very presence and character that shamed calumny into silence; so he was bitterly disappointed when, having lost his money, he found that the whole monkey-tribe had ceased to consider him worth imitating, and devoted their energies to the imitation of those malignant apes which belonged to a species from time immemorial hostile to such creatures as Mr. Holmes. The great majority of his acquaintances were suddenly affiicted with shortness of sight and shortness of memory; they were many of them quite unable to see so far as to the other side of a very narrow street; and one of them who had drunk many a bottle of Mr. Holmes's best wine, and with tears in his eyes had poured out his gratitude for the friendship of so generous a man as poor Frank Walker's benefactor, had been prostrated by so complete a paralysis of recollection that he could with difficulty be brought to recognise even Mr. Holmes's face. Poor Robert had suffered many disappointments already, and this man's brutality was the last straw that breaks the camel's back. Mr. Harris passed him in the street, not far from the new shop in Islington; he seemed in a great hurry, he was looking across the road at—

perhaps a lamp-post. At any rate, it might be only a mistake, Harris couldn't have *forgotten.*

"Hollo, Harris!" he said, stepping up to him, and touching his shoulder as playfully as he could, "how are you? In a hurry?"

"Who are you, sir?" said Harris.

"Who am I?" said Mr. Holmes; "well, that's a nice little joke. How's Mrs. Harris and the children?"

"Well, you're confoundedly familiar, my dear fellow, for a perfect stranger, but I haven't the honour of your acquaintance, and am rather in a hurry; so perhaps you'll excuse my bidding you good morning."

Mr. Holmes stood for a second or two perfectly confounded, while the broad back of his old friend was hurrying up the street; and then for a single instant the devil of common honesty got the better of him, and totally regardless of assault and battery, the paralysed memory of Harris and the six-and-eightpences of Harris's solicitor, he seized him by the back of his coat in the open street and flung him round till he couldn't help facing him, important as his business elsewhere might happen to be.

"Now, then, do you know me now?" he said, foaming with rage; "I don't think you're a fool, Harris, I think you are a knave. If you were a lunatic, you might have forgotten me; but you're not a lunatic, and so you haven't forgotten me, and you're a contemptible coward. You know as well as possible that we've been in each other's houses hundreds of times, and you really seem to imagine that I'm going to take off my hat to all the lying pretences by which you are trying to cut my acquaintance. I don't want your acquaintance now, God knows; you're not worth having. But if you think I can't see through you, you may understand as soon as you like that you're quite mistaken. You're a mean, cowardly, lying fool; and now, if you like to give me in charge for an assault, you can do it, and I'll tell the magistrate what I assaulted you for."

Mr. Harris didn't give him in custody for divers reasons; but he thought he might as well try, with what little bit of spirit he had left, to give a farewell sting to an old acquaintance.

"Well, good morning, Holmes," he said; "I don't want to get you into trouble for this very gross insult in a public street, and indeed I wanted to spare you the pain of any explanations whatever; but you know you're a disappointed man, and not unnaturally perhaps just a little out of temper with everybody. But I really can't afford to be connected with a person who has, of course quite innocently, got himself involved in a bank robbery."

Thereupon he raised his hat in the most graceful manner possible, and hurried along the street as fast as his legs could carry him.

So Mr. Holmes began to understand what it was to have seen better days, and when his wife was mourning over the dulness of those evenings that no visitors enlivened now, he would tell her with an anger that almost terrified her, and made her fancy sometimes he suspected even his own wife of treachery, that the fewer visitors they had the better—that there was not a human being worth trusting. And this was perhaps scarcely the worst effect of calamity on Mr. Holmes. He almost began to think that he was not worth trusting himself; he bitterly reproached himself for what he now considered his extremely reckless generosity to Frank Walker. He had felt sure when he became Frank's surety that his wife would sympathize, as in truth she did, with his unselfishness, and would rather visit his grave a poor widow than be the rich widow of a grasping and covetous man. But it's one thing to visit a man's grave, and quite another to live in a much smaller house than you've been used to; and to be bereaved of our little comforts and luxuries is sometimes nearly as painful as to be bereaved of an affectionate relative. If this remark sounds cynical, I can only plead as an apology that it is unquestionably true. And I may say, moreover, that what seems so hard-hearted is not, after all, wholly selfish; for reduced circumstances are for many purposes no better than a premature death. People who have seen better days are already dead to most of their old acquaintances, only unfortunately they can't get decently buried; they keep continually appearing to their old acquaintances in a corpse-like, ghastly way, and they themselves cannot help haunting the scenes of their old enjoyments with fruitless, miserable longings, like unresting ghosts.

Moreover Mr. Holmes was weighed down by the feeling that there was not the smallest hope of his ever being a prosperous man again. He had an inexhaustible perseverance, but even after selling the business near the Quadrant he was still considerably in debt to Messrs. Goulburn and Sons. Of course they were very sorry and very accommodating, and all that sort of thing, but the most fascinating of creditors are comparatively disagreeable. The shop in Islington was not likely to make a man immoderately rich even if all the profits could have been invested as capital; but all the profits could not be invested as capital, for there were perpetual remittances towards getting rid of the liabilities that the suretyship had produced. So Mr. Holmes became, at least compared with what he had been, a hard, ungenial, suspicious man; a man who had lost heart, who almost believed that he deserved his calamities, and who completely believed that everybody else thought he deserved them.

But how, all this while, did Effie manage with her reduced circumstances? A place of business in the city is not the home a lady would choose, if choice were free; it is utterly without romance. Sometimes there is an excess of business so thoroughly fatiguing, that many a night Effie went to bed unquestionably more tired than an average bricklayer. Then in the dull and quiet season, or I suppose I ought to say when it isn't the season at all, what are you to do with yourself? All the girls in places of business are neither ladies nor agreeable companions; and for that matter it would be difficult to say that all parsons or attorneys are gentlemen. But there's a certain fundamental human nature in everybody that one may build upon rather hopefully. At any rate Effie managed to make something of most of her companions, and even to make friends—well, I don't like to say of any. For, in truth, friendship is one of those things so extremely rare, that the great majority of mankind have never seen a specimen, and are entirely in the dark as to what it is. And among girls, too, there is a gushing sort of behaviour which seems at first sight to mean a good deal, and really means nothing. They kiss one another, for instance, in the most promiscuous and reckless way; and the male mind might for a few moments be completely deluded by this frantic affectionateness. And then again, though not exactly resembling Nestor in wisdom, and extremely anxious not to resemble him in age, they are like him, if we may believe Homer, in the honeyed sweetness of their language.

It needs some slight experience to discover, what is nevertheless an admitted fact, that a girl finds no difficulty in calling another "dear," though she will turn round in a few minutes and do her every spiteful little injury that jealousy and envy can prompt. Of course all the girls in the Wood Street house called Effie "dear;" though many of them tried their utmost to dislike her, because they had a faint suspicion that she was more of a lady than they were. But as to *friends*, Effie was one of those who have seen better days, and so perhaps she had caught a glimpse, in the old times, of some ideal friend, the like of whom was not to be found in the Wood Street house of business. And then, how many of the friends of the old time had vanished; gone into that unknown world, compared with which the world beyond the grave is a familiar country; the unknown world of hollow pretences and heartless conventionalisms, where men and women judge one another by utterly inhuman standards, and walk, as the Scripture has it, "in a vain show!" They were not dead, these friends of the old times, they had by no means lost their memories; to the people of their own set they would have seemed unchanged, and perhaps if they had met Effie in a quiet country lane or in a back street where they could be quite sure nobody could see them, they might just have stopped for a minute, and out of the mere force of an unmeaning habit called her "dear." But otherwise they had quite forgotten her; for they had, and I'm afraid all of us have in some degree, a double life; the one true, and the other false; the one genuine and hearty, the other cruel and hypocritical; and unfortunately it is the true and loving life that we seem to be half-ashamed of, that we keep hidden out of sight; that we only retire into now and then when we think we are quite alone, or into which we introduce, at the most, only two or three of all the millions of human beings that are our sisters and brothers.

So in respect of friends Effie was in the position of those blessed ones who are not disappointed because they expect nothing; and for companions some of the Wood Street girls were agreeable enough. Sometimes, when it was not the busy season, she read aloud tales or poems; not without a recollection of reading aloud elsewhere, in the better days, when she was the listener. And in the evening, when work was over, and she might sit in her own quiet room, she never forgot that now more than ever she was to take care of her truest self, seeing that she had no longer appearances and conventionalisms to rest on. She read with avidity, and with an ever-growing quickness of comprehension, the best books of the day. She wrote abstracts of those which most pleased her, and essays on kindred subjects, and even (must I confess it?) little lyrics that Fritz afterwards (but of course he was no judge) thought very musical. She was determined that poor though she might be, and cut off, by the mere fact that she earned her own living, from a position in society for which she knew she was fit, she would never cease to be *fit* for it, nor suffer the dull routine of Wood Street life to break her spirit. It was a rather dull routine, and often she felt more than sufficiently rebellious against it. She was beginning to think it a hindrance to intellectual and spiritual growth, and to cut it off more and more from the delightful labour of her leisure hours. In that way both learning and work began to suffer; she was often impatient in the one, and her sorrow and self-reproaching for an impatient and undutiful spirit spoiled the pleasure of the other. Was the curse to fall on her also? Was she to become one of the people whom calamity sours? Was she to become suspicious and defiant, looking upon everybody as in a conspiracy to defraud her of her just rights, scorning and hating even the honest work which had once seemed her only true friend, helping her onwards to independence and comfort? No, she was not to become this; but she little knew who had been sent to save her.

She was walking one Sunday morning, a splendid morning in June, along St. George's Road; and as she passed the chapel she heard through the open windows the music of a delicious organ. It was the voluntary, and the organist had chosen the air which is so well known and so universally admired, which seems so full of hope and rest even to those who do not know to what words the music has been adapted—the air, "Oh! rest in the Lord," from Mendelssohn's "Elijah." She listened till the music ceased and the minister began to pray.

"Whose chapel is this?" said Effie to a woman passing along.

"This? It's Richardson's chapel," said the woman.

"Richardson's!" Well, at any rate there was a sweet organ charmingly played; so Effie thought she might as well hear "Richardson" for once, as go further and be late at her own chapel.

"How long has Mr. Richardson been here?" she asked.

"Oh! years and years," said the woman, "ever since afore I was born."

Effie entered the chapel. Plainly Mr. Richardson carried age better than most men—bald and grey, at least Effie fancied so, though she was not sitting where she could see very well, the light of a window opposite dazzled her, but a wonderful vigour for so old a man. No trace of seventy years in his voice either, for it was loud, and clear, and firm, and there was a something in his voice too that seemed to Effie strangely and sweetly familiar. She looked and listened eagerly. Where could she have seen Mr. Richardson before? But it was no use guessing;

she took her part as well as she could in the whole service. The singing really *was* singing; everybody sang, minister and people. She began to feel sure that it couldn't be Mr. Richardson; no old man of seventy could sing like that. At any rate, what did it matter to Effie if it were a stranger? Anybody in that pulpit would be a stranger to her. So she tried to fix her wandering thoughts on the worship of God. The Psalms were ended, and the minister began to pray. Effie had no trouble to fix her thoughts now; truly, those were the very blessings she needed, those temptations from which she was hearing prayers for deliverance were her very own; those mercies for which thanks were rising to heaven she actually had received; and she could at any rate ask, with a child's sense of weakness and a child's confidence also, that in all the mysteries and perplexities of life she might be able to trust all to her heavenly Father's love.

And then came more singing, and the sermon. The stranger could not know how tired she had been growing of the Wood Street routine; how mean and poor and remote from spiritual life that routine had often seemed to her; how eagerly she hurried away from it. And yet why, with that strangely familiar voice, did he give out the text, "Whatsoever ye do, do it heartily, as unto the Lord and not to men?"

There was nothing extraordinary in the sermon,

it was in one sense extremely commonplace. It was in plain English, without a vestige of the technical jargon which so often mystifies the plainest subjects, and seems to separate Sunday by a great gulf from the common work of week-day life. The preacher said that work was very hard, and often very disagreeable; that it often seemed a mean and stupid routine, quite beneath the serious attention and genuine interest of any but the most meagre intellects and grovelling spirits. Effie was quite certain, as she listened, that this man had some message for her, whoever he might be. "And many spirits," said the preacher, "were grovelling; and the common business of life seemed to make them more sordid, and to harden their hearts. But what were they working for? For their wives and families? Even for themselves? Scarcely; for if they were, they would make a better use of their leisure for self-culture, they would cherish a loving disposition, they would care more to leave their children a good example, and to adorn and strengthen them by the ornaments and armour of righteousness, than to toil through a joyless life of unremitting labour, only to leave them rich. Men were oftenest working for the world; for the sake of a position in society; for the flattery and smiles of people who did not sincerely care for them, and who would forsake them to-morrow, if they were to fall into poverty, even though that poverty might be the triumphant proof of their generosity and virtue."

"You will work happily, you will work generously, you will find your work a spiritual and intellectual help and stimulus," said the preacher, "if whatever you do you do to the Lord and not to men. The labour will never seem mean to which you feel *He* sends you. What you would otherwise tire of, as dull routine, will become to you a type of the Divine order, and the blessed force of habit hurrying you away from your own idleness and selfishness. You will never cease to desire the esteem of your fellow-men, but you will rise above the insincerity either of praise or blame. And be sure that sloth is the fruitful parent of an innumerable progeny of vices, in whatever station of life you may be. And though the necessity of honestly working for your daily bread may seem to lower your social status, or even bring upon you the contempt of ignorant vanity; you will cease to care for that when you remember that you are doing the Master's bidding, and rewarded by His love."

Yes; there was nothing the least clever in the preacher's sermon; but that did not matter to Effie. He had brought a message from God to her, whatever he might be.

"Is that Mr. Richardson?" Effie asked the pew-opener.

"Lor, no, Miss; Dr. Richardson's been left this nearly three years: that's the new minister."

"What's his name?" said Effie.

"Rivers—the Rev. Frederick Rivers."

Yes! of course it was! Some ten years make a difference in everybody, but it was unmistakeably Fritz. Effie hurried home, sad and happy. Would she ever meet him again? Would he dislike or shun her because she had to work for her living? Surely not, after such a sermon. Perhaps some day she would try. And yet, she had seen something of what common friendships are; and for Fritz, *he* was under no sort of obligations to remember the happy Shiloh days because *she* was unable to forget them. Well, reader, if you have ever been in deep need of love and help, if one after another has betrayed or disappointed you till you have almost lost faith in the possibility of sincere affection, you will know better than any words of mine can tell you, what Effie felt after that Sunday morning service, of loneliness and grief, of hope and fear. And yet, somehow, she could not help persuading herself that in the darkness of her sorrow she could at least see the first, faint, beauteous beams of a day of joy and rest.

All through the week she was trying, not in vain, to work for the Lord; and it was, perhaps, no mortal sin if she thought sometimes upon him who had brought to her the Master's message.

CHAPTER XIV.

FRIENDS.

Fritz's wife was a tall, slender girl, with black hair and eyes. Anybody could see that, and as I said before, I'm not clever at description; and so I wont spoil Hetty's face by any miserable botch of my painting. She was a Manchester girl; not a relation, but the daughter of a very old friend of the Rivers's family. Fritz couldn't have made a better choice, if he had searched half over the world, and waited through twenty years of courtship, till he colud make up his mind to marry. He did nothing of the kind. He became "engaged" without any approach to romance; he didn't go down on his knees, or say any of the pretty speeches that we may read in story books or hear at the theatre. A lover on his knees Hetty would most certainly have refused. She was even more unsentimental than Fritz; and at the time of his marriage Fritz was not nearly sentimental enough. But one evening, when they were going to hear a lecture on something or other, he proposed right in the middle of Market Street, and she said "Yes;" and in eight months they were married. They had been friends for years; now they were man and wife. Every man and woman knows the likeness and the difference; and that it would be better to be friends and never married, than to be married and not friends.

The children were boy and girl; and Fritz had every reason to expect the blessing of the "man that hath his quiver full of them." The boy was fair like Fritz; the girl was dark like Hetty. There was no such manager of babies as Hetty among all Fritz's acquaintance or congregation. She had a perfect passion for babies; if a waggon-load of babies had been left at the house she would have provided for every one of them. She had a profound contempt for those young ladies who are always reading, or writing, or playing the piano, or drawing, or arguing—arguing was her special aversion—and who scarcely know the difference between a plum-pudding and a cauliflower, or a night-cap and a pair of shoes. She was assuredly not a "blue-stocking;" but often when "learned ladies" had been talking what Hetty called "rubbish" for hours at a stretch, floundering about in all manner of moral and religious bogs and "sloughs of despond," waiting for Fritz to help them out, she would administer a shrewd, common-sense, perfectly suitable slap on the back which helped hysteric intellects to the firm ground in half a minute. "I don't see the least meaning in all that," she would sometimes say—there being, in fact, no meaning to see;—and that settled a discussion incomparably more rapidly, and far more effectually, than all Fritz's talk could have done if he had talked for centuries. Young ladies who with very slender reasons thought themselves intellectual were rather in awe of her, for they never could "make her out." How much did she know? And Fritz had a way of talking to her with his eyes, which was very bewildering to strangers. Sometimes in the very midst of the most brilliant display of female rhetoric, Fritz would give a quiet look at Hetty that in a single instant took off all the polish from the most shining sentences, and left nothing but a mass of rust; while even Miss Demosthenes herself began to stutter. Hetty had a quiet way of asking people what they meant, which was very embarrassing to those who didn't quite know what they meant themselves; and they could never make out whether she was a simpleton asking for information, or a quiz asking for fun. In truth she was not averse to quizzing, though she had none of the malice which genuine quizzing includes. She thought women should be anyhow domestic, and then as accomplished as possible.

She could play well on the piano, and besides that, she had a most charming voice and a thorough knowledge of music. Moreover, knowing two or three modern languages well, and as much as most schoolboys know of Latin, she often rendered to her husband really valuable service; copying Latin or translating German and French for him with great accuracy and taste. She had, too, that gift or acquirement invaluable to a minister's wife, perfect command of her tongue. Her reticence was absolutely marvellous; unconquerable by hints, suggestions, confidential communications on the other side, or even direct questions. A congregational church is almost an unknown region to the outside world; though even congregational churches are not quite what they used to be, and London churches are very different from country churches. Many breaches have been made in the "walls" by which these "little gardens" are enclosed. For one thing, congregationalists are much more wealthy than they used to be; and a pious man with fifteen shillings a week takes not unnaturally a very different view of worldliness from that of the pious man with fifteen pounds a week. But the theory is that every "member" is "truly converted;" and the signs of true conversion are almost all reducible to "other-worldliness." There are very few country "churches" that would hesitate to excommunicate any "member" who had been seen in a theatre; but I never heard of an expulsion for bad temper or malicious gossiping. On the contrary, as every member is personally interested in the "purity of the church," which means the personal character and private habits of every other member, it is a part of piety to be a busybody in other people's matters. So bankruptcies, breach of promise of marriage, and almost as many errors or vices as used to come within the jurisdiction of the unreformed ecclesiastical courts, may be submitted to examination and judgment at a "church-meeting;" and everybody knows that gossip and accusation begin a long way on the safe side of judicial decision.

"A minister's life must be very harassing, my dear," said Mrs. Lush, a deacon's wife, to Hetty one day; "I'm sure I sincerely sympathize with Mr. Rivers. This new case of inconsistency must very much trouble him."

"You're very kind, Mrs. Lush," said the minister's wife, "but I don't quite know which case you refer to."

"Ah, dear, you may well say so; no doubt you've heard of others."

"No, no; I didn't mean that, of course; but I couldn't tell what you were thinking of."

"No, certainly, Mrs. Rivers, how could you? I was meaning that most unfortunate engagement of Miss Jones with young Sparks—a young fellow in Goulburns' Bank."

"Oh! then are they really engaged? I heard the report contradicted."

"Engaged, my dear? Yes, indeed and to be married in a month; and there are all manner of whispers. I'm afraid he's a gay young man; very, very worldly."

"I hope not," said Hetty; "she's a sweet girl. But, in fact, I know nothing whatever about young Sparks, and so, of course, can have no opinion about the match."

"Just like you, my cautious dear," thought baffled Mrs. Lush, who quite hoped to fill up the details of her narrative about Miss Jones and Mr. Sparks by her call at the parsonage. "By the way," she said, "have you noticed a girl who has been sitting the last few Sundays, in front of the Skinners?"

"I can't see so far down the chapel," said Hetty, "and I don't like to look about; though, indeed, I sometimes wish I could see just enough to tell Mr. Rivers if anybody is absent whom it might be right to call on."

"Well, she seemed quite a lady, and in fact took a sitting on Wednesday week. So last Sunday I asked her if she would come to the Dorcas meeting on Tuesday—it was at my house; I told her you would be there, and most likely Mr. Rivers would just look round for a few minutes at the end, and she would get to know the people. She seemed very much confused, and blushed quite ridiculously, and begged to be excused. In fact it turns out, to put it in plain English, she's a mere shopwoman. I don't think I've been so disappointed for a long time."

"Do you know where she lives?" Hetty asked.

"At some house of business in the City, in Wood Street—I don't remember the name."

"And what is the young lady's own name?" said Hetty.

"I think it was Holmes; but really the young woman looked so confused and shy and ridiculous, I scarcely heard what she said."

Mrs. Lush was not a learned, arguing, intellectual lady, but Hetty didn't like her. She was not unkind; at least never unkind as yet to the Riverses. But she had a hard business-like way of dealing with human nature and its most refined and delicate manifestations, which even to unromantic Hetty was utterly repulsive. She seemed to think that affections and conscience, and almost religion, might be weighed or measured as easily as sugar or silks. The prosperity of St. George's Road Chapel and the success of Fritz's ministry meant with her a certain amount of pew-rents. She thought people ought to be "kept at their place" by any amount of conciliation or compromise; for, as she triumphantly asked, "You may want ever so much to do them good, but how *can* you do them good if they're not there?"—and as to doing them harm, if they *were* there, by unworthy and cowardly compromise, *that* never entered Mrs. Lush's thoughts.

"Getting *harm* at our chapel! stuff and nonsense." At the same time, what was the use of filling the place with people who could do nothing? We want subscribers to the schools, the societies, and that sort of thing. "Oh yes! poor people have souls, and there are plenty of free seats and ragged churches; but chapels like ours have expenses, and it's no use expecting to pay them without money." So a shopwoman was a disappointment—possibly might get in arrears with pew-rent, and certainly could do nothing extra. Besides—"Well, one can't ask a shopwoman to one's house with young men there, and such like. It would never do at all." Of course it wouldn't, Mrs. Lush, particularly if the shopwoman were pretty and good.

This good lady, in fact, cared nothing about the reality if it hadn't the conventional form. The "young woman" who had taken a sitting "in front of the Skinners" was very lady*like*, had unimpeachable manners (apart from the blushing, which showed that her feelings were not sufficiently under control), spoke the correctest English, dressed with perfect taste, and indeed, as to the actual stuff and substance of her nature and training, *was* a *lady*. But is a Lush to find out her good qualities if she chooses to appear in the disguise of a shopwoman? Even uncle Alfred couldn't have expressed the matter better than Mrs. Lush. "We surely owe *something* to ourselves and society." Who ever said we didn't, Mrs. Lush?

But, at any rate, when she was gone, Hetty thought how vexed Fritz would have been if he had heard Mrs. Lush talking about "a *shopwoman,*" in her hard-hearted, snobbish, worldly way. What had God's priests to do with such distinctions, except to show that they belonged only to the surface of life, and were in the sight of our Father in Heaven but "as the small dust of the balance?" Was it not against mere shows and unrealities of all kinds that he was continually preaching? Though Hetty didn't look about her on Sundays, she would manage to see the pew in front of the Skinners next time she went to chapel, and form her own opinion of "the young woman," the disappointing shopwoman, who had taken a seat there. She told Fritz what Mrs. Lush had said, and he fancied he knew the name Holmes quite well, but couldn't remember the person; anyhow he'd find out. As to Miss Jones, it was quite true that she was to be married to young Sparks of Goulburns' in a very few months.

And that, of course, explained why young Sparks had taken to chapel going. It was not much, as we know already, in his natural line; but Miss Jones was rich and her parents were pious, and a certain thin coating of religious properness was a necessary part of the matrimonial investment.

Moreover, he found a kind of pleasure in exercising his ingenuity upon a class of people so different from those with whom he had been in the habit of associating. To learn the evangelical and dissenting dialect was like learning a new language; which was very easy, and at the same time so like English, as to afford the utmost facility for an everlasting supply of puns and double meanings. He was soon able to talk in the most "gracious" and savoury manner. Even Mrs. Lush began to think him a very "hopeful" young man, and felt quite sure in her own mind that he would soon be "proposed for Church fellowship." It was his great delight to "trot out" his intended wife's pious connexions, in fact "fooling them to the top of their bent." They seemed to him, and in fact they often really were, so charmingly green that he could scarcely help laughing in their faces. The publication of one or two books of a sceptical tendency had produced quite a panic in the religious world, which, in spite of Fritz's most earnest endeavours, had extended even to St. George's Road. It would have been a most favourable omen if Sparks could have been persuaded to read them; his favourite literature was, unfortunately, of a very different kind, more in the direction of Don Juan or the cleanly poems of Swift. In fact, to do him justice, he cared very little for literature of any kind, and found conversation much easier and quite as decently

—dirty. But, at any rate, the panic-stricken orthodox were quite certain that there must be some grace in a young man who assured them that "he wouldn't be seen reading such books as these sceptics were writing for any consideration; he couldn't afford to have his religious principles weakened"—which would have been strictly true if he had had any religious principles to weaken. He was quite amused to be so earnestly warned against giving to religion the slightest thought or examination, to which he never felt for a single moment tempted; while the temptations which really did assail him, and to which he was in the habit of continually yielding, were never so much as mentioned, and were apparently unknown. Pious old ladies seemed to think that when a young man was out till two or three o'clock in the morning he was wasting his valuable time upon infidel speculations. Sparks could lay his hand on his bosom and declare, before heaven and earth, that the small hours of *his* life were occupied by no such inanities.

Of course, the piety of Sparks's new friends had a practical form, chiefly negative. He found the theatre regarded with profound horror, for which horror every wrong reason was offered that the imagination of people who had never seen the inside of a theatre could devise; reasons, in fact, which were of far greater force against walking down Regent Street or the Haymarket. At the worst, however, the slight restriction of his amusements which prudence dictated would not last long, and he was not without reason for believing that Miss Jones would be more tolerant of worldliness than Miss Jones's pious friends. It was in an interview, however, with Fritz that Sparks's cleverness and new attainments in piety shone out with their brightest lustre. That charming young man had, like almost all his class, a very firm belief that every minister of religion when venturing even a single step beyond the limits of his own profession was just a fool or a girl, which such young gentlemen consider the very same thing. It seems never to occur to them that a grown-up human being is under no kind of obligation to tell everything he knows. For instance, when Sparks was telling some enormous lie to Fritz with the utmost coolness, Fritz never felt it in the least degree necessary to say that his young friend was a hypocritical scoundrel, though he quite well knew it. Moreover, sometimes, there did just now and then pass over the young gentleman from Goulburns' the faintest shadow of a suspicion that playing with a parson was highly amusing, but required so much skill and tact that it amounted almost to making a labour of a pleasure. The young gentleman from Goulburns' was in plain English a jackass, with just enough education to make him anxious to appear like a nobler animal, and just enough wickedness to gain for him the reputation and privileges of a rather "fast" young man. An odd mixture, surely. And I'm not quite sure whether his having the reputation of being "fast" did not add a peculiar charm to that piety which quick-sighted Mrs. Lush could discover rapidly ripening to a glorious maturity. Think what a charming letter of experience he would write to the church meeting, and how eagerly all the young ladies would listen to it on the night when he should be "proposed for fellowship." In fact already Fritz thought he detected the young banker's style in a similar document presented to the church by the prettiest scholar in Miss Jones's Sunday-school class. He had just a smattering of all manner of ologies, from theology to entomology; and as Fritz had a somewhat perplexing manner of acknowledging his own extreme ignorance of many of those subjects of which Sparks was even more ignorant still, that charming young man, visiting the parsonage with Miss Jones, and anxious to display the versatility of his genius to her too partial affection, was not unfrequently beguiled into prematurely revealing the most startling discoveries in almost every one of the sciences. "Yes, Mr. Sparks," the parson used to say, "it is, as you say, most astonishing, and indeed to me quite new; indeed, I I had always understood—but what's the use of my saying *I* understood?—because you know I don't pretend to know anything about these things, and you do." And then sweet Miss Jones would look at Sparks with the fascinating blindness of love, and say in her heart, "Oh, you brilliant darling! Of course Mr. Rivers can't expect to be as clever as you are." In fact, Fritz did really know very little of the physical sciences, though it happened to be far more than enough to protect him from being in the least degree deceived by Sparks's pretensions; and every now and then he put that extremely accomplished young gentleman to almost as exquisite torture as the Sparks' nature is capable of. With a diabolical cruelty, and without the slightest provocation, he would sometimes appeal to him for information, or ask him to be kind enough to solve a difficulty. One evening, for instance, he was listening to a conversation, and to the extent of asking questions, joining in it, about some new discovery in chemistry. The gentlemen with whom he was talking were two thoroughly accomplished physicians. They were the more interested in the new discovery, because on the one hand, it seemed to promise to throw new light on one of the great difficulties of physiology, and on the other, to furnish some rational foundation for the treatment of a dangerous and ill-understood disease. But the new discovery was itself somewhat doubtful, and even for the understanding of what it professed to be, Fritz had to tax very heavily the patience of his two friends. Just at that very moment, as some demon would have it, the self-satisfied smirk of Sparks arrested his attention. He also was evidently explaining something to a little circle of ladies, and looked for all the world like a living illustration of the frog in the fable, who did his humble best to attain the gigantic proportions of the bull.

"Mr. Sparks," Fritz called out, "if those ladies will let you tear yourself away from them, I wish you'd come here for a minute."

"We were just talking," said Fritz, "about that new chemical discovery you have no doubt read so much about in the scientific papers during the last few weeks. I wish you'd just tell us what the thing actually is, and explain the reactions that seem so complicated, and that in fact we can't quite make out."

"Oh yes, Mr. Rivers," said the charmingly unconscious clerk from Goulburns', "I shall be delighted; it seems to me exceedingly simple."

The two physicians stared at one another in undisguised astonishment, while Sparks floundered away out of one absurdity into another, telling how one element was changed into another element, and in fact turning all nature into chaos.

"Ah!" said one of the physicians, "now it never struck me before that that could have been the explanation: indeed, you're quite a genius, Mr. Sparks."

In short, with the most guileless desire to receive information, they began asking Sparks all manner of questions. "How did this happen? How did that happen? And what did Sparks mean precisely by this and by that?" And one of them had just produced a pencil and a detestable blank piece of paper, with a child-like desire to see in plain black and white Mr. Sparks's simple statement of what the mistiness of mere conversation seemed slightly to cloud. With an extremely red face that charming young gentleman was really, with a courage worthy of a better cause, preparing to ruin for ever his scientific reputation, when Miss Jones by a merciful Providence came to his relief. She was very sorry to deprive the gentlemen of his society, but the ladies could not really do without him any longer, and wouldn't he come? The graceful and gallant Sparks was only too thankful to come, and it was long before he ventured upon another "everythingological" conversation with the Rev. F. Rivers.

But we need not stay any longer with Mr. Sparks, at least in this chapter; he is not yet "proposed for fellowship," nor is he yet united in holy matrimony to Miss Jones; and the other people who visited Fritz, even though some of them came exceedingly often, were by no means all of them friends; indeed, unfortunately, with more or less of disguise, some of them were becoming enemies. The rest were what we call acquaintances; they paid and received visits, they were on the footing of exchanging little engraved notes if any of them happened to be confined or if their friends died, to the effect that Mrs. A. thanked Mrs. B. for kind inquiries. Even when they shook hands, or when the ladies kissed one another, they knew quite well that even between their very lips and palms there was a great gulf of reticence; in fact, in many cases it was not so much reticence, as the absolute impossibility of communicating that for which there was no receptivity. But Fritz and Hetty *had* friends who could give and take with perfect fellowship, and there was an inner circle of their lives in which all was warm and genuine. Indeed it was this very thing which gave so much offence to some of the most influential of Fritz's congregation. There was Mrs. Lush, for instance, the wife of one of the deacons, who couldn't imagine what Hetty could see to like so much in Mrs. Parkinson, the wife of another deacon. Hetty was always exceedingly courteous to Mrs. Lush, and even consented to be kissed, though she used to tell Fritz she had a bad taste in her mouth for hours afterwards. She used to call quite as often as any deacon's wife could expect to be visited; she listened with exemplary patience to all Mrs. Lush's gossip, though she had the misfortune to be utterly unable to communicate any gossip in return, and yet that exacting deaconess was far from satisfied. It was unquestionably her private opinion that Mrs. Rivers was "a very stuck-up piece of goods," and it very ill became a minister's wife to have favourites, and to endanger the harmony of the Church by her whims and partialities.

"And who's Mrs. Parkinson?" said Mrs. Lush. "She hasn't been long connected with our cause at any rate. And why am I to be put into the background by any Mrs. Parkinson? and if we're not of some use at St. George's Road, I should be glad to know who is. There's Lush a deacon, and a very good deacon too; does a good deal more visiting of the poor than Mr. Rivers ever does, that's one thing; and then there's Rebecca, superintendent of the Sunday-school, and Sarah meets the mothers, and Jane's secretary of the Dorcas Society, and Henrietta looks after the poor lying-in women that have boxes, and I don't know what there is that we haven't something to do with. Not that I wish anything of the sort," she once said to her husband, "but I've been thinking it would make rather a large hole in the cause at St. George's Road, if we were all to go away."

Persons with such sentiments often become rather chilly as friends; often even without knowing it themselves. When we begin to think how immeasurably our friends are in need of us, the temperature of our affections gradually cools; and Mrs. Lush was already doing something towards fulfilling the prediction of the Rev. John Veneer. As to partiality, nobody could doubt for a moment that Hetty *loved* Mrs. Parkinson, and was *scrupulously polite* to Mrs. Lush. Well, how can we help it? Are we to give no expression to our affections, and go down to our graves without giving any utterance to our love, for fear of offending those who unquestionably are not to us "as our own souls?" Are we to love nobody until we can love all alike? and what's the use of loving people if we can't say that we do—if from that good tree of genuine affection every blossom is to be nipped as soon as it appears? Hypocritical nonsense! we might as well refuse to light a fire in the winter for fear of offending the North Pole!

But if Mrs. Lush was scandalized by Hetty's sisterly regard for Mrs. Parkinson, how much more was she scandalized when she found that disappointing shopwoman who had looked so much like a lady, admitted with heartiest welcome into the inner circle of Fritz and Hetty's friends! The Sunday after the mother of so many useful daughters had told Mrs. Rivers the low estate of the young person who had taken a sitting in front of the Skinners, Hetty had an unexpected opportunity of making "the young person's" acquaintance. The morning had been very bright, and almost everybody had come to chapel without the slightest preparation for rain. The service, however, was just closing when a heavy thunderstorm began, with drenching rain. The people were still crowding about the passages and doors, venturing out one by one as their courage, or clothing, or distance from home suggested, when Fritz and Hetty, nodding to their weather-bound friends on all sides, set out to brave what yet remained of the storm. Just as they were turning the corner of St. George's Road, they met, coming from the other side of the chapel, the girl from whose sweet face Hetty had been scarcely able to take her eyes all through the sermon time. It was the girl who sat in front of the Skinners, the young "person" who had so much disappointed Mrs. Lush —it was Effie Holmes.

"Have you far to go, Miss Holmes?" said Hetty.

"Thank you, ma'am, it is rather far; I have to go to the city—but I daresay I shall soon get a seat in an omnibus," said Effie.

"I fancy the omnibuses are sure to be full," Fritz said; "and at any rate we shall be very pleased if you'll go home with us to dinner."

Effie thanked them, and accepted their invitation. Fritz could not make out what it was that made her name, her voice, her face seem so familiar, while they walked home together; and for Effie, she was almost in a delirium of hope and fear, joy and pain. What would come of this new meeting? Would she be recognised? Should she tell Fritz at once who she was? And yet what did it matter?—the present was not less real, even if the past were forgotten—she might at least wait. So she went upstairs with Hetty "to take her things off;" and Fritz sat by the fire in a reverie, trying to think of all the Holmeses he knew, and what face it was that Effie's so reminded him of. She soon came down, and now that she had put off her bonnet her face was more like than before to that other face that Fritz was trying to identify.

"I can't make it out at all, Miss Holmes," he said; "but you're wonderfully like somebody I know, and I can't think who the somebody is."

"Very likely you've seen Miss Holmes at chapel, and just remember her face without connecting it with any particular person," said Hetty. "Have you always lived in London, Miss Holmes? You know we're country people."

"Yes," Effie said, "I'm Cockney enough for anything. I was born in London, schooled in London, apprenticed in London—scarcely ever out of it except at the holidays, years ago, when I sometimes visited an old bachelor cousin in Derbyshire."

"No!" said Fritz, starting to his feet, and seizing Effie's hand; "not old Moses Holmes of Shiloh? What a fool I am!"

Hetty looked surprised, and Effie rose from her seat, while Fritz introduced her as an old friend, a friend who strangely bound up for him the past with the present, and quiet home scenes with the stir and harass of London. Hetty was charmed to find that the intelligent, beautiful girl, who had so disappointed Mrs. Lush, was in very fact a lady; one in whom, she already fondly hoped, it might be *proved* that a human spirit is greater than the circumstances in which it is placed, and "a man's life consisteth not in the abundance of the things that he possesseth." And there was talk all dinner-time of Manchester and Shiloh; and Effie remembered (oh, how well) the library, and the fir-plantation, and the books she and Fritz had read together. And Hetty half envied one who knew so much more than herself of that little piece of Fritz's past; and, perhaps, Effie half envied one who knew so much more than herself of Fritz's present. But each, as far as might be, enriched the other; and Effie, too, had her own tale to tell—all about poor Frank Walker, and her own efforts to get a living, and where she was now—and, in fact, everything she could think of to fill up those long years since she and Fritz had spent together that delicious autumn holiday, boy and girl.

And did he despise her, because in an ordinary London warehouse she was earning her own living? Despise her! He looked upon her as a kind of heroine; he thought every bit of her conduct so brave and thorough, so perfectly genuine. He liked her all the better because he knew full well what society thinks of misfortune and self-help; and that a "lady" may without social disgrace be an idler or a burden to her friends, but must assuredly lose caste if she works. Instinctively he felt that he must be in some sort her protector, and vindicate her honour and the beauty of her soul against even the silence and coldness of the world. He felt what most people have felt one time or other, how irresistible is the power which our abstract principles acquire when they become incarnate in a living person. He had never failed to set the substance above the form. In sermons, and the ordinary intercourse of society, and even already in print, he had made it his chief business to urge men to *be* rather than to *seem*. He had told them to love work and to honour workers: to honour them far more than idlers, though the idlers might be rich and the workers poor. But a wondrous new form had all this teaching taken now, in Fritz's mind and heart. It was henceforth EFFIE. It meant love Effie, admire Effie, honour her independence, her perfect unselfishness, her strength of character, the tender grace of her whole being. The ordinary judgments of a cold, mercenary world, were henceforth, for Fritz, slanders against Effie; and he denied and refuted them, not with the calm assurance of a logician, nor even with the impartial benevolence of a Christian, but with the passionate energy of wounded affection.

Does it surprise you, reader, that these two were in one short afternoon drawn so closely together that it seemed as if they had never been separated;

while even that autumn holiday, years ago, was brightened with a new glory? Perhaps it was strange; and yet in a mystic way they had been working together, even though Fritz had all but utterly forgotten the sweet companion of those happy weeks. The one in thought, the other in life—they had been solving the same problems, grappling with the same foes. And now they seemed almost to be conscious of what had never really been, the present and the past were one. In fact they were lost in those relations which are independent of time altogether; they only knew that they had met once more, and that the life of each was fuller and more complete and far happier for their meeting. But they could not have said how much belonged to Shiloh and how much to London.

And neither Fritz nor Effie seemed more pleased by this strange recognition than was Fritz's wife. She could have predicted with absolute certainty what Fritz would have thought of such a girl as Effie, even if there had been no Shiloh experiences to bind them together. She knew it when Mrs. Lush was talking her worldly rubbish about "the young woman in front of the Skinners." She knew it because it was the thought of her own heart also, and because she and Fritz were one. So when the evening came she kissed Effie, and told her that she must be sure that she would ever find a hearty welcome with Fritz and her. She was not to come now and then as a stranger might, on set invitations, but with perfect homeliness as an old well-loved friend.

Poor Effie! How bitter are the sweet pains of joy. She felt as if her true life were at last beginning. He who had been so much to her in imagination was even more in plain reality than she had ever dared to imagine. And what a sweet girl was his wife! And how genuine and happy was their home—the home that they had, in a manner, made her home also. Yes, young reader, especially if you are a girl, more especially still if you are a gushing, impetuous girl, with ill-regulated mind and undisciplined affections, Effie loved Fritz with her whole soul, with unfathomable depths of love that you, likely enough, have no line to measure—far too fondly, deeply, truly, to be what you would call "in love with him." She loved him with the love that excludes envy and jealousy; the love that drew her near to everything he loved, to everything who loved him; the love that bound her fast in most genuine affection, above all, to Hetty.

And yet—was it not dangerous? Would the world let them be happy together? Could anybody see how it would all end?

"Sufficient unto the day is the evil thereof."

CHAPTER XV.

HERESY.

Whatever the world might be disposed to do with Effie's happiness, the Church was gradually making up its mind that it was high time to come to a somewhat clearer understanding about Fritz's orthodoxy. Religious people were, as I have already said, panic-stricken by the appearance of a few books which, from various causes, had obtained a popularity and an influence which their intrinsic merits could scarcely account for. Indeed it is very difficult to understand what all the fuss was about. I should have thought, from simply reading them, that they were written by very good men who were so clever and learned that they might be excused for believing that they were justified in publishing to the world the opinions to which, after careful thought, they had arrived. I never found out that they were liars and infidels, though a great many very religious people say they are; and of course religious people never call their neighbours liars and infidels without knowing them intimately, and taking the utmost care that there is no mistake. However the Church, and especially those little scraps of Churches that are found among dissenting sects, were in a most bewildering muddle; and seemed to expect nothing less than the demolition of Christendom, as the result of the publication of one or two thin octavo volumes, containing three or four hundred pages apiece. Anyhow it was not for the Church and congregation over which, hypothetically at least, Dr. Richardson and his sainted predecessors had presided, to be either less frightened or less furious than meaner Congregations. And yet nothing was being done. The trumpet of the Rev. Frederick Rivers was giving no certain sound; and how could Bung and Lush and the Sunday-school teachers prepare themselves for the battle. Not indeed that the Sunday-school teachers needed much trumpeting; for they had a capital brass band of their own, and were in excellent practice. To do them justice, they were so far from wishing to trouble their minister for his opinions and advice, that they considered his trumpet decidedly out of tune, and that their band was much better without it than with it. They had already settled, not so much by study as by a pious instinct, all those questions which were being so hotly discussed on every side. Had they read those dangerous volumes—those "Lectures on Sacrifice;" those "Essays and Reviews;" those "Criticisms of the Pentateuch;" which were supposed to prove that the Church of England at any rate was a mischievous nest of Jesuits? "Read them indeed! No! You wont catch us reading such books as those as long as we've an open Bible!" They unquestionably had an open Bible, and a very much more open mouth; and with that last, at any rate, was it not their plain duty to testify?

And yet at St. George's Road absolutely nothing was being done. The minister had never once availed himself of the numerous opportunities that had presented themselves for warning his hearers against those dreadful heresies and that fearful contempt of God's holy word, which were sapping the foundations of Christianity. Long ago, the Rev. John Veneer had delivered a most convincing course of lectures on "Infidelity in Lawn Sleeves." He had proved to demonstration that everybody who has the smallest doubt about the authorship of Genesis denies the divinity of Christ, and even disbelieves in the existence of a God. Nothing but Christian charity prevented his going to the end of his invincible argument. He knew, though he was much too generous to say so, that everybody who has a single doubt about the authorship of Genesis is incurably insane, and is a perjured villain hurrying along the broad road that leadeth to destruction. Nor could anybody accuse the Rev. J. Veneer of having preached this course of lectures without the most careful preparation. For as much as three calendar months he had devoted a whole hour a week to the study of the Hebrew tongue, under the invaluable guidance of a converted Jew.

Moreover, had not even the minister of the Primitive Methodists given a course of week-day orations on "Our precious Bible;" proving to the entire satisfaction of his enlightened audience everything that they had already made up their minds to believe? And the Rev. Ebenezer Dickson, too, quietest of men, solitary and sallow, with a delivery cautious even to hesitation—had not even he risen superior to his customary timidity and unburthened his soul; and were not his discourses, at the request of an enraptured congregation, already in the press? "The Bible Infallible; Seven Discourses by the Rev. Ebenezer Dickson." Infallible in science, infallible in history, infallible in grammar, infallible in poetry, infallible in prediction, infallible in theology, infallible in morals. Ah! didn't they catch it, miserable sceptics—at least, wouldn't they have caught it if they'd been there? *They* were *not* there; but Mr. Dickson's congregation was. Every one of his people was more than ever convinced of the truth of what he had always believed; the infidel men of straw which Mr. Dickson set up, had been duly battered down again; and his delighted hearers sang "Io Triumphe" accordingly.

And what a glorious peroration was that which concluded the course of sermons by the evangelical rector of the parish church! "What should we be," he asked, "what, my brethren, should we know, what, oh what, beloved, should we do without the Bible? We should know nothing about the creation of the world, nothing about that glorious Eden in which our first parents spent the blessed days of their innocence and perfection. We should know nothing of the water that drowned the world or the fire that burnt up the cities of the plain. We should know nothing of the fall, of the serpent, of our lost and ruined state by nature. We should know nothing of a Saviour, nothing of heaven or hell, nothing of God. Keep your Bibles, my beloved brethren, at any cost. Clasp them to your bosoms, through fire and sword, through persecution and derision, through evil report and good report. Let no profane or sacrilegious hand tear them from your grasp, though prisons yawn, and fires blaze and crackle, and swords gleam. Keep your Bibles, and rest assured that your Bibles will keep you."

And all this while St. George's Road was doing absolutely nothing. How different it would have been in the days of the good old doctor! With what a gentlemanly properness would he have put the infidel down! Even now, old though he was, a pamphlet had appeared from his pen, falling like a snowflake on the raging sea of controversy, to be soon swallowed up by—oblivion; not, however, before the evangelical magazines and newspapers had duly chronicled its appearance and trumpeted forth its praise. And all this while Mr. Rivers was silent, or worse than silent. What was to be done?

Couldn't they, at any rate, *pray* for him; and under the forms of devotion delicately hint at what they were so eagerly desiring to receive? The prayer-meetings were not well attended; and a prayer to heaven was not always so carefully listened to, but that its secondary object, information for earth, might fail. But at any rate the attempt might be made, and the prayer-meeting was a capital nucleus for—anything. So it was privately arranged, between Bung and Lush and a few others, that the next Monday evening should be devoted to special application for the spiritual enlightenment and ministerial prosperity of their beloved pastor. It was, of course, quite uncertain which of them would be first "called upon to engage." They all hoped it might be Lush, they all hoped it might not be Bung; while it was even possible that Mr. Rivers might call upon some brother not in the secret of the special object, and Lush might positively have no opportunity of conveying to his minister those delicate suggestions which he had already, not without effort, translated into the form of a petition to Almighty God.

The hymn was nearly over—the pious conspirators, with daggers of supplication hidden in their bosoms, could scarcely sing the last verse, so great was their excitement—when the minister made the usual sign, and, as soon the hymn was ended, announced in a clear voice the disappointing words—

"Mr. Bung will engage in prayer."

The distracted deacon looked imploringly to Lush, but it was of no use. It was impossible for the father of so many useful daughters to affect to believe that Mr. Rivers had called on *him*. Fritz had a perfectly audible voice, and though neither Bung nor Lush was a pretty name, they had quite different kinds of ugliness. There was nothing for it but to go on; already the pause was becoming painful, so Bung must screw his courage to the sticking-place, and plunge his diaconal dagger into the obdurate bosom of his minister—*viâ* Heaven. It was not so easy as it looked; and already the faint heart of this excellent brother began to fail him.

Of course, he had often prayed at the prayer-meeting before; so often, indeed, that any memory present that evening could, under ordinary circumstances, have acted as prompter. And why not? Mr. Bung's prayer was a very good one, and why wasn't it as good for one Monday as for another? In fact, it included a prayer *for* "Thy servant who ministers to us in holy things," and it wanted no amendment beyond the addition of a prayer *to* "Thy servant," ditto. Yet that was "the rub." Mr. Bung, though eminently pious, was not a man of quick invention or artistic genius. With unutterable labour he had composed two or three new sentences for this special Monday evening, but he was utterly baffled by the enormous difficulty of getting any of them to fit into the original composition; and he shivered with despair as he reflected that if they once got in there was not the smallest chance that he would ever be able to get them out again. And in that case he would have sacrificed for a single Monday the prayer that had lasted for nearly twenty years and was still as good as new.

At any rate he began. The rising anxiety of the little band of worshippers began to grow calm as he jog-trotted through the first score or two of the oft-repeated, well-remembered sentences. Indeed, so great was the fascination of the accustomed road that, like an old horse, he began to feel that he must trot on to the very end or perish; and his one hope was that he might remember not to say "Amen" till he had tacked on the two or three new passages which were to stimulate the dilatory soul of the Rev. Frederick Rivers. With increasing and still increasing terror he drew nearer and nearer to the fatal spot. Could the old horse be pulled up with the very stable-door open before him? Bung did his best, but alas! the force of habit was too strong. He stuttered and stammered, he grew white with fear, and his weak knees trembled; in the agony of his excitement he quite forgot how the new sentences began, and without having deviated by a single syllable from the form of words which had edified the prayer-meeting for twenty years, he flung out the conclusive "Amen."

"Oh! Bung's a poor creature," said Mrs. Lush, in a whisper to her daughter.

"A perfect idiot," responded her mother's darling.

"I suppose Lush will make a great show-off now," said Mrs. Bung to *her* daughter.

"Yes; don't you see it brewing?" said the irritated daughter of Bung; "and I can see Mrs. Lush making game of 'pa."

But these affectionate "asides" were of course interrupted by Fritz's reading a lesson and giving out another hymn. He then said—

"Mr. Parkinson will pray."

"I am very glad of it," said Mrs. Bung to her daughter, as she bent her head; while what seemed almost the ghost of a lost smile glided miserably over the ashy countenance of her poor bewildered husband. At any rate, Lush's triumph must be deferred for another quarter of an hour.

Mr. Parkinson was not in the secret of the special object of the prayer-meeting; moreover he was, like Mr. Cave, one of Fritz's *friends*, and would not have been trusted with the secret of a conspiracy. He was an intelligent, well-educated man, and his prayer was simply a *prayer*, and not a lecture or an advertisement; moreover, it was short. There was next a very quiet address from Fritz, and then—

"Mr. Lush will pray."

The ladies exchanged glances and whispers as before, and Bung put his face into his hands with the air of a man who was saying, "Now, Lush, let's hear how *you'll* do it, as you *are* so ready."

Mr. Lush was a very tall, abdominous man, with a very small head, ridiculously out of proportion to the large scale on which the other parts of his person had been constructed. He had a very apoplectic complexion, thin, light-brown hair, and a small voice (to match his head) which seemed to emerge with oily softness from the inmost recesses of his being. He had a habit of constantly playing fancy tunes with his fat fingers on his bald crown, and of every now and then thrusting out his arms at full length to free his wrists from the adhesion of his shirt-cuffs. He had in respect to business many irons in the fire, but he was by profession an auctioneer, and was a perfect master of the gorgeous rhetoric which is almost peculiar to the gentlemen of that profession. Like his esteemed partner in life, he had a way of regarding religion as an investment, and thought that the blessings of salvation should be knocked down to the highest bidder, with a kind of spiritual workhouse for paupers. He was inclined to think a chapel or church might be a capital business investment if properly managed. "Pay well," he used to say, "get your talent, have a large place, and the thing's done. But there must be pulpit talent. Men must be attracted." He thought courses of lectures, anniversary services, bazaars, everything that could be advertized and puffed, almost necessary to the progress of piety. "We must make ourselves known, sir," he said; "that's the order of the day." His beginnings were comparatively humble; his father began life as a vendor of dog's-meat; he had then invested his well-saved earnings in a small tripe-shop, and risen by degrees to be a man of considerable property. Lush junior, however, was extremely anxious to forget "the hole of the pit from which he had been digged;" and the slightest allusion to tripe or dog's-meat would throw his wife and daughters into paroxysms of indignation and anger. His own success in life had been very considerable; and he was anxious to make the best of both worlds, and willing to make a fair "bid" for the glories of Paradise. But he had no notion whatever of a religion that didn't succeed; he didn't care to belong to a chapel that didn't succeed; and he began to have an auctioneer-suspicion that the ministry of the Rev. Frederick Rivers was a ministry that wouldn't succeed.

His public prayers were of the nature of an "air with variations." The air was taken from "Family Devotions," by the Rev. W. Jay. The sentences were long and sonorous, the doctrines strictly evangelical. The variations were required to adapt the prayer in the family to the necessities of a larger company. Sometimes the whole air was retained with a kind of prelude, in which the little company of believers was *compared* to a family; sometimes the strictly domestic parts were left out, and the empty space filled by a variation on the petitions for "our beloved monarch." This Monday night both family and nation were omitted that there might be ample space for variations on "our beloved pastor." The pious auctioneer had much on his mind. He asked for the prosperity of "our cause," and that "multitudes might flock to hear the blessed Gospel and gladden the heart of our devoted minister." Above all, he asked that "our minister might be enlightened and guided, and that in these dangerous times his trumpet might give a certain sound, and the banner of salvation wave triumphant from his faithful hand." He gave thanks for the fidelity of the majority of Christian people, and especially of the neighbouring Churches, and humbly desired "that we might not be found lagging behind those we ought to lead in the vindication of the blessed Bible and the Glory of God."

Like a dog out of a pantry, or "a guilty thing surprised," did each conspirator betake himself to the vestry after that Monday evening prayer-meeting. Bung, indeed, had done nothing; but then he had meant to do something and had failed, and that was even harder to bear: it was as if "the artful dodger" had been imprisoned for *attempting* to pick pockets.

Isn't it right to pray, then? Why should poor

Bung have looked so crestfallen? Why should Lush's complexion have been so unusually apoplectic, and the tunes he played on his bald crown, as he sat in the vestry chair, so many and so fast? In plain English, each of these amiable brethren felt himself for once a mean and miserable sneak; he knew that his prayer had been a cowardly hypocrisy; that he had been taking liberties with Almighty God because he daren't take liberties with the Rev. Frederick Rivers. As to God—was He really there at all? Whereas, "our beloved pastor" was most unquestionably there, sitting in bodily presence at that wooden painted desk, able not only to *hear*, but in most transparent and unmistakeable language to *answer*. And these were the men, forsooth, to deliver Christendom from infidelity and atheism!

Fritz had for some time been expecting, not, indeed, the mingled blasphemy and humbug of such a prayer-meeting as this, but at any rate complaints. He knew quite well what Bung had intended, and what the auctioneer had done. But it was not for him to begin a quarrel which would be only too soon begun by others, and which would require his utmost nerve and patience and integrity, and might end—he could not guess how. So he passed into the vestry for his hat and coat; he waited a minute or two to see whether those miserable cowards were ready to say out what was so plainly weighing on their minds, and then he bade them good night, and went home to Hetty. Mr. Parkinson and Mr. Cave left at the same time; and Bung and Lush, soon joined by Mrs. Bung and Mrs. Lush, and Miss Bung and Miss Lush, remained to consider the state and prospects of the conspiracy.

"I thought he would have said something after to-night," said Bung.

"Well, Mr. Bung, I thought *you* would have said something," said Lush.

"And why should everything rest on me, Mr. Lush?" said injured Bung; conscious, at the same time, that he had done very little for the conspiracy that night, at any rate.

"I thought you understood," said the auctioneer, "that to-night was to be special."

"Well, Mr. Lush," said Mrs. Bung, "I *may* be partial, but *I* thought Mr. Bung's prayer beautifully suitable. Did you notice the emphasis he laid on the words *light* and *grace* when he was praying for the pastor?"

"Besides," said Bung, hitting for once the right nail on the head, "if you're to be so very personal, you might as well tell Mr. Rivers what we mean straight out, without the means of grace."

"Well, well, Mr. Bung," said Lush, "I'm sure we don't disagree; I always enjoy your prayers exceedingly."

"He's only got *one* prayer to enjoy," said Miss Lush, in a malicious whisper to her mother.

"At the same time, what's to be done now? I'm afraid Mr. Rivers will be a rather awkward customer."

"Shall we mention it at the deacons' meeting?" said Bung; "though, perhaps, Mr. Parkinson and Mr. Cave would be a difficulty."

"Why not ask him to my house?" said Lush; "and Mrs. and Miss Bung can come round, and we can talk it over."

"Capital," said Bung; "and suppose you come round to supper to-morrow with us, and we can determine what to say."

So, with this understanding, the deacons, deaconesses, and useful deacons' daughters, parted; feeling satisfied that there was just ground of complaining, and quite determined before to-morrow evening to find out what that just ground of complaining was.

Meanwhile Fritz had hurried home, walking fast to keep pace if it were possible with his quick thoughts, pondering what would be done and what he ought to do; trying to get fast hold of his *principles* of action, so that no mere details of difficulty or temptation might take him by surprise. I dare-say he looked pale and his brow was clouded when he entered the dining-room.

"What's the matter, darling?" said Hetty; "has anything happened?"

"Oh, nothing particular," said Fritz; "indeed, I might truly say nothing at all."

"And yet something worries you. Do you think I can't read your face well enough by this time to know that you are troubled? What is it, dearest?"

"Why, my pet, it's really nothing. Only at the prayer-meeting——"

"I hate prayer-meetings," said Hetty, with passionate energy.

"That Mr. Lush——"

"And I hate Mr. Lush," Hetty continued; "I believe he's a very sneaking, mercenary coward."

"Well, my little pet, he only *prayed* for me. There wasn't much harm in that, was there, Hetty?"

"Oh, of course not—but I understand; he prayed *at* you."

"Well, he certainly managed to tell me he thought me sadly remiss in these very dangerous times. Poor old Bung tried to do the same, but habit got the better of him, and he went right to the end of his old sing-song without a single variation."

"What! wasn't *Mrs.* Bung there? Didn't she prompt him? She's much the better man of the two. But, really, what do you think? What are you afraid of? What do you mean to do? Which of them can you rely on?"

"Which of them can I rely on? That's a very hard question to answer. So long as I don't *need* them, I can rely on almost all. So long as I can *ask* their help, I can rely on many. But if I were really to find it necessary to take an independent course which would separate me from some of the ordinary customs and traditions of our "denomination," I could not then *ask* anybody to stand by me; I could not make the controversy a personal one, or divide the Church into those who like *me*, and those who don't like me; and it is very likely I might be left almost alone."

"Alone! Fritz."

"Well, I think Cave would stand by me, and Parkinson too. The young people will go with their parents; and, generally speaking, it is better they should. We wont begin by distrusting anybody; but we mustn't live for applause. Ministers, above all men, should set a far nobler example than that. And we mustn't whimper and affect to be martyrs, however acutely we may have to suffer. Besides, the trouble hasn't come yet; it *may* never come at all."

"But it will come, darling; and when it does, you wont try to hide it from me, will you, Fritz, and bear it alone?" and Hetty kissed him, not without tears.

"Why, you sly little thing," he said, "it's no use trying; you find me out so easily. Besides, a misunderstanding with the chapel people would scarcely be small enough to hide."

"What do they want?" said Hetty; "what are they dissatisfied about?"

"I don't think they quite know."

"I should think they don't," Hetty said; "I wish they had old Dr. Richardson to supply for a month or two; a change might do them good and help their digestion."

"However, darling," said Fritz, "we needn't worry ourselves; we can wait till trouble comes; and even then we may find help we little expect."

So they settled down as calmly as they could. It was well for Fritz that all his troubles were outside his own house. When he came home to his library, his children, his bright and loving wife, he was sure to find peace and hope. It was well for him that not a single word was ever uttered by Hetty to tempt him from the straight and manly course. "No, no!" she would say, even in their bitterest troubles, "we can't help it, Fritz, we must wait, and put our trust in God. But never be tempted to preach what you don't believe, or shun to declare the whole counsel of God. Above all, never be tempted to do it *for my sake.* If I led you into such sin, I should feel that I was a curse and a disgrace to you. I should never dare to look you in the face. It would break my heart."

Brave and loving Hetty; and not alone in your loving courage! Would that men could see how much they make women suffer when they are cruel and selfish and grovelling for the sake of their wives and children!

The preliminaries of the conference with their

pastor were duly arranged next evening by Messrs. Lush and Bung, not without valuable assistance from the ladies; and an invitation was duly forwarded to Mr. and Mrs. Rivers, who were to spend Thursday evening at Mr. Lush's house,—"no party, quite in a friendly way." In truth, with all the Lushes and three Bungs there was party enough, even if there were some little lack of friendship. They had tea in the dining-room; and when it was over, Mr. Lush suggested that the ladies should retire to the drawing-room, "for a little music or something of that sort," (scandal, for instance) while the gentlemen had a little chat. The Lushes and Bungs exchanged meaning glances as they went away, carrying Hetty with them, "for a little music." Miss Lush sang first, "Eve's Lamentation;" and then one of her sisters played a fantasia. Miss Bung was not herself musical, but would be charmed to hear Mrs. Rivers sing.

Hetty, sing! and what, meanwhile, was going on in that other room, where they were putting her husband to the torture? Could she get a note out? It must, at any rate, be something she could *mean*, into which she could throw her soul, or she would utterly break down. So she sat down to the piano to sing a song she had quite lately learned. It was a wondrous melody, into which the composer, careless of plagiarism, seemed to have introduced the sweetness and pathos, the indignation and earnest purpose of almost every master of song. It was adapted to the words of the first six verses of the 137th Psalm. So Hetty sang—

> By the waters of Babylon we sat down and wept, when we remembered thee, O Zion.
> As for our harps we hanged them up upon the trees that are therein.
> For they that led us away captive required of us then a song, and melody in our heaviness; saying, sing us one of the songs of Zion.
> How shall we sing the Lord's song in a strange land?
> If I forget thee, O Jerusalem, let my right hand forget her cunning.
> If I do not remember thee, let my tongue cleave to the roof of my mouth; yea if I prefer not Jerusalem in my mirth.

Hetty sang like one inspired. Almost everybody has noticed the peculiar richness and beauty which deep passion gives to a woman's voice. And just then Hetty's whole being was possessed with love for Fritz, with indignation against those who she thought were persecuting him, and with the foreboding of loneliness and grief. So she poured all the fulness of her own emotion into the wailing of the captive Jews till she forgot where she was, and sang to herself and Heaven. Her cheek was flushed, her large dark eyes were full of tears when the music was ended, and she heard the low murmur of wonder and delight, almost of awe, with which the enchanted listeners acknowledged her power.

It was plain that nobody else would sing that

evening, so the ladies subsided gradually into other occupations, while the gentlemen were in deep consultation on the state and prospects of St. George's Road Chapel.

"We have been very anxious," said Bung, whose face was getting extremely white, and eloquence extremely impeded, "about the condition of St. George's Road, and we thought perhaps a little friendly conversation might help to set matters rather right."

Mr. Lush, with a very red face, was playing fantasias or galops on his bald crown with the most brilliant execution.

"I'm sure, Mr. Bung," said Fritz, "I'm always very pleased to hear all you may wish to say about St. George's Road. And what are these matters that are rather wrong?"

"Well, Mr. Rivers," said Lush, "perhaps you don't quite know the reason why Mr. Edwards has left our place?"

"I didn't know he'd left at all," said the minister.

"Ah," said Lush with a heavy groan, "I really almost half suspected it. And yet, Mr. Rivers, Mr. Edwards was a man of very considerable means, contributed to nearly every one of the Societies, and subscribed to the general income of the place quite five times as much as his ordinary pew-rent. I'm sure we can't afford to lose such men as Mr. Edwards."

"Well, but Mr. Lush, if he chooses to go how can we help it? You know we can't nail him down to his pew and drag money out of his pocket whether he wishes it or not; and I'm sure I don't know what he has left for."

"Perhaps," meekly suggested Mr. Bung, "it might be well to call upon him and inquire; he's not a man to be lost for nothing."

Lush nodded his head and groaned.

"Well," said Fritz, "I think it would be much easier if you were to tell me at once, because it's quite plain you know."

"Well, sir," said Lush, "Mr. Edwards didn't feel quite satisfied. We've a good deal to battle with in the world Mr. Rivers, and we come on the Lord's Day to chapel that our souls may be fed, and Mr. Edwards remarked to me in confidence that he didn't think his soul *was* fed."

"Oh," said Fritz, "so his soul wasn't fed. Well, now, as we are talking in a nice friendly way, quite plainly and confidentially, would you just like to explain to me what you mean by a person's soul being fed?"

"Well, sir," said Lush—with a rather fat cough, which unfortunately prevented him finishing his sentence.

"Why, sir, as to *fed*," said Bung, "fed, you know, means the marrow and fatness of the Gospel; that's what fed is."

"Oh," said Mr. Rivers, "*fed* means the marrow and fatness of the Gospel. And so poor Mr. Edwards hasn't got the marrow and fatness of the Gospel; I'm very sorry for him, and all I can say is, it isn't my fault, is it?"

Grim silence—while Bung contemplates his boots and Lush plays a kind of dead march on his bald crown.

"Well, gentlemen, is it?" said Fritz.

"Well, Mr. Rivers," said both deacons at once; though Bung hearing Lush's voice thankfully collapsed into silence, and left Lush to finish the sentence. The sudden pause, however, of Bung, brought Lush's eloquence also to a premature conclusion.

"So I suppose you mean," said Fritz, "you think it *is* my fault. Did you know Mr. Edwards was going to leave, Mr. Bung?"

"Well, Mr. Rivers, I did just hear a whisper of it some little time before it happened."

"Yes, I thought so," said Mr. Rivers; "I suppose you mean, Mr. Edwards whispered it to you, and then you whispered it to Mr. Lush; that's it, Mr. Bung, isn't it? I'm sure it's a pity to disguise the matter, because I can see quite easily from one end of it to the other, and it saves so much time to be plain."

Fritz spoke with perfect coolness, and even with a quiet-looking smile, though indeed he was red-hot with indignation; moreover, distrusting the reticence of his hands, he thought it desirable to put one in his pocket, and rest his head on the other.

"Well, Mr. Rivers," said the oily Lush, "I don't see how we can help people coming to us and mentioning their dissatisfaction. It's one of the little sacrifices of our office that we're obliged to bear. Indeed we most sincerely wish that Mr. Edwards were the only person who has become dissatisfied."

"It's very kind of you to say so," said Fritz; "and of course any right-minded deacon would be sure to feel as you feel. However, I'm sure you need not be troubled, Mr. Lush; it can't be more than one or two who are discontented."

Nobody could have believed that such a small head as Mr. Lush's could have expressed so much meaning by a mere shake, while Bung grasped his feeble knees in speechless horror.

"No, Mr. Rivers," said the latter, still looking on the ground, and shaking his head mournfully; "no, it's not so; it's our painful but bounden duty to inform you that there's a general feeling spreading among the members of St. George's Road that there's a something."

"Oh, a something," said Mr. Rivers, "a something—I'm sure I'm not at all surprised to hear it; but what particular something do the discontented members allude to?"

"Well, sir," said Lush, "it's not so much a something; it's a want."

"Yes, yes, Mr. Lush," said Mr. Bung; "you've said exactly what it is; it *is* a want."

This definition might seem very exact to the deacons, but it seemed very far from complete to their minister.

"Yes, yes," continued Bung, "there's a want. There's a deal we've been accustomed to hear from the good old doctor that we don't seem to hear through your ministry; and I've noticed, Mr. Rivers, there's a number of our sweetest hymns that we never have the privilege of singing. And last Sunday night, too, Mrs. Bung assured me that the blessed name of Jesus was mentioned only three times during the whole of your sermon."

"Very well, Mr. Bung, and what of that?" said Fritz.

Bung looked at Lush, and Lush looked at Bung, and there was grim silence again.

"What of that?" said Fritz again—"eh, Mr. Bung?"

"Well, Mr. Rivers," said Lush, "it's my opinion that every sermon that any minister of the Gospel preaches should contain a full and simple account of the plan of salvation. Very likely, sir, some poor sinner may have entered the sanctuary that evening for the first time, and we none of us know," laying his hand on his capacious waistcoat, "whether it mayn't be our last opportunity; and it's my opinion, Mr. Rivers, that a minister wouldn't like to have it on his conscience that he hadn't led that poor wanderer to the foot of the Cross, and told him exactly what to do to get his soul saved."

"Oh! that's your opinion, is it, Mr. Lush?" said Fritz. "Well, then, I may as well be plain, and tell you that it's really very far from being mine. I don't believe that what you call the plan of salvation can be squeezed into half a dozen sentences, and tacked on to the end of every sermon a minister preaches. Besides, I always thought Mr. Edwards considered himself a very good Christian, and knew the plan of salvation well already. So what is he discontented about, Mr. Lush?"

"Well, sir," said the auctioneer, "he didn't consider you altogether sound; and at any rate he said there was a something, and he thought his soul would be better fed under the ministrations of the Rev. John Veneer."

"However," said Bung, "we only wanted to mention the matter, just that you might be on your guard, Mr. Rivers, and consider whether something mightn't be done. Of course we've no doubt that you can explain it all, and tell the people that you quite disapprove of all these infidels, such as Mr. Maurice, 'Essays and Reviews,' the 'Pentateuch,' and all that lot. Indeed, when Mr. Edwards told me that Mr. Veneer told him that you had nearly all Maurice's books in your study, I told him at once that I was quite certain that was a lie, whoever said it."

"Ah, thank you, Mr. Bung," said Fritz. "But as such a remark as that might to a perfect stranger sound rude, I would advise you to be rather careful before you make another of the same sort; at any rate, until you've made a complete catalogue of my library. The fact is, that nearly all Mr. Maurice's books *are* in my study, and very good books they are, too."

"Mr. Rivers!" said Bung, with pious horror; "why, Mr. Maurice is an infidel."

"Oh, is he?" said Fritz. "Who told you so, Mr. Bung?"

"Well, it was—it was—Mrs. Bung that told me so," said the deacon, with just the faintest suspicion that Mr. Rivers might not consider his esteemed spouse a fountain of infallible wisdom. "But it's not Mrs. Bung alone—everybody knows it; indeed, there was a complete exposure of him only a few weeks ago in the *Gospel Flag*."

"Well now, look here, Mr. Bung," said Fritz, rising from his chair; "I can't pretend to argue about Mr. Maurice's books with anybody who hasn't read them, not even with you. I've all manner of books in my library; some I like, and some I very much dislike; some of them are true, and some of them, I think, are false; some are very pious and edifying, others are extremely indecent and demoralizing; it's a very small library, but for all that it contains theological works, histories, novels, plays, poems, and all manner of odds and ends. Now, in plain English, I don't mean to be interfered with as to my private reading, and I solemnly declare to you that I wouldn't turn a twopenny tract out of my library to keep ten thousand Mr. Edwardses at St. George's Road Chapel. As for the rest—"people not getting fed"—"a something"—and all that sort of thing—I'll think the matter over. And now we'd better go to the ladies; they'll be getting quite frightened and wondering what's the matter."

They went to join the ladies accordingly, who received them with that exaggerated welcome which a sense of uneasiness almost always produces in those who have something on their minds. They tried to keep off chapel affairs as much as possible, but people like Lush and Bung had really very little else to talk about, except their own private business, auctioneering or otherwise. Perhaps that may be the reason why Bungs and Lushes seem so pious—they've nothing but their own sort of religion to fall back upon for conversation when they are in the company of comparative strangers. So the conversation soon turned, as by a kind of dissenting instinct, to the discussion of private character, and for once took the direction of praise and hope; Mrs. Lush having, for a long time, been able to see nothing but spots in the face of the sun, had, by a strange optical illusion, come to see all the sunshine in the spots themselves.

"You remember my mentioning to you, Mrs. Rivers," said the auctioneer's wife, "that young Sparks of Goulburns' was engaged to Miss Jones; well, I've really come to be agreeably disappointed with the young man, though I dare say it's owing a good deal to his regular attendance at St. George's Road. Have you noticed Mr. Sparks much, Mr. Rivers? He seems to me quite a promising young man."

"Yes," said Fritz, "I have taken a good deal of notice of Mr. Sparks, and I'm very glad you've found out the favourable points in his character, Mrs. Lush."

"Yes, indeed; he had a most charming conversation with Rebecca the other day. Of course, you know, now he's engaged, Mr. Rivers, he feels at liberty to be much more easy and comfortable with our girls. Indeed, he was telling Rebecca quite a little bit of his own experience, and how thankful he was for the company of good, sober, pious people, instead of his own old, wild companions." Neither Rebecca nor her esteemed mamma had the faintest suspicion that, on the occasion referred to, Mr. Sparks was simply availing himself of a favourable opportunity of testing his recent acquirements in the dialect and customs of the saints.

"Oh, then, Mr. Sparks has given up his old companions, has he?" said Fritz.

"Oh yes, sir," said Rebecca, "quite; and I was really almost sorry for the young man, for he said to me, 'I dare say I oughtn't to think it so, my dear Miss Lush, but it is rather a sacrifice to give up these enjoyments.'"

It was with the most charming little tremble that Miss Lush reported this outburst at once of affection and piety, for it was extremely seldom that any member of the male sex had so far forgotten himself as to call her "dear." She was, as I have already said, superintendent of the Sunday-school, and useful in many other ways. She was almost as good as a detective in hunting out a scandal. She was not so young as she had been years ago, for she had been a kind of right-hand woman in the days of the good old doctor. She was a tall, gaunt, bony creature, with perhaps the reddest face in all the world. Her hair was one of those tempting subjects of speculation that very few observers could resist. It was beginning, in fact, to turn grey, but that was not the peculiarity; for of course the hair of many people turns grey, and dark-haired people often get grey at a comparatively early age. But Rebecca Lush's hair rebelled against the ordinary operations of nature, and would only turn grey in stripes and patches; and for the head of a deacon's daughter to look like a zebra or a tabby cat was enough even to provoke a saint to impatience. So with that delightful generosity which cannot bear to leave a kindness unrequited, the people into whose private affairs the detective propensities of Miss Lush had been in the habit of prying, rewarded her kindness by whispering malicious slanders about the private affairs of the Sunday-school superintendent. They were in the habit of inquiring, with the nearest approach to a wink that sterling piety admits of— "Whether you had ever noticed the faintest tinge of blue on Miss Lush's head, and whether sometimes symptoms of inflammation were not discernible." "In fact, dear," these wicked whisperers were in the habit of insinuating, "she dyes her hair, and the dye doesn't always seem to take quite rightly, and I shouldn't be a bit surprised if she came to chapel some morning with a perfect rainbow on her head. And what a beautiful type that would be of her natural disposition!"

Poor Miss Lush was very much to be pitied when she fell into the hands of irreverent jesters like these. But there was always one consolation; she was quite able to give as much as she got. Not, indeed, that she could have made a joke, if her life had depended upon it; but her weapons of defence were far more effective; indeed, they were truly dangerous. She could snap off the head of your reputation with a single bite, and do you more harm in half-an-hour than the utmost prudence could undo in half a year. And now, in spite of her peculiar hair, inadequately protected from the ravages of time, in spite of her emphatic features and her complexion glowing with fiery earnestness, this smart young man from Goulburns', used to such excellent society, and engaged to one of the prettiest girls at St. George's Road, had called her "dear." Positively there did remain some faint hopes that some one might be found some time or other to call her "dearest."

"Yes," she told Fritz, "young Mr. Sparks found it a great struggle to give up those worldly amusements to which he had been addicted. 'I haven't been to the theatre, Miss Rebecca,' he said to me, 'since I began to attend St. George's Road; I scarcely think it's consistent; though, of course, Mr. Rivers doesn't say so much about that sort of thing as many ministers do.'"

"What do you think about the theatre, Mr. Rivers?" said Henrietta, the female Lush who had the management of the maternal boxes.

"What do I think about the theatre, Miss Henrietta?" said Fritz; "how do you mean?"

Mr. Bung looked at his feet, as he always did in cases of perplexity, and Mr. Lush looked at his wife, with a look that seemed to say, "I'm afraid the trumpet will not give a certain sound in respect of theatres."

"Well, sir, the theatre—what do you think about the theatre?" continued Miss Henrietta, without the slightest consciousness of ambiguity or vagueness in her question.

"Well, I really haven't an opinion, Miss Henrietta."

"But you surely don't mean, Mr. Rivers," said Mrs. Lush, "that you would think it right for anybody to go to the theatre?"

"Why, to tell you the truth, Mrs. Lush, I have not been into a theatre since I was ordained; and though I think it highly probable I shall go some time soon to judge for myself, yet, until I do go, I know far too little about them to have anything to say on the subject worth hearing."

"Well, sir, everybody knows it's wrong to go to the theatre, Mr. Rivers; where are we to draw the line?"

"It's very hard to say where we're to draw the line. At any rate, it will be somewhere or other in the region of our motives and intentions, and not merely our outward acts; so that even when we've drawn it, it wont be quite as visible as a chalk line on a black board. However, I'd advise you to ask Mr. Sparks some day; he knows all about the theatre, and has given it up apparently; and therefore he can tell you exactly what it is, and why he thinks it wrong to go there."

And so the talk went on, frightfully uninteresting; Fritz and Hetty knew quite well that all these questions were directly or indirectly parts of the conspiracy. Moreover, Hetty was on the rack of suspense, eager to hear what had been going on in the dining-room while the ladies had been away. Nobody was at ease; and in fact there is scarcely anything so irritating as enmity under the disguise of friendship. So Fritz and Hetty seized the very first opportunity of making their escape from this nest of vipers. Outside the door they seemed to breathe more freely, and they were at any rate on their way to that quiet retreat into which trouble and vexation could never follow them without being transformed into good. For did not all the outside griefs make home happier, and bind them together by those bonds which only time and common experiences can produce? It is the silliest of all mistakes to think that courtship and the honeymoon are the happiest part of life; for love and joy depend far more upon the experiences of the past than upon hopes of the future.

CHAPTER XVI.

"HOME, SWEET HOME."

"WELL, dear, what do you think about it all?" said Hetty to Fritz, when they were sitting quietly at home at the supper table.

"I can hardly tell what to think," he said; "but I've no doubt that there's a storm brewing. They tell me, to begin with, that Mr. Edwards has left."

"Oh dear, has he? I'm afraid that'll do a great deal of harm."

"Yes," said Fritz, "of a sort, of course it will; he's been connected with the place a long time, and has been in the habit of setting the fashion as to giving, and all that sort of thing; and then, just because he's been so long connected with the place, his leaving will make a sort of panic. Besides, old Bung says there are a great many other people getting dissatisfied."

"Why, what do they want? what are they dissatisfied about?" said Hetty.

"Oh, I don't know," said Fritz; "but they say there's a something, and a want, and people don't get their souls fed, and a lot more of the same sort. Of course it's all stupid, unintelligible jargon, but it does quite as well for the watchword of a conspiracy as if it were the soundest sense."

"But really, Fritz, what do these people mean by getting their souls fed?" said Hetty, who was deplorably ignorant of the dialect of saints.

"I'm sure I know no more than you do, but it seems to be the same thing as getting comfort. Old Bung says that "getting fed" is the marrow and fatness of the Gospel. But then old Bung's a noodle. Lush, on the other hand, as nearly as he dares, says that "getting fed" means getting every sitting let, and a clear income of 600*l.* a year; and perhaps on the whole Lush is as near the truth as Bung. But I'm sure I don't know what on earth to do with the people. I'm sure I don't know any other Gospel to preach to the people than the one I do preach. And if people like Mr. Edwards choose to leave, and others don't choose to come, I don't see how I can help it."

"Well, dear," said Hetty, "I don't know what you can do. And yet there are plenty of people about who seem to get on very well, such as Veneer and Dickson. I dare say our folks, for instance, would like to have courses of lectures and that kind of thing."

"Yes, I know they would. That's the very thing they were praying for on Monday night.

And in truth, dear, they shall have a course of lectures; but I'm quite certain it will only make bad worse. To tell you the truth, I feel that I've been rather a coward up to this time. I don't think I've preached anything that I didn't believe, but I've managed to leave unnoticed a good many things that I do believe. Of course it ought to have been impossible for a man like Bung to venture to say on my behalf what he did say to Mr. Edwards."

"Why, what did he say?" said Hetty.

"He said he was quite sure that whoever told Edwards that I had Maurice's works in my study told a lie."

"Really," said Hetty, "what a stupid old donkey that Bung is!"

"Yes," said Fritz; "but think of a man hearing me preach for some three or four years, and never finding out in all that time that I was independent enough to read even the books of those from whose opinions I might very widely differ. You know I can't be a good preacher, Hetty darling, for that to be possible."

"Well, what courses of lectures are you going to give them?"

"I'll give them three courses, one after another. I'll give them one course that will involve the points of special interest in the doctrine of sacrifice, and the doctrines that are nearly related to that. And then I'll at any rate give them a single sermon about the way in which I think we ought to deal with such books as "Essays and Reviews." And then I'll give them another on the Old Testament and the Bible as a whole. And I'm quite certain they'll dislike every one of them."

"You're not going to be very rash, darling, are you?" said Hetty; "it would be hardly worth while to make the people more angry than they are, would it, Fritz?"

"No, dear, of course it wouldn't, if I could fairly help it. I thought myself a perfect model of prudence in keeping quiet so long, and simply saying nothing. But Veneer's been coming out with his "Infidelity in Lawn Sleeves," and Dickson with his "Infallibility of the Bible," and the people don't seem satisfied that I should remain silent any longer. So I must speak, I suppose; and when I speak I must say what *I* think, and not what Bung and Lush think. And if I were to say what I think I should most likely tell Bung that he knows a good deal about hosiery, and Lush that he's very clever in drawing up catalogues of 'all that valuable furniture to be sold by auction' and the like, but that it's sheer impudence for either of them to have an opinion about the authorship of Genesis. There's Farmer, for instance, that paltry shoemaker down the street; am I really to get up into the pulpit, and virtually ask that poor jackass to pass an opinion on Maurice and Professor Jowett?—not if I know it!"

"Oh, of course it's unspeakably stupid," said Hetty, "perfectly ridiculous; but doesn't it seem to you it's only part of what they call our system. Suppose they had a Church-meeting and discussed your doctrines—Farmer's vote would go for just as much as Cave's or Parkinson's."

"Yes, Hetty dear, you're quite right; and that's exactly what makes me feel so frightened. I'm perfectly certain that before many months are over, it will have come to a regular stand-up fight. I shall maintain the right of free inquiry and the free expression of one's belief, whatever that belief may be; and so you'll find they'll call me an infidel. I shall be sure to have to say before long that Farmer's vote is *not* worth so much as Cave's or Parkinson's—in fact, that it's worth nothing whatever; and they'll say that it is entirely opposed to our principles, and that I deny the Gospel to the ignorant and poor. And they'll say that my love of order, and my endeavour to get something approaching to a decent ceremonial in public worship, is Popery. Of course all these different accusations would neutralize one another if they were all put down on paper, and shown to the same person at the same time; but that's not the way it will be done. One person will undertake the infidelity part, and another person will undertake the Jesuitry part; one set of people will be told I'm too hot, and another set of people will be told I'm too cold. So, at any rate, they'll all have something against me, and for practical purposes it doesn't much matter what the something is. Moreover, of course I shall have no opportunity of defending myself; and even if I had, I do not know whether it would be worth while availing myself of it. Nothing but time will work a cure, if even that does; and meanwhile——"

"Yes, meanwhile, dear," said Hetty.

She was beginning to look very miserable, so Fritz took her hand and kissed her. "Meanwhile," he said, "what's the use of letting our supper get cold? All this makes no real difference to us two, darling; we should have been sure to meet with some trouble wherever we had been. And then we've the children and just our two or three friends that we do feel sure of; and Effie, too, turned up so lately and so unexpectedly, and already such a treasure to both of us."

"Yes, indeed," said Hetty, "there's nobody in the world I love so much, excepting you and your sister Peggy."

So they went on with their supper, generally the snuggest meal of the day at Fritz's house. By that time, of course the day's worries were over. Fritz and his wife were not likely to be interrupted by unwelcome or merely formal visitors; for though they were very seldom alone at supper, their supper-guests were comparatively few, and were almost always really trusted friends; and of course they had friends who were not members of Fritz's congregation, and who were none the worse for that. Everybody almost is brightest at night. We wake in the morning burdened with an awful weight of care, not knowing what the day will bring forth. But by supper time we have found out its secret; and if it has brought trouble it has done its worst, and we have got through, after all.

Sometimes among the supper friends would be a "brother minister." Fritz's heresies were not as yet so widely known that it was unsafe for an orthodox parson to be seen associating with him. When they were, a number of his ministerial friends of course discovered that they might love Cæsar much, but that they loved Rome more; in fact, that they "owed *something* to their own reputation, and to the Churches over which they presided." After that time the minister of St. George's Road was always in possession of a test by which, with the utmost ease, to distinguish the true from the false. He had but to propose an "exchange of pulpits," or that his reverend evangelical brother should attend a meeting at his school-room, and every little flattery was nipped with untimely frost and forthwith began to die. Why evangelical brethren of the time-serving, imbecile kind should ever take the trouble to flatter him, even when nobody was there to see, was to Fritz an inexplicable mystery. He always knew where it would end; and until the matter grew too serious, a grim life-and-death struggle, he used to laugh as one after another wrote himself down a coward and went to his own place. There was also a swarm of nobodies who were disposed to be patronizing. They confessed that they really thought it a pity their young brother should be doing this or that, and getting himself so much misunderstood. They were quite disposed to be friendly, and some of them ventured, even in public, to pat their young brother on the back. Their own orthodoxy was above suspicion, and they were quite sure their dear young brother was sound at the core, however oddly he might express himself. Patronage must be very agreeable to the patron, for it is often received with base ingratitude; and I regret to say that Fritz, on the whole, preferred most of his enemies to his patronizing friends.

"Patrons" are generally to be found among that class of dissenting ministers which contains some very excellent men, and which also furnishes the most pestilent, mischief-making "old fogies" on the face of the earth. It is composed chiefly of parsons who, being utterly unable to persuade any congregation to listen to their preachments for six consecutive months, have a good deal of spare time. Fortunately they are often possessed of "private means," and so occupation is even more necessary for them than cash; "for Satan finds some mischief still for idle tongues to do." "Necessity is the mother of invention," and the necessity of finding something for parsons to do who can't get congregations to "sit under them" has been the mother of many "societies." Nor let anybody find fault with the arrangements of Providence. Do not flowers and fruit grow all the better for having very nasty manure at their roots, and hasn't the whitest loaf-sugar been refined with bullock's blood and all manner of abominations? We eat the fruit and smell the flowers, and put the sugar in our tea, "asking no questions for" digestion's "sake." And are we to grumble at our great societies because they are manured and refined by—never mind who? Besides, very few people know anything about it.

The Reverend Josiah Bulky, for instance, D.D., LL.D. was a burning and a shining light—D.D. of the University of Chicago, and LL.D. of the University of *£ s. d.*—represented in this country by a gentleman speaking broken English and "bearded like the pard," who advertizes in the *Daily Telegraph*, and "gives information" about foreign diplomas to the learning and worth which an ungrateful England has overlooked. And why should not modest merit be decorated, and in fact become changed into blatant self-asserting merit. Modesty, after all, is a poor, mean, grovelling virtue; and if a violet chooses to hide itself and be discovered only by the scent, that is no reason why the

Rev. J. Bulky should hide himself and run the risk of not being discovered at all. Besides, having bought a diploma from a wandering foreigner to whom he had been kindly introduced by the British Press, was in itself a plain and convincing proof that he was a great man. And yet not a congregation would have him, not even gratis. No—he had offered his valuable services as a free gift to the frequenters of a country conventicle, and he had been ignominiously refused. Could it be then that no sphere of usefulness had been provided by Providence for the natural gifts and acquired accomplishments of the Rev. Josiah Bulky, Doctor of the Universities of Chicago and the *Telegraph* Office? Was there nothing that he could do for the Church and the universe? Yes—there was something; he could found a society for supplying country churches with useful and devoted ministers. Not indeed with himself, for it was all too plain that they declined to take him; and indeed he began to feel that he could do far greater service to mankind in other ways. Was it for a Doctor of Divinity and Laws to waste his sweetness on the desert air? What a thrilling speech did he make at that large meeting in Leeds, when he was sent down to that rich and thriving town as a deputation from the parent society; "the society for providing snubbed and uneducated ministers for congregations who can't afford to keep them." "These brave and noble men may have no great preaching power," said the man who had been quite unable to get anybody to listen to himself; "they may be humble and comparatively unknown. Humble, did I say?" and the orator raised his head and his right hand, and gazed at the ceiling as if appealing to Heaven; "yes, humble—and, my friends, let us thank God that they are humble. Humility may seem to the carnal mind, to the haughty spirit of the unregenerate man, a mean and grovelling virtue; but it is the virtue that keeps the stars in their courses, and for the want of which Lucifer the Son of the Morning was flung down into the nethermost pit of despair and fire. My friends, I well remember the time when I was myself the humble pastor of a village church. I was not then possessed of those distinctions which have, I fear with too indiscriminating a partiality, been bestowed upon me; and my humble charge—it might well have seemed to you almost insignificant. When I look at your Belgrave Chapel and your East Parade Chapel, when I see the vast assemblies that crowd those spacious edifices, drinking in like parched and thirsty pilgrims the waters of life; when I see at the doors, awaiting the conclusion of the service, the equipages of wealth and the carriages of prosperity, I reflect with a thankful bosom that the Kings of Sheba and Seba are offering gifts—for are not our merchant princes kings? When I see these things, I reflect with a sigh, and yet with a holy delight, on that little village church where I broke for nearly twelve months the bread of life. No carriage rolled to and from the doors of that humble meeting-house. My single deacon was a pious baker, and the wealthiest member of my congregation was a tallow-chandler whom I had been blest as the humble means of converting. No—my friends," said the orator, melted if not to tears, at least to perspiration, "when I appeal to you to aid that noble society which I was one of the unworthy instruments of founding, I feel that I am not pleading for a name or a theory; I feel that I am pleading for that humble village. Before the eyes of my imagination rise the cheerful countenance of the converted tallow-chandler and the consistent sobriety of the pious baker; and are these, I ask myself — no, my friends, I ask YOU—are these to be left without the means of grace—without a preached Gospel—without their eyes seeing their pastor—without a faithful shepherd and guide through this weary wilderness? But I know I need not appeal further to your generosity and kindness; already I am assured the object of my mission to this prosperous and wealthy town is more than accomplished; and when the collection is made, and above all when our earnest-minded and devoted friends visit you at your own abodes, urging upon you the claims of this noble society, let me beseech you to remember, not the humble deputation who so feebly laid its claims before you ,but the spiritual necessities of that converted tallow-chandler and the unobtrusive worth of that pious baker."

In a perfect tempest of applause the Rev. Dr. Bulky resumed his seat. And yet, who would have thought it? Apart from the beneficent laws of a free country, he would without compunction have wrung the neck of any humble pastor who had ventured to apply to the secretary of that society for an increase of salary. Hadn't Mr. Mason, for instance, been refused a grant from the society, and been therefore compelled to resign the pastorate of Broadstones, Derbyshire, for venturing to suggest that because God had blessed him with fifteen children, it was plainly the will of Providence that he should have more than 50*l.* per annum; and wasn't Broadstones a "vacant church" in consequence?

Then, again, there was the Rev. Robert Cinderton, a tall man, one of those lean, hungry-looking wretches that Julius Cæsar was so anxious to keep at a distance from himself — with a face like vinegar, and a temper to match. He was another of those unappreciated divines that no congregation could tolerate; indeed, he'd have curdled the pure milk of the Word with the acid of his own ill-nature, before he had preached it for a month. But he was a secretary. He had more to do with arranging who should speak at our great public gatherings, and who should be honoured, and who snubbed, than he could possibly have expected to have, even if he had deserved it.

But I need give no lengthy descriptions. Everybody knows this tribe of divines; everybody knows how many birds they manage to kill with one stone; how they are neither more nor less than incarnations of religious red-tape; how the glories of the whole universe are represented for them in some society or other, and would be, if it were nothing more than a society for feeding the manufacturing districts on tadpoles. These are the gentlemen who go out on deputations to Killarney and the Highlands in the summer-time, and to all the most fashionable watering-places whenever it happens to be the season. They are the men who carry the gossip and scandal of London churches all over England, Ireland, and Wales, and who confidentially blast the reputation of every minister they don't like.

But really I was provoked into these digressions by the recollection of those exceedingly few instances of official patronage which made Fritz so indignant and angry. The graduate of Chicago and Mr. Secretary Cinderton were never at Fritz's supper-table; and so I may very well let them alone. Though, to do them justice, they were at the supper-tables of a good many other people, and managed to say their spiteful little say, not against Fritz only, but against every minister in the denomination who had any independence either of thought or action.

Nearly all Fritz's ministerial friends were much more prudent than he was, and many of them were much more clever, and all of them were quite as honest. And so they could talk together with the utmost freedom on subjects of the deepest interest; just as, in ordinary life, outside the narrow boundaries of the religious world, one gentleman talks to another gentleman without irritation about politics or the money-market. A conservative doesn't find it necessary to accuse a liberal of high treason, and even a protectionist doesn't find it necessary to regard every free-trader as a cut-throat or a thief. So Fritz and his friends talked together about doctrines and ceremonies and ecclesiastical discipline—and all manner of subjects, with the utmost unreserve; and they were almost as jolly together as Fritz and his college companions had been. Fritz's deacons considered some of these ministers as very models of propriety, and never ceased to wish that their own beloved pastor would follow such wholesome examples. *They* would never have entered into religious discussions with such people as Bung and Lush; and they would even have paid them the compliment of practising upon them a little pious deception.

"You know I should say to such a chap as Bung," said Johnson to Rivers one evening—"at least, I don't quite know what I should say, but at any rate I should trot him out. If he said, for instance, that 'Essays and Reviews' were very dangerous, I'd pull a very long face and say, 'Yes, Mr. Bung, they are indeed very dangerous.' And if he said to me, 'What do you think of the theatre?' I should say, 'What do *I* think of the theatre? How can you ask me such a question? Can there be two opinions?' That's what I should do with such a fellow as Bung, Rivers."

"But on what principle could you do that sort of thing?" said Fritz.

"On what principle? Why, on this principle, that Bung's a lunatic and ought to be treated accordingly, and that it's no use throwing pearls before swine; that's my principle, Rivers."

"Well, not a bad principle either, for he is a lunatic, of course. Still, unhappily I happen to be, as it were, head doctor in the asylum in which he is confined, and I feel it my duty to do my humble best to bring the poor patient back to sanity."

"Oh, Rivers," said Johnson, "you're a hopeful beggar, but Bung's incurable, take my word for that! And, by the way, there's another of your leading conspirators, the sweet Miss Lush, the one with the hair and the complexion. The last time I was preaching for you I dined at Lush's house. A most wonderfully developed animal he looks when he pins his table-napkin under his chin and begins to carve.

But that's, however, neither here nor there. It's his sweet daughter that dwells in my recollection, 'Though lost to sight, to memory dear.'"

"Which of them do you mean?" said Fritz; "the Dorcas, or the Sunday-school, or the Baby-linen?"

"Which of them, Rivers? Can you ask? Will you lacerate my feelings by suggesting that there is *any* comparable to *that one?* Of course you must know. It was the Sunday-school; it was thou, Rebecca. I really believe, Rivers, that that fascinating creature would have married me if I had proposed to her, and if I had not had a wife and four children already. And it was all my orthodoxy, and my unspeakable affection for the Rev. Dr. Campbell. 'Did I know,' Miss Lush asked me, 'with what courage and fidelity the good Doctor was taking up the cause of true religion? Ah,' she continued, 'the Doctor's doing a great work, Mr. Johnson; don't you think so?' Now, that last remark, Rivers, was my salvation. They're first-raters in conversation, women are. They ask so many questions all in a breath, and mix up with the questions so many assertions of their own, that you can answer just whatever question you think proper, and leave all the others to look after themselves. Now, if that delicate-looking Miss Lush hadn't volunteered the remark that the Doctor was doing a great work, I should not in the least have known what to say.

As to Dr. Campbell helping on the cause of true religion, of course that's all my eye; but as to his doing a great work, I can't see how anybody can doubt it. At the same time, the moment Miss Lush began to talk in this strain I was on my guard. I said to myself, that poor young female's a lunatic, and I must keep my eye on her. I must humour her little oddities. Perhaps if I don't love and adore Dr. Campbell, she may put strychnine in my soup, or get her father to pray for me some Monday evening."

"Ah!" said Fritz, "but you know you've such capital command of your face."

"Well, yes," Johnson said, "perhaps I have; but I should be sorry to be discomposed by a Lush at any rate. But gravely, I really think you waste a good deal of feeling, and expose yourself to a good deal of danger, where it's quite unnecessary. You're a capital fellow, Rivers, in your way, and I'm sure you would not think me capable of condescending to any mean dodges for the sake of what you call peace. But we know one another a great deal too well to be wasting time in compliments, don't we? And I think, that for you to be bothering yourself with such people as your conspirators, does a great deal of harm to you, and does no good to anybody. And yet of course I can see well enough that the thing's more complicated than at first sight it seems. There's the theatre, for instance."

"Yes," said Rivers, "that's just one of the things they're bothering me about now. There's that charming creature, 'Baby-linen,' Rebecca Lush's sister, who's always teasing me to know my opinion about it; in fact, there's a young jackanapes who's courting a very pretty girl in my congregation, as conceited a coxcomb as you could wish to meet anywhere. I wonder how the girl could fall in love with him, for he's nothing to look at. Well, I've taken this young gentleman down just perhaps one single button, on one or two occasions, and he would no doubt be very glad to do the same thing for me. Mrs. Lush thinks him an extremely hopeful young man because he's always trotting Rebecca out—not literally, but metaphorically; and he's certainly extremely ingenious, and has learnt the evangelical dialect wonderfully well, considering he does not care a straw for what it means. He's constantly telling the Lushes of his former worldly life, and especially letting them know just enough about theatres to make them wish it was not extremely wicked to go. Now what am I to say to them when they ask me what I think about the theatre? Of course nothing would be easier than to make a long speech with nothing in it, and to leave them rubbing the dust out of their eyes for another twelvemonth. But that wouldn't altogether do; for there are other people in the congregation asking the question with the utmost sincerity, and really anxious to be guided in the right way, and I can't give one answer to one person, and a totally different answer to another person, when they both ask the same questions."

"No, of course you can't," said Johnson. "And I can't either. And in truth I'm more bothered with things of that sort than with doctrines. Besides, I had a lady at supper at my house not long since, a very accomplished actress, and who made me, to tell you the truth, feel very small indeed. For of course she asked me whether I thought theatrical entertainments really wrong; and if not, why ministers of religion always acted towards them as if they had been already proved incurably vicious and mischievous. We know the stock answers well enough, don't we? But what could I make of *them* in such company? The lady *was* a lady. She had been brought up, moreover, in a strict family, and in all the traditions of a most rigid Puritanism. Her career had been in every respect most honourable; and she is now the wife of a gentleman well known in literary circles, and in a very good position. So what was I to say about 'the notorious bad character of actors and actresses?' In truth she anticipated me. 'You don't imagine,' she said, 'that all the stories that are told about actors and actresses are true, do you? Of course some of them are; but there's nothing to make it necessary or inevitable that actors and actresses should be worse than other people. Moreover the stage will always depend very much upon the spectators; and if *all* the good people of England had left the stage to all the bad people of England, actors and actresses would no doubt by this time have been the mere scum of society.' And in fact, Rivers, it's plain enough that our horror of the theatre is only the result, or at any rate is chiefly the result, of our Puritan traditions. Dissenters, indeed, belong for the most part to a dreary little world of their own, and almost unavoidably think everything wrong which lies outside of the conventionalisms of their own class."

"Yes, of course they do," said Fritz; "there is a relation of mine who's very well off, but he evidently does not know what to do with his money; at least he knows well enough what to do with it, but somehow he thinks it rather wrong to spend it in anything like a stylish sort of way. I wonder he didn't think it worldly to get it; but of course piety must draw the line somewhere, as the barber said to the chimney-sweeper. They were thinking, for instance, of keeping a snug little brougham some time ago, which they can very well afford, but they gave it up because they thought it a little worldly, and it would make a talk among the enlightened members of the Church to which they belonged. I only wish he'd keep a brougham for me, and the members of the Church might practise elocution as long as they liked."

Though Rivers and Johnson and one or two other ministerial friends were in the habit of talking together at the supper-table and far on into the night, in a way that would have dreadfully scandalized such people as Bung and Lush, they were very well aware that the work that lay before them was one of great difficulty and even danger; their complaint was not that their congregations were too godly and sincere, but in fact that they were not godly and sincere enough, and that their religion was formal and conventional instead of being real. They never forgot, and they very often reminded one another, that greater external freedom could be obtained only by a far more rigid adherence to the true principles of life. At the same time they were sure that the narrowness and hardness of Puritanism, its inability to avail itself of a very large number of those blessings which God has bestowed on men, and its stern refusal to recognise as sacred and divine the common life of mankind, was neither more or less than to declare that it had excommunicated itself from the true Church. In London, too, it would have been impossible for Fritz and his friends, if they had wished it ever so much, to silence the young men about them, as it would have been quite easy to silence them if they had been living in a quiet country town. For young men in London know a good deal of life, whether parsons do or not; and they simply laugh at those fancy pictures of the world with which sermons to the young are frequently so profusely illustrated. So the little band of friends to which Fritz belonged would have been compelled, even if they had tried to avoid it, to make known their real opinions both about doctrine and practice; or else to shut themselves up in that narrow dungeon of dissenting asceticism and the dull routine of mere sermon-making, which they were beginning more and more to abhor and despise.

But after all, that would be a very poor, dull home that could not dispense altogether with visitors; and Fritz was often glad enough when even his best friends had gone, and he and Hetty could just sit down quietly together to talk or read. The intellect of a man would be almost sure to be ruined who had no companions but women. He would be in the greatest danger of losing his powers of abstraction and generalization, and of regarding almost all questions in a passionate, personal way. And yet there is something extremely fresh in the criticisms of a really clever woman, which even the brightest of men seem thankful to avail themselves of. Whatever may be the cause of it, there is unquestionably a wide difference between the intellect of a man and the intellect of a woman; and as half the population of the world consists of women, it must be worth any sensible man's while to find out as far as possible what that side of truth and life is which a woman sees most readily and most heartily approves. Moreover there is one whole department of literature which appeals almost as much to the ear as to the intellect, and which needs as much to be heard as to be read. Of course this is obviously true of the drama and of all poetry. Why should the poet be at such pains to make his verses musical, if they are to be perused in silence? And the people who can enjoy a quiet reading of a poem are either prosy people, who are quite indifferent to the form, or people who have the faculty of mentally reproducing and clearly remembering beautiful sounds. But even for the best musical memory, the true way of enjoying poetry is to read it aloud, or to hear it read. And there are poems too, as there are songs, which seem made for women's voices, and which men can never read with good effect. At any rate those were delicious evenings which could be spared for readings in which both Hetty and Fritz could take a part; and better still those evenings when Effié could join them, and it became practicable to read, not separate poems only, but plays. Nobody will ever understand Shakspeare thoroughly, as even Coleridge, one of the very best of his critics admits, without seeing his dramas performed on the stage. But next to that, the best commentary on Shakspeare is a thoroughly good reading; especially if there are several readers, each of whom will carefully study a play, and try to give full and adequate expression to the intention of the dramatist. Indeed in some respects a good reading is somewhat better than the stage; for nothing can be more ridiculous than to divert the attention from poetry to scenery, and it may well be questioned whether some recent representations of Shakspeare's plays have not done irreparable mischief both to poetry and the theatre. Of course there were many books that neither Hetty nor Effie cared to hear; but for Hetty, with a steadily increasing number of little babies to look after, reading was becoming more and more impossible, and she had to depend for her literature almost entirely upon those evenings when Fritz could read aloud, and was himself engaged with books of general interest.

Among those books which Fritz read on the evenings when Effie could be at their house, was the "Life and Letters of Schlaiermacher;" and perhaps there was scarcely any book that produced so marked an effect upon their life. Fritz himself was far enough from being a Schleiermacher, and yet there were certain points of far-off resemblance which helped him to understand the life and work of that illustrious man. But what made the book so fascinating to the three who were hearing it together was the fact, that it suddenly explained to them their own relations to one another; and made them understand the peculiar value and danger, and at any rate to many eyes, the strangeness of their fellowship. For Effie seemed both to herself and to the other two, as they were reading Schleiermacher's letters, to be in a position almost exactly corresponding to that of Henrietta von Willich. She was now extremely often at Fritz's house; they were unquestionably exceedingly fond of each other, and they never pretended to disguise from each other, and least of all from Hetty, their mutual affection. They never hesitated to write to one another if they had anything to write about; and they never wrote coldly. While they were reading Schleiermacher's letters, it seemed to all three, Hetty and Effie and Fritz, almost as if they had found in the house of a perfect stranger portraits of themselves. Nor was it only that they, like Jette and Ehrenfried and Schleiermacher, were united by the ties of a most complete and hearty affection; the union in both cases had the same foundation and was exposed to the same dangers. They belonged to each other by virtue of irresistible natural affinities, and why should they try to keep apart? And yet, if Hetty had been jealous, or Effie a weak-minded flirt—well, *then* they would never have been united at all.

Home was all the happier for Effie's love. Impossible as flirts and fast young men may think it, it bound Fritz and Hetty more closely together than ever. Fritz was proud beyond all measure of his bright and beautiful wife; he felt himself honoured by her deep and true affection, and regarded her perfect confidence in him with the profoundest gratitude. In her love he found perfect rest. When the fast-increasing persecutions and annoyances which he had to endure seemed almost breaking his spirit and souring his temper, she never failed to cheer him, even though her efforts to strengthen him were exhausting the springs of her own life. She never reproached him, she never complained. Her tears and sad forebodings were for herself, her smiles and hopes for him; and indeed for her, dear loving woman, wife and mother, these battles of creeds were "with confused noise and garments rolled in blood." A flippant gossiper might accuse her husband of Popery or infidelity, and then go about his daily business as unconcerned as ever, while his idle, lying words were robbing Fritz's children and breaking Hetty's heart. And she could do nothing, even Fritz could do nothing; they could only suffer and wait. But more and more closely they clung to each other. As friend after friend forsook them, their love of each other became stronger and more precious. And yet when some some new calamity came upon them, some fresh unlooked-for treachery, when Fritz looked on the pale face of his wife, and saw the traces of that weeping which she tried so hard to conceal; when sometimes as she knelt at night to pray he could hear her sobbing, and knew that she had put out the light that he might not see her grief, he almost felt as if *he* were *killing* her. Could there be no compromise? Was even victory at last, if it ever should come, worth the cost of such suffering as this?

"It's hardly worth going on with, dearest," he said, one day; "how miserable it makes us! Nothing will ever satisfy these men. They don't care what we suffer; perhaps they think they are 'doing God service.' I'd better give in—and yet—I don't know *how* to give in."

"No, no, my own darling, never, never. I never loved you, dearest, so much as I do now. We can bear whatever comes. Go on, Fritz; think of the end—'Enter thou into the joy of thy Lord."

Well, well, it was hard to bear, but

> Knowledge by suffering entereth,
> And life is perfected by death.

CHAPTER XVII.

THE CHURCH MEETING.

Everybody knows that in a Protestant country there is no persecution. There is no persecution because it would be quite absurd for people who had forsaken the ancient Church, on the ground that it was the right and bounden duty of everybody to think for himself on religious matters, to refuse to allow other people to think for themselves. Least of all could there be any persecution among Protestant dissenters, who have separated from the Established Church in the exercise of that right of "private judgment" which belongs to every responsible human being. And yet, is it not a pity that persecution should have entirely died away? There was something very genuine and hearty about it, and moreover, could anything be more scriptural? Don't we know what we are to do in case of heresy or false doctrines, to the wife of our bosom, or the friend that is even as our own soul? "Thine eye shall not pity, neither shalt thou spare, neither shalt thou deliver, but thou shalt surely kill him;

thine hand shall be first upon him to put him to death, and afterwards the hands of all the people."

Yes, that was something like. We live in degenerate times—and yet there are redeeming features; and institutions still survive to remind us that we are of the same flesh and blood with those who stoned heretics to death or fried them on gridirons. To the disgrace of civilization and religion in merry England, *persecution* has died away; but by a merciful Providence, to save us from utter Atheism, there still remain, little as we may deserve them—*Church-meetings.*

Very few people in the world at large have ever seen a Church-meeting. And perhaps it is a good thing that they have not. Not by any means would I insinuate that a Church-meeting cannot bear the closest inspection. A Church-meeting is an assembly of the truly converted, a gathering of saints. It is generally opened by prayer, and closed with a benediction. From that sacred enclosure every demon of selfishness, pride, vain-glory, hypocrisy, anger, hatred, malice, and all uncharitableness, has been for ever exorcised. An insignificant assembly a Church-meeting may appear to the unregenerate observer; but do we not all know that God prefers the foolish things of this world, and that, in actual fact, every member of an Independent Church is inspired by the Holy Ghost? Mr. Bung, for instance, *as* Mr. Bung, was perhaps as ignorant a human being as could be found under heaven; but Mr. Bung, as deacon and Church-member, was neither more nor less than infallible on every point of Church doctrine or ceremony. For what was the use of prayer if you did not get what you asked for? And hadn't every member of the Church assembling in St. George's Road Chapel been praying through the mouth of Mr. Lush, auctioneer, and father of a large family, that the "Blessed Spirit might guide them in all that it might be their painful duty to undertake on the evening of Monday, June 24th."

For that was the evening of *the* Church-meeting. Of course the conspirators had said nothing to Fritz about what was to be done that night, but for all that, there had been very considerable preparation for that eventful Church-meeting. Hadn't Bung, for instance, made a point of visiting all the old women who received the sacramental money, and given them to understand, in one way or other, that however old and shaky their limbs might be, they must manage to get them dragged to the Church-meeting on the 24th of June, inasmuch as a subject of great importance was to be brought before the Church? Hadn't Miss Rebecca Lush imparted her anxieties to all the senior scholars in the Sunday-school who happened to be in Church-fellowship, and besought them to do their duty as members of the Church, however painful that duty might be? Hadn't the teachers of the Sunday-school held at least fifteen special prayer-meetings, in which they had given the minutest directions to Almighty God as to the manner in which it was their fixed and unalterable determination that He should deal with their minister? Hadn't the good old doctor been consulted; and hadn't he said to Bung and Lush that deeply as he sympathized with them, he felt it, as he might say, almost a matter of etiquette not to interfere in so grave and painful a quarrel? Hadn't he told them how serious a disappointment it was to him to see a cause that he left so prosperous and flourishing withering away? Didn't he tell them that he reflected with awe upon that mysterious Providence which, in its inscrutable wisdom, permitted false doctrine to be proclaimed from that sacred desk where, for more than a century, the simple Gospel had been preached to men? Hadn't one or two of the neighbouring ministers expressed their sympathy and their regrets, and their pious desire, that though they were not in a position which warranted their taking any prominent position in the coming struggle, all might be for the best, and that the spirit of wisdom might be poured down upon the deacons and the flock? Yes, indeed! Bung and Lush, and the rest of the conspirators, had left no stone unturned to make this Church-meeting all that they wished it to be. And they had every reason to believe that Parkinson, and Cave, and Fritz's staunchest friends, who I regret to say were not in the habit of attending Church-meetings, knew nothing whatever of their plots, and would almost certainly be absent on the 24th of June.

They *were* absent on the 24th of June. An ordinary Church-meeting wasvery much like a prayer-meeting. There were hymns, a lesson out of the Bible, prayers, a short address, and then whatever business might be necessary. On this particular Monday there was no business, at least so far as Fritz knew. No one wished that month "to join the Church;" not even Sparks; and as Mrs. Lush very truly remarked, "How was it likely that that dear young man would ever be brought to the Lord while there was such a coldness and want of Gospel truth in the pulpit?" So Fritz was just beginning his address when the first shell was fired by the conspirators, and exploded in the very middle of the schoolroom. For up rose—yes, it couldn't be anybody else—up rose Farmer; occasionally maker, but for the most part humble mender, of shoes. He was very pious, and rather small; with a bald head, which of course he couldn't help, and a very lamentable deficiency in English grammar, which perhaps was his misfortune rather than his fault. He had a very drawling, nasal utterance, and in fact it was hardly fair to put so poor and humble a

Christian in the forefront of the attack. Hardly fair, and yet not unwise. As to Farmer himself—why, poor man, he made the shoes for all the Lushes, and he really couldn't afford to refuse to go into the front when he was asked; and if he was shot down by the enemy there was scarcely a conspirator who could be better spared. It needed an effort for Farmer to make his trembling voice heard; and it was only when Fritz had finished reading a text, and lifted up his head, that he became aware of the apparition of the embarrassed shoemaker. "I should like," said Farmer, "just to be allowed to make a few remarks and propose a resolution. I'm sure I don't wish to be anyways offensive to our minister, but I must say there's a good deal that many of us would like altered. We've been accustomed to a very pure Gospel at St. George's Road; it's been our privilege for many years, when the Word's been preached, which it always has been so preached by our honoured pastor, Dr. Richardson, whose age and infirmities compelled him to leave us, and indeed it was a heavy loss to all this parish, when the pure and undefiled Gospel was held forth to perishing sinners, and we don't like to miss it. Many of us is in very humble walks of life, and when we come on the Lord's Day, or a prayer-meeting, to the means of grace, we 'ope to 'ear that which will comfort our 'earts, and 'elp us to journey through the wilderness to Canaan on our way rejoicing.

And I really feel obliged to say, and I shouldn't like to hurt Mr. Rivers's feelings, that when we come on a Sunday morning to the Lord's 'ouse, and when we p'r'aps have been late to bed on Saturday night, and our wives and families, that we don't feel prepared for such hargumentative preaching; it isn't what we want, nor yet what we've been used to. What we want, Mr. Rivers and Christian friends, is the pure milk of the Word, which shall comfort our 'earts and feed our souls, and prepare us for a better world when time with us shall be no more. I'm sure there's nobody I want to give offence to," said Farmer, trembling with apprehension lest every sentence that he spoke should cut off a customer; "but I hope there's no 'arm in saying what's on many people's minds in this room, that we should like something done; and I should like to propose, Christian friends, that a special Church-meeting should be appointed to be 'olden, to take into our prayerful and careful consideration, the doctrines and preachings of our beloved pastor, the Rev. Frederick Rivers." Thereupon little Farmer vanished, being not only small of stature, but so heartily ashamed of himself—so much grace yet remained—and so fearful lest he might have alienated more customers than would be an equivalent for the large family of Mr. Lush, that he would gladly have taken refuge, if it had been possible, in his own shoes.

Another voice was heard at the far end of the school-room, jerking out the words, "I beg to second that resolution." When Fritz said—

"I understand you to say, Mr. Farmer, that you would *like* to propose a certain resolution. Have you quite made up your mind whether you *will* propose it or not?"

There was silence for a moment while Farmer was picking himself up out of his own shoes, and trying to comprehend what was expected of him.

"Did you speak to me, sir?" he said, emerging once more into public notice.

"Yes, certainly," said Fritz; "I want to know whether you've got anything to propose?"

"Yes, sir, please, the resolution."

"Then perhaps you'll kindly write it on a piece of paper, and pass it up to the desk," said Fritz.

Here was a difficulty; Farmer had no paper handy, except a few bills. There was considerable delay, and at last Rebecca Lush handed the back of an old letter to Farmer, and he wrote out as coherently as he could, the resolution which he had already expressed a wish to propose.

There was another pause. There was no other member so dependent upon Lush's custom and Bung's patronage, as to feel bound to sacrifice himself for the interests of the conspiracy; and it was evidently of the utmost importance that the deacons themselves should not appear as the leaders of insurrection a moment sooner than was necessary. So Fritz rose again, and said—

"If nobody seconds this resolution, I may as well go on with my address."

Thereupon, up rose Mr. White, husband of Bung's housemaid, collector of rents from the cottage property belonging to the son and heir of the successful tripe-vendor. White also, like Farmer, had much more piety than education. It had been his heart's desire to devote himself to the missionary work. He had offered himself as a champion of the Cross, willing to carry the Gospel to the most unhealthy climates and the most ferocious wild beasts. He would probably have been accepted, and transported for life to one of the West Indian islands, for he had been butler to one of the largest contributors to the London Missionary Society, and he attributed his conversion to the prayers which his pious master had offered at the family altar. But White had a mother and a sweetheart; and the sweetheart had a medical man. There is many a slip between the cup and the lip, even when both the parties to a contract to marry are residing in the same parish. But what could Matilda hope if her beloved were to pitch his tent in a West Indian island? She implored her medical man to warn the intended missionary of the dangers to his feeble constitution which threatened him in those distant climes. Why should he throw away in the space perhaps of one short year, a life which might be a blessing to his own countrymen for perhaps a quarter of a century? Why, indeed! And thinking the matter over—the mission-field or matrimony—need we wonder that the susceptible heart of White inclined to marriage and Matilda? The wedding-breakfast was at Bung's. The Rev. Dr. Richardson officiated at the marriage ceremony, without assistance. Mr. Lush presented Mr. White with a situation as a marriage present, and White had collected rents and read his Bible and conducted a little service in one of Lush's cottages, ever since.

He was by no means wanting in fluency, but this was a great occasion and he felt it necessary to secure accuracy. So with very considerable labour he had committed to writing his charge against the Rev. Frederick Rivers, and he now rose to read it. The manuscript was a formidable mass of inked paper, and calculating from the first page might have required a couple of hours for effective delivery. It was an essay upon Christian doctrine in general: proving, firstly, what St. George's Road had been used to; secondly, what it wanted and liked; thirdly, what the Bible taught us; fourthly, what Mr. Rivers didn't teach us. Upon this formidable statement of the case poor little Farmer picked himself up once more, and felt that if he were given to understand that he would make no more shoes for

Mr. Parkinson, it might be possible to borrow White's essay and make everything right again.

The eloquence and logic of poor Mr. White were, however, nipped in the bud. At the end of the first page of his carefully prepared manuscript he had arrived at no definite complaint against his minister, much less at any distinct resolution. If "the Church" was in need of elaborate instruction on dogmatic divinity, it was not quite clear that Mr. White was the man to give it. At any rate, Fritz, with ruthless severity, put a stop to his reading, and recalled his attention to the unwelcome fact that he had risen to second a resolution and must do so or sit down again. "Mightn't he read the paper he had prepared?" "No, he mightn't. If everybody, without permission and without notice, brought a long paper to read, the Church meetings would last for ever, and all order would be at an end. He must speak, not read; and he must speak to the resolution or not at all."

A loud "hear, hear," at the other end of the room indicated the unexpected arrival of Parkinson. He had been passing the chapel and just looked in for something he had left in the vestry the day before, when to his astonishment he heard from the chapel-keeper that there was some kind of unpleasantness in the room above. He just entered in time to hear White's question and Fritz's answer. He rose immediately, and with a loud clear voice said, "he was quite sure they were all much obliged to Mr. Rivers for his firmness. It would be quite intolerable if they were to be at the mercy of everybody who chose to write out long essays for the edification of the Church." A good deal of applause made the conspirators understand that the iron was not yet quite as hot as they had expected, while poor White folded up his fourfold testimony and returned it to his pocket, saying—

"At any rate, I second Mr. Farmer's resolution."

Parkinson marched up to the top of the room and took his place on one of the forms reserved for the deacons, and then with the utmost coolness looked round full into the face of Bung and Lush to see how much they were implicated in this unexpected revolution. A single glance was sufficient, for sneak and coward was written on every line of their faces.

"It has been moved by Mr. Farmer," said Fritz, "and seconded by Mr. White, that a special Church-meeting be held to consider the doctrines and preaching of the Rev. Frederick Rivers. Perhaps somebody else would like to speak on the subject before I make the very few remarks upon it myself which may seem to be necessary."

"Yes," said Parkinson, "*I* should like to say a few words on the matter. I consider it in the highest degree irregular, and most ungenerous, to introduce business of this kind at a public meeting without notice, and without previous conference with the minister and deacons. As I am a deacon myself I of course am in a position to know that there has been no such notice or conference. My colleagues in office, Mr. Bung and Mr. Lush," here he looked those worthies in the face, "are far too honourable to have suffered anything of this kind to happen, if they had in the least suspected it, without communicating with our minister, and with Mr. Cave and myself. As to the complaints that have been made I attach no importance to them whatever; and I think if any complaints had been necessary the very last person to make them should have been Mr. Farmer, and the last person but one Mr. White. I protest against this resolution as being wholly irregular and ridiculously impertinent."

Nobody seemed inclined to say anything more, so Fritz rose.

"As to this resolution," he said, "I quite agree with Mr. Parkinson, that it is extremely irregular. As to its being ungenerous, I say nothing; people who bring this sort of business, and in this manner, to a public meeting, are quite incapable of perceiving what generosity *is*. Nor am I misled by the fact that Mr. Farmer and Mr. White have consented to be most conspicuous in this movement. I am sincerely sorry for them. They have set out upon a course which will disturb their own peace and the peace of many others; and *nobody* will respect them for it. They have both been, so far as I know, very pious, consistent members of the Church; and I would not for a single moment pretend to set up myself as their superior in the graces and virtues which belong to a true Christian. But neither of them is competent to discuss those grave matters which they propose to submit to the consideration of the whole Church. They have not time for such work; and they must excuse my saying that, if they had the time, they are very far from having given any proof that they possess the ability. The discussion to which they invite you has nothing to do with Christian experience, nor even with the 'simple Gospel;' but would be devoted to an examination of technical terms which many of you know nothing whatever about. It would be the silliest affectation in me to pretend that I think the Church-meeting a fit assembly for such discussion; and therefore I refuse to allow any Church-meeting to be held for that purpose. I shall submit to no examination, and answer no questions about my doctrine. If I can't make you understand what I believe by preaching three times a week, I don't think I should be able to make you understand me by submitting to be cross-examined. But, to speak plainly, you *do* understand me. So long as I am your minister, I consider that I am here to teach *you*, not *you* to teach *me*. That is a chief feature of our relation to each other; and I will do nothing incompatible with that relation. From many of you I have received most valuable help and real benefit, both spiritual and intellectual; and from such I most sincerely hope I shall ever be willing to learn. But they are not the people whose intelligence and wisdom could have due weight in a Church-meeting. Indeed, they would scarcely think it worth while to discuss technical theology with Mr. Farmer and Mr. White, and to have the result determined, not by learning and thought, but by the ballot-box. Once for all, I will not to-night, and I *never* will, put this or any similar resolution to the Church. I will never be present at any meeting for the public discussion of my doctrines. I shall do my best to preach plainly and faithfully; and in that way I shall in time set before you what I really believe. And I am quite sure that, in private, not the humblest nor yet the proudest of you has ever found me unwilling to answer your questions or do my very best to guide and instruct you. I shall conclude this meeting by a few verses of a hymn and the benediction."

Yes! Bung might look at Lush, and Lush at Bung; Mrs. Bung and Mrs. Lush might exchange glances, and their daughters might whisper to their hearts' content; but that was Fritz's *ultimatum.* Those who didn't like it could of course leave St. George's Road, but it was clearly impossible for Fritz to submit to preach only what Farmer and White thought proper to sanction. The ballot-box is no doubt a noble institution, but in theological controversy and for the determination of the truth it is not a whit better than a dice-box. And as to "our principles as Congregationalists," they seemed to Fritz to be undoubtedly subordinate to our common sanity as men. If "our principles" meant that a majority of ignorant people is more competent to decide the meaning of a Greek word or the history and development of a dogma than a minority of instructed people, then "our principles" at St. George's Road would have to be modified. Moreover, the pensioners who received "sacrament-money," and the scholars in Rebecca Lush's class, were not even the numerical majority of the "Church," though they might be a majority of the Church-meeting; and Fritz had no notion of sacrificing a whole congregation, even though they were not enamoured of Church-meetings, to a clique of ignorant fanatics. So that was his *ultimatum*. Congregationalism does, as yet, recognise the existence of a ministry, and a minister Fritz meant to be; and, in order that he might truly be the servant of the congregation, he steadily and emphatically refused to be the slave of Bung and Lush, White and Farmer.

But though Fritz, even at this early stage of the conflict, had given his *ultimatum*, the conspirators had by no means determined upon theirs. Indeed, how can there be a last before there is a first? And the conspirators had not yet decided upon the real grounds of their dissatisfaction. There was "*a something*," which may be very effective in private gossip, but is inclined to fade into thinnest insignificance under the process of cross-examination. Moreover, who were the conspirators? Farmer and White? Nobody believed that; and yet nobody else had been conspicuous at the Church-meeting.

But Fritz was not to be put off any longer. A Church-meeting, an adverse resolution, a public statement of objection and dissatisfaction—these are not trifles in a dissenting chapel. So, when the minister and Mr. Parkinson, with Bung and Lush, met in the vestry that Monday evening, the minister was quite determined to get as near to the bottom of the whole affair as possible.

"Now, Mr. Lush," he said, "what does all this mean?"

"All what, Mr. Rivers?" said the flushed and excited auctioneer.

"This resolution, proposed by Farmer and seconded by White. Did you know of it before?"

"I think that's hardly a fair question," said Bung.

"Did *you* know of it before, Mr. Bung?" said Fritz, with increasing indignation.

Bung and Lush looked at one another, as only mean and cowardly sneaks can look.

"Then you mean you wont tell me, gentlemen; that is what I am to understand, is it? You are my enemies, and you have not the courage to say so," said the imprudent minister.

"At any rate, gentlemen," said Parkinson, "I ought to have been made aware of this, being a deacon, even if it be true that the deacons and the minister have different and opposing interests."

"You were not at our deacons' meeting, Mr. Parkinson," said Lush.

"What deacons' meeting?"

"The one last Tuesday," said Bung.

"Did you send me a notice?" said Parkinson.

"I think it was mentioned in the vestry," said the auctioneer.

"When Cave and I were not there, I suppose?"

"I don't remember."

"Don't you, Mr. Lush? Then perhaps next time you want to hatch a mischief of this sort, you'll take care to give such plain notice that it will be impossible not to remember."

"Well, Mr. Parkinson," said Lush, "you're very warm, but what have Mr. Bung and I done?"

"Yes, indeed," said Bung.

"Done! suppose you've done *nothing*, it's scarcely possible to be worse than indifferent and silent while ignorant humbugs like Farmer and White are plotting all kinds of wickedness."

"Well, they're not satisfied," said the auctioneer; "we can't help that, can we?"

"Yes, you can," said Parkinson.

"No, no," said Bung, "that's too bad!"

"Well, they can hardly be expected to control the tastes of the shoemaker and rent-collector," said Fritz.

"I never knew before," said Lush, taking advantage of Fritz's indiscretion, "that shoemakers and rent-collectors were less valued by God than deacons and ministers."

Pious Lush! virtuous protest against a mercenary view of religion!

"You're quite right, Mr. Lush," said Fritz; "it's not their trade that anybody need find fault with; it's their impudence in pretending to understand what they know nothing about, and their wickedness in beginning a quarrel that nobody can see the end of."

"Pooh, pooh! Mr. Rivers," said the fiery Parkinson, "*they* didn't begin it, did they, Mr. Bung?"

"I don't know what you mean," said Bung.

"Well, then, I mean that *you* began it—you and Mr. Lush, and your wives and daughters; that's what I mean. Do you understand now?" said Parkinson.

"I think, Mr. Rivers," said Lush, all oil, "we had better go for to-night; Mr. Parkinson is a little violent, and we'd better not lose our tempers."

"I don't know what you mean, sir, by losing our tempers" said Parkinson, "but to tell you the truth, I don't care to see our minister annoyed in this sort of way, by people who sneak behind Farmer and White, like Irish murderers behind a hedge."

"Well, but, Mr. Parkinson," said Fritz, "we don't *know* that Mr. Bung and Mr. Lush have had anything to do with this affair; though I quite agree with you that Farmer and White are only a pair of very silly, unfortunate dupes. But let us talk it over as quietly as we can. The mischief has been set rolling, and the thing is to stop it."

"Yes, that's the thing to be done, of course," said Parkinson; "and if you'd seen the rate at which the old pensioners' heads were wagging as they went down stairs, you might guess how long it will take to stop them. I expected to see every curl drop off Miss Berrick's head before she got to the first landing. But at any rate, Mr. Bung and Mr. Lush, are we agreed here in the vestry? I entirely disagree with Farmer and White in their opinions about Mr. Rivers. I'm perfectly satisfied —more than satisfied—and so is Cave. Are you two gentlemen perfectly satisfied, or are we to understand that you sympathize with the grumblers?"

"I think we've a right to ask that," said Fritz.

Bung looked helpless. Poor fellow! even his knees were not so weak as his brains, and he was sorely puzzled. To defend the faith against his own minister, seemed easy and even meritorious, when he was talking to the pensioners, and watching them as they shook their old heads, and groaned, and lifted up their hands in awe and fear. But it was quite another thing to be shut up in a vestry with Parkinson and Fritz, and only Lush to help him. It was much pleasanter to talk about Fritz's heresies behind his back, with Mrs. Bung as prompter. For that was the secret. *Mrs.* Bung was really *Mr.* Bung. She always told him what to say and do. If she had foreseen her poor husband's temporary imprisonment in a room with the man he was doing his best to ruin, she would have supplied him with a whole host of texts of scripture that she and Miss Bung had often quoted as proofs of Fritz's unsoundness. But she had not expected this vestry interview; and so, while she and her amiable daughter were waiting with the female Lushes in the schoolroom, nearly bursting with impatience, the unhappy Bung was left to his own resources, and his own resources were—*nil.*

"Well, sir," he said, addressing the toes of his boots, while Lush was playing every tune he knew, on his bald, red head, from a polka to the Old Hundredth, "I don't quite feel able to say that I'm perfectly satisfied, though I have no intention of leaving or making mischief. Mrs. Bung and my daughter think——"

"Never mind what *they* think," said Parkinson, with an abruptness that quite startled the unhappy Bung, and almost reduced him to sheer idiotcy; "we can consult them separately, when it becomes necessary. Just please to give us your own opinion. What's the matter with you, Mr. Bung?"

The oracle in Bung's boots was plainly dumb; so was the oracle in his weak knees. As a compensation for want of speech he shook his head from side to side in a mournful manner, and said—

"Ah!"

"Ach!" said Parkinson, manufacturing on the spot the most guttural interjection his organ of speech could frame, "I thought so. That's all you've got to complain of! 'Ah!' And so, when a Church is disturbed, and a minister insulted and wronged, we're to be content with people shaking their heads and saying 'Ah!' Beautiful! and most religious!"

"Well, Mr. Parkinson, I'm *not* much of a speaker—indeed, in argument, I feel when I'm talking to Mr. Rivers as ignorant as a Hottentot; but I am not quite satisfied—there's a something."

"And at any rate," says Lush, "we're all anxious for the success of Saint George's Road Chapel, and I suppose you hardly think we *are* successful, do you, Mr. Parkinson?"

"Yes, I do," said the uncompromising Parkinson; "I do think we're succeeding. Why should I think otherwise? There are good congregations, and people are evidently made to *think*. Even this humbugging disturbance proves that."

"It's all very well, Mr. Parkinson, for people to *think*, but they don't take sittings. They come, stay for a quarter or so, pay nothing, and then go away again, because they don't think Mr. Rivers is orthodox."

"Do *you* think I'm orthodox, Mr. Lush?" said Fritz.

"Well, Mr. Rivers," he said, "you must know that your way of explaining Scripture is very different from what we're used to."

"I don't quite know what you're used to," said Fritz; "but what does it matter? You hear me expound Scripture over and over again. When my view differs from what you were used to, do you think, generally speaking, that I'm right or wrong?"

"Oh, I've no complaint to make, exactly; I think you're generally right. But it doesn't suit the people, it doesn't take. And what's the use of preaching what nobody wants to hear? I'm sure, Mr. Rivers, you're anxious to do good, and my advice is, get the people together first, and then do good to them afterwards."

"I don't quite understand what your suggestion is, Mr. Lush," said Fritz; "at the same time, I think that I might, if I tried, make my sermons more popular than they are. Do you mean to advise me, then, to cultivate a more popular style; to avoid any subjects that might perhaps give slight offence, and wait for the complete expression of my opinions until the seats are all let, and the congregation well settled? Very likely we might get a good congregation in that way," said Fritz, with the meekest voice.

"Yes, Mr. Rivers, I'm sure you would, and nobody would be more delighted to see it than myself; and I'm sure it would be very easy to get people used to your way of thinking, if you only did it by degrees."

"Yes," said Fritz, "perhaps it would. What do you think, Mr. Parkinson?"

"I think that way of treating a congregation," said Parkinson, "would be a mean, cowardly, sneaking, wicked way of treating a congregation, and what's more, I'm quite certain it would be a complete failure, and I'm very glad of it."

"What do you think about it, Mr. Bung?" said Rivers.

"Well, sir," said Bung, "I don't see how preaching the Gospel to a large congregation can be mean and wicked."

"No, of course you don't," said Parkinson; "neither you nor Lush understands it. Can't you see, Mr. Bung, that it wouldn't be preaching the Gospel at all, but only preaching pew-rents; and that Mr. Rivers would have to consider, not how he could do us most good, but how he could best fill his own pockets with pounds sterling?"

"I'm quite of your opinion, Mr. Parkinson," said Fritz, "and I don't think I'm likely to try the popular style. However, it's getting very late, and we shall settle very little to-night. We must of course talk this matter over carefully as soon as we can find an opportunity. Meantime for the present, good night, gentlemen. We may as well walk together, Mr. Parkinson, as far as you go."

So Parkinson and Fritz walked together, in fact, all the way to Fritz's house; and Parkinson went in to have supper with them. Of course Hetty saw that something had been amiss, and was evidently frightened.

"Good evening, Mrs. Rivers," said Parkinson; "we've had a jolly row at the Church-meeting, and you needn't be at all frightened. But who do you think were the chief actors on the occasion?"

"Well, I dare say Mr. Lush was one of them," said Hetty.

"No, he wasn't one; guess again, Mrs. Rivers."

"I'm sure I can't guess: I don't think Mr. Bung often speaks in public, or else perhaps he might be one."

"Oh no, Mrs. Rivers; you're very wide of the mark; a very much more learned man than Bung, and a much more brilliant orator than Mr. Lush. Indeed the two chief speakers were two gentlemen of great learning, with ample leisure, devoted to literary pursuits, and men, moreover, who fortunately have made theology a hobby, and know everything about every doctrine from beginning to end. Come, can't you guess now, Mrs. Rivers?"

"No, indeed I can't," said puzzled Hetty; "I think I'm further off than ever."

"Well, then, I'll tell you," said Parkinson. "The two learned orators were Messrs. Farmer and White."

"What do you mean, Mr. Parkinson?" said Hetty.

"I mean," said Parkinson, "that that humbugging little shoemaker, and that canting collector of Lush's rents, did positively get up in the middle of the Church-meeting with a resolution, that there should be a special Church-meeting to examine your good husband's doctrines and preaching."

"Yes," said Hetty, "I knew it would come to that soon. Well, what then?"

"What then? Mr. Rivers very properly refused to put it; and all the old women went downstairs wagging their heads, as if they were quite tired of carrying them on the top of their necks any longer, and wanted to shake them off."

"Well, and what then?"

"Well, then we'd a long talk in the vestry, and then Mr. Rivers would have me come home to supper with him; and here I am, Mrs. Rivers."

"All right, my dear," said Fritz. "I'll tell you

all about the Church-meeting another time. It's nothing more than we've been long expecting, indeed it is not quite so much."

"But how odd people are," said Parkinson. "Now there was Lush, for instance, deliberately advising you to alter the very Gospel itself for the sake of pew-rents; and yet I suppose if he knew that I'd been hearing Miss Glyn play Lady Macbeth last night he'd open his pious eyes with horror."

"Of course he would," said Fritz.

"And how did she play?" said Hetty.

"Oh gloriously! she's a real artist. It doesn't matter what the scenery and stage apparatus may be, —*she's* Lady Macbeth. Modern stage effect almost dispenses with poetry, and I might say with actors and actresses."

"I'm afraid it's very conceited," said Hetty, "but I often wish I might *myself* try a part in a thoroughly good play."

"So do I," said Fritz. "When I was seeing that poor stupid—what's his name? playing Romeo at the Princess's I felt tingling all over; and to be honest, I thought if I were a better figure I could have played Romeo more effectively myself."

"Did you hear the anecdote about him?" said Parkinson.

"No; what was it?"

"When Juliet was sitting in the balcony, saying,

'Oh Romeo, Romeo, wherefore art thou Romeo?' somebody in the Pit called out, 'That's exactly what I want to know.' Of course it's too good to be true."

"Yes; but it's exactly the question I was asking myself."

"By the way," said Parkinson, "how's your friend Miss Holmes? Don't you think that young Sparks is a little inclined to think she's a shade superior to Miss Jones?"

"I don't know," said Hetty. "I think he'd like to flirt with Effie, and marry Miss Jones. Effie's the best girl, and Miss Jones is much the richer."

"Of course a young gentleman must have an eye to the main chance, Mrs. Rivers; and I fancy Sparks knows as well as anybody that twenty shillings, or even two hundred and forty pence, well saved, are worth a sovereign."

"Well, he may try Effie," said Hetty, "whenever he likes."

It was quite his intention to try Effie; and when Mr. Parkinson was gone, Fritz and Hetty remembered a good many little indications that Sparks thought Miss Jones by no means such good company as Miss Holmes. Of course he would never marry a penniless girl; besides, he was tolerably intimate with Effie's uncle Alfred, meeting him frequently at the Bank. They had often had a gossip about Effie, and the noble uncle had given Sparks his own version of the past and his prophecies of the future. Sparks thought Effie fair game—unprotected, pretty, clever, able to take care of herself, a most delightful girl to flirt with, if she only could be persuaded to flirt, and, being only a shopwoman, easily got rid of when the flirting was over. It wasn't perhaps very likely; but Sparks thought himself a match for any girl. It was a difficult undertaking, requiring both courage and craft; but at any rate he would try. Even Miss Jones herself was rather tame; and the insufferable tameness and slowness of her pious friends was at last boring poor Sparks alm st to death.

And Effie was a glorious girl, growing more accomplished and almost more beautiful every day. She was not ashamed or tired of her common daily work; but every day she was better able to understand the reasons which make ladies and gentlemen dislike or despise shopwomen. For though any lady might be a shopwoman, every shopwoman was not a lady. Most of Effie's companions were ignorant and frivolous, and were utterly astounded at her mode of life. When their work was over they seemed to have nothing to do but read sensation novels, or seek some exciting amusement. They could by no means understand what pleasure there could be in going to one's own room and spending the whole evening in reading dry books; and their s.rprise passed all bounds when they discovered that the friends at whose house Effie spent so much of her leisure time were a very quiet parson and his wife. They could scarcely be made to believe that the letters which so often came to her were not from some adoring "lover;" and, in fact, though she always assured them that she had no lover at all, it would be well for every girl if the man to whom she is "engaged" loved her half as well, or half as reverently, as Fritz loved Effie.

In spite of Hetty's boast that Sparks might try Effie whenever he liked, both she and Fritz were very sorry that he was only too likely to put their confidence to the test. And yet, not their confidence—they never doubted Effie—but Fritz knew that Sparks was a thoroughly worldly, unprincipled fellow. Of course he knew also that he had been a fellow-clerk with poor Frank Walker, and that he had made himself very acceptable to his employers by his (happily fruitless) efforts to discover poor Frank's hiding place, and bring him to justice. Fritz and Hetty were sure that if he found Effie what they knew he would find her, he would be deeply mortified, and have no scruples whatever about doing her all the harm he could. They didn't know that he could do her any harm, but they feared him with that strange unaccountable foreboding of evil which so often warns us of unseen and unknown danger.

And for themselves all seemed growing darker—

all but their own love. Hetty seemed losing spirit and health. She would sit for hours together in melancholy reverie. Her womanly instinct compelled her to see all their coming troubles in minutest detail, penetrating their daily life. She knew quite well what the next move of the conspirators would be. They would "stop the supplies." And then?——

At least she hoped that they would all be beggars together sooner than Fritz should yield.

CHAPTER XVIII.

THE LOST LETTER.

Of course Sparks thought himself a match for any girl. Doesn't every young man think so, and especially every young man who "knows the world?" Hadn't he already been a match, in a perfectly respectable way, for Miss Jones? and though winning her had been rather a dull game, it had not been without its difficulties. Had it not been necessary for him, for instance, especially for the winning of her parents, to acquire a totally new language, and to become conformed to the world in which they lived and moved? Poor Miss Jones was a very pretty girl, and what people call a sweet girl: one of those girls, moreover, who fall in love on the slightest possible provocation. She had the best of tempers—a temper, in fact, which it was almost impossible for anything to ruffle. When Sparks proposed to her, she of course took it for granted that he was violently in love; indeed, he told her he was, and she had no reason in the world to think it strange that a young man should be in love with so pretty and good-tempered a girl as she was. Of course her parents felt it necessary to make the customary inquiries, having extremely little confidence in the felicity of "love in a cottage." Two qualifications they considered indispensable; or, at any rate, one indispensable, and the other highly desirable. The one absolutely indispensable, was a good position in society and good prospects; the other, highly desirable, was piety, or a hopeful tendency to become pious. As to the first of these, Sparks was all that could be desired; and as to the second, he was much that could be hoped.

"I don't want to be a hypocrite," he said to Mr. Jones; "I don't pretend to be much better than other fellows of my own age and position, and of course I shall be very happy to attend chapel with Miss Jones, and all that sort of thing."

Surely such frankness and docility were a charming addition to a position in society! I don't know that Sparks would have found going to chapel absolutely intolerable, for of course a person must go somewhere on a Sunday; and being of a somewhat active temperament, he cared less than young men sometimes do for the privilege of sweltering in bed till about noon, and dawdling through the rest of the day like used-up scamps. But, after all, Miss Jones's pious friends were a horrid nuisance. There were the Lushes, for instance; father, mother, and three fascinating daughters. What was a young fellow like Sparks to make of them? Into how many caricatures had he not introduced the demonstrative features of Miss Rebecca! How often had he relieved his feelings when walking home alone on a Sunday night, by swearing at "Baby-linen." And as to "Dorcas," she was a poor imbecile, washed-out looking thing, that couldn't keep a conversation going for two minutes. Poor Sparks! he had a weary time of it. There was noth ng approaching to amusement in the pious circle to which he had been introduced. The wildest dissipation in which Miss Rebecca Lush ever indulged was the May-meetings. And though Sparks was prepared to make great sacrifices for—shall I say the love of Miss Jones?—he could scarcely be brought to demean himself enough to attend a May-meeting. The news which seemed most interesting to his new acquaintances was the news about a "week of prayer," or a series of "lectures on prophecy," or the glorious results of the "midnight movement," and the regenerating effect of tea and toast upon "social evils."

It was very different indeed when he spent an evening at the Riverses, and met Miss Holmes there. Both the Riverses and Effie spoke ordinary English, and avoided the dialect of saints as carefully as they would have avoided broad Cockneyisms. They were so far from confining their conversation to meetings, and lectures, and movements, and causes, and all that sort of thing, that they seemed, with the utmost rapidity, to change the subject whenever such matters were introduced. They knew quite as much about politics and the ordinary affairs of society as Sparks himself could pretend to know, and were a great deal more familiar than he was with the sterling English literature which every educated Englishman is expected to know something about. Moreover, Effie was so thoroughly genuine, so perfectly unembarrassed, and at home. She never made a parade of her knowledge, though it was really very considerable; but she never made a remark that was not sensible, and simply kept quiet if she had nothing to say worth hearing. Poor Sparks scarcely knew upon what part of her nature and accomplishments to fix a compliment. There are people, and Effie was one of them, who hate compliments more intensely than they hate insults; and really compliments were poor Sparks's strong point. In an extremely blundering kind of way, for instance, he once tried to flatter Effie about her reading.

"I wonder how you can find time, Miss Holmes, to read so much, and to read it so carefully. You seem to have read nearly everything, and to have forgotten nothing."

Effie looked up at him, as if expecting that perhaps he might say something else; there being simply nothing in what he had said already. When, instead of receiving a blush, or a pretty little simpering answer, you're obliged to reduce the poetry of a compliment into the dull prose of common truth, you naturally feel a little bewildered.

"How do you manage it?" said Sparks, a little crestfallen.

"How do I manage what, Mr. Sparks?" said Effie.

"To read so much, and remember it so well, Miss Holmes."

"Don't be too modest, Mr. Sparks," said Effie; "it doesn't make me more clever when you underrate your own attainments; I never met with an accomplished gentleman yet who didn't perceive in a moment how much assistance I need, and contrive in an unobtrusive, good-natured way to give it to me. I really have very little time, and read very little, and don't remember half of what I do read; and, besides that, reading isn't everything. I sometimes think that if I had the ability patiently and thoroughly to master one good book from end to end, it would be better than all the reading I have ever done since I left school."

"Ah, very likely," said Sparks. "But that's what seems so extraordinary in you, that you should have such views about books and reading; very few young ladies would ever dream of studying in that way."

"I don't know," said Effie; "I suppose you wouldn't say so without some experience; my circle of friends is so small, that I could scarcely give an opinion, or even *have* an opinion, about young ladies in general."

In fact, Effie extremely disliked Sparks; disliked him at all times, disliked him when he was talking glib nonsense to anybody else who cared to listen to him; disliked him most of all when he was offering ridiculous flatteries to herself. However, though he was often exceedingly annoyed by her slights, he managed to get excuses oftener and oftener to call at Fritz's house when he thought Effie would be there, and one night he called when he knew that Fritz would *not* be there; having, in fact, seen him in an omnibus on his way to the city about half an hour before. He contrived to wait, pretending to be expecting Fritz, until it got tolerably late, and Effie rose to go. He of course immediately offered to see her safely so far as she had to go alone. She was much obliged, but it was quite unnecessary; she should ride home in the first omnibus she could get. Well, then, Mr. Sparks would see her to the omnibus; it was a dark night, and he was sure Miss Holmes would find it very disagreeable to be waiting about alone. The first omnibus that came up was full, and so was the second; moreover, it began to rain. However, in another minute or two an empty cab drove up, and Effie asked Sparks if he would be kind enough to stop it for her. Of course he would; and perhaps Miss Holmes would allow him to ride part of the way with her, as he had to go in the same direction, and it was now raining fast. They both got into the cab, and were driven towards the city. Sparks found it much easier to pay pretty compliments in a dark cab than in a lighted drawing-room; and as Effie disliked him far too much to enter at all heartily into conversation, he imagined from her half-embarrassed silence, that on the whole he was making himself extremely agreeable. Yes, of course *he* knew the world well enough! It was all very well for Miss Holmes to look so proper and steady when she was with the Riverses, but *she* liked a game, Sparks was sure, as well as any other girl. So he went on from one little advance to another, until at last he put his arms round Effie's neck and kissed her. Effie wasn't a prig, and among real friends she might have seen nothing to resent even in a kiss of genuine affection—but a kiss from Sparks! that odious monkey, with his fine speeches, his miserable jokes, his impertinent flatteries! She pushed him off, and put her head out of the cab window.

"Cabman, the gentleman wishes to be set down here."

"No, no, Miss Holmes," said the baffied young gentleman who "knew the world."

But the cab stopped, and Effie got out.

"I needn't leave you yet," Sparks said; "I have time to see you to your journey's end."

"Thank you, no," said Effie; "I wouldn't for the

world put you to so much inconvenience; in fact, I wouldn't on any account ride a yard further if I were taking you out of your way with me. Good night, Mr. Sparks."

So she got into the cab again, and was driven away.

"Good night, you she devil," said Sparks; "I suppose you'll tell it all to that snivelling parson and his wife, and they'll tell it to the Joneses. And yet you're hardly such a fool as that, I should think. But I'll serve you out, you young humbug, I can assure you. I'm not going to be beaten by a girl, I can tell you that."

He needn't have been afraid that Effie would make a fuss about so ridiculous a trifle. For it was a trifle. It was nothing at all for Sparks at any rate to kiss a pretty girl whenever he could get the chance; the thing that vexed him was that Effie unmistakeably considered him a very stupid and conceited ass. He had often had his ears boxed; but it had hitherto been by young ladies who wanted another "kiss for a blow." This time it was plain that he was considered a nuisance, and his endearments an insufferable impertinence. Besides, the Joneses were dreadful prigs, and they would think that kissing Effie was little short of breaking the seventh commandment.

At any rate Sparks took the very earliest opportunity of finding out how matters stood. He called on the Riverses when he knew Effie would be there, and was received just as usual. Of course he visited Miss Jones, and found in a moment that no mischief had been done in that quarter. So he decided with himself he would let Effie alone until he could "serve her out" for thinking so slightly of those attractions which hitherto had been victorious wherever they went. He thought it a tolerably good and safe beginning to throw hints and suggest suspicions to the Joneses and Lushes. He knew that Mrs. Lush would talk it over with Mrs. Bung; and he rightly judged that a good deal of harm can be done by clever gossip without incurring any risk for defamation of character.

Mr. and Mrs. Lush and their lovely daughters were spending an evening at the Joneses, when Sparks made his first experiment. They were talking of the Riverses, and he said—

"By the way, how extremely intimate Miss Holmes is there. I wonder Mrs. Rivers likes it. But there's no accounting for tastes."

"Do you know what Miss Holmes is too?" said Mrs. Lush.

"Yes," said Sparks, "a shopwoman; or at any rate in some business place in the city. And really a wonderfully clever girl for being in such circumstances."

"Well, I never could see it," said the auctioneer's wife.

"I can see nothing in her at all," said Rebecca, "and she's decidedly plain."

"Of course Mr. Rivers doesn't think so. I'm sure a stranger would find it hard to guess which of the two is Mrs. Rivers, and which is the friend. I daresay it's all right; but, to a person who knows anything of the world, it has a rather queer look."

"Miss Holmes must be a very bold girl," said Mrs. Lush, "and I deeply sympathize with poor Mrs. Rivers; she's many a miserable hour, you may depend upon it."

"I've noticed a great difference in her lately," said Rebecca; "she seems much paler and quieter. Of course Mr. Cave and Mr. Parkinson say it's the misunderstandings at chapel. I know better. 'Ma doesn't look pale and ill, and she's quite as much interested in the chapel as ever Mrs. Rivers was."

"But your mamma is a lady of unusual fortitude and strength of mind, Miss Rebecca," said Sparks.

"No, no, Mr. Sparks. It's a skeleton. Weren't you telling me a quotation out of one of your books," said Rebecca, "about everybody having a skeleton in a cupboard? Well, Miss Holmes is Mrs. Rivers's skeleton."

"Oh, I daresay it's all our fancy," said Sparks, "and we shall be getting into scandal if we don't mind. But my principles are rather strict in such matters. I think a girl's a girl, and a man's a man, and you can't be too particular."

It would be doing Mrs. Lush and her trio of useful daughters great injustice to suppose that they had never before, at least in the confidence of the family circle, discussed the relations of Effie and the Riverses. Mrs. Lush had long thought it "perfectly indecent," and that Hetty was "a poor creature not to put a stop to it." And she thought it rather hard that if the minister must have a pet he could not have chosen one from among his old friends—"not indeed that she would ever suffer Rebecca to be on such terms with a married man—but their minister was very peculiar." "And now," she said, "that young Mr. Sparks notices it, and he's pretty knowing. Yes, yes, it has a queer look, you may depend upon it. Be sure, girls, that you avoid such snares. Don't be too familiar even with your minister. A man's a man, as young Sparks said. I do admire that young man's principles. Miss Jones has found a treasure."

"And she's not much in her, either," said Rebecca.

"She has money, at any rate," said Baby-linen.

"Oh yes, a pretty good fortune, *I* know," said Mrs. Lush; "I wonder they're making such a long courtship of it."

Mr. Sparks congratulated himself on the success of his generous scheme for increasing the happiness of the girl who declined to be kissed by him. And quite independently of his own little grievance, it was extremely exhilarating to a bored young man to get up a scandal, especially when a parson was concerned in it. His detective instincts and acquirements had been sadly rusting since the robbery at Goulburns'; and this little affair between Effie and Fritz was exactly the thing to polish them. Besides, it was charming to see with what zest the Lushes and Bungs entered into the matter; and what innumerable and ingenious devices they had for making mischief. They would watch Effie with a persevering effrontery that made her half crazed; and then, if she seemed embarrassed or turned away, they would sigh and gaze languishingly at Hetty, or perhaps go and sit by her and talk in a soft, pitying tone, till Hetty grew quite frightened, as if some mysterious trouble was coming upon her. Sometimes they would sit listening with affected raptures of delight while Fritz and Effie were talking; and then apologize and say "it's really so charming to hear you two talk, you seem made for one another."

"Well, I do think," said Mrs. Lush to Hetty, "you have an angel's disposition. How kind you are to Miss Holmes."

"I don't see anything very angelic, Mrs. Lush, in being very fond of a girl like Effie. Besides, she's a very old friend of my husband's, and that alone would be quite enough to make her a friend of mine also."

"Yes, dear," said Mrs. Lush, "that's what I

like so much in you. These horrid newspapers and divorce-courts seem making almost everybody so suspicious."

It is extremely annoying to be complimented for a very commonplace virtue, the possession of which it would be an insult to doubt—but what can you say? And really Hetty was beginning to feel a little uneasy. She knew Effie far too well, and trusted her husband far too completely, to be for an instant jealous; but could it be that their enemies were going to strike them *there?* Was the pretended zeal for truth to end in such detestable cruelty as a conspiracy against the love and trust of husband and wife and friend?

Meantime Effie was venturing upon an experiment which she had only just confided to her two friends. She had collected a considerable number of her ballads and songs, the best, as she thought, of those which had been the amusement and delight of many a quiet evening when her city work was done. She had retouched them with great care, almost rewriting some of them, and had found a publisher who was willing to undertake the whole risk of their publication, giving her half of whatever profits there might be. And now she brought the manuscript to Fritz to ask his advice. She wanted to read some of the songs to him, and to decide upon a pseudonym for their author. Many of them he knew already, but many were quite new; and now that they were all arranged in what seemed to Effie the best order for indicating the development of thought and feeling out of which they had sprung, she was just a little proud of them. She had, indeed, good cause to be proud of them; and yet she was half bashful about reading them aloud. They seemed all to belong to Fritz and Hetty; and to herself at least, they seemed a series of confessions,—a revelation of what she knew so well, and felt so deeply, that her whole heart and life were bound up with her two friends. She could not help singing out her love and joy; and surely there was no harm if they who had inspired her songs should hear her sing them.

When, in fact, she came to read them over, it was quite plain that the development of thought and feeling out of which they had sprung was neither more nor less than the growth of her intimacy with Fritz, from the Shiloh days till that very moment when she was reading her songs to him. Perhaps he was too partial a critic to be able to give her any advice worth having; and yet, on the other hand, his love was not of the blind sort, but in fact morbidly quicksighted. He was painfully alive to anything that might make Effie disliked or misunderstood; and he would have felt far more annoyed by any unfair or ungenerous criticism of her poems, than by anything that the most ungenerous critics could say about himself. But still there was really nothing he could advise her to leave out. Of course there were some peculiarities which might or might not please. There were modes of expression, strong and unconventional, which were very likely indeed to be misrepresented. But still they were thoroughly genuine; even the shallowest or bitterest of critics would scarcely pretend to regard them as affectations.

"So let them go, Effie," he said. "It's no use trying to sing just like everybody else. If you've anything to say beautiful enough to be worth saying, say it out in the way that pleases yourself, and if it be truly beautiful every true ear will be sure to find it out. And if not, well then, you know we shall all be disappointed, and I daresay get over it in time too."

"And as to the name?" she said.

"Well, I don't know. You see you want the name to be tolerably like your own, and yet sufficiently unlike to escape detection. As to the name Hope, I daresay that would be well enough instead of Holmes; but it's no use calling yourself *Effie* Hope. However, I'll think it over. There's no hurry, and it will do very well when I return the manuscript."

Fritz returned the manuscript in two or three days with a letter.

"St. George's Road,
"*Friday Night.*

"My very dear Effie,—I think you seem more than ever like Schleiermacher's Jettchen, now that I have to write to you about a book of your own. Indeed, Hetty and I often laugh together as we read his letters to his clever little favourite, especially the passages marked with pencil, and we are almost compelled to believe that our own letters are nothing more than miserable imitations. There is indeed one difference; ours are not half so affectionate, or I might say, so passionate as his. If I were to call you all the pretty names he used to call Jette, you'd think I was trying to excel in quite a new department in art—to wit, flattery. Indeed there's nothing after all like excelling in a variety of accomplishments; and I sometimes think it might almost be worth while to compose some twenty or thirty extremely neat compliments, and have them arranged in order, graduated like a thermometer; each compliment corresponding to a certain temperature of affection, from zero up to boiling-point. You know how puzzled I often am to find something suitable to say to the younger members of the B. and L. families, not to mention their esteemed mammas; and a few well-prepared flatteries, constructed on the principle of saying nothing and seeming to say a great deal, would do almost as much towards winning the hearts of my refractory deacons as preaching sermons in the style of the Rev. J. Angell James. Very good sermons, by the way, his often were; though I need scarcely stop to make a parenthetic explanation to you on such subjects.

"But for yourself, my dear little Effie, I often wish there were some English style of address corresponding to the German '*thou*;' of course '*thou*' itself wouldn't do. '*Thine*' isn't a bad way, perhaps, of ending a letter; but to '*thou*' and '*thee*' a letter all through would be making it almost as stiff as a State-paper. And even without the '*thou*,' I often wonder what such priggish, insincere, superficial people as some we know of, would make of our letters if they happened to get hold of them. We shouldn't care to make explanations; and what is more to the purpose, no explanations could possibly be made to such people as they are. They seem to be quite incapable of what we think and feel; and even our quiet letters would seem to them the wild extravagance of doubtful or sinful passion. What would they make of Schleiermacher's?

"And now as to the poems:—Of course you know quite well already what I shall think of them. Indeed, are they not written out of a common experience—out of that one life which we three have in a manner been living together? Of course, my dear Effie, you won't think for a moment that I mean I could have written them myself. Even if I ever have the good fortune to think beautiful thoughts, I never can manage to find beautiful forms in which to express them. So I must be content just to have an ear and an eye, and to know the beautiful when I see it. Well, of course I like the poems exceedingly; and I daresay you would prefer that I should say so, even though you must know it already. At any rate, in similar circumstances, I should prefer your saying so. That's the mystic power of words. Clear utterance, distinct affirmation and revelation; while, at the same time, of course words themselves are miserably inadequate, and *are* not that which they reveal, but are only *of* it. I don't mind writing to you in this way, because you understand me. I wonder what they would think at St. George's Road Chapel, if I were to try to illustrate the doctrine of the 'Logos' in the same way, and the expression 'God *of* God' in the Nicene Creed?

"But I'm getting a long way from your poems. As to the first of them, your translation, in our English ballad-metre, of the last part of the sixth Iliad, do you remember my silly version of it? the one I read to you at Shiloh? I can assure you that I thought no small things of those jingling rhymes. It was only a few weeks ago that I happened to find a copy of them, which I needn't say I tore up and burnt. And yet I am half sorry for it now, because it's rather useful to have some means of testing ourselves—some better evidence than mere memory can furnish, of what we actually were in the past. It would be quite silly of me to ask whether you thought of that translation when you were writing yours; because of course I know you thought of it, and of the old library, and a great many other things. But you had to take all your knowledge of Homer in those days second-hand. How little we thought then that we should one day be reading the original together; and, by the way, some of your renderings seem to me wonderfully happy. I'll show you the parts I mean when I see you again.

"Then there's that little song about 'work,' which I flatter myself is a very pretty memorial of a sermon you once heard on the same subject. So you must be on your guard against all my praise, for after all it may only be another form of vanity. In fact, I think that both Hetty and I have a very fair share in all these songs, and that without ceasing in the least to be yours, they are also ours. How many happy, quiet evenings do they recall, when we have talked on all these subjects together! And yet this is a new gift, this poetry of yours—a fresh treasure for all of us. God bless you, my dearest Effie! I am charmed with your poems, and so is Hetty; and we both wish and expect for you a great success of the kind you most desire. But we'll talk about it next time we meet. Hetty is expecting you to spend Sunday with her; of course you know I shall be, for once in my life, preaching elsewhere.

"Good-bye, my little Effie. You're a good, brave girl; and at any rate you have, what I wish was worth more, the hearty affection of

"Your very sincere friend,

"*Effie.*" "FRITZ.

On a separate piece of paper was written—

"P.S.—As to the name, I had almost forgotten that important matter. The disguise will be better if you change *both* names— *Julia* Hope, for instance, instead of *Effie* Hope, which is too like Effie Holmes. But there is plenty of time for that, which is one of the last arrangements we need make.

"Thine, FRITZ."

Of course Effie went to St. George's Road Chapel on Sunday, and went home with Hetty after the morning service. Sparks was walking behind them, and as Effie took out of her pocket her gloves, or pocket-handkerchief, or something or other, she pulled out at the same time Fritz's letter and dropped it. The noble Sparks could surely do nothing less than pick it up and—surely not read it? The ladies were not far in front. Could anything be easier than to run on and restore the letter to its owner? Yes, many things would be easier; and above all it would be easier to read the letter first. Men may laugh at women as they like, but they have just as much curiosity as Eve's daughters, and are quite as fond of poking into other people's secrets. Silly little Effie, too, to carry letters about in her dress-pocket with gloves and pocket-handkerchiefs and all manner of odds and ends. Besides, hadn't she read it already, and what's the use of reading a letter more than once? and to read a letter over and over again, say twenty or thirty times, could anything be more weak-minded? And yet somehow Effie always liked to have Fritz's last letter in her pocket. It seemed almost as if he himself were with her, and they were talking together in their perfectly genuine unconventional way. Indeed she had a silly habit of every now and then wanting some perfectly useless thing out of her pocket for no reason in the world, it would seem, but just to put her hand on Fritz's letter, and so make his nearness more real. It was not, therefore, very long on that Sunday morning before she wanted something out of her pocket, and found to her dismay that the letter had gone. She instantly stopped, saying to Hetty, "I have lost a letter;" and she turned round as if intending to walk back till she met it wherever it might be. Seeing Sparks, however, she walked quickly up to him and told him what she had lost.

"You can't have lost it, Miss Holmes," he said, "since you left the chapel; for I've followed you every inch of the way, and in truth I've been watching both you and Mrs. Rivers, and should certainly have seen the letter if you had dropped it."

"Oh dear, dear!" said Effie, "I must have lost it in the omnibus."

"Was it a private letter, Miss Holmes?" said Sparks, with the very letter itself in the breast-pocket of his coat.

"Why all letters are private, are they not?" said Effie, "and at any rate I did not want to lose that one."

"So much the better," thought Sparks, "you little wretch! So much the better for my chance of serving you out. I know the handwriting on the envelope at any rate, whatever's inside it.

"I think you're very likely to get it back again," he said, speaking to Effie; "any good-natured person who picked up a letter would be almost sure to drop it into the first letter-box he passed, and the letter-carrier would be very unlikely to have a quarter of an hour to spare to read it; so it will come to you just as good as ever I have no doubt."

Sparks walked by their side till they came to Fritz's house, and bid them good morning with that lingering uncertainty which seemed to say as plainly as could be without actual speech, "wont you invite me to dinner?"

They didn't invite him to dinner. So as soon as they had shut the door, and he had turned the next corner, he took Fritz's letter out of his pocket and quietly read it.

"Ah, charming," he said, "charming, Mr. Rivers. Isn't she a darling little Effie? Isn't she a bright, clever girl; exactly the person for Mrs. Rivers number two? Really all the delights of bigamy without its little drawbacks. So you're a poetess, are you, my fair prig? Or a third part of a poetess.

Well, well; if I can't make something of this affectionate effusion my name isn't Sparks."

So he put the postscript into his purse and the letter into the next letter-box, and went on his way rejoicing.

"What a very disagreeable young man that Mr. Sparks is," said Effie to Hetty, as soon as the front door was shut; "I have a perfect horror of him; and he seems to me so mean and cruel."

And yet she knew very little of him beyond what we have seen already. But she shrunk from him with the instinctive antipathy which often warns us of the presence of an enemy when we are quite unable to justify our fears. He was soon forgotten, however, and even the lost letter seemed a slight trouble as in sisterly love the two friends passed that quiet Sunday together.

Effie was very much surprised and half afraid when the lost letter was brought to her on Monday morning. The envelope was dirty and open, yet the contents might have been unread, and the stranger who had picked the letter up and re-posted it would not know who "Fritz" and "Effie" were, and it would make no matter if he did, and at any rate the letter had come back, and she would read it once more, and then lock it up in her desk. It seemed all right; and it was not for an hour or two that she remembered that the postscript was missing. She fancied it might perhaps be in her desk, or drawer, or dress-pocket. No—it was gone, stolen out of the letter. She instantly thought of Sparks, and fancied she remembered a peculiar look, an unusual meanness of expression, as they met and parted on Sunday morning. She could not imagine why he should care to steal a piece of her letter, or what he could do with it; but all day long she was oppressed with that dull foreboding of misery which is sometimes almost harder to bear than acute pain.

And was it absolutely unknown to Mr. Sparks that to read, without permission, a letter addressed to somebody else, is a mean and detestable action? No, he knew it quite well. He knew that he was meditating a piece of cruelty which might bring utter ruin, and certainly would inflict the acutest suffering upon people who were, he was sure, utterly innocent of what would be imputed to them. And Effie had done him no harm, and he was not even seriously angry about what she had done when he tried to kiss her. His own little mistake was the merest trifle; and he admired, in his way, a girl of high spirit. But here was a letter, and a secret. What fun it would be to see what the Joneses and Lushes would make of it. And besides that, it *was* odd. Married men don't often write such letters to unmarried girls, and wives don't generally prefer that they should, and prudent young ladies don't often take part in such correspondence. What could they make of the matter? How could they explain it?

Would there be a scene? Would Effie, "to avoid scandal," come seldom or not at all to the Riverses' house? Or would they defy scandal? And what would people say? Sparks wasn't proof against the temptation to let Fritz's postscript introduce to the outside world the inner life of the three friends at the parsonage; and nobody would know how the secret had been found out, least of all would anybody suspect *him*.

So, on his way to the bank the day after he picked up the letter, he meditated with the postscript in his pocket what should be the first move in his little game. Why not drop it, or just show it, "in confidence," that very day at Mr. Jones's house; where he was to spend the evening, and where he knew the Lushes would be also? Of course it *would* be "in confidence," and the confidence would not be betrayed; any high-spirited young gentleman who steals letters is sure that he can trust his fellow-creatures to that extent. At any rate he would take it with him that night to the demure little party of saints, and see what turned up. As they had neither dancing nor cards, nor anything worldly with which to amuse themselves, a little scandal might relieve the monotony of pious conversation.

But Sparks had scarcely taken his seat in the Bank when he saw enter his esteemed friend Alfred Holmes, Esq. What an odd coincidence. Alfred Holmes was not of a playful disposition, and his feelings towards his niece were not what one would call affectionate. If any human being was willing to do Effie harm it was the benevolent uncle who had offered her a home, as upper nurse without remuneration. Fritz's postscript in *his* hands would be no joking matter. His philosophy of life in general, and of the intercourse of the sexes in particular, was at any rate simple. "Don't tell *me* of ladies and gentlemen being intimate *friends*, or any such rubbish. I know the world, and have known it a good many years. It's marriage or ———;" and he filled up the blank by knitting his brows and giving a sharp fierce nod. Moreover, he did really hate Effie. Sparks didn't mind having what he considered a lark even at the risk of doing her serious harm; but Alfred Holmes *wanted* to do her harm, and had been watching his opportunity for years. Surely Sparks knew better than to show the stolen postscript *to him*. Yes, he *knew* better; but young gentlemen who read other people's letters are not to be trusted too far.

"By the way," said the playful banker, "I found out a rum little game yesterday."

"Did you? why where were you yesterday? I thought you always went to chapel like a good little boy, that 'pa' and 'ma' might see you weren't in mischief," said Holmes.

"Well, I was at chapel, and the little game's at chapel, and that's the fun of it."

"Not much fun at chapel, I should think; what was it?"

"Why it's a little—I don't know what to call it—not, of course, flirtation, and much less anything worse—but, at any rate, a little affair between a parson and a very proper young lady. Would you like to know the particulars?"

"Just as you like," said Holmes, "but it isn't much in my way."

"Not much, perhaps," said his young friend, with a grin; "but what do you think of that for a young parson with a wife and family?" and he handed the postscript to Mr. Holmes.

"What the devil's this?" said Holmes, with a ferocity that almost frightened Spark out of his self-possession.

"That? It's a bit of paper with some writing on it. Give it me back. It isn't much in your way, is it?" said Sparks.

"And who's this damned scoundrel with a foreign name?" asked Holmes, white with rage and the fiendish torturing joy of gratified hatred. "I'll get to the bottom of this, you young——"

"No don't," said Sparks, interrupting him, "don't call names; and especially don't call a young lady names. But, by Jove! old friend, you *are* in a tantrum. What the deuce does it matter to you?"

"No, indeed; but it shall matter to somebody

else. But who is this damned foreigner she's off with; where is he, what is he?"

"Foreigner! Off with! what do you mean?" said Sparks, with delightful innocence.

"Why, I should think you don't pretend not to know what this bit of paper means, eh?" said Holmes.

"Means? It's a little joke about something or other, of course. That's what I told you at first. Here, give me the paper," said Sparks.

"Well, you *are* a fool. But of course it's all gammon; you know all about it. At any rate I'll just take a copy of this precious document, if the Bank can spare a slip of paper."

He copied it, and handed the original back to Sparks.

"Now, what do you think it means?" said the young gentleman.

"Why, it means that that shopwoman means to go off, with a false name, with some damned German—that's what it means."

Sparks roared with laughing, till Holmes took hold of his arm and shook him.

"Now then, are you going out of your mind?" he said.

"Lord bless you, no," said Sparks, "not if I can help it; but you are such a loving uncle; and I can't help laughing at the 'damned foreigner.' Why, it's our parson, the Rev. Frederick Rivers, mild as milk, meek as Moses, tame as a tabby cat, innocent as a new-born lamb. Now, what was the use of getting in a passion? I told you it was only a little game."

"Well, parson or not, it's not a little game that I mean Effie to play at, if I can help it," said Effie's uncle, inspired with a new affection and a disinterested anxiety for his niece's welfare. "I shall just walk over to Islington, and see her father about it."

"Mind what you are up to," said Sparks, a little alarmed at the unexpected form his joke was assuming; "you'll find Rivers a pretty tough customer; and if you threaten or bully him, he'll be torn to pieces before he'll give in."

"Well, we'll see; good morning. By the way, you can swear that's the parson's handwriting?"

"I should think I can, indeed; good-bye."

Sparks sat meditating for awhile when his friend had gone. It was rather a mistake, he thought, to have said anything about the matter to that grim old bear; his hug was not exactly the caress to be mistaken for affection. "However, it can't be helped. If it's all right, it doesn't matter who knows it; and if it isn't all right, that's their fault and not mine," said Sparks to himself. So he put Fritz's postscript into his purse again, for the entertainment of the pious circle which he was to join in the evening.

Meanwhile Alfred Holmes, Esq., stalked on to the shop of his long unvisited brother, Robert Holmes. Disappointed and broken-spirited, Robert looked so worn and old that even Alfred was alarmed and almost grieved.

"Good morning, Robert," said Alfred; "you don't look quite up to the mark to-day. How are you, and how's the wife and family?"

"Oh, much as usual, thank you, brother," said Robert.

"You'll be surprised to see me," said Alfred, "and I wish my business were agreeable; but we can't control these people, and at any rate I thought I ought to let you know."

"What is it?" said Robert; "haven't I troubles enough?"

"You'd be a very remarkable man, Robert, if you hadn't," said his brother. "But though I'm grieved at what I have to tell you, I'm not surprised. I knew that place in the City would bring Effie to grief."

"I'm sure Effie seems happy enough," said her father; "what do you mean?"

'Ah, happy indeed;" and the little new-born pity died in his heart as he remembered his niece's scornful letter, and his own detected hypocrisy; "but let's go into the house—we can't talk these matters over in a public shop."

They went into the house. "Mother" was

there, and rose to go when the two brothers entered.

"No, no, Emma, don't go," said Robert; "it's something about Effie—stop and hear it."

"Well," said Alfred, "it's no use putting the matter off; talking wont mend it. But Effie's assumed a false name for the sake of disguise, and made a secret appointment with some man, who seems to be a foreigner. I'm told it's the minister of the chapel she goes to. It's likely enough; I believe parsons are the meanest scamps alive."

Neither father nor mother could speak a word, while with stony indifference Alfred Holmes, Esq., drew from his pocket-book the copy of Fritz's postscript—and read with solemn emphassis—

"As to the name, I had almost forgotten that important matter. The disguise will be better if you change *both* names—*Julia* Hope for instance, instead of Effie Hope, which is too like Effie Holmes. But there's plenty of time for that, which is, indeed, one of the last arrangements we need make. Thine, Fritz."

"The friend who gave me that," said Alfred, "saw Effie drop it, and picked it up himself. At least, he picked up the paper that this was copied from."

Still father and mother sat without a word. They dared not trust themselves to speak; above all they could not speak to each other, or speak at all about

Effie and this new dark-looking mystery, before that cold-hearted, cruel man, who never entered their doors but with bitter reproaches or evil tidings. At last, with the utmost effort, Robert said—

"I wish, Alfred, it were your good fortune sometimes to visit us when you have good news to bring. However, we'd better know this, if it is so; and we'll inquire. We can't talk about it now."

"No; and I won't stay any longer. It's a bad business, Robert, and I'm sorry for you. Good-bye! Don't trouble to come into the shop; I can find my way."

And still the two sat silent—stunned. Effie, their pretty queen, so good and brave and true, as they thought her—had it come to this? To what? They could not understand it; but it must be bad if Uncle Alfred had thought it worth while to be interested in it and to bring the news. But they had never spoken a single word of doubt, or fear, or blame of Effie, and it was hard to begin.

"Father, speak," said the wife, kissing him, and putting her arm round his neck; "say something—it will relieve you. What must we do?"

"Oh, mother!"

He could say no more; but those two words were better than the utter dumbness that had been choking him. He put his head on his hands, and wept and sobbed in a convulsion of agony. His wife sat by him with her hand on his shoulder. It was no use speaking yet; it was better for his grief to have its way. She knew that Effie was more than life to him—his joy and pride and comfort. She knew that her death would kill him; and even death would have been better than shame.

"Don't cry so much, darling," said his wife, in a little while; "perhaps it's all a mistake. Effie *cannot* be so cruel and wicked. Alfred doesn't make the best of our misfortunes, and he's very vexed with Effie for being so independent. Hadn't you better send for Effie?"

"Yes, mother, yes," said Robert; "I don't believe a word against Effie—nothing could make me. And yet I don't know what to think. I'll send for her."

So he wrote a short note:—

"Effie, my own darling, come home to us directly; we're in great trouble. Come directly—directly!"

He quite forgot to sign it, but sent it at once by the errand-boy to Wood Street. It seemed an age before Effie came. He had no doubt that if she came all would be well—he felt sure she would come. And yet—if she were already gone with the false name, and the yet more false companion. At last she came, bursting into the room.

"Father, what's the matter? What new trouble have you, poor, dear father?"

"Oh! Effie, my queen, this will kill me," and he could speak no more; she was in his arms, and he was sobbing and weeping as if his heart was breaking indeed.

"Mother, what is it?" said Effie.

It was long before they could grow calm enough for any sort of explanation; but at last Mrs. Holmes made her understand that her uncle had been, and brought a copy of a letter to her which a friend of his had found in the street, and shown to him.

"Yes," said Effie; "most wicked man. Let me see the letter. I know what it is—I never dreamed that human beings could be so fiendishly cruel."

She gave what explanation she could, and promised to send the letter of which what Uncle Alfred brought was only a postscript. They knew, of course, how often Effie was at the Riverses' house, and that she regarded it as another home. They were half jealous, indeed, of the new friends who were so dear to her. Moreover, Mr. Holmes was *not* "a man of the world," and was therefore incapable of seeing vice everywhere, even in the very heart of virtue. But he was puzzled by these intimacies and confidences; and "Thine, Fritz," seemed to him dangerously unconventional. Effie he knew was good and pure, nor could he doubt her most trusted and best-loved friends; but people will talk, and they don't believe in genuine friendship and disinterested affection. And Effie's literary relationship to Fritz Mr. Holmes could scarcely understand.

"Do you often write to one another in this way, Effie?" said her mother.

"I'm so often there, mother, it isn't necessary; but I write whenever I like, just as if he were my brother, or as if I were writing to father."

"Well, darling, I don't understand it; it will be long before we get over this shock. You must come and stay a day or two with us, if you can. Bring Mr. Rivers's letters, and let us see them, and talk it all over."

So that was agreed upon, and Effie went back to the City to get leave of absence, and returned that night to stay at Islington until Thursday. Whatever they might think of Effie's prudence, and it was only in the first moments of alarm that they doubted that, her father and mother were quite certain that she had never contemplated anything like that which uncle Alfred had led them to fear. For the first time since his misfortunes, Robert Holmes went that very afternoon to his prosperous brother's house. He would not sit; he had few words to say, he wanted to say them and begone.

"Alfred," he said, "you came to my house this morning, with the malice of a devil, to ruin our happiness and blast the reputation of my child. You knew there was no ground for fearing what you pretended to believe. You have never, since my trouble, entered our house without leaving tears and misery behind you. Never enter my house again, Alfred;

and be sure that if there be a just God in heaven, you'll suffer bitterly, bitterly, for the misery and shame you have brought on me."

With that Robert left the house. It was all very well for Alfred to sneer, but in his inmost soul he felt the curse already working; and it was many hours before he regained his wonted composure, and could enter with his accustomed serenity of coldness into the routine of his daily occupations.

The little party at the Joneses, assembled in due course at half-past six o'clock. There was the customary tea and talk, and then "a little music," and whatever could be devised for getting through two or three hours without approaching worldliness. At last dulness would assert its supremacy; and the small stock of subjects comparatively general having been exhausted, the elder members of the party returned, as by a fatal necessity, to "chapel."

"By the way," said Sparks, "I picked up this in the street yesterday. I show it you in confidence. It looks very much like Mr. Rivers's writing; I can't make it out."

Mr. Jones was certain of the handwriting, so was Mr. Lush. And what did they think of the written matter?

"Well, I should think Parkinson's eyes will be opened now," said Lush.

"Are you going to take the sacrament from that

man's hands any more?" said Mrs. Lush. "Oh, poor, poor Mrs. Rivers; *you're* a suffering creature, I know."

There was much pantomime on the subject, groaning, resolving, protesting—nearly everything but knowing the merits of the case. At any rate, Lush was to call next morning on Mr. Parkinson, and lay the case before him; and meanwhile, the ladies knew what to do with Effie.

Mr. Lush called on Mr. Parkinson the next day, and showed him Fritz's note.

"What do you think of *that*, Mr. Parkinson?"

"Most extraordinary; where did you find it?"

"Mr. Sparks saw Miss Holmes drop it, and he picked it up, and very properly gave it to us."

"So you really approve of what Mr. Sparks did, Mr. Lush? Do you know that you've been simply receiving stolen goods?"

"Stolen goods!"

"Yes, sir. Is this letter, which I mean to restore to its proper owner, *yours?* Is it Mr. Sparks's? Mr. Sparks is a detestable sneak; and, to tell you the truth, I don't think you people who listen to him are much better. If I hear another syllable of this impudent slander, I'll put Sparks into the hands of my solicitor. For shame, Mr. Lush; a man of your age ought to know better. Good day."

Lush had scarcely gone when Parkinson put on his hat and went forthwith to Goulburns' Bank. Of course he found Sparks there.

"I just want a word with you, Mr. Sparks, in private," said Parkinson.

"Certainly, sir," said Sparks.

"You found the *postscript* of a letter, Mr. Lush tells me, from Mr. Rivers to Miss Holmes; you read the letter and reposted it," said Parkinson, making a lucky guess; "you stole—*stole* the postscript, and have been making a mean, cowardly, ungentlemanly use of it. Will you settle the matter with me or with my solicitor?"

"I don't understand you, sir," said Sparks.

"Don't you? Then I'm not in a hurry, and I'll wait till you do."

"Well, Mr. Parkinson, if you've anything to say, it's a pity to have a solicitor."

"Just as you like," said Parkinson.

"Besides," said Sparks, "it was quite in confidence I mentioned the matter to Mr. Lush; he had no right to tell you that I saw Miss Holmes drop the letter."

"He did tell me," said the immovable Parkinson; "one sneak ought never to be such a fool as to trust another sneak."

"What do you propose? What do you want?" stammered out Sparks.

"A full confession and a complete apology."

Sparks hesitated.

"Just as you like, Mr. Sparks; as you thought proper to publish your utterly detestable meanness to a whole roomfull of people, it doesn't much matter what you choose to do. I really want to spare Mr. Rivers pain; but if you don't choose to help me in that, I'll add the additional allowance to you also. Just as you like."

"I don't see that it's any business of yours, Mr. Parkinson," said the letter-stealer.

"Well, I know Mr. Rivers, and Mrs. Rivers, and Miss Effie pretty well, and so I think it my duty to spare them all the annoyance I can. But it's as you like, Mr. Sparks."

"Well, sir, I don't mind apologizing. I'm very sorry."

"Yes, Mr. Sparks, apologizing must be as easy as stealing; but I must have it in writing; black and white. You know very well what your defamation of Mr. Rivers and Miss Holmes amounts to, and it must be stopped."

The unhappy Sparks produced paper and pen and ink; and Parkinson, prince of deacons, wrote as follows:—

"I confess that I saw Miss Effie Holmes drop a letter in St. George's Road on Sunday last. I picked up the letter; I read it; I took out the postscript, which was written on a separate piece of paper, and stole it. I showed it to several persons. I acknowledge that this was most ungentlemanly and abominable conduct; and I hereby apologize to Miss Holmes for the same."

"Now, Mr. Sparks, that's pretty clear—quite true and right. Date it and sign it—that's all."

Sparks hesitated.

"Well, you're very considerate; it's not quite all. You must write on this paper, 'This is the postscript I stole,' and sign your name to the endorsement."

"And what shall you do with it?"

"Send it to Miss Holmes."

There was a little more talk and explanation, in which Parkinson spoke his mind; and then Sparks signed and dated and wrote as the deacon required. Parkinson enclosed all to Effie, with a note; assuring her that he had taken care Mr. Rivers should be spared the pain of knowing of this most abominable wickedness, and that he (Parkinson) was almost glad of *any* opportunity to express his profound respect both for the Riverses and Miss Holmes.

So ended Sparks's little joke. And Effie? Yes, she *was* capable of friendship. "Father," she said, "I *do* love Mr. Rivers more than I can tell. I believe he loves me. I am sure our love is true and good. I should be as wicked as I should be miserable if I tried to alter it. But if you doubt whether it is right, let *Mrs.* Rivers decide."

Effie knew right well what Hetty would have decided.

In this poor cold world it is hard to find people who can truly *love;* it is even harder to find people who can really and heartily *be loved.*

CHAPTER XIX.

STOPPING THE SUPPLIES.

It was some years before Fritz knew of the danger from which Mr. Parkinson's honest firmness had saved him. If Sparks's wickedness and treachery had taken the form that he half wished it would take, Mr. Veneer's prediction would most likely have been fulfilled, and St. George's Road become "vacant." Courageous enough for himself, Fritz was easily terrified when his friends were threatened; and he would never have consented to expose Effie to the annoyance of unchecked gossip, or the scarcely smaller annoyance of a public vindication. Moreover, would any vindication have sufficed? True love and genuine affection can never be discovered by the dissecting-knife of vulgar curiosity.

Meantime there were more Church-meetings, notwithstanding Fritz's *ultimatum*. It was of course useless to propose any more resolutions like that of Farmer and White; but it was quite possible for a disorderly "member" to get up and resign his membership in a loud voice, and with his reasons for so doing. Moreover, Bung and Lush resigned their deaconship; and it became evident more and more that the "Church at St. George's Road Chapel" was applying the ultimate dissenting test for the discovery of truth, and was "stopping the supplies." When a considerable number of persons refused to pay their pew-rents, it was not easy to see that much new light had been thrown on the questions at issue between Fritz and his flock; but it was very easy to see that new and difficult financial problems might present themselves in Fritz's domestic economy.

Many of the discontented took refuge with the Rev. John Veneer, many more with the Rev. E. Dickson. They were received, not perhaps with enthusiasm, but with the interest attaching to the people who are continually reminding us even by their mere presence of our own superiority. Some of the young men who had heard Fritz with patience and attention, if not with pleasure, now went nowhere; their friends assured them that it was wrong and dangerous to attend St. George's Road, and they found out for themselves that it was disagreeable to attend Dickson or Veneer. They might have been content enough to go with their friends, for the sake of peace, wherever they chose to wander; but to be congratulated for that reason on their orthodoxy and spiritual religion was more than they could stand. So they stayed at home, read the newspapers, went walks, anything in fact but church or chapel. A parcel of quarrelsome people, constantly trying to damage one another, and doing dirty tricks of which any man in business would be ashamed—what was the use of bothering with them!

Meantime Fritz and Hetty were exposed to that terrible temptation which the voluntary principle furnishes in its strongest and worst form. Fritz's salary was to be in inverse proportion to his honesty. "Preach what Bung and Lush, and Farmer and White believe, and have 500*l.* a year. Preach what you believe yourself, and be a beggar;" that was the alternative. It doesn't seem hard to decide, at least at a distance, but "distance lends enchantment to the view." To brave the fury of an enraged mob, to awe them by a calm undaunted presence, to sway them by the mystic force of words, and conquer them by the irresistible might of weakness, even that had been an easy task compared with the labour that was to be laid on Fritz. Even suffering much more acute he could have more easily endured, if he might have borne it in the open daylight, surrounded by sympathizing friends, cheered by their love and strengthened by their approval. But now friend after friend forsook him, hard and bitter words, cruel insults, and malicious calumnies gave a sterner hardness to the daily conflicts of his life. And with the vexations which were coming upon him more and more thickly he could not even reason. Rent and the price of bread and meat are deaf to every argument. He could, in a manner, blame nobody about him; and, after all, that was a comfort. The real wrongdoers had disturbed the peace and gone; it was no use finding fault with the few who remained true and firm. Even their true friendship had its bitterness; for how hard it was, Fritz thought, for Cave and Parkinson to feel fastened to a sinking ship. He felt wronging his very friends by letting them love and help him; and yet he sometimes comforted himself with the reflection that he would have tried to do as they did if he had been in their places. And when he tried to separate in his thought their courage and fidelity from the good which that courage and fidelity brought to himself, he could never doubt that it was better for them, as it was better for him, to prefer truth and a good conscience to ease or popularity. Sometimes he ventured to tell them so. But far oftener he was silenced by the thought that from *him* the praise of their fidelity might seem scarcely better than an appeal to their compassion. It was almost impossible, too, amid all the calumnies that had been uttered against him, to avoid the appearance of an unbecoming directness of application even in his sermons. He shrunk with the acutest sensitiveness from any intrusion of his own sufferings, or affectation of the superior sanctity of a martyr. And yet, how could he overlook the promises to the persecuted and distressed? While, even against his utmost effort, his voice would sometimes tremble as he prayed for those who "in this transitory world are in any sorrow, need, or adversity."

Johnson and a few of his most valued minister-friends were still faithful, and they could almost make him forget his trouble sometimes in their genial society and hearty sympathy. Even if they had before thought him indiscreet, they could not regret now, tempted as he was on every side, that he had so heartily and entirely committed himself to what he believed the cause of truth and liberty, that any compromise would have been so utterly disgraceful as to be virtually impossible. Some, also, who might almost, from their experience and ability, have "patronized" him without offence, were content to be friends. Of course the majority "erred on the safe side." Veneer, at luncheon in Paternoster Row, feeding like a parasitic animal on the respectable publisher, repeated with embellishments and illustrative examples every silly slander he had heard of the minister of St. George's Road. Some of Mr. Dickson's flock, zealous for truth, stood in front of Fritz's chapel on Sunday mornings, warning strangers that it was Socinian and Popish. Even the Principal of his old College, having made his peace with the religious world, thought it necessary to administer a few gratuitous insults to the pupil who followed the example of independence which he himself, in his stronger days, had set.

Well, it was no use grumbling; and at any rate something must be done. No economy can make one pound go as far as two, and the piety of Fritz's congregation had turned his two into considerably less than one. He must get his own living. Preaching the Gospel was not a trade; and if those to whom he preached couldn't or wouldn't keep him, he couldn't alter the article he had to supply to meet the demand of average customers. He must keep himself by some independent work, and take for his preaching exactly what salary his people thought fit to give him.

Getting a living! It is hard work for anybody in a crowded country and a fiercely competing age. But a minister getting his living otherwise than by "the ministry" has to contend with peculiar difficulties. There are very few occupations for which he is fit. Moreover, to try to make an independent living is an acknowledgment of "reduced circumstances," of "having seen better days," which few people care to make. At the same time Fritz's circumstances unquestionably *were* reduced, and he could no longer live on what his people gave him. Was not that the very object of Bung and Lush, to starve him out of St. George's Road; and were they not lurking about in the neighbouring chapels waiting for the exhausted foe to surrender? Fritz felt that in this battle he was fighting not for himself alone, but for the liberty of every Christian minister to preach the truth according to his conscience; and he was determined, like the first preachers of the Gospel, to live to preach, not to preach for a living.

The first attempt was to take pupils; that he was sure he could do. It needed no new outlay; it would be sufficiently in harmony with his ordinary work to be comparatively a very slight hindrance.

"A graduate of the University of London receives a few pupils to board, and educate, and prepare for University and Civil Service examinations. For particulars apply to the Rev. F. R., Post Office, St. George's Road, London."

Miserable delusion! "*receives* a few pupils?" Nothing of the kind; only wishes he did. With charming regularity, three times every week, did those few lines present themselves to the British public in the columns of "*the Times*." The people who read them little knew how anxiously every morning's delivery of letters was waited for by "the Rev. F. R.," in hope that it might bring some answer to his advertisement. Sometimes an answer came. "Q. Z. would be much obliged if the Rev. F. R. would kindly forward a prospectus." But sending a prospectus was a very different thing from receiving a pupil; the prospectuses were many, printed with the utmost neatness, on the best of notepaper, but the pupils as yet were none. Meantime Fritz could write; and he liked that far better even than teaching. Writing, too, was, as yet, far more profitable; and, in fact, just paid for the costly advertisements that brought no pupils. But, writing with an easy mind out of the mere fulness of the heart is one thing; and writing for bread, embarrassed and disheartened, is another thing. Sometimes, when he came into his study after an unusually early breakfast, just in the very mood for writing, determined to make a long day of fruitful work, the post would bring a manuscript, of appearance all too familiar, with a slip of paper enclosed—"Returned, with regret—Editor of ——." "What is the use of writing?" he would think. "I work hard, I'm willing to do anything. I don't find fault with my congregation: I don't want to be a trouble to them. I only want work, and to be paid for it, like the poorest workman in Edwards's factory; and I can't get it. 'Returned, with regret,' God help me."

So that day's work would be spoiled. Memory and imagination alike roaming over a dreary desert of disappointments, what writing could be done that anybody would care to read? A few paragraphs, pointless and dull, composed with infinite difficulty, amid the wandering of sad thoughts and gloomy forebodings, and then Fritz would put paper and pen aside and try to read; or he would sit and talk with Hetty in the dining-room; or he would walk over to Johnson's—anything to forget how unhappy and unsuccessful he was.

Sometimes the post would bring an anonymous

letter full of calumnies and bitterness, or a letter of abuse from some dissatisfied "member." Sometimes a letter would come full of love and regrets, but none the less containing the now so common resignation of all connexion with St. George's Road Chapel and its minister. He felt almost as if smitten by paralysis. No thoughts would come or stay, excepting, indeed, those which came unbidden and refused to go. How often he asked himself if indeed he were right, if these evil days were not God's judgment upon his error and blindness. Even wicked calumniators could sting and hurt him, but they never made him waver in his determination. Whoever was right, *they* were clearly wrong. But could those be wrong who evidently were pained to grieve him, who almost wept when they bade him farewell, who seemed to tear themselves away from him *because* they loved him, and felt how easily he could fascinate them into error? Could both they and he be right? Yes, surely—not both right in forms of doctrine or intellectual processes; but right, equally, in heart and in the honest desire to please God. And yet they must separate, and he must do his work, more and more, alone. Sometimes, even friends would leave him, "for the sake of their children;" the children whom he had baptized, who had sat on his knees as trustfully as if he had been their father, who had run, hundreds of times, to meet and kiss him. And they must be taken from him, lest he should persuade them to trust too much to the love of their Father in Heaven! Hatred robbed him of his people, and so did love; some left him because he could not persuade them of what he believed to be the truth, and some because they were quite sure that he could. It was, at any rate, more and more necessary for him to get a living in some way quite independent of his chapel. Get a living! How could that be done with a breaking heart, and an ever-increasing pressure of disappointment and grief? "The spirit of a man will sustain his infirmity, but a wounded spirit who can bear?"

But I will not attempt to describe the hard struggle of those dark days, and better days were coming. The chapel in St. George's Road was being rapidly emptied of the dissatisfied, and the new-comers were all aware of what they were coming to, and came because they liked it. At last, moreover, the advertisements began to be of use; and a few pupils found their way to the house of "the Rev. F. R.," and Fritz's spirits, always elastic, were not slow to recover from the pressure of hard times. His intellect became brighter. He wrote with greater ease, and power, and even brilliancy. The manuscripts "declined, with regret," were fewer and fewer, and he seemed at last in a fair way of making his own living.

Moreover, was Fritz to be the only person in the

world to experience the grief and hardship of "stopped supplies?" Why should not Bung have a share of the same wholesome discipline, or Lush experience the blessedness of them that mourn? Bung was too weak to be ruined. He could go through the ordinary routine of business very profitably; but he had no brains for speculation either on the right side or the wrong. But Lush had many irons in the fire; he was always looking out for a profitable investment; and hitherto he had managed so to balance his risks, that he had never lost ruinously, and had for the most part been exceedingly lucky. With his increasing fortune, and his persistent good luck, his speculations became more and more dangerous; his greatest risks had indeed been his greatest successes, and he began to think that there were other things, much better than fair ladies, which faint heart never won. He had just made a most lucky hit, unusually lucky even for him; so he had an unusual amount of uninvested money lying idle, and idleness in money Lush rightly considered a most costly and extravagant vice. He was therefore exactly the man for Mr. George Plymouth, who, being eminently speculative, and beyond measure ingenious, and at the present moment deplorably low in ready cash, was looking out, not for an investment but for an investor.

Mr. George Plymouth, was like Mr. Lush, an auctioneer. He was, like Mr. Lush, an auctioneer, *et cetera*—a man with many irons in the fire, mostly other people's irons. And why blame him? He *had* no irons of his own, or of course he would have used them; but he had *copper* of his own, so entirely his own that it was absolutely impossible to part with it, or even to show it. It was as yet (hypothetically) in the bowels of Cornwall, and really in the deep, fruitful, unexhausted, inexhaustible mine of Mr. George Plymouth's lying invention. Mr. George Plymouth was, like Lush, abdominous; but he was short, and his flesh was firmer and less jelly-like than the flesh of Lush. His head was large, while Lush's head was small; and his intellectual superiority was proved by the fact that, though Lush could make a fortune out of impudence and a very little, Plymouth could make a fortune out of impudence and nothing at all. Like Lush, Mr. George Plymouth had for a little while attended St. George's Road Chapel; like Lush, he had left because Mr. Rivers was not sound; and he, Plymouth, would put up with nothing that was not pure Gospel. Like Lush, he now attended the ministry of Mr. Dickson; and so did Mr. Jones.

Mr. Lush introduced Mr. George Plymouth to Mr. Jones, and the three became exceedingly friendly. They were often at each other's houses, and a supper at Mr. George Plymouth's was worth going to. Of course no one cares to eat a supper; but it's gratifying to see it there—fish, soup, joints, poultry, game, pastry, jellies, creams, sparkling wines, wines of all sorts, punch, everything. The grandest dinners Lush ever gave were nothing to Plymouth's suppers; and Plymouth could carve without splashing himself, and never pinned a table-napkin under his chin like Lush. But Plymouth had rather an unfair advantage, for he had years ago been landlord of "The Cross Keys," where there was, in his time, a first-rate ordinary; and Plymouth knew what was what. At any rate, he knew that Lush and Jones were much more chatty and cheerful, and much more disposed to look hopefully into a copper-mine, after a liberal supply of champagne and punch. And, after all, it was not such extravagance as it looked. Plymouth was living entirely on credit, and had quite determined to retrench in a quiet continental town as soon as the spare cash of Mr. Lush and Mr. Jones had passed into his own pocket. Besides, his accomplished daughters were anxious to perfect themselves in German and French.

It came on by degrees. In a moment of confidence he told his friends how he had made his fortune—it was in mines. Soon after there was, he found, a chance of a new investment of the same kind; and he meant to take advantage of it. Splendid specimens of ore at his office in the City—would they like to see it? If they had money lying idle, he thought it a capital chance; though of course it was no business of his. They *would* like to see it. Then they would like to take shares. I'm not able to explain the different stages of the transaction; they were as complicated as deceit could make them; but I know that all the idle money of Lush and Jones seeking investment found its way somehow into Plymouth's pocket; and that when he was safe in a quiet German town, Mr. Lush and Mr. Jones found themselves swindled and ruined, with mining liabilities as deep as the deepest mine that was ever dug. As to Mr. Jones, he was a most innocent and unhappy dupe, greatly to be pitied. Yet he was better off, as he deserved to be, than Lush. His wife had a private fortune, settled on herself; not large enough to admit of their old ease and style, but enough for comfort. Lush was a mere beggar.

The first cut the world gave the Joneses—and indeed the last, for they were above want—was administered by Mr. Sparks, in the form of a letter to Miss Jones.

"GOULBURNS',
"*City*.

"MY DEAR MISS JONES,—You may be sure I was very much grieved and mortified when I heard of your papa's losses through that scoundrel, Plymouth. We would have warned him, if we had imagined he was in any danger; for we know only too well about that swindling humbug. However, it is done now and can't be undone. Plymouth will not visit England till this affair has blown over; and he always takes care to keep out of the reach of law.

"But I most of all regret your papa's misfortunes, though, perhaps, it is selfish in me to say so, because of the effect they must have on our relation to each other. I need not tell you, my dear Miss Jones, how much I love you; but love and poverty are very unsuitable companions—it is the very expression your papa made use of when I waited upon him to ask his consent that I should ask your hand and heart.

"I have been accustomed to a stylish life, and we should feel poverty insupportable, so I will not subject *you* to so much suffering; you, whom I love so dearly. I shall always wish you well, and remember you with respect and affection; but under your altered circumstances we can never marry. Is it not better for both of us?

"I return your letters in a small parcel, by Parcels' Delivery Company, and remain,

"My dear Miss Jones,

"With the most respectful affection,

"Yours sincerely,

"*Miss Jones.*" "J. SPARKS.

It didn't cost Sparks much to write this letter. He was tired of his pretty little sweetheart long ago. And what could her father say? That pretty sentiment about poverty and love was really his own, bitterly as he wished that he could recall it. And after all, Miss Jones had only lost a heartless scapegrace; and he was better lost than won. But he was to her the very man, her ideal of all manliness. She believed what she could not see; and glorified him with every virtue and accomplishment that she wished him to have. And so she mourned according to her love and trust, not according to his worthlessness.

The Lushes were made to understand their altered position in society by a far rougher method—their instructors were the suburban tradespeople in the neighbourhood of St. George's Road. And, indeed, they owed Mr. Lush a lesson; a return of frankness. On the occasion of stopping Mr. Rivers's supplies, had he not made the most careful inquiries, and hinted to them the most solemn warnings? "Were they aware that the minister's circumstances were seriously altered? He thought it right to tell them of that lamentable fact; he should like them to deal candidly iwth him under similar circumstances, and he tried to do to others as he should like them to do to him." Of course, they were much obliged. They quite saw to the bottom of Mr. Lush's meaning; but that was neither here nor there. A suburban shopkeeper can't afford to be magnanimous; he has generally a wife and children. He can't afford to give credit; at least, he can't always—he can't when he doesn't choose. So they all sent in their "little bills" to the Rev. Frederick Rivers; due or not according to the usual terms of credit and payment. They had themselves heavy payments to make; they were very sorry, but—in fact they meant to have their money forthwith. Of course, it was embarrassing, it might have been fatal. Fortunately, it was not fatal.

But now it was Mr. Lush's turn to experience the affectionate and delicate attentions of the suburban shopkeepers. The four principal drapers were riding on horseback together one Saturday evening, according to their brotherly custom—their names were Brown, Jay, Pipe, and Thorn.

"Did you hear of old Lush's smash-up, Brown?" said Jay.

"What about Lush?" said Brown; "he's one of mine."

Brown was the chief draper, but the worst rider: and was too far behind to hear distinctly what Jay was saying. He had a quick ear, however, for the name of a customer.

"What about Lush, what about Lush, eh, Mr. Jay?" he said, riding up.

"Why, the poor old boy's gone to pot, that's all. Is he one of yours?" said Jay.

"I'll send his bill in to-morrow," said Brown.

"To-morrow? Why to-morrow's Sunday," said Pipe.

"Oh dear, so it is," said Brown, "what a pity."

Brown had left St. George's Road Chapel because he'd seen Mr. Rivers in a railway carriage one Sunday afternoon, thereby breaking the fourth commandment.

"Wont Monday do?" said Thorn, who rather enjoyed "chaffing" the pious Brown.

"Don't you think it rather hard on him?" said Jay.

"Well, if I don't somebody else will, and why should I miss my chance?" said Brown.

"Does he owe you much?" said Jay.

"Perhaps five pounds: luckily it's only the beginning of a quarter, or it might have been fifty," said Brown.

At any rate, lucky or unlucky, Brown was seized on Monday morning with serious and dangerous and unexpected poverty. The symptoms of this painful malady were not apparent to the ordinary observer. The shop was full of customers, the stock was abundant, the assistants busy and cheerful. No gloom as of approaching dissolution darkened the establishment. With undiminished soapiness did the smiling Brown himself glide from customer to customer, with a pretty compliment or a polite inquiry. About the middle of the morning, too, Mrs. Brown drove to the shop from the country house, in the smartest of pony-carriages, with a little page behind, all buttons. It was plain, from a single glance at her beaming countenance, that the tender-hearted Brown had concealed at any rate from her the impending bankruptcy. On a sea of crinoline she floated upstairs to the show-room and began forthwith to examine and exhibit those miracles of millinery which she had been to Paris the week before (in a City omnibus) to select. And yet amid all this seeming prosperity and skin-deep cheerfulness, Brown was in imminent peril; and nothing could save him from ruin and disgrace, but the sum of four pounds, sixteen shillings and fourpence, due to Brown, draper and milliner, from Lush, auctioneer. At least scarcely due; for Mr. Lush never pretended to pay oftener than once in six months and in ordinary circumstances Brown was quite offended if he did. "Oh, dear no, sir, let it go down in the bill," that soapy sinner would say, "we're sure to have many little trifles that will please the ladies when Mrs. Brown returns from Paris; we'll send the bill in half-yearly. Any time will do for that, Mr. Lush." Yes, under ordinary circumstances; but with impending bankruptcy delay might be fatal, and cash could not fail to become welcome long before the customary credit was over.

So the errand-boy brought a note to Mr. Brown as he glided, cat-like, from customer to customer.

"Please, sir, will that do, Miss Wilkins says?"

Brown reads to himself.

"Mr. Brown presents his respectful compliments to Mr. Lush and begs to call Mr. Lush's attention to his small account enclosed, amounting to £4 16*s.* 4*d.* Mr. Brown has some very heavy engagements this week, and would feel obliged if Mr. Lush would send a cheque by the bearer for the above amount."

Mr. Brown took a pen, underlined the words "*by the bearer*," fastened the envelope, wrote "*wait*" in the corner, gave the boy a receipt stamp, told him there would be an answer from Mr. Lush—and then glided about again, with soapy smile, as if the crisis of his fate were not come, and the fortunes of the great house of Brown were not depending upon the cheque "by bearer" for four-sixteen-four from Lush, auctioneer.

Mr. Lush was just leaving home, just coming out through the front door, when Brown's errand-boy came up and presented him with the affectionate letter which the draper had so smilingly approved. Lush put it into the letter-box unopened, shut the front door and was walking away, when the errand-boy interrupted him.

"Please, sir, I was to wait, Mr. Brown said."

"Wait? what for?"

"For an answer, sir."

"Oh! very well."

He went in-doors again and read Brown's letter. In his prosperous days he had been sharp enough himself; but none the less for that did he feel wounded and insulted by the sharpness of Brown. He wrapped up the money in paper, and gave it to the errand-boy with a note.

"Sir,—I am perfectly amazed at your demand. You'll never have another penny from me or anybody I can influence."

Brown was half-sorry he had sent for the money. Perhaps Lush hadn't "gone to pot" so completely as the draper thought. Perhaps Jay had made the worst of it that Brown might offend Lush, and Lush take his custom to Jay. What was to be done? Brown would have been the most consummate liar in all his parish, if it had not been for his wife. She soared so far above him in power of imagination and neatness of execution, that his mendacity seemed absolutely contemptible in comparison with hers. He called Mrs. Brown therefore from the show-room, and gave her Lush's note.

"All right, dear," she said; "it doesn't matter; I'm sure he's smashed up. However, I'll answer his letter, it won't take a minute."

"My dear Madam," she wrote to the wife of the auctioneer—"I deeply regret that, by an oversight, your account was sent in so much earlier than usual. It was another Mr. Lush's account that should have been demanded, and the mistake was entirely our clerk's. I the more regret the error as we hear you have suffered some losses through the dishonesty of ne we hoped better things of. Hoping you will accept this apology, I remain,

"My dear Madam,

"Yours truly,

"*Mr. Lush.*" "ISABELLA BROWN."

"What a liar that woman is," said Lush, when he read the letter.

Yes, she was indeed; and she hadn't taken pains. It was a poor, clumsy lie, a transparent lie that anybody could see through. But it didn't matter. Lush was done for. It wasn't worth while to use Mrs. Brown's talents for answering him; Brown himself could have lied well enough for that. At any rate, the four pounds sixteen shillings and fourpence, had been paid; the great house of Brown was rescued from ruin; and Mr. Lush had exactly three shillings and eightpence remaining of his last five-pound note.

We may let him alone now, and part company. He had not been without friends; but they were the friends of his prosperity. They measured him, as he measured everybody else, by his money. Now he had no money, and had he not, therefore, himself become nothing?

Meanwhile, the cheerful Sparks was making love to Effie's cousin, Matilda Holmes, eldest daughter of Alfred Holmes, Esq.

CHAPTER XX.

ALONE.

Fritz's spirits improved far more rapidly than his finances; for they had by no means yet regained their old position. Nevertheless, the tide had turned; the discontented had gone, and their places were being filled by friends and admirers. Pupils were not very remunerative, and the profits of tuition were scarcely worth its trouble; but literary work was far more profitable, and was, moreover, a positive delight. Above all, the coldness of the outside world seemed to have made home happier than ever. Even when Fritz was half-inclined to yield if he could to his enemies, that so the "stopping of supplies" might cease, and their old comforts return, Hetty was always unflinching.

"I know you're grieving about me, darling," she used to say, "and I'm sure you needn't. I don't care about these little privations; at least, not much. And at any rate we can't help it. We might as well steal what we want out of a shop as get it by *your* being dishonest."

"I'm sure, dearest," Fritz said, "I don't know what to do. It makes me utterly miserable when I think of what you would like and really need, and I *can't* give them to you. And yet *this* isn't our own fault. I've done many a wrong and silly thing, but it's not wrong or silly to preach the truth, and we may leave what comes of it to God."

But Hetty, brave and patient as she was, was far too frail and tender for the rough fight to which she was called with such people as Bung and Lush, and the rougher conflict still with the vexations of straitened circumstances. When the tradespeople, who had been so unselfishly warned by Lush of Fritz's reduced supplies, sent in their bills, and had to wait till the quarter had turned for payment, Hetty dared scarcely shew herself in the street. She knew she had done no wrong. Indeed, the most importunate of the petty shopkeepers was a man who owed eighteen months' pew rents, and refused to pay them because "Mr. Rivers didn't preach the Gospel." But for people to come for their money and go away without it seemed to Hetty disgraceful.

"You know we do owe it them, darling," she would say.

"Yes," said Fritz, "but there's no hurry; they've no business to teaze in this way. They daren't treat other customers so."

"But it's so horrid to pass their shops; I always

feel so hot, and walk so fast—indeed I never go out if I can help it."

"My darling little Hetty, you're a good girl; you're quite right to be so sensitive. But really is there one of our people in decent circumstances who hesitates to have quarterly bills? Is there any harm in it?"

"No, dearest, I am a stupid thing."

That indeed she wasn't; but she was very miserable. And yet it was not her fault that their income had been reduced by a full half, without a word of notice, or the possibility of preparation. It was not their fault that Lush had gone from shop to shop, creating a panic among the mean-spirited shopkeepers; who afterwards, in his own misfortunes, combined to complete his ruin. Hetty knew perfectly well that everybody would be paid, and that the tradespeople were very rude and ungenerous—but still——

Yes, that was not all. For Hetty had really loved some of the people who had gone; and their desertion and treachery had seemed to her like the piercing of a sword. It was all very well to say that Mr. Rivers was not sound, and that truth was more than friendship. So it was, but at any rate Hetty was lonely, and knew not whom to trust; and she felt quite as keenly for Fritz as for herself. She thought he had been *cruelly* treated; she knew he *felt* far more than he ever said. Nothing seemed to go right. Nobody seemed true. Honesty and courage seemed to lead only to poverty and grief.

Yet some were true; Parkinson and Cave, and always Effie—who indeed was one of themselves, never reckoned as a stranger. Parkinson was most gentle and considerate; and in fact growing more and more concerned about Hetty's pale, thin face, and ever increasing feebleness.

"Is your wife ill, Mr. Rivers?" he said to Fritz one day.

"I'm very anxious about her," Fritz said, "she's had too hard a life lately."

"I wish you'd let me ask our physician to call and see her."

"I don't know, Mr. Parkinson," said Fritz. "I'm very much obliged to you, but it might only alarm her and make her worse. Perhaps if we go on better at chapel she'll get stronger."

"Well, I hope so, most sincerely," said Parkinson; "but she's been abominably treated, and everybody can see how much she has felt it—far more than her cruel tormentors were worth."

"Yes, far more," Fritz said; "but I'll talk to her about it; I should be most thankful for advice. I'm much more alarmed than I care to confess even to myself."

That very evening when Fritz came home from the service—it was chapel night—the servant met him crying and frightened. "Mrs. Rivers," she said, "was very ill; they didn't know what to do with her."

He hurried upstairs; Hetty was already in bed, white as a ghost.

"What's the matter, darling?" he said, "are you very ill?"

"No, my pet; don't be frightened. I only fainted, and the servant didn't know what to do with me. But I'm better now; coming to bed was the best thing. I don't know how they managed to carry me up. They're very kind."

"How do you feel now, dearest? let me send for the doctor."

"No, thank you; not now, at any rate. Perhaps when it's all over, and baby is born, I shall be quite strong again. And yet I don't know; I feel very weak. I can't rouse myself. I'm very happy, my dearest pet, but yet I can't help crying and feeling low. Perhaps we had better have advice. Just as you like."

Fritz gave her such restoratives as he thought best, and sat by her till she was asleep; a quiet, placid sleep. He looked at her dear face, so thin and white, almost corpse-like, and he wondered he had been so slow to see the change that sorrow and care had made. He wrote at once to Parkinson, to ask that he would kindly send the physician he had recommended the next day.

The next morning the physician came. Parkinson had told him all about the Riverses; far too much for a favourable prognosis, as he looked at Hetty.

And yet there seemed to be no well-marked disease; there was a dreadful weakness, utter want of tone every way. But what could physic do? For some ten days Hetty was unable to rise, was scarcely able even to speak; she had no acute pain, but her prostration was so terrible that she sometimes lay for hours as if she was already dead. It was more than a month before she could venture downstairs; and then as Fritz looked at her, he began to know that it was only for a little while, only "to put her house in order because she must die, and not live."

He tried to put away this horrid fear, and sometimes when they were all three in the study together —Effie came every evening now, that Hetty might never be alone—and he was quietly reading some favourite book, the flush of pleasure or excitement would almost persuade him that his wife's face was becoming more like itself. But the flush soon passed away, and the awful paleness came back again, and the short excitement was followed by a reaction which seemed to threaten a return of the alarming prostration from which she had so slowly and so imperfectly recovered.

Fritz never left home till evening, when Effie could come and take his place. And how sad and changed the chapel services seemed when he looked into Hetty's corner, and felt that she would perhaps never be there again; never again to sing, to pray, to hear him preach the Gospel of the "Common Salvation;" never again to weep. How little had his persecutors considered that every blow they aimed at him was striking her; how little some of them would have cared. When she hid her tears, and bore herself bravely in the midst of Fritz's enemies, how proud and hard they thought her; and more than ever determined they were that they would make her wince, and him too, before their wicked work was finished. They had gained their end now. Nothing could bend her spirit, but it was all too easy to set it free from its frail and beautiful dwelling-place.

"Is Fritz very dull about me, darling?" said Hetty to Effie, one Sunday evening, when Fritz was at chapel.

They were sitting close together in the study; Hetty in an invalid chair, Effie on a stool by her side. Effie kissed the poor, thin face, but she could not speak a word.

"Is he, dearest—is he very dull? poor, darling Fritz."

"I know I shall never get better, my Effie," she went on in a little while, "and I must be content; I *am* content. But it cannot be wrong to tell our Father what we have thought and wished. I thought I should be able to bear up till these chapel-worries were over, and then be quite well and strong. We should have loved one another all the more for these troubles; and they *are* nearly over now. But it may not be, darling; *my* rest will come in another world."

"What are they doing now at chapel?" she said again, looking at the timepiece. "Seven o'clock; they will be singing the Psalms. What Psalms are they, Effie dearest?"

Effie opened the Prayer-book and read the Psalms for the eighth evening of the month. It was not easy to read such verses as these with a clear and steady voice:—

"The Lord comfort him when he lieth sick upon his bed, make Thou all his bed in his sickness.

"I said, Lord, be merciful unto me; heal my soul, for I have sinned against Thee.

"Like as the hart desireth the water-brooks, so longeth my soul after Thee, O God.

"My tears have been my meat day and night; while they daily say unto me, Where is now thy God?

"Why art thou so full of heaviness, O my soul; and why art thou so disquieted within me?

"O put thy trust in God, for I shall yet praise Him, which is the help of my countenance and my God."

"Yes, yes, Effie; so I shall, 'Where the wicked cease from troubling and where the weary are at rest.' I know the music they will be singing to those Psalms; I almost fancy I hear them," she said, leaning forward as if to listen—"all the parts—and Fritz's voice, too, quite plainly, singing, 'Why art thou so heavy, oh my soul?' Now it's over. I shall never hear it again, Effie. Poor, dear Fritz."

She leaned back again in her chair, and closed her eyes. Her lips moved, and Effie knew that her spirit was with Fritz, and that she was joining in the prayers at St. George's Road, as truly as if she were really sitting in the old corner where she had wept so many bitter tears, when her head was bowed before Him "who despiseth not the sighing of a contrite heart nor the desires of such as be sorrowful."

Soon she opened her eyes, and looked at Effie with unutterable love, and kissed her.

"We mustn't cry any more, darling; we must have cheerful faces for Fritz when he comes in. Let this Sunday supper be as much like old times as we can make it."

Fritz soon came. He seemed in better spirits than usual. There was some good chapel news to tell; he had received some little kindnesses, that were doubly precious after long coldness and neglect. Surely the clouds were breaking at last. And Hetty, too, seemed to rouse herself; she asked about nearly everybody at St. George's Road; she seemed more herself than she had ever been since she came downstairs after her last illness. In about a quarter of an hour Parkinson came in, merry as ever, but as gentle now and quiet as a girl, and he would not stay long.

"Good-bye, Mr. Parkinson," said Hetty; "we shall never be able to thank you enough for all your kindness."

"I am thanked more than enough already, Mrs. Rivers," he said; "get better as fast as you can; that will be the best thanks for all of us. Good-bye."

Why was he so strangely moved by that parting? Why did the "good-bye" sound so final? He could not tell. But he said to himself, "I'll just call in and ask the doctor to look round there pretty early to-morrow. God bless her. They've managed to kill her among them."

He stayed chatting with his friend the doctor far into the night, their talk returning continually to the Riverses. About one o'clock there was a ring at the door; the servants were gone to bed, and Parkinson ran to open it.

"Please will the doctor come to Mrs. Rivers directly?"

"Yes; is she worse?—is she very bad?"

"Oh, sir, I don't think she'll be alive when I get back," said the girl who had brought the message; "do come directly," she said, passionately weeping.

"Good night, Parkinson," said the doctor, "it's come at last."

So *that* was the work that Church-meetings, and

refractory deacons, and Veneers, and Dicksons had done. They had cast fresh light on no text of Holy Scripture, they had smoothed for no human being the rough path of common duty, they had brought no troubled spirit nearer to God; but they had saddened the brightest years of a good man's life, and they had brought as pure, and gentle, and loving a woman as ever breathed to an untimely grave. A lonely, desolate home, and four motherless children! So much evil had lying gossip, cruel slanders, and ignorant fanaticism wrought.

"Thou shalt not KILL."

Would it be wrong sometimes, even at a special Church-meeting, to offer up the prayer—"Lord have mercy upon us, and incline our hearts to keep *this* law?"

And where should Hetty be buried? It could not matter much; and yet Fritz could not bear to leave what he had loved so fondly, far from all associations of gladness and peace. He had an utter abhorrence of great town cemeteries. That the body of his darling should be regarded as a thing for some Company to make a profit of, he could not endure. And in those mercenary tombs, what was there of hope and promise? He wanted a resting-place for what was left of Hetty, near some House of God; over which, though she would never hear it, might float every Sunday the music of devout worshippers, praising their heavenly Father. He fancied she would be less lonely if the feet passed over her grave of bride and bridegroom going to God's altar, and coming back after holiest vows, such as *she* had taken, and kept so well; of fathers and mothers carrying their babes to God's holy Baptism; of God's ministers coming out again and again, when for one after another of their flock all the world's cares should be over, to tell the mourners of the sure and certain hope of a resurrection to eternal life.

So he made up his mind at last that Hetty should be buried at Stonecroft, or rather in Mellor churchyard, about a mile and a half from the White House, where he was born. Parkinson went down to make all needful arrangements, and Effie stayed in London with the children. It was a very small funeral party, and was to assemble at the White House—Fritz and his father, and Peggy, and Parkinson. The carriage-road to the church was long and winding; but they came at last to the top of the hill, at the gates of the churchyard. The same clergyman was there still whom Fritz had seen so often when he was a little boy. With snow-white hair, eighty years old, and still straight as an arrow, he came out of the porch as the little company of mourners were alighting from the coach.

"I am the Resurrection and the Life, saith the Lord, he that believeth in Me, though he were dead, yet shall he live; and whosoever liveth and believeth in Me shall never die."

And it was all over. There she lay, under the very path to God's house, two-hundred-and-twenty miles away from St. George's Road. Parkinson and old Mr. Rivers went to the White House, in the coach. Fritz and Peggy walked back together, the old way, over the fields they knew so well. How strangely all was changed. Peggy was married, with little children about her at home; and Fritz—it was all over. How could he look into the faces of *his* little ones and hear their questions? No, mamma would never come back again; never see them any more till the Great Judgment Day.

CHAPTER XXI.

SPARKS'S LOVE.

AND all this time Mr. Sparks was diligently making love to Matilda Holmes. She was very unlike Effie, she was very unlike Miss Jones. Her relations were not pious, and she herself had no horror of conventional worldliness. Courting therefore was, for the young gentleman at Goulburns', less tedious, but much more costly than in the quiet, dreary days of Jones, Lush, and Co.; and Matilda was in every respect a different sweetheart from the gentle girl of whom poverty had robbed him. To begin with, she was unquestionably, even in intellect and knowledge of life, Sparks's superior; and she knew it. If he had taken Miss Jones to the theatre, for instance, she would have been awed, half-frightened, totally bewildered by the novelty of the scene, utterly unable to give, or even form, an opinion. She would have received whatever her guide told her. If he assured her that a ballet-girl was the Princess of Wales she would scarcely have ventured to doubt it; and his criticism of actors and actresses would for her have been final. Not so Matilda Holmes. If her admirer ventured to express an opinion on anything superior to the legs of a dancer or the brilliance of a transformation-scene, Matilda simply curled her lip and was silent. Unless, indeed, the opinion was unusually outrageous, and then she affected to consider it a joke; and the more earnest Sparks was, the more she laughed. Indeed, she had so excellent a judgment in almost all departments of art, and histrionic art among the rest, that the young gentleman from Goulburns' began to take it for granted that she must be very fast; and ventured by degrees to entrust to her such confidences as are generally reserved for dubious male companions.

Especially it did not occur to him—always identifying knowledge of the world with actual participation in its worst vices—that she would do more than laugh at his mild flirtations with divers "young ladies" inhabiting the border-land of chastity and shame. By degrees Matilda discovered that he fancied that all the prettiest bar-maids or confectioners' girls in his part of London were in love with him. An extremely lovely waiter at a coffee-house he had treated to the Crystal Palace. In fact, he was so delighted with making Matilda think him a fine free young fellow, that the vices of his invention became far more numerous and serious than the vices of his real life; for, in actual fact, parsimony kept his profligacy in check. Matilda was growing more and more distressed at the connubial prospects opening up before her; and her courtship was not wholly without those lovers' quarrels which are not always the renewings of love. But what could she do? Sparks always apologized, promised, vowed, swore the distraction of his love; and, above all, stuck like a leech to the chance of Matilda's fortune; while Alfred Holmes, Esq., thought the match an exceedingly good one, and laughed to scorn his daughter's priggish objection to a young fellow "sowing his wild oats."

So the courtship went on; for no better reason, it would seem, than that it had begun, and nobody had energy enough to stop it. If Matilda and Sparks were married they would have a very nice establishment, much better than Alfred Holmes, Esq., had begun life with; and an establishment is everything. So they really were to be married. Poor Matilda was far from satisfied; was, indeed, without the smallest doubt that, with Sparks, she would remain for ever *un*satisfied. But her father would as soon have cut her throat as see her earning her own living like Effie; and he had given her plainly to understand, when she pleaded at least to defer the marriage, that he thought it very undutiful of her to wish to be a burden to him when it was no longer necessary. So it was agreed that in six months those two should take one another, "for better, for worse, for richer, for poorer, to *love* and to cherish." A solemn, far-reaching vow!—a most evil vow for them at any time; but if it must be taken at all, let it be taken now, not in six months.

For, little as anybody would have suspected it, there was a fountain of real love in Sparks's heart—not for Miss Jones, not for Matilda Holmes, but for little Polly Warren, daughter of one of the porters at Goulburns' bank; a beautiful, bright girl, with black hair curled all round her head; and eyes, eyebrows, eyelashes—though I can still see, in my mind, that young, innocent face, as if it were actually present before me, I can't describe it. She had come to the Bank one day to say that her father had broken his arm, and could not be in his place for a few days. She was very frightened and distressed, weeping bitterly; and Sparks had to go home with her, and see what could be done for the porter. That was their first meeting. She was so pretty, so sorrowful, so loving to her father, so grateful to Sparks, so perfectly simple and genuine, her artlessness fascinated the young clerk more than all the artifices of all the most accomplished flirts in London could have done. He very often visited her with one excuse or another. At first her father's accident furnished abundant opportunities of meeting; and by the time of his recovery there was sufficient intimacy, and on their side, the Warrens thought, more than sufficient obligation, to make the young clerk a welcome visitor whenever he chose to go. Very bright the little house, in a dingy Walworth square, seemed to Polly when Sparks came. Even the very square has vanished now; a row of houses built through the middle of the garden, has turned it into two narrow streets. But any house would have been a Paradise to Polly Warren, if only Sparks were with her. He was greatly her superior in education; though for a girl in her station she was well taught, and she was naturally quick and clever. In her society, therefore, there was no temptation to the silly show-off which made Sparks, in ordinary company, so insufferable a nuisance. He needed only to be himself to be by far the most accomplished gentleman Polly knew. And he really loved her; for he did see what was beautiful and loveable in her, and his heart responded accordingly, as every man's heart will. It seemed quite a new world in which Polly Warren lived, a world of truth and sincerity. Very likely it too had its little shams and concealments, but they were not the kind which Sparks had been used to, and they did not affect him. An evening spent at the porter's home was the quietest of enjoyments; and the time had been when he would have laughed to scorn "a cup of tea" there, and the homely virtues of that happy household. Now, it was the greatest delight he knew; for indeed it touched the true man in him, and over all was there not also the wondrous enchantment of love?

Polly's heart was given long ago irrevocably. Sparks might not care for her love, but none the less for that she loved him, and could not cease to love him. He seemed far too great, far too much above her station, to be ever more to her than he was then. He was, we know, no great hero; but what had Polly seen of him but affection and generosity? and greatness is only relative. We may smile or wonder at the porter's pretty daughter spending her whole wealth of love and reverence on such a one as Sparks; but many of the world's gods have been meaner than their worshippers, and when Sparks cast off his conventional outside, he, like every one of God's children, was in God's image. At any rate, she had grown into the habit of reverie, half sad, half glad—playing with her heart, like Gretchen with her flower. "Does he love me? He loves me—he loves me not—he loves me"—Endless uncertainty! what flowers or guesses could put it to rest?

But in truth, Sparks *did* love her, and couldn't help letting her know it. How she thought of every tender word he spoke! How much *she* would have meant by it! And yet he was not for her, perhaps; it was only his gentlemanly way of talking. Poor little Polly! That great, dreadful, glorious tyrant had usurped the throne of her heart, and now her whole life was only for love. If Sparks told her where he had been—at a party, a play, a quiet evening with intimate friends—that poor little heart throbbed passionately till Polly had hardly breath to speak. "Was anybody there he *loves*, loves *really*, is in love with, means to marry?" And yet, wouldn't he bend down and kiss her when they were quite alone, and say—"My dear little Polly, there's nobody like you; I love you better than all the rest put together."

And Sparks really meant it.

But what about the outside world? He belonged to that also; even more to that than to the little, genuine world of tea and honesty in the Walworth Square. Would he give it up? He hardly knew how much he belonged to it till there was a chance of giving it up. He wrote to Miss Jones without much grief; for his engagement had been rather with her father than with her. But still he felt that *she* was not her father, and perhaps he was making her miserable. And then——

Why not *marry* Polly Warren? He had never offered *that* to her; he had never even written to her; and yet he did really love her. It was no use talking to himself about her being poor, about her being a porter's daughter, about his losing caste, and all that sort of thing. He just *loved* her, in spite of caste, porterage, poverty. Moreover he felt it was right; it was genuine love, and she was worthy of it—and at any rate he had made her love him. He knew it quite well every time he saw her; and her attempts at concealment only revealed the secret more completely. One evening she seemed busy when he called, kept out of sight; her customary place was empty by Sparks's side. What was the matter? She came in at last, half-crying, talking as if she were half-afraid to speak, half-choked with some suppressed emotion. Moreover a strange restlessness possessed her; her busy fingers and lips and eyes all betrayed her.

"Wont you sit in your old place, Polly?" said Sparks; "you don't seem well to-night."

Then poor little Polly fairly broke down; she came to her accustomed chair, and cried till the great load was somehow moved, the heavy cloud gone.

"What's the matter, Polly?" said Sparks, very tenderly. He somehow *knew* what was the matter. Such wonderful insight does love give! He knew he had never spoken a cross word to her; that, in fact, she was becoming more and more to him every day. Perhaps *that* made her cry. Perhaps she wished, hoped, feared, doubted, was in a mere labyrinth of perplexities, the perplexities of a loving little heart, full of its first passionate affection; and *that* made her cry. Perhaps she wanted to know the truth, and yet feared lest it should be a killing truth. Perhaps she wanted him to know she loved him, and didn't want to tell him so, and did and didn't want her open secret to be found out—and *that* made her cry. Poor, silly, darling Polly.

"Nothing's the matter, sir," said Polly, wiping her eyes. "I don't know what's the matter; I've been crying so—it's done me good. I'm quite better."

She'd been thinking she would keep out of the way, would just be as if Mr. Sparks were anybody else—would—she didn't quite know what; but she would be somehow different, and not let her heart's secret be known. And now Sparks knew every bit of it as well as if she'd written it all down on paper with pen and ink and shown it to him.

And why not? As she sat in the old place by his side how happy she was! She *did* love him; and if he found it out, it would only be finding out the truth. And she had done no wrong; how could she help loving him? Why not, Sparks, why not shake off that other false life of yours, and take this pretty creature, so strong in love, so true and faithful, to your heart and home? An "establishment" is much, but what is it to such a heart as this?

Sparks felt it was nothing when he was with Polly. But at the Bank, or when he was visiting Alfred Holmes, Esq., and spent the evening with Matilda—what then? Suppose he were to say one day to the enemy of shopwomen and undisciplined charity, "I'm going to marry Polly Warren, our porter's daughter!" He could never bring himself to that. He was getting rapidly bewildered, half-crazed in his mental conflict. His part in the engagement with Matilda was, like her father's, a mere matter of business; but if it ended in marriage, what about pretty Polly Warren?

I suppose there would be no more sin if everybody could be compelled to look carefully at a wrong action before he committed it, and to give himself time for reflection. And many actions are not wrong; it is only the actions which follow them that are wrong, because the others have gone before. Was it wrong, for instance, for Polly and Sparks to be married at one of the very quietest of the Walworth churches?

Not wrong, but perhaps unwise. Or, if not, why have the marriage so secret—not even poor Porter Warren himself to know. And the mother could not make out what ailed Polly, when one morning she came home from a walk and cried hysterically for an hour. Polly felt that Sparks really did belong to her now; but she was never to put on the ring, and they were not to live together, and it was to be a profound secret for two years—until Sparks could see his way clear. The ring was in *his* purse, much safer there surely than in Polly's; but nevertheless, through his private marriage, he was at a disadvantage in every respect. And still—yes, still—the courtship with Matilda Holmes was going on, and the last six months of delay were going out. He tried more and more to make Polly understand that a *private* marriage, at least until he could "see his way clear" to take her to live with him at his own house, was only a rather unusually solemn form of engagement. Nobody knew of it; he thought nothing would come of it; it was no better, no worse, than a mere ceremony.

The six months had gone—the day of marriage with Alfred Holmes's daughter was *to-morrow*. How could it have been put off without acknowledging *the* reason for delay? Sparks had seen Polly two days before, and told her he was going for a trip to the Continent, and would not be back again for a month. How she cried! And *he* cried. Why not go to Matilda and tell her he could never be hers, for he was already the husband of Polly Warren? No, he could never bring himself to that. The *fascination* of sin was on him, the *power* of darkness! What could come of it? He could not *think*, he seemed driven on by some terrible irresistible impulse to utter ruin.

No good brother Robert was to be at the wedding—no hard-working Effie; the shopwoman, the disgrace of the family. From the least plebeian of his friends had Alfred Holmes selected the company who were to grace his daughter's marriage with —— Polly Warren's husband. It was to be all in the best style. And when it was over, the happy pair were to go first to Paris, and then wherever else they might choose to go.

As the last day was wearing out, Sparks became more and more restless and bewildered; he seemed almost to think that he *must* go through the wicked and unmeaning ceremony in which he had promised to take so conspicuous a part the next day. Unmeaning—for no splendour and pomp, no gay dresses and costly wedding gifts, no customary congratulations of insincere worldly friends, could give it half the significance, or even the smallest fraction of the significance, of the quiet service in the most obscure of Walworth churches, in which he had promised to take Polly Warren "to be his lawful wedded wife, for better, for worse . . . . until death should them part." And assuredly, however mad or blind poor Sparks might become, no Alfred Holmes, Esq., would be able to part them.

He almost felt that he was going mad. Did he really mean to go through the insane and cruel farce of a wedding ceremony with Matilda Holmes? And if he did, what would he do next? When would he make up his mind to tell her that all was a hideous mockery together, and that she was not, and could never be, his wife. He thought it all over in that utter distraction, of which almost everybody has had some slight experience; in that utterly stupefied condition in which a man seems the mere sport of irresistible power and unrelenting fate; in which one feels as they say birds feel when they are fascinated by serpents. Would nothing break the spell?

Yes; it was broken at last. He made up his mind he would go and see Polly and tell her all about it. He would go to the Continent for a month, but it should be with *her;* and even as the thought came into his mind he was a new man, rejoicing and free, forgetting even what bitter disappointment, what mortified vanity, what shame and rage he would leave behind him in the midst of all those splendid preparations which next morning would be waiting for him at the church in vain. At any rate he set off to Polly's house walking very fast, life and determination overflowing as it were through his whole frame, and speeding him on with a vigour that he had scarcely known before. He tapped at Polly's window as he passed it, and before his long quiet knock at the door was over Polly was there to meet him.

"You darling," she said, "you must surely have known I was quite alone sitting thinking about you, and wondering how the dull month would ever end while you were away."

"Alone, my little pet?" he said, "you dear little Polly!" and he kissed her over and over again standing at the street door, as if their faces could never separate.

"But come in, my love," she said. "Is anything

the matter with you? How very hot you are, how fast you must have been walking, and your hand trembles." And indeed he was trembling; and when he got into the house and sat down it was some minutes before he could speak.

"Polly," he said at last, "do you know who is going with me to Paris to-morrow?"

"No," she said, with an anxious look; not of jealousy or distrust, but a look expressive of the sense of danger and the misery of concealment or disguise in that part of one's life where all should be most open.

"I'm going with you, my sweet little wife," he said, taking the wedding-ring out of his purse and putting it once more on her finger; "get your things ready as fast as you can, for we must set off the first thing in the morning, and I'll take you with me to the hotel to-night. We will never be separated any more, Polly."

Polly looked as frightened as if they were never to be *together* any more; but it was only the fear that possibly there might be some mistake, and that the utmost blessing her heart could conceive had only come in a false dream to mock her. But Sparks was there real enough; and she clung to him with such fond embraces that he could only curse and scorn the folly that had kept them so long apart. And would he tell her father and mother all about it? Might she show them her marriage certificate and explain her strange reveries, her wayward fancies, her tears which had so awed and grieved and alarmed them? Yes, she might tell them everything now; tell all the world.

And then he told her of Matilda Holmes, of his folly and baseness, how near he had been to utter madness and ruin. And she cried and kissed him, and somehow (can any woman believe it?) her love so blinded her that she felt him a mere martyr for her sake—throwing himself away on a girl who had no rank, no fortune, nothing but love and truth.

"My own darling," she said, "my dearest, dearest love, what can I do to recompense you? I am not worthy of you; but I should have died if I had heard to-morrow that you had married somebody else and left me. You never could have done it, my pet."

And then she thought of Matilda Holmes, and they talked together how best the bad work might be undone. But, alas! what woman could have flung herself out of such a heaven as Polly Warren had been raised to for the sake of a mere stranger?

"Get ready, Polly," said Sparks, "tell your father and mother all about it, and I'll fetch you at ten o'clock."

And so Sparks went home. Everything he needed for his wedding tour was already packed, and nothing now remained but to write to Miss Holmes as best he could. Everybody knows what it is to write a really important letter, every sentence and word of which will be read over and over again by unfriendly critics, in which we are anxious to do justice, and at the same time to do it as tenderly and safely as may be. All such letters are stiff and formal, they often seem cold, and tricky, and hypocritical, with no more affection or manly feeling than a lawyer's letter. However, Sparks sat down and wrote.

"MY DEAR MISS HOLMES,—You will receive this letter to-morrow morning when I am far away, and not until you have suffered bitter humiliation and sorrow. I am afraid you will scarcely believe me when I tell you that I am deeply grieved and ashamed and penitent, and would with the greatest thankfulness make you all the amends that lie in my power for the wrong I have done you. I must have been a fool, indeed; but somehow I dared not tell you what I really was, and I humbly thank Almighty God that I am able to tell you now before worse harm was done. I am married already. I have been married for some time.

My wife is the daughter of one of our Bank porters, and I know very well how those to whom you may show this letter will scorn me even more for being true to her than for being false to you. Perhaps you will scorn me also, and I am quite sure that I deserve it.

"I can only offer you my sincere regret, and my

solemn promise that if in any way I can make amends for my cruelty to you I will.

"I remain, My dear Miss Holmes,

"Yours truly,

"J. SPARKS."

The next morning Sparks and Polly, sad and happy, were crossing from Folkestone to Boulogne, while Alfred Holmes, Esq., and all his proudest, richest relations, were waiting before the altar at the parish church of Islington—waiting for the bridegroom of Matilda Holmes. Her father had been talking, not without growing annoyance and even alarm, to some of his friends, of his daughter's match, and had even tried to get a kind of joke out of Sparks' unpunctuality. But unpunctuality on the morning of a man's marriage must be confined within very narrow limits; and half-an-hour, even of suspense and fear, hurries too rapidly away. There had been much whispering and wonderment; and, in fact, some of the friends of the bride and her father were already retiring, lest they should be compelled to take part in a tragedy that they had by no means rehearsed. It was no use sending to Sparks's house, for no messenger could be there and back again within half-an-hour; and surely, they thought, he must be close at hand. But the minutes hasted on, and as the silence and perplexity grew deeper, every tick of the church-clock could be heard;

nay, could be felt, as if a hammer were beating on the brain. At last the clock in the tower began to strike, and the clergyman in the vestry took off his surplice, only too thankful to escape from a scene of so much pain and confusion. The friends of Alfred Holmes, Esq., bid him adieu with such expressions of sympathy or encouragement as their puzzled brains could suggest. Mr. Holmes sent a stern message to his own house, that every guest and waiter should be sent away, that the marriage feast should be removed with all celerity, and that in less than an hour his daughter and he would return as they had gone out. In grim silence they drove round Hyde Park and Regent's Park, through streets and squares, till they felt sure that all at home would be quiet; and then they drove to their own house, to find Sparks's letter and make the best of it.

No woman could receive such treatment as Matilda Holmes had endured without bitter indignation. But though she felt that she had been deceived and humiliated, she knew full well that from end to end the marriage arrangements had been heartless and hypocritical. She knew that she did not love Sparks; she did not believe that he loved her. She hated more than ever the hard, worldly policy of her father; and she knelt down and thanked God that even by so rough and stern a grasp she had been held back from misery.

And her father cursed his own feebleness for yielding to his child the fatal six months of delay. If it had not been for them, he thought, all would have been well. But he had been struck with too heavy a blow; his spirit was crushed within him; the untasted wedding-feast was the last feast that was ever prepared in his house; he could not believe that any of his old friends really loved him; he was sure that whenever they saw him, they were making themselves merry with his calamity. Ever more and more suspicious, broken-spirited, lonely, before the end of that year he was dead.

CHAPTER XXII.

EFFIE TAKES A NEW SITUATION.

Who shall tell the utter loneliness with which Fritz resumed his work at St. George's Road when he came back from Derbyshire, leaving his darling under the pathway in Mellor Churchyard? He dared scarcely look on Sundays into the corner where Hetty had been used to sit, and whence he had been able to hear so well the rich music of her voice in Psalms and Hymns. Through the long dreary day he could never any more go out of his study to her room, for a few minutes' rest, to tell her how his work was going on, or to read to her something he thought would please her; and no more could she come to him, to cheer him amid all his worries, or even to ask his help in her graver household cares. Perhaps it was more bitter than all to Fritz that he could not tell her of his returning prosperity, his increasing comfort, the reward which seemed coming at last to his faith and patience.

It was so hard that she should have shared with him only his troubles, and have gone away before she could know of his honour and success.

For he was succeeding now, though there had been much suffering even since Hetty's death; and it seemed as if people knew that his wife had been killed by the cruelty of narrow-minded and vulgar bigots, and were trying by unobtrusive love to comfort him. The battles of the Creeds had acquired for them quite a new significance; and in a way they had little thought of, theological controversy had connected itself with real life. To Fritz's little band of friends the least word of calumny, the merest whisper of the personalities of religious wrangling, sounded horrible as the warning rattle of a venomous serpent. "No, no," they would say, "we will not hear another syllable. Pray to God to give you light, and above all, to give you love."

Effie was a constant visitor at Fritz's house, just as before. Was there not all the more need now for her sincere affection? And if the world chose to talk, it might talk; Fritz cared nothing for that sort of world, or for what it might think and say. Parkinson never missed having supper with Fritz every Sunday night; and in time when they gained courage to talk of Hetty, it almost seemed as if she were with them still. They knew exactly what she would have said, if she could have joined in their conversation; and they could scarcely believe that she had not heard of all that had happened since she went away.

Did not Fritz often in spirit talk to her, when more than two years of his loneliness had passed away, about his sore need of such comfort and fellowship as he had been used to find in her? Did he not often tell her, as if they still "could hear each other speak," how his children were needing more and more a mother's loving government, and how much there was of the work of his own ministry which he could not do now that he was alone?

"Hetty, darling," he said, "if I thought you could for an instant doubt my unchanging love to you, I would live alone for ever. But you cannot doubt it, looking down on me from where you are. You must know me now, dearest, better than you ever knew me here; you must be more sure than ever of my love."

So he said one day to Effie—

"I want you and Parkinson to come down with me for our summer's holiday to Derbyshire, to Little Stonecroft; Parkinson has agreed, and I've arranged to have the White House for a month—the house where I was born. What do you say to it, Effie?"

"I'll ask in the City," she said; "nothing would please me better."

"And then," said Fritz, "we shall see Mellor Churchyard, where my darling Hetty is buried. We shall seem almost nearer to her there than anywhere; and I want to be very near to her just now."

Effie said nothing. The tones of man's or woman's voice so change when love is speaking, that Effie knew quite well what Fritz was going to say.

"I want you to marry me, Effie. Nothing can bring back our Hetty, nothing can make up for the loss of her. But what should I do, my little pet, if I lost you also? Will you take me, Effie, to be your husband?"

She put her arms round his neck and kissed him, and sobbed out—

"Yes, Fritz."

What need of more words?

So it was at Mellor church, one bright June morning, Parkinson, and Fritz, and Effie were standing before the altar. They had passed over Hetty's grave as they walked up the steep pathway in the glorious sunshine. They had no wish to forget her. The new love that could have found no room in Fritz's heart without first casting out the love of Hetty, would have been a curse and a disgrace. So in the clear memory of the past, as if in the presence of the pure spirit of her who had been, and ever would be, so dear to both of them, Fritz and Effie spoke the irrevocable words.

And was not that holy union a more genuine tribute of honour, and affection, and undying loyalty and love, than any marble monument,

SACRED

TO THE MEMORY OF

HETTY,

THE BELOVED WIFE OF

FREDERICK RIVERS?

THE END.

CPSIA information can be obtained
at www.ICGtesting.com
Printed in the USA
LVHW100511130422
716029LV00002B/62

9 783752 592030